TIMETABLE FOR THE GENERAL

When France fell in 1940, General Alain de Forge, whom Hitler described as worth forty divisions to the Germans, was captured and imprisoned in the impregnable fortress of Koenigstein in the heart of Germany. There was one difference between de Forge and the ninety-nine French generals held with him: de Forge was determined to escape. Yet everyone agreed escape was impossible. The fortress was perched on a towering rock. The French frontier was hundreds of miles distant. Without outside help, nothing could be done.

Patiently de Forge contrived to contact a specialized 'travel service' which arranged a de luxe itinerary for him. But before he could return to lead France to the destiny he believed awaited her, he had to get down off the rock and a courier had to be sent in. Not only had the courier to cross Occupied France and half of Germany: he had to escort an escaped general whose height alone made him conspicuous. And then the carefully worked-out timetable went wrong . . .

BERNARD FRIZELL

Timetable For the General

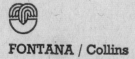

FONTANA / Collins

First published by Wm. Collins 1972
First issued in Fontana Books 1973

© 1972 by Bernard Frizell

Printed in Great Britain
Collins Clear-Type Press London and Glasgow

*Tout ma vie, je me suis fait
une certain idée de la France.*
   —CHARLES DE GAULLE

Contents

Author's Note

This fiction is based on fact. The escape described in these pages actually occurred, but the characters, their relationships and many of the incidents, though not the technique of that little masterpiece of patience and ingenuity, have all been imagined; any resemblance between these fictional characters and actual people, living or dead, is coincidental.

As a matter of historical interest, the escape that suggested this story was made from the fortress of Koenigstein in Saxony in April 1942 by General Henri Giraud, who was picked by President Roosevelt to lead the French when the Allies invaded North Africa later that year, but who was subsequently eliminated from his position of leadership by General Charles de Gaulle.

PART ONE

The Plan

ONE

A French armoured car sped along the black asphalt road less than fifty miles east and somewhat to the north of Paris through a countryside sweet and tender with spring. It was a painfully beautiful day in early June – painful because the year was 1940, and armies of Nazi Germany were overrunning France. Although the three men in the armoured car did not know it, German tanks and troops were all around them. A general, his star-studded kepi flat on his head, sat beside the driver; his aide, a lieutenant so young the down was still on his cheeks, swayed on the rear seat of the high-slung vehicle. Like so many others under the general's command, the lieutenant had always feared and respected him. But during the past few horrible weeks the lieutenant's feelings had changed. The lieutenant would never have put it in such words, but he had come to love the general.

Lieutenant Leclerc was mildly astonished when he realized the intensity of his emotion, for on the outside at least there was nothing lovable about General Alain Georges Marie Jean-Claude de Forge. Indeed, he was easier to hate than to love; and the lieutenant well remembered how he had hated the general until, as he told himself, he understood that the outer shell was not the inner man.

The outer shell was forbidding – if for no other reason than that de Forge willed it so. De Forge did not aim to be liked; he aimed to be effective. He created a distance, erected a wall, between himself and others to mystify his person and augment his authority. It worked – in both directions: his prestige rose, his popularity fell. It did not matter: the price of authority was solitude. So de Forge looked down at the world over his powerful nose with a profound air of knowing what was wrong with it, why, and how to correct it. The distressing thing for those who knew and disliked him, and they were many, was that de Forge almost invariably did seem to know what was wrong and how to set it right. Even when he did not, the force of his personality and the power of his logic overcame such opposition as he met and prevailed.

His attitude towards his military superiors was conveyed in his eyes and bearing, in the tone of his voice and his precise but ambiguous phrasing. It all said, 'I may be your subordinate, but hardly your inferior.' This disarmed those whose duty it was to give him orders. For the general had mastered the art of imposing his will to the edge of disobedience without leaving himself open to the charge of insubordination.

Towards his own subordinates, de Forge played God— distant, omnipotent, fearsome. It produced results, but with them a schizophrenic reaction towards the deity of resentment splintered by awe. Small wonder that Lieutenant Leclerc had been surprised to find himself so completely under de Forge's spell. In those terrible days Lieutenant Leclerc had asked himself the ultimate question (would he lay down his life for his general?) and had solemnly replied in the affirmative.

Lieutenant Leclerc felt a sickness in the pit of his stomach as the armoured car hummed and bounced along. Nobody spoke; nobody had spoken since they had jumped into the car ten minutes before. The lieutenant's eyes were fixed on the back of the general's weatherbeaten neck, but what he saw was de Forge's face. He now lived with the image of de Forge's face burned into his mind. That is how it had been since the German attack began, and the worse matters became the more the general's face haunted him. De Forge was withdrawn, as distant as Olympus though bodily present, and this multiplied the impact of his person: somehow he created the impression through his imperturbable serenity that there was something he knew, something he could do that nobody else imagined. But Lieutenant Leclerc, who was with de Forge more than anyone else, was not fooled. For each day, as evening brought even worse news than the dispatches they had awakened to, the lieutenant, in those almost secret moments together, saw de Forge's face grow longer, the lips tighter, the nose more pinched, the circles under the eyes deeper and darker, and the eyes, the eyes burning always more feverishly, set aflame and fed by the tinder of successive catastrophes.

Lieutenant Leclerc suffered with the general. He felt like the witness to some awesome natural disaster, as if, while he watched, a mountain crumbled or an entire continent sank beneath the sea. It was France that was crumbling before the lieutenant's eyes, a world and way of being that was coming to an end. The lieutenant did not know it as it was happening so much as he felt it, and all that, not in the movement of troops or by markers on a map, but in the general's face, in the knowledge and emotion de Forge never spoke but that his face could not hide. Day by day, hour by hour, the nation fell apart. Nothing could now be done to stop it. All this de Forge knew, suffered and unconsciously reflected. For Lieutenant Leclerc, by some mysterious process of transference, de Forge became the embodiment, the incarnation of France. The cataclysm was too great for the young lieutenant to conceive. De Forge gave it a human dimension. Lieutenant Leclerc lived the tragedy in that image of de Forge's face as he might suffer a woman's death from the pain in her lover's eyes.

Swaying in the back of the armoured car, Lieutenant Leclerc was overcome with drowsiness and began to doze. He had a muddled sense of unease as his eyes closed under the heat of the day and the smell of flowering trees swept over him; vaguely he felt that if a June day could be so glorious when his world was coming to an end, the universe was indifferent even to the most conclusive events. The car squealed around a curve. In his somnolence, Lieutenant Leclerc knew the driver was trying to please de Forge and was certain he was not succeeding. Speed was what the general always demanded, but no matter how high the supply, the demand was never satisfied.

'Faster,' de Forge said as if to confirm the lieutenant's suspicions. 'Can't you go faster?'

That was when the shell struck. It fell short and to the left of the speeding armoured car. Shell splinters cracked against the front and side of the car with a swift metallic drum roll and fragments shattered the windshield; under the percussion the heavy car bounced on its fat tyres. The left front tyre burst, wrenching the vehicle against the driver's grip. To the terrifying sound of metal smashing, glass crashing and rubber squealing on asphalt, the car skidded, turned over twice, then slid to a stop right side up. The driver quivered over the steering wheel. Lieutenant Leclerc lay stunned in the back of the car. De Forge was thrown clear and lay unconscious in a patch of grass beside the road. In an instant a dozen German infantrymen were around them. Their officer, a captain who looked tough because of a squashed nose and a black stubble of beard, stood over the inert figure beside the road. His tired face brightened when he saw the stars on the khaki sleeve.

'A general,' he said, his eyes sparkling.

De Forge opened his eyes, meeting those of the German captain. It would be a long time before the general's captor forgot that look of disdain mingled with contempt. De Forge rose with some difficulty, pushing away the captain, who tried to help him. The older man limped with his right leg, which had been hurt, but he drew himself erect without complaint and, a full head above his captor, glared down at him over his large nose and flowing grey moustache, reducing those around him to an uneasy silence. Nothing about him seemed defeated; he had the air of a monarch glowering at delinquent subjects.

Lieutenant Leclerc, who was inexperienced, had not imagined how swift and conclusive the violence of war could be; it was finished almost before he knew it had begun, so suddenly that he felt neither fear nor triumph at surviving. In those first moments, watching from the car, he did not think of himself but only of the unimaginable fact that his general, Alain de Forge, was in German hands. For youthful and loyal Lieutenant Leclerc, and not for him alone, de Forge was the best general the French army had, a fighting general and one with vision. Now he was a prisoner.

Holding their rifles laxly, their sweaty faces creased with dirt, the German soldiers stood around the general in an embarrassed circle under the gloriously blue June sky. De Forge made them feel uncomfortable, even guilty in a way. He looked through them as if they had done something irretrievably wrong, something obscene, in obliging him to submit when his withering presence, his inner size, told them he was not a man meant for submission but for command.

Silence. De Forge's chin went higher. The sun beat down. One of the soldiers picked up the general's kepi. He handed it to the captain. The captain offered it to de Forge. De Forge put it on his head.

'I'm very sorry,' the captain murmured apologetically in broken French.

Unbending: 'Not as much as I.'

Another long awkward pause.

'Shall we go?' the captain asked, gesturing vaguely.

De Forge led the way, limping.

As Lieutenant Leclerc and the driver were led out of the car to follow the others, the young lieutenant said, 'Can you imagine anyone like General de Forge a prisoner? The poor man.'

'Can you imagine the life he'll lead his captors?' the driver replied. 'The poor Germans.'

Accompanied by Lieutenant Leclerc, de Forge was taken back to division, then to army headquarters, where he was treated with due protocol. The commanding general of the army that had broken through at Sedan insisted on meeting him, but when the German general offered his hand, de Forge pointedly refused it. Projecting strength and serenity in the absence of both, de Forge never lowered his head or raised his voice. The Germans were correct. Facts are facts. There was no need to insist on them.

De Forge and Lieutenant Leclerc were driven across the Rhine to a big house on the outskirts of Bonn. It was a luxuriously furnished old mansion set in the middle of a rolling lawn surrounded by towering trees in full leaf that cut off the grounds from the roads around it. Even de Forge was impressed by the elaborate meals served in the cheerful dining room. Lieutenant Leclerc expressed surprise at such generous treatment.

'It won't last,' de Forge said dryly. 'The Germans want something.'

'From a prisoner?'

'There are three things you can do with a prisoner. You can hold him, kill him or use him. The Germans will want to use me. I don't think they will try with much conviction. After all, they know me. But the setting they've chosen is agreeable.'

De Forge was pensive.

'I tell you, Leclerc, there is only one reality now: the nation. A Frenchman must think of France, only of France, and nothing must stand in the way of his duty to that idea.'

'But what can we do about it as prisoners?'

'I shall escape.' The words fell from de Forge's lips as if the fact were evident. 'One does not refuse France. Nor one's destiny. It's an imperative, an absolute imperative.'

'Escape?' Lieutenant Leclerc said gently with a gesture at de Forge's sprained right leg, which was stretched out stiffly. 'But, *mon général*, you can barely walk.'

De Forge considered the young lieutenant over his large strong nose. 'You don't have to be able to walk to escape,' he said. 'You have to want to escape, and you have to know how to do it. I escaped once before, you know, in the last war. I escaped because of an inner compulsion. This time I must do it because of an outer call, because France needs me.'

Lieutenant Leclerc was politely silent.

'There's a solution to every problem,' de Forge said, answering the silence. 'A solution to every problem no matter how difficult it may be. Every soldier should know that and every statesman too. When mind is applied to matter, matter must always give way.'

'Nobody,' Lieutenant Leclerc ventured, 'has ever squared the circle.'

'And nobody,' de Forge replied, 'ever will. Squaring the circle is not a true problem; it aims at what is by definition a contradiction. But there are no contradictions in nature; they exist only in the mind. It's like the pseudo-problem of what happens when the irresistible force meets the immovable object. I can assure you that something happens when the irresistible force hits the immovable object in nature. We then learn if the force is resistible or the object movable.' De Forge paused, then

12

leaned on his words as if the new emphasis would help turn faith into fact. 'I must escape,' he said. 'Therefore I shall escape.'

The next day an emissary of the German High Command, a colonel, came to see de Forge. He was a handsome Baltic baron with silvery temples, got up in an impeccably cut uniform, who kept opening his eyes wide and letting his monocle drop on the black ribbon to which it was attached. De Forge readily conceded that there was little doubt about the outcome of the current phase of the war, and the baron asked what conclusions he drew on subsequent relations between France and Germany.

De Forge's answer was elaborate. The battle of France was decisive, but however devastating its loss might be to the nation it was still only a battle; the war, of course, would go on. Even if all of France were occupied, the French fleet was intact, the Mediterranean wide and a new, if difficult, beginning could be made from North Africa. England, too, would fight on, and Hitler would simply redden the deep waters of the Channel with German blood if he was foolish enough to attempt an invasion.

Then de Forge spread his wings. Since the baron came from the Baltic region, he spoke of the Baltic and its exposure to the east. The German accord with the Russians could not last forever. The European balance of power was already basically altered by the events now taking place. The dynamics of that situation had their own laws of motion which would ineluctably follow their course. Besides, the German-Russian pact was an unnatural one, calculated on both sides for temporary reasons that could not long remain valid. Ideological differences exacerbated national differences and natural antagonisms in the heart of Europe. Inevitably, on one side or the other, the non-aggression pact would be denounced and broken. And then on the other side of the Atlantic there was a giant that could not remain forever asleep. America was potentially the greatest power in the world. De Forge spoke eloquently of that power and of the impulse that would bring it into play. France still had many friends. The war would spread and the forces against Germany would become overwhelming. In war there was only one vindication: victory. In the end France would be vindicated.

The baron listened politely until de Forge finished, then thanked him for confiding his views so frankly.

'Our conclusions are different,' the baron said. 'We believe that collaboration between France and Germany would greatly benefit both our countries. And of course if you agreed, it would make a very great difference in your own personal situation.'

De Forge focused on the baron's small, upturned nose. 'One doesn't collaborate with the enemy,' he said, 'especially after losing a battle. One strikes back.'

The baron's light blue eyes widened and his monocle dropped. He rose. 'You should know,' he said, 'that the High Command has not forgotten that during the last war you were taken prisoner and escaped. We don't think it will happen this time.'

De Forge was awakened very early the following morning and told to get ready to leave immediately without his aide. Lieutenant Leclerc was very depressed.

'Courage,' de Forge said as they parted. 'It will come out right in the end.'

De Forge limped out into the early morning sunlight and got into the back of a powerful Mercedes sedan painted a dull dirt brown. He was followed there by a Wehrmacht captain; a sergeant sat beside the driver. The Mercedes circled the town and was soon speeding in a northeasterly direction through the flourishing June countryside deeper into Germany. After they had passed a few towns, de Forge, who had spent some time in Germany between the wars, recognized their route. Towards noon he was hungry and asked where they would have lunch.

'We'll have sandwiches while we drive,' the captain said.

'That's not good enough. There's an excellent restaurant in the next town where I ate several years ago. We'll lunch there.'

The captain was startled by his prisoner's tone of command, but after a moment's hesitation he said, 'At your orders, General.'

The muddy brown Mercedes nuzzled into the parking space in front of the restaurant, and de Forge, limping, led the way into the crowded restaurant followed by the captain, the sergeant and the driver. As the French general walked in, kepi flat on his head, every eye in the restaurant turned towards him and the steady hum of voices suddenly dipped into silence. With a gesture, de Forge directed the group, including the enlisted men, to sit down at a table in a corner of the room. De Forge ordered first, then the others in turn of rank. The lunch was excellent and de Forge ate with high appetite. The captain paid. As the limping general led the group back to the car, all the eyes in the restaurant once again followed them with curiosity.

They drove all afternoon and into the evening. Every minute, every kilometre put a greater distance between de Forge and France, between de Forge and freedom. They crossed most of Germany and came at last to Saxony, not far from the Czechoslovakian border. The sun was setting as they drove through a long valley beside a stream, the immense evening shadows of the tall trees cast far ahead of them. On either side hills rose majestically around them. Presently they turned left into a thickly wooded area and began a steep climb. As the incline became sharper, the road began its twists and turns upward. It snaked through the mountains higher and higher in hairpin turns that turned smack around on each other. The air became cooler. The driver was forced to shift the Mercedes down into second, then into first to make the turns and pull the heavy car up the sharp incline. The powerful car continued to grind upward, slowing down almost to a full stop at the twists of the road, then gathering a little speed, then slowing for the next turn. The landscape was rocky, broken and savage, with an air of doomsday about it.

At last the dust-covered car stopped at the foot of an immense rock. All of them got out. The sun had already gone down, but the last feeble light was still in the gathering night sky. Against it, de Forge saw the black outline of an ancient fortress on the top of the rock soaring overhead. It hung above de Forge, suspended against the darkling sky like a beast that would swallow him. Moment by moment the night became darker, enveloping them like a shroud, and the mass of stone above bore down more heavily, seeming to crush de Forge under the inexorable weight of its masonry and malevolence.

They were at the end of the road; the car could go no farther. High up in the craggy night, they might have been at the butt end of the earth.

The rest of the distance to the fortress had to be covered on foot. De Forge and the others toiled up a path that mounted even more steeply than the road. It led to an arched portal. A massive wooden door swung back, squealing on its hinges; then when the group had passed through, it swung closed with an echoing crash of wood and metal. It sounded more sinister and definitive to de Forge than a rifle shot.

He found himself in a bare cobblestoned courtyard. A group of guards stood at the huge door. De Forge gathered from the exchange between the guards and the Wehrmacht captain that they were expecting him but something had gone wrong with the welcoming ceremony. In a moment a noncom detached himself from the group, crossed the courtyard and, pushing hard, opened a second huge fortress door. De Forge went through the doorway and climbed a small stairway cut into the rock. In the darkness he made out a small tower above him. As he reached it a lieutenant with a narrow face and receding chin rushed towards him, very much out of breath, from inside the fortress. It was the aide of the colonel in command.

'Forgive me, *monsieur le général,* for not having met you at the door outside,' he said. 'We expected you much earlier and had no idea you would still be coming at this hour.'

De Forge waved his excuses aside, treating the officer like a receptionist leading him to the hotel suite he had reserved. As the lieutenant spoke, they continued their progress inside the fortress grounds. They kept going up, always up, still more stairs, and yet more again. At last there was a final stairway, this one rising in a spiral. At the top of it a door with three locks on it. The noncom threw the door open. De Forge saw that he had arrived at his new home.

It was nothing to warm his heart.

The room was high above the interior courtyard, looking out on it through a small window blocked by iron bars. In the room were a bed, a table, a worn armchair, a straight-backed

16

chair, a pitcher and a washbowl. In a corner there was a hole in the floor with a flush attachment above it: the toilet.

While the lieutenant and noncom remained near the door, de Forge strode into the room and, nose high, eyes quick, made a fast turn of inspection. The window had been left open during a heavy storm that afternoon, and the old wooden planks of the floor were soaked. In places there were puddles of water.

'Have you seen this?' de Forge demanded harshly.

The lieutenant's receding chin seemed to recede further as he stammered an excuse.

'I wouldn't have thought the German army would be so incompetent behind the lines.'

The lieutenant reddened and again begged to be excused with the promise that things would fall into place now that the general had arrived.

'Would you like something to eat, *monsieur le général*?' the lieutenant inquired, happy to have found a way to change the conversation. 'It's late, of course, and all we have to offer you is some bread and sausage. But there's plenty of that and it's very good indeed.'

De Forge shook his head and unceremoniously dismissed the lieutenant and noncom. 'It's late,' he said. 'I wish to be alone.'

After the door closed he heard the locks slip into their bolts. For the first time since he had been captured he was alone. He sank into a chair, his head in his hands, sitting there woodenly as if in shock. This bare, drab room was his new reality. Command had been taken from him – the command of armies – and he was reduced to nothing. Locked up, cut off, emasculated.

Like others of his class and generation, de Forge had grown up with a certain idea of France, an idea of France as a fairy princess whom kings and armoured knights fought and died for. He had clung to that idea as a child playing with lead soldiers, as an adolescent passionately reading the history of France, as a youth at Saint-Cyr; nor had he ever faltered in maturity. He had always dreamed that he would be the saviour of his fairy princess, and his particular hell now was that just when he was most deeply needed he could not serve.

He undressed and crawled between the icy sheets. It was a room in an ancient fortress and it was cold and damp. De

Forge lay in bed and stared at the barred window. The night was quiet. It was as bitter a moment of stillness as he had known. He wondered how many hundreds of days and nights he would spend here while the world outside turned without him as if he were dead.

TWO

After a bad night de Forge rose early, unrefreshed. He went directly to the barred window but saw disappointingly little from it. Above, a patch of blue sky; opposite, a blank wall; to the side, a path skirting a curved crenellated wall. Beyond the wall, de Forge guessed, there would have to be nothing: a sheer drop down the rock on which the fortress was built into the wooded valley below.

De Forge cast a practised eye on the construction of the buildings. They were solid. He speculated that the fortress must date from the seventeenth century. Built as such buildings were built, magnificently in thick-walled stone to last forever, and anchored on the rock. How could anyone dig tunnels or underground passageways in such a place? And if one could, where would they lead? Holding on to the bars and gazing out, he felt the full weight of his imprisonment in this eerie, high-flung stone enclosure.

Suddenly, without any advance warning, like a shot in the heart, he missed his family, his four children and his wife, Suzanne. Suzanne. He saw her face, worn, patient, suffering his moods and rages. The surge of love brought tears to his eyes. 'I'm falling apart,' he told himself. 'I must get a grip on myself.'

He passed a bitter hour while a shaft of sunlight crept into his room and silently crept out again. Heartsick, he wondered if he were indeed doomed to rot here when he was most needed to fulfil the mission for which he had been trained and destined. But destiny, he thought in despair, is what happens, not what might have happened.

In the middle of the morning the locks turned, the door

opened and the commander of the fortress entered accompanied by his aide, the slack-chinned lieutenant. Colonel Wilhelm von Bardsdorf was a dour old reserve officer from Hamburg with a narrow parchment face, a sour expression and alert brown eyes. He struck de Forge as one of those men whom life had disappointed and who had now accepted with more or less bad grace the smaller portion he found distasteful. De Forge stood erect in the centre of the room. None of the emotions he had suffered only moments before could be divined. He felt his battle was about to begin.

After introducing himself, von Bardsdorf began speaking in German. He had said only a few words when de Forge, scarcely listening, interrupted. Speaking French, de Forge demanded an interpreter.

'What need is there for an interpreter?' von Bardsdorf demanded. 'We know you speak German.'

Speaking with deliberate precision, de Forge launched his words at the German colonel like mortars. 'Let us be very clear from the outset so there is no confusion afterwards, *Herr Oberst*,' he said in French. 'The fact that I am your prisoner in no sense means or implies that I am in any way your inferior or am to be treated as if I were. You are German; I am French. When we speak officially, I demand an interpreter. I shall speak my language, not yours.'

Von Bardsdorf understood every word. His yellowed, leathery face seemed to turn yellower. He had been warned about de Forge, told that this man, of all the general officers who would be in his charge, would be his prize prisoner and without doubt his *bête noire*. The word had come directly from the High Command. The Fuehrer himself had taken note of his capture. Von Bardsdorf had been told that when Hitler learned that de Forge was a prisoner he had jumped up, his eyes alight, and had cried, 'They're finished. We've got their best general, their best soldier. He's worth forty divisions.'

Von Bardsdorf was now faced with the man and felt rather intimidated. He was not at all sure that he would know how to deal with him. The German colonel now had fifty French generals in the fortress and had been informed that he would soon receive another packet of fifty generals. He hoped, as he dropped his eyes from de Forge's steady gaze, that there would not be another like this one.

'Lieutenant Hetzel,' he said, turning to his aide, 'tell the general he is here in reprisal.'

The lieutenant translated.

'I don't understand.'

'In reprisal for Marshal Foch's unspeakable conduct in nineteen-eighteen towards Colonel von Golzte.'

De Forge shrugged. 'Your military establishment has a long memory,' he said ironically. 'I never heard of that gentleman. This is entirely arbitrary on your part.'

'It's a decision of the High Command,' von Bardsdorf said firmly. 'The order has been forwarded to me; I shall execute it.'

De Forge spread his hands, lifting his shoulders; irony was his only defence. 'If it's a decision of the High Command . . .'

'It means that you will be kept here in solitary confinement.'

'For how long?'

'Until I have instructions that the reprisal is terminated.'

Von Bardsdorf marched out with Lieutenant Hetzel in step behind him.

De Forge interpreted the reprisal as the High Command's reaction to the unsuccessful probe by the Baltic baron to win his collaboration. He felt at once pleased and contemptuous that the Germans had marred the correctness of their treatment of him.

At noon de Forge's door opened again. In marched a noncom followed by a soldier bearing a tray with de Forge's lunch. The soldier placed the tray on the table near the window. De Forge was famished and immediately sat down to eat. The lunch consisted of a liquid that passed for soup in a metal dish, a piece of bread and a pitcher of water. De Forge tasted the soup. His expression changed like a sky suddenly swept black in a storm. Watching him, the noncom recoiled as if from a blow. Without a second's hesitation, de Forge picked up the metal dish containing the soup and hurled it over his shoulder at the open window. It clattered against the bars, exploding metallically as the liquid splashed over the floor and out of the window. The noncom and soldier were paralysed.

'Get me the adjutant,' de Forge snapped.

The adjutant, a pudgy lieutenant with close-cropped hair, puffed into the room, his face beet-red. 'Why, why, how could you do such a thing, *Herr General*?' he stammered.

Balancing himself up and down on the balls of his feet, de Forge pronounced from a great height, 'I would like you to know, *Herr Leutnant*, that on my country property in France I raise pigs. I would also like you to know that I would never dream of serving them the filth I have just been served. I would be afraid of killing them.'

The lieutenant's face became still redder. How could a prisoner, even if he was a general, speak to him like that? But de Forge towered there like offended Justice personified, a breathing slab of rock such as the mountain on which the fortress was anchored, and the adjutant climbed down from his indignation like a boy creeping away from a dangerous height.

'*Herr General*,' he said defensively, 'the regulations are spelled out, they are spelled out for prisoners in your situation. You cannot get anything else.'

'In that case,' de Forge announced as if meting out a sentence on the lieutenant and everyone else concerned, 'in that case, I shall manage to subsist on bread and water and nothing else. My campaigns in the Sahara have taught me abstinence. I shall manage.' Turning away and dismissing the man with the back of his hand, de Forge then fired the single shot in his entire armoury. 'But of course,' he murmured, 'this will become known in due time in France.'

The lieutenant raised his arms and let them fall, his hands slapping at his sides. 'But, *Herr General*,' he said, 'what is it you want?'

De Forge wheeled around. 'I want the food the Geneva Convention defines as right and proper for a prisoner of war, namely, the same food eaten by my guards. In other words, the very food, *Herr Leutnant*, that you eat, for we all know since you have repeated it enough that German officers eat the same food as their men. I therefore demand exactly the same food that is served you, sir, in the officer's mess. Neither more nor less.'

'That's beyond my competence. I shall have to speak to the colonel.'

As the pudgy lieutenant left, de Forge told himself he was too weak to do anything but attack; otherwise his jailers would walk all over him. 'I'm the man God made me,' de Forge said to himself, 'and they must never be permitted to forget that. This is the moment, in the full flower of my impotence, without weapons, ammunition or allies, to force them to consider me, to respect me and to bow to me.'

Presently Colonel von Bardsdorf burst into the room followed by the adjutant and Lieutenant Hetzel. For a moment the colonel stood boiling before de Forge; then he spluttered into a violent denunciation, accusing the French general of everything from ungentlemanly behaviour unworthy of an officer to simple ingratitude for the correct and gentle treatment with which he had been favoured.

A few icy words reduced von Bardsdorf's head of steam to a simmer. 'You're breaking the Geneva Convention,' de Forge said. 'I can't allow myself to be a part of such scandalous behaviour. What, you pretend to be heroes on the field of battle and you treat prisoners, general officers, worse than cattle! If an officer under my command behaved like that towards any of you people, I'd have him court-martialled.'

The word set von Bardsdorf off again. 'Court-martialled, court-martialled! Are you mad? Court-martialled for following orders?'

'There are laws and international agreements as well as orders. There is also, just to the west of barbarism, something we call civilization and humane treatment, all of which has a special importance in relation to prisoners who are physically at the mercy of their captors.'

'I'm a soldier. An order is an order. It must be obeyed.'

'You're a soldier, yes. But I didn't think you were an automaton.'

'I shall obey my orders none the less.'

'And I shall obey my conscience.'

Von Bardsdorf felt dissatisfied with himself especially before the two lieutenants. He felt as if he had been turned in a circle and cornered. It was something in the tone of the dispute even more than in the substance that made him feel he had come out a bad second, that he had adopted an official position familiar to all that somehow did not stand examination.

'I cannot satisfy your demand,' he said curtly. 'Nobody here can, not even I.'

'Why not?'

'The decision to put you in this situation was made by the High Command.' Von Bardsdorf's tone was cajoling, to make de Forge see he was fighting windmills. 'Any change in your status would have to be referred to Berlin.'

'Refer the matter wherever you like,' de Forge said with an air of indifference. 'So far as I'm concerned the question is settled: until I obtain satisfaction I shall manage on a ration of bread.'

Von Bardsdorf looked unhappy. 'You'll be the only one to suffer.'

'No doubt. But anything would be preferable to eating that slop. In any case it's a matter of principle. I cannot even passively, even as a victim, co-operate in the arbitrary and cynical flouting of an international agreement to which all civilized nations subscribe.'

'This is madness,' von Bardsdorf said. 'You're simply making life harder for yourself, indeed unbearable.'

'And perhaps not for myself alone.'

'What do you mean?'

'Even as a prisoner I'm not without arms. It will do neither you nor your High Command nor the Third Reich nor the hopes of your government any good when this gets back to France.'

'And how will it get back to France?'

'Everything worth knowing becomes known sooner or later.'

It was a bluff, but it was a good bluff because of the element of truth in it. Von Bardsdorf had to consider the International Red Cross and one hundred French generals who would soon be in the fortress; some would eventually be released because of sickness or any of a dozen unpredictable reasons. Everybody in the fortress would know if this unmanageable man decided to starve himself; and of course if it became generally known in France, that would not be good.

Von Bardsdorf left de Forge's room worried, and de Forge knew it. De Forge was certain that the last thing von Bardsdorf would do was to refer his problems to the High Command. On the other hand, by bringing the High Command into the picture he had created the fiction that the battle was not between him and de Forge but between de Forge and the High

Command. That meant he could capitulate more easily without loss of face. De Forge stood at the window and sighed. However von Bardsdorf viewed the matter, de Forge felt he had to win. He had an excellent appetite and thought that it would be a long time before it was satisfied again.

That evening the same abominable soup was brought to him. This time he simply left it untouched. He merely nibbled at the black bread and drank the water. His mood turned even blacker, the hunger gnawing at his stomach.

For three days de Forge ate no more than a bit of bread at each meal and grew visibly weaker as the days passed. On the third day Lieutenant Hetzel paid him a visit. De Forge received him lying in bed. It was the first time he had not been erect and at attention in the presence of his captors.

'Don't you feel well?' Lieutenant Hetzel asked.

'No.'

'What is it?'

'Nothing important.'

'Do you wish to see a doctor?'

'I don't think a doctor could help.'

'Can I?'

'Do you know how to cook?'

On the fourth day, knowing the word would get back to von Bardsdorf, de Forge did not get up at all. The following day at noon the private and the noncom arrived with a different platter of food. It came directly from the German officers' mess and included a dish heaped high with steak and home-fried potatoes. Showing no surprise, de Forge rose with great dignity, and before the curious eyes of the enlisted men he sat down to table and picked up knife and fork as if this were the meal he had ordered. He ate slowly but with huge appetite, wiping up the blood from the steak with the bread. He could not remember when he had so enjoyed a meal. Small victories, he thought, will lead to bigger ones.

De Forge remained under reprisal for two weeks and saw no one but his guards. His only consolation was that he ate well. But his isolation was complete and no fragment of information from the outside world penetrated his cell. To his captors he seemed inhumanly distant and unmoved; he emanated a quality of godlike serenity that had them tiptoeing around him, awed. The reality did not match the emanation. De Forge was suspended in an eventless continuum, the victim of every empty crawling second; accustomed to action, to decision, he found the paralysis of prison like living without air. But quite alone with himself, he had the sardonic humour to muse that if his own company was the best he knew, who else could stand him?

One morning in the latter part of June, Colonel von Bardsdorf came to see him again. De Forge received the colonel standing up and did not invite him to sit down. Some colour seemed to rise in von Bardsdorf's sallow complexion, and his eyes were lively and malicious.

'I have good news for you,' he announced. A slight smile creased his parchment face. 'You go off reprisal today and join the others as another prisoner.'

De Forge looked blandly down at von Bardsdorf. 'Well,' he said mildly, 'you're finally putting me on the normal schedule I should have had from the start.'

'But you would have remained on reprisal twice as long had it not been for an important event that's just occurred.' Von Bardsdorf paused to give greater effect to what he had to announce. 'Your government has signed an armistice at Compiègne. That's why the High Command is giving you a reprieve.'

'I would have preferred to remain on reprisal.'

'In any case you shall not. The war between our countries in effect is over and – '

'I'm not as sure of that as you seem to be.'

'We shall see, we shall see,' von Bardsdorf said lightly. 'At least the shooting and the killing is ended. A few weeks to settle England, and we shall see.'

'As you say, we shall see.'

'It puts an entirely new perspective on the situation here. The closer we are to a peace treaty, and an armistice brings us much closer, the sooner you'll be freed. For your sake, for all our sakes, I hope it happens quickly.'

'I appreciate the generosity of your sentiments.'

Von Bardsdorf let it pass. 'There are things we should discuss, now that you'll be circulating around the fortress grounds,' he said, and launched into a description of the virtues of the fortress as a prison: its height, its isolation, its construction, the impossibility of emerging in any secret way. De Forge concentrated on every word.

'It will not surprise you to learn,' von Bardsdorf concluded, 'that we went to great pains in choosing a place to house you and your fellow generals. The reason this fortress was chosen is quite simple: it's escape-proof.' Von Bardsdorf let the idea sink in. 'You'll have ample opportunity to examine our little institution for yourself. I urge you to do so. Consider it from all angles. I think you'll come to the same conclusion we've come to.'

He offered de Forge a cigarette and when it was refused lit one for himself.

'I need hardly tell you,' von Bardsdorf went on, puffing out a cone of blue smoke, 'that we know your history. In fact, we know it quite well. We know, for example, that you escaped from us in the last war. So we have an idea of your resourcefulness.' Von Bardsdorf smiled. 'Be that as it may,' he continued with assurance, 'there will be no escape this time. You'll see that soon enough, and it will be greatly to your advantage.'

De Forge began to see what the colonel was leading up to.

'I'll be frank,' von Bardsdorf said, 'We want your co-operation. What sense does it make in your situation not to co-operate? No matter what the propaganda abroad says, we're not ogres. If we can manage to work together instead of against each other, your life will be a lot more agreeable.' Von Bardsdorf hesitated, then added, 'Considering the circumstances, we ought to come to an agreement.'

'What kind of agreement?'

'I would be very happy if you gave your word as an officer that you will make no attempt to escape.'

A slight smile modified the gravity of de Forge's regard. 'But such a promise,' he said, 'would be meaningless. You've just told me the fortress is escape-proof. In that case a promise not to try to escape is worthless.'

Von Bardsdorf's smile was as dry as his parchment face. 'The proposal is a matter of form. It's made in your own interest.'

'I'm just as concerned about your interest.'

'Then you'll give your word?'

'But I wouldn't offer you something that's worth nothing.'

The two men looked at each other steadily. 'Very well,' von Bardsdorf said. 'You'll have a chance to look around and you'll judge for yourself. You may change your mind.'

He went to the door with a quick, decided step, stopped, turned and said, '*Herr General,* I've studied the matter most carefully. I cannot imagine you will try anything foolish, worse than foolish – suicidal. There are two ways, and only two ways, any prisoner can leave this fortress. One, if we release him. Two, feet first.'

After the door had slammed behind von Bardsdorf, de Forge sank on to his cot and sat there a long time, his chin on his fists. He was troubled. Von Bardsdorf was very convincing about the virtues of his fortress.

THREE

The first person de Forge met when he moved into his new and permanent quarters later that day was General Hubert Bonniot, a chunky little man de Forge remembered as almost invariably bouncy and gay, and who was probably the French army's outstanding quartermaster expert. He looked neither gay nor bouncy.

'Hullo,' Bonniot said. 'So you're here with the rest of us after all.'

'As you see.'

'That was the rumour. We knew there was a general in solitary, but all we got was a rolling of the eyes from the Boches and something about a *"derrible bersonage."* Some of your worst friends said it could only be you.'

'I can always depend on my worst friends.'

'I was betting against it.'

'Oh?'

'My assumption was that since you were always out of step with everybody from the General Staff down –'

'That I wouldn't fall into step now.'

'Something like that.'

'Well, as you see, I fell into their hands like everyone else.' Bitterness tempered with irony.

Uncharacteristically, Bonniot was glum. 'You can say "like everyone else." We're all in their bag, all of us. It's pathetic, appalling. The one time I came up close and paf! in the bag. Me, back at quartermaster. One inspection tour to get the idea and it's the end. I never imagined it could be so bad, such a total hopeless mess.'

De Forge shrugged off the past. 'How is it here?' he asked.

'They're correct.' Bonniot looked at de Forge soberly. 'I'd almost rather they weren't so damned correct.'

De Forge nodded approval. 'And our people?'

Bonniot spread his hands. 'Hopeless.'

'How so?'

'Resigned. The spirit knocked out of them.'

'Not all of us,' de Forge protested. 'It's not possible.'

Bonniot shrugged. 'Of course, but it's still variations on a theme. Look at me. I've never felt so beaten in my life. I don't want to feel that way but I do. Most are in effect playing the German game: "We're beaten. The war is lost. We may as well co-operate. What else can we do?" '

'The lesser evil for the greater good.'

'Not quite. More likely the only alternative.'

'There must be another choice, there has to be.' De Forge was suddenly angry. 'They're not men; they're sheep. It makes me want to puke. Courage! Resolution! They don't know what it means. And they're supposed to be soldiers. Why did God decide to populate France with Frenchmen? It must have happened on the seventh day when He was reading the Sunday papers and not paying attention.'

'At least we have Reboux and Palisse with us,' Bonniot said. 'They're the best of the lot. They want to escape. They can't talk of anything else – among ourselves, of course.'

'Have they found a way?'

Bonniot shook his head glumly. 'This place is a can without a can opener. There's no way out.' A look of despair came into his eyes. 'I've got to get out, I've got to. They could keep us here for years, for years. It's like death for me.'

De Forge had never imagined Bonniot could be so intense.

'How do Reboux and Palisse see the problem?'

'You know how different they are. Reboux: attack, attack. Palisse: plan, plan. Well, here they agree on the most depressing premise. They don't know if there's any hope, but they're sure that at best it will take a long time. For me that's no hope at all.'

He was begging for it. De Forge asked, 'What's your hurry?'

'Haven't you heard? I was married a week before I was captured.'

Bonniot wanted to talk more about it, but Palisse walked in. He was a husky, good-looking man and a fine staff officer. His light blue eyes had a direct, untroubled regard.

'Sorry to see you here,' he said, shaking de Forge's hand.

De Forge liked him. 'Let's arrange to see each other elsewhere.'

'Difficult. Probably impossible.'

'Nothing is impossible.'

'That's the principle I'm working on, but it's discouraging. Can't find any way of getting out of this damned place – alive.'

They talked for half an hour, but the talk turned on itself, reached a dead end and came back in a circle. It wasn't very good talk because it didn't strike reality. There was only one reality: escape.

When they left, de Forge felt depressed but was determined not to show it. His room was much like the last one. It was in a small building in the middle of the fortress inner grounds. On one side of it was a long structure where most of the other prisoners were housed; on the other side, towards the fortress wall, was a series of casemates where the balance of the imprisoned generals lived. Only three other prisoners lived in de Forge's building – Bonniot, Palisse and Reboux. Pierre Reboux was a fighting general, a first-rate divisional commander. He was a wiry, saturnine man, a little bowlegged, who did his own thinking and prided himself on his realism. In the afternoon he showed de Forge the fortress grounds.

De Forge quickly saw that the grounds were contained on an oval-shaped plateau of several acres that sat sky-high on top of a mountain of rock. One end of the plateau was narrower than the other and was covered with trees and shrubbery like a small park. The balance of the area was open space broken by seven or eight ugly stone buildings of varying sizes and shapes with a group of hump-shaped casemates on one side. As they walked, Reboux identified each building – those where the generals were housed, the one for the French enlisted men who served the generals, the one at the far end opposite the park where the German command was located, the canteen and the building that served as a sort of club room.

The worst part was when de Forge came to the crenellated wall. The battlement surrounded the entire plateau. Reboux led him to one of the holes in the parapet. De Forge looked down. Instantly the vertigo grabbed him by the bowels. There was a sheer drop of 150 feet. Below, a thickly wooded area; this in turn dipped steeply at least another five hundred feet to the bed of a valley. It was breathtaking.

De Forge drew back and closed his eyes. Then, his teeth clenched, he leaned forward, gripping the stones, and looked again. It was not the majesty of the scene he saw but the terror of the empty space below him and its unscalable dimension. At last he turned back towards Reboux, silent.

'You see?'

De Forge nodded. How the hell could anyone who couldn't fly get out of this place? As if pulled by a magnet, de Forge turned back again to the broad, deep, seemingly fathomless empty space. Yes, he thought, it was the very place he himself would have chosen for the purpose. They might as well have been on another planet for all the chance they had to get down to the earth so far below. It was an aeroplane view. De Forge's stomach dropped away. Bonniot had to be right: a can without a can opener.

'What other way out is there?' he heard himself ask.

'The front door,' Reboux said sourly. 'The only exit is the entrance, the way you and the rest of us came in. You saw it. There are two huge vaulted doors, one after the other. Each has its complement of armed guards. Even if it were conceivable that anyone could get past the first door, it's unthinkable that the second could be breached as well. Force, in any case, is out of the question. If by a miracle, and we're hardly saints to depend on miracles, someone got out that way, what chance would he have? The alert would be given immediately. He'd be dragged back. Or shot. No, there's only one way out: over the wall.'

They were walking away from it.

'Without wings?'

Reboux grunted. 'There's no answer to that one. The battlement swings out. You can't even see the wall below, but obviously it's a straight clean drop. The wall is suicide.'

'Bed sheets . . .'

'You saw the distance. Even if there were enough bed sheets. No, that's daydreaming.'

'A rope. A cable.'

'That length? Where would we get it? And even if we did, and even if it were strong enough to hold, would we be strong enough to hold it?'

The two generals walked in silence. De Forge had merely been probing. These were the obvious ideas, the unworkable ones. The problem was baffling. They were barehanded, without arms, tools, equipment, walled into a fortress on the top of a mountain.

'It's worse than I thought,' de Forge said. 'I'll have to think about it.'

'It will take a lot of thought.'

FOUR

It did. But de Forge got no further along than Palisse or Reboux. His depression deepened as the days and weeks passed. The summer was splendid, a mockery to the turmoil inside him. He often went to the parapet and gazed at the majestic panorama spread below. There lay the world, visible but beyond reach. Somewhere beyond the full-leafed forest, the valley, the river, the distant horizon, lay freedom and the possibility to do what he felt he had been destined for. There it was, and here he wasted away day after interminable day without purpose or hope.

But though his spirit darkened, he presented the same

serene face to the world. It was not easy, but fortitude lent him grace. As one of a hundred French generals being held captive, de Forge felt humiliated and demeaned; the low tone of the prisoners and the climate of resignation intensified his shame. The others had given up. He could not.

But he was blocked. He soon stopped discussing the problem with Palisse, Reboux or Bonniot. The surface assumption was that for lack of a plan they had abandoned the dream of escape and accepted imprisonment. Reboux was grim and taciturn. Palisse seemed impassive, but his eyes and an occasional twitch betrayed him. Between waves of forced gaiety, Bonniot, who longed for the bride he had so quickly lost, would suddenly find himself becalmed and his face, disconcertingly, would decompose. De Forge shored up his resolution against despair, refusing to believe he would suffer the same fate as the others and be disposed of like an object without a will of his own.

One fine summer morning he ran head-on into Colonel von Bardsdorf between the casemates and the Kommandatur. Von Bardsdorf was in crisp good humour.

De Forge bowed stiffly and walked past the smiling German colonel towards the parapet, but von Bardsdorf turned and caught up to him.

'Did I mislead you the last time we spoke? Now, tell me, did I? Isn't it just as I said it was? Look there. A wall. And it goes all around the place. Not really much of a wall, but enough, eh. And what a beautiful view! Do you know that in peacetime (may it come soon again!) tourists come from all over Germany and many other countries, too, just to see this view? It's one of the most spectacular views in the whole world. I hear you enjoy it very much. I hear you come here very often just to enjoy our fine German scenery. Enjoy it. That's what it's here for.'

As von Bardsdorf chuckled and left, his triumphant high spirits crystallized what de Forge had been repressing. Von Bardsdorf had pronounced the fortress escape-proof; and after weeks of stretching his mind against the challenge, de Forge had to admit he was right.

That night as de Forge lay in bed he faced the rock-bottom reality that he had no way or even any possibility of getting out. The truth struck him like a blow. He couldn't do a thing. His dreams of destiny, visions of service, élan towards glory were empty illusions. They had unmanned him; he was like a gelded beast turning blindly under a yoke in an endless circle. He buried his face in the pillow and wept. He wept the loss of the man he had been, wept for the strength that had been torn from him.

Nobody ever knew. But because he wept from strength, from the rock of courage that was his centre of gravity, de Forge emerged from his crucible of tears cleansed and tempered. It was his worst crisis. After it he realized that even in prison, especially in prison, a man had to have a purpose and work towards it with whatever hope he could summon from the resources within himself. Otherwise he withered and died.

De Forge imposed an exercise on himself: to rationalize the problem despite the evident impossibility of solving it. He used Bonniot to bounce ideas against. Giving voice to his rationalizations was important since it gave them a sense of reality. The idea of escape had become so remote and improbable that any trick lent substance to this frailest wisp of a dream.

De Forge and Bonniot went for daily walks. They had total freedom to circulate on the fortress grounds but were as safely enclosed as animals in a cage; for wherever the prisoners might go, eventually they came to a dead stop against the parapet. In addition, armed guards constantly made the rounds, circling the parapet at a relaxed pace.

Watching the guard one afternoon, Bonniot said, 'If we ever worked out a plan to escape, those bastards would complicate things.'

'I've thought about it,' de Forge replied. 'They set some of the conditions.'

'How so?'

'It would have to be a daylight operation. With the guard doubled at night the risk at that time would be too great.'

'But there are enough of them in daylight too. They come around every fifteen minutes.'

'Don't I know! I've timed them often enough. And yet the only way is over the wall.'

'Suicide canyon.'

'There's no other way. But fifteen minutes is more than enough time. It just takes guts and decision.'

'And a cable.'

'And a cable,' de Forge echoed. 'If there were a way to get a cable or make one, the first half of the problem would be simple.'

'A cable long enough and strong enough to lower a man to the bottom of the rock.'

'A hundred and fifty feet long.'

Bonniot shook his head at the dimensions of the problem. 'That's an awful lot of cable,' he said.

'And only a small part of the problem.'

They had been over this ground many times, but they liked to gnaw at it in the hope that somehow, perhaps by endless repetition, a light would break where there had been only darkness. It was their way of exorcising evil spirits and beseeching the gods to set them free.

'In sum,' de Forge recapitulated, 'the operation is divided into two parts: one, getting out of the fortress; two, even more difficult, getting out of Germany and into France or Switzerland. For the first we need a cable; for the second we need help from the outside. After all, what point is there to risking our neck, getting out, then being dragged back because the escape is badly conceived?'

That was how de Forge always recapitulated. He treated the problem like a practical military exercise. De Forge knew all too well what an escape of this sort entailed; he was no novice. Having been left for dead on a World War I battlefield, he had been picked up by the Germans and had barely recovered from his wounds when he made an escape so notable the Germans never forgot it. That problem, however, had been a lot easier than the one de Forge now faced. Though weak from his wounds, he was much younger then; and his escape had been engineered from a hospital, not from a fortress hung in the sky; in addition, his major effort had been to move through occupied Belgium, where the population was friendly, and not across hostile enemy territory, where he could not count on the sympathy of a soul.

But the previous experience had burned certain axioms into his blood and bones: that an escape could not be improvised without throwing oneself rashly into the hands of fickle gods; that an escape had to be meticulously planned and executed; that it demanded an infinitude of patience and perseverance; that his captors had to be lulled into the deepest sense of security, though here that was no problem. He also knew from having suffered through it that at the point of action it demanded the utmost in courage, decisiveness and tireless strength. He was aware of the implication: that if anyone stood in his way, he would kill him.

Bonniot often became discouraged. 'All this talk,' he would say. 'It's like masturbating.'

'Patience,' de Forge would reply. 'It needs lots of patience.'

'Just what I don't have and don't want.' And Bonniot would think of the bride he couldn't touch and his face would fall apart.

Once, in his room, de Forge spoke of the complexity of the problem to Reboux, who disagreed with de Forge's conception.

'If a way could be found to get out of here,' Reboux maintained, 'the rest would be simple. I'd dash for the border. Then over it and free.'

'But how would you get there?'

'I'd get there if I had to crawl.'

'Eight hundred kilometres?'

'I'd walk a bit, then hitchhike.'

Nobody could tell from Reboux's German that he was French. De Forge lacked that advantage.

'Still,' de Forge objected, 'your chances would be nil.'

'Any way you look at it our chances are nil.'

'All the more reason to raise them by preparation and organization.'

'Doing it your way you should hire a travel service.'

'Precisely,' de Forge said. 'A French travel service.'

Despite an edge of irony, de Forge meant it. The idea had been flowering slowly. There would be time enough to tell whoever had to know when the moment was ripe. But if he mentioned it now, they would surely think he was mad.

FIVE

A somnolence fell over the fortress as the drowsy, eventless summer days passed. Every morning at seven o'clock de Forge's orderly, a sturdy young private from a village in Normandy, would awaken the general, who would then take his breakfast of ersatz coffee and black bread. The orderly's name was Gabory, and he was devoted to de Forge. Their morning conversation invariably began the same way.

'What's new this morning, Gabory?'

'Not very much, *mon général*.'

Then Gabory would plunge into the intrigues, discussions and problems of the French enlisted men. There were as many of them in the fortress, about one hundred, as there were generals. They did all the basic work in the kitchen, the various details and served the generals. It was Gabory who kept de Forge informed in a casual way of what was going on at his end of the fortress. De Forge learned from the start that the spirit among the enlisted men was much better than among the generals. The enlisted men were younger, to be sure, but they also approached the Germans with less of a desire to understand them and less resignation in defeat. They were at once less civilized than the generals and more hardheaded. Apart from a few who were used by the Germans as their instruments, the vast majority of the enlisted men were resistants. The vast majority of the generals, on the other hand, were resigned to defeat. About a dozen were open collaborationists; and an equal number were, like de Forge, irreducibly defiant. But none envisioned escape. Even if escape had seemed possible, they were too old, too tired. Many hoped to be released for reasons of health. These would go on sick call almost daily. But though many were sick, they were not sick enough. Higher headquarters had imposed rigid criteria, and the German doctors were sympathetic but ungiving.

One French general finally made it; he would rather not have. After weeks of examination and tests, the ailment was

36

diagnosed as an advanced and generalized cancer. The general was given no more than a few months to live. On two hours' notice, they shipped him back to France to die. It happened so fast and de Forge found out about it so late that he did not have the time to prepare a message the general might have hidden and taken back with him.

Later that day de Forge's path crossed Colonel von Bardsdorf's. The colonel stopped him.

'Please accept my sympathies,' von Bardsdorf said, referring to the sick French general. 'A most regrettable case and I am deeply sorry.'

'It might be a good thing,' de Forge quickly replied, 'if such cases could be sent back home a good deal faster.'

'They have to be checked and tested. Those are the rules. We're obliged to abide by them.'

'There are special cases that can be expedited. It's a question of simple humanity.'

'I'm aware of it, and you can be sure that I will push such cases to the extent of my authority. In any case, as you see, we don't want any of you to die here.'

'But it doesn't look so good for you if those you send home die off as soon as they get there.'

'We can't send you people home just because you turn up for sick call.'

'But if the only ones you send home are those who die after a couple of months, what will people think and say?'

'They will be wrong,' von Bardsdorf said heatedly. 'And you know it as well as I. The treatment you get here is exemplary. It's to the letter of the Geneva Convention.'

'That won't prevent people from drawing conclusions from the fact. I say this not from my point of view but from yours.'

De Forge felt that he had shaken von Bardsdorf and was pleased with the exchange. He felt that there might be a change in attitude, however slight. The criteria might be lowered. And what vistas the release of the general opened up! It could happen again. In that case he could get a message to his wife, a secret message the Germans would not see. He inquired discreetly about who was really sick, so sick that he was likely to be sent home. Nobody. The worst case was that of a collaborator, who added a little too much faking and a touch of obsequiousness to his ailment. De Forge was disgusted. Just his luck that there was no one trustworthy who was sick enough to have the prospect of release. But the idea was planted. He felt that sooner or later he would have a means to put his private travel service into operation.

Meanwhile, a more normal service began to function. Towards the end of July the first mail from France arrived. De Forge was authorized to correspond with his wife. When he received an answer to his first letter he felt connected again; a life line was established: it was like blood flowing into his veins.

Letters took a month in coming, but they were something to live for. This link with the outside world was an open one, to be sure: the letters he sent had to be submitted unsealed and the seals of those he received were broken. But even though foreign eyes read every intimate word (and some of the letters, as he learned, even went to Berlin), it was a glorious living contact not merely with the human being closest to him, but through her with the outside, with the world. He thought of her, of Suzanne. She knew him in some ways better than he knew himself. She would know what his thinking was, know that his single, all-devouring thought was escape. He read every word of her letters a dozen times, searching for meanings that weren't there. Then he began to puzzle over a simple code. If, somehow, he could establish that with her, the link would become private – private enough, in any case, for his purposes.

With the mail service, a post office was established at the fortress. It was placed in charge of a bright little corporal from Paris named Picoche, who had strong left-wing sentiments and nurtured a special irreverence for his German captors. Nor did Picoche have much reverence, indeed any at all, for the generals he served, but almost in spite of himself he had an affinity and deference for de Forge. He had been an infantryman in a regiment under de Forge's command and in the fortress had had some casual contacts with him. De Forge did not have the exasperating attitude of most of the other generals, who spoke to Picoche as if he were an inferior animal specimen.

In the middle of August the first packages from home arrived. They were carefully examined at the post office by the Germans to verify that nothing unauthorized was in them, then they were distributed. Picoche delivered a package to de Forge that his wife had sent. It was filled with canned food, homemade pâtés and the like.

'I have something good for you, *mon général*,' Picoche said as he entered de Forge's room. 'A package from your wife.'

'So they've started to come at last,' de Forge said, then added over the package, 'Don't leave yet, Picoche. What's your hurry?'

The package had been redone, and de Forge untied the string around it and dumped out its contents on his bed.

'Did you get a package, Picoche?'

'No, *mon général*.'

'Take what you'd like.'

Picoche looked at the pile of food with big eyes. 'I couldn't do that, *mon général*.'

'Nonsense. Go ahead.'

But Picoche held back, and finally de Forge selected a pâté and a can of sardines and handed them to the little corporal.

'Thank you, *mon général*,' he said with a broad smile. 'I have a pal back there, and he and I will put this to good use and drink to your health at the same time.'

'And how are our German friends?'

'I wish the rest of us had the same concern about them that you and I have, *mon général*.'

They had been over this ground once before. De Forge knew how Picoche felt about the attitude of most of the imprisoned generals.

'Never mind, Picoche. In the end, we'll have them.'

'Not our own generals!'

De Forge laughed. 'I was talking about the Boches.'

After Picoche left, de Forge arranged the food on a shelf. He was gathering a small stock of supplies. Every month the Kommandatur distributed scrip to the generals; it served as their pay and as money in the fortress. The generals could spend it in the canteen for cigarettes, canned food, German newspapers, German books and a host of necessities. They were not authorized to have real German currency, for that had the smell of freedom. But the scrip sufficed.

De Forge tidied up. He placed the carton near the door,

where his orderly, Gabory, would find it the next morning and remove it. He stuffed into the carton the paper with which the food had been wrapped. Then he threw on top of that the string that had held the carton closed.

De Forge went to the shelf once again to contemplate his riches. They were the ones he felt Midas-like about. These were the poor riches that would satisfy his hunger and free his mind, his true fortune that would prevent his body from dominating his spirit. But just as he was about to give in to greed something in his mind clicked and his heart leaped out of him. He stood there frozen a beat, remembering with brilliant lucidity what he had seen, then, whirling around, in two strides he was bent over the carton. Out of it he took the string. He held it up between the thumb and index finger of his right hand. It was about four feet long and thin. De Forge took it in both hands and pulled on it, making it snap. His eyes were alight, his face illuminated.

'A cable!' he said aloud. '*The* cable! My cable!'

He paced the room excitedly, the length of string clenched in his hand. I've got it, he thought; finally I've got it. He gazed at the pitifully frail bit of string thinking that it would be his lifeline to freedom, and brought it fervently to his lips. There's always a way, he told himself, there has to be. A phrase of Mao Tse-tung came into his mind to the effect that if one must walk a thousand miles, one must begin by taking a first small step. Yes, he thought, it would take a long time to fashion his cable out of such bits of string; but in his thousand-mile march this was his first small step. At last he had the concrete beginning of a plan of escape. He was exultant. It was half an hour before he calmed down.

De Forge carefully hid the precious length of string and left his room to look for Picoche. His step was jaunty; he was a man going somewhere. Outside the building he met Palisse and Reboux.

'Where are you off to?' Palisse demanded. 'What's your hurry?'

'Things to attend to,' de Forge called over his shoulder.

'Packages have arrived,' Reboux called after him.

'Yes, yes, I got one.'

De Forge ran into Gabory near the canteen.

'Have you seen Picoche?'

'About ten minutes ago, *mon général*. He's distributing packages.'

'Tell him I want to see him.' De Forge hesitated. 'It's about the package I received. I just wondered if the Boche had removed anything. But be discreet. There's no need for anyone else to know I want to see him.'

While de Forge was waiting for Picoche, Colonel von Bardsdorf passed and stopped to chat with him.

'I understand you received a package.'

'*Monsieur le colonel* is well informed.'

'I trust you are pleased.'

'Immensely. Beyond my powers of expression.'

Von Bardsdorf smiled broadly. It was the first time de Forge had replied with unqualified approval to any advance von Bardsdorf had made. The German colonel beamed. Here was this cantankerous French general, the pride of his catch and the most unmanageable, being positively enthusiastic.

'Delighted, delighted. I hope there'll be many more, *monsieur le général.*'

'And so do I, *monsieur le colonel*, so do I.'

A quarter of an hour later the lively little corporal from Paris appeared.

'Gabory told me you wanted to know if something was removed from your package, *mon général*,' Picoche said as he came up to de Forge. 'I was there all the time and – '

'No, no, Picoche. That was just a dodge. I wanted to talk to you about something else.'

De Forge led the bright-eyed Parisian aside.

'Tell me, Picoche, were there many packages today?'

'Quite a few, *mon général*. Perhaps forty or fifty.'

'They should keep coming now, eh?'

'I should think so.' Picoche looked puzzled. 'Why do you ask, *mon général*?'

'Picoche, can I have confidence in you?'

'Of course, *mon général.*'

'Absolute confidence, Picoche?' de Forge demanded over his protests of loyalty. 'What we say now must remain only between us. You must not whisper a word of it to anyone, not even to your best pal.'

'It's sworn, *mon général*.'

'Good.' De Forge hesitated, then plunged. 'There's string around the packages, Picoche. I would like to have that string, as much of it as possible.'

Picoche looked up at de Forge with wide eyes. De Forge returned the look. It lasted longer than de Forge liked. For an instant doubt struck him and his heart fell.

'Very well, *mon général*,' Picoche said at last. 'But how much do you need?'

'I tell you as much as possible. It will be months before I have enough.'

'Very well. I'll put it aside and get it to you.'

'It is very delicate, Picoche. You understand that, of course. No one must know. It will be better for me and better for you.' De Forge hesitated. 'And in the end better for France.'

'I'm not asking any questions, *mon général*. If you need this string, that's good enough for me.'

'The less you know the better. There's no need to know anything.'

'But how will I get it to you?'

'Put it aside in lengths of three or four feet. I'll let you know soon enough, tomorrow probably, how to get it to me. Above all, there must be no direct contact between us. That way, no matter what happens, there can be no suspicion thrown on you. In any case, you could convincingly deny knowing anything about it.'

The following morning over his ersatz coffee de Forge asked Gabory if he would serve as a go-between, getting the bits of string from Picoche and bringing them to him in the normal course of his duties. De Forge appreciated Gabory: he was simple, straight and true, and there seemed to be no complexities or reservations behind his open, blue-eyed regard. De Forge was certain the sturdy Norman peasant would agree; he was as sure of him as he would be of his own son.

'There will be no problem, *mon général*,' Gabory said. 'It will be as simple as drinking a glass of good cider. And as great a pleasure.'

Gabory was right. As packages arrived in successive shipments, he was handed castoff bits of string by Picoche under the noses of inattentive guards and delivered them, bunches at a time hidden under his tunic, to de Forge. Deliveries were usually made in the morning and never failed to brighten de Forge as he awoke to another day of imprisonment. Having hidden the string, de Forge anticipated all day long that secret moment after the late German check at nine o'clock when, safely alone at last, he could turn to the instrument of his escape.

He braided the lengths of string together, twisting and knotting the strands in place, thickening and overlapping each length to increase its resistance. Progress was agonizingly slow. It required five or six yards of twine to fashion one yard of cable, the twine sometimes taut and strong, often weak and mediocre. But each bit of string, however poor its quality, added to the length or thickness of the growing cable – a yard at first, then a bit more, then two yards, then three. De Forge learned to work the string as he went along. He braided each new length into the cable, twisting it tightly with other lengths, his hands red and burning on the rough twine, the nerves and muscles of his hands, wrists and forearms strained to numbness.

Those tedious hours of mindless labour braiding and twisting the strands together in the night-soft silence of his room were hours of joy and fulfilment that de Forge looked forward to with the longing impatience of a lover for his mistress; and he regarded and fondled the cable in progress with an emotion something like love. It was this amateurish object he was fashioning that would be the instrument to change his condition; it was this derisive, this ugly, inanimate thing that would alter his existence and enable him to realize his destiny. He pondered upon how little relation of grandeur there was between cause and effect. Yet for him these bits of string entwined strand by strand into a mediocre cable strong enough, he hoped, to hold his weight were nothing less than a poem, a poem chanting his conviction that destiny had pointed its gnarled finger at him for affairs of great moment: he envisioned himself as the saviour of France.

With so far-reaching an ambition to feed his imagination, de Forge redoubled his efforts in all areas. He was richest in time but it no longer weighed on him, for now he filled it purposefully – until suddenly there seemed to be hardly enough each day. He devoted himself to reading, studying, speaking German, taking every possible occasion and manufacturing others according to the circumstance to engage the guards and their officers in conversation. He would need the language to cross the country – or he might need it.

Just about every day there were long periods when he stretched his mind against the other half of the problem that resisted him. He kept at it as if it were an exercise, feeling that somehow he would find an answer, somehow he would find a way to communicate secretly with his wife and through her with others in France who could help him. He knew that that was what he had to do if he were to succeed in his escape; it was not possible, to his thinking, to do it alone. And he felt that just as he had seen the string and from it deduced a cable, in the same way he would find a solution to the other half of the puzzle. He felt that the problem had to be fought, that no matter how hopeless it seemed to be, if he kept at it, kept fighting it, the solution would finally, like a vanquished enemy, bow to him. So he kept going stubbornly after it, round and round in circles, refusing to abandon the battle. It was wearisome; yet no matter how he stretched and pulled at it, he remained baffled.

He came to the conclusion at last that the only way he could count on getting word home was if one of the generals he trusted was released. But he knew none who was sick, certainly none who approached being sick enough. Then he thought that if the reality did not exist, it should be invented. The idea was illuminating. He puzzled over it the better part of a week. How could he invent a sick general? How could he invent a general so sick it would convince the able and suspicious German doctors that the ailment was the real thing and that the man had to be repatriated?

De Forge was certain he was now on the right track, but he found it harder than ever to find his way. He searched his mind for all the medical lore he had ever heard; the answer eluded him. Then he reluctantly concluded that this solution was an impossible one. It was too simple. If sicknesses could be invented and doctors tricked, everybody would do it and the fortress would be empty in the time it took to say tuberculosis. He abandoned that line of thought.

But as he walked away from it, one reflection remained in his mind and stuck stubbornly like a bit of food in a tooth: it was symptoms that doctors based their diagnoses on, symptoms, and very often the symptoms fooled them. He kept wondering, on and off, what set of symptoms could be fabricated so that no group of doctors could read them correctly. If he could inflict these symptoms upon a friendly general anxious to get out – and which of them was not anxious to get out? – then it would be the same as inventing a general so sick the Germans would be obliged to ship him home. Then he did not need a sick general, but a general who seemed to be sick. That was easier, he thought, but still difficult. To be effective, the appearance would certainly have to approach the reality. It might take an act of will. But a psychosomatic ailment would surely not be good enough, especially one that was deliberately manufactured. Nor would faked madness do. Nor anything that could be checked. They would simply discover the fraud, and it would make them that much more suspicious even of the real thing.

There was no solution.

Wherever he turned the doctors were there before him. Whatever gambit he tried the doctors could always check him. He had to find a set of symptoms that could not be checked for a malady that did not exist.

De Forge was persuaded that an expert would have a simple solution, and every time he attacked the problem he tormented himself that no specialist was at hand to reveal the elusive secret – perhaps an ancient case in the man's own experience or in the literature that had baffled a generation of specialists and that could be reconstructed here in the fortress. It was beyond de Forge's means. He told himself he would have to be patient and not push it, that he would have to put the problem aside and plan a new line of attack. It was too much for him, perhaps too much, after all, for anyone. No doubt he was knocking on doors that could never be opened.

Then, suddenly, out of the blue, he had it. Or thought he did.

If there was anything de Forge abhorred, it was abortive acts, projects that fell apart midway because they were ill-conceived, badly organized or shabbily executed. He was a man whose dreams were based on realities, who deeply believed that the nature of things contained and limited by its brute facts and complexities the goals and ideals that could be wrested from the flow of time. De Forge therefore spent two thoughtful days examining his idea from all sides before he was satisfied that he could initiate it. On the third day he sought out Bonniot.

The chunky quartermaster expert had lost his bounce. As the war continued and the golden days of summer without his bride succeeded each other in mocking splendour, the horizon of imprisonment stretched endlessly ahead, turning him morose and dull-eyed. De Forge took him for a turn of the grounds, casually mentioning that he had thought of something quite promising in the escape department. They had been over the same ground too often for Bonniot to light up.

'I've given up,' Bonniot said. 'Fighting windmills just depresses me. The fact is there's no way out. We'll just rot here until the war is over. Months, years, all of them lost.'

'For most of us, yes. But not for all of us.'

'All you need to get out is a generalized cancer in an advanced state.'

'That would be doing it the easy way.'

'On a stretcher without trying,' Bonniot mused. 'Not really my style.'

'The trick,' de Forge suggested, 'is to be sent home sick, but not so sick that you won't recover and enjoy it. But of course,' he added, 'that takes ingenuity and effort.'

Bonniot assumed that de Forge was merely expressing a laudable principle and did not immediately pursue his lead; but as they approached the parapet, he came back to it.

'I've thought of that,' Bonniot said. 'I suppose all of us have thought of it. I thought if only I could will myself to be sick. I used to do that, probably we all did, when I was a child. I would make myself sick. You know how you can make yourself look miserable and feel miserable and then your mother or father or nurse clucks over you and for a day you can stay at home, in and out of bed, and not have to do any homework. But how the hell can you make yourself sick enough so that a Boche doctor pronounces you unfit to be kept imprisoned and recommends that you be sent home?'

De Forge looked down at Bonniot sideways as they walked. 'I think I've worked that very thing out.'

Bonniot was still unimpressed. 'Then why don't you put it into effect?'

'It's no good for me.'

'Ah! . . . That's always the problem,' Bonniot said ironically. 'The good ideas aren't workable.'

'Oh, this one is workable all right.' De Forge spoke with infinite assurance. 'It's just not workable for me.'

'Why not for you if it's workable for someone else?'

'Because the Boches have a particular concern for me. They know me and I know them, and we both know it. It would be foolish to have illusions: they wouldn't let me out of here alive unless I were on a stretcher heading for my deathbed.'

They had reached the parapet and stopped. Both of them gazed at the splendid scene spread out below them.

Bonniot was thinking. He turned to de Forge. 'Then who would your idea be good for?'

It was the question de Forge had been waiting for. 'Someone with iron in his soul. Someone who would rather die than rot while life passes him by. And more than that – someone who is ready to suffer, perhaps for months, to succeed in an enterprise he can never really be certain about.'

'But, de Forge, you're talking to that man.'

Bonniot was excited now, but de Forge regarded him coolly. 'How can you say you're the man when you don't even know what you would have to do and what you would have to suffer?'

'You know I'd do anything humanly possible to get out of here. And you know why.'

De Forge nodded. 'Yes,' he agreed, 'you have a stronger reason than most to want to get out.' He hesitated, as if reaching a reluctant decision. 'It's really very simple,' he said, almost apologetically.

'Like the best ideas.'

'It will be a test of how much you want to get out.'

'That's a test I can pass. Just tell me what I have to do.'

De Forge studied Bonniot's eager round face, then said, 'Starve.'

Bonniot's face fell. 'Starve?'

'Yes, starve.'

'That's all?'

'That's all. But it will be enough.'

'I don't understand.'

'The Germans are a very methodical people,' de Forge explained. 'You have noticed that we have regular medical checkups. They take our pulse, they listen to our heart, they check our weight. What do you deduce from that?'

Bonniot shrugged.

'They don't want us to get sick,' de Forge said, 'not without their knowing about it. They're concerned about us. We're generals. They feel a responsibility. We're important people, *mon cher* Bonniot. They would be distressed if one of us died while in their care. That would not be as bad as losing one of us in an escape, but it would be very bad. It would be a kind of *lèse-majesté*, the patent failure to fulfil an obligation. None of us must escape, but none of us must die here. That is their principle. And they will do as much to fulfil the second part as the first.'

'What has starving got to do with that?'

'They will not know you are starving. Nobody will know except you and me.'

'So?'

'So they will be puzzled at the apparent and precipitous decline in your health. You will not push it, for that might arouse their suspicions. It will require immense self-control. But you will report for medical checkup. They know how much you weigh. They will observe that you are losing weight. They will see that you are fading away, that you are getting weaker. All that will be true. But they will be unable to explain it. You will become their problem. They will see you waste away and they will not know how to stop it, for they will ignore its cause.'

'Suppose they send me to a hospital for observation.'

'I doubt that they will. They don't do that so easily – especially if the prisoner doesn't ask for it. In any case, by that time you can plead loss of appetite. You will stop eating. For them that will be another symptom of the malady and not its cause. After all, you will be perfectly docile. There will be no question of a hunger strike. On the contrary.'

'And then?'

'And then at a moment you judge the situation to be psychologically ripe you must say to them, rather wistfully, how you would love to see your family, especially your bride, before you die. That will do it. They know your situation. Who doesn't? They know that you hardly had the chance to embrace your bride before you were taken prisoner. The Germans are brutes, but they are sentimental brutes. And they will be afraid to be held responsible for a death they don't understand. They will therefore release you, but not until you're very far gone. That will allow them to enjoy the luxury of their humanity while dumping a problem they couldn't solve.'

De Forge regarded Bonniot to observe the effect of his words. Bonniot seemed to be stargazing.

'It could work,' he said. 'It could work.'

'Would you have the strength and fortitude to do it?' de Forge asked. 'That's the question. If you're able to go through with it, it will work.'

'I'll do anything to get out,' Bonniot said fiercely, 'anything. I'm dying here. I die every moment . . . But it's so simple, so very simple. Will the German doctors really fall for it?'

'Think about it. Take your time and think about it. And ask yourself, too, what else you might do to get out. Is there a better plan, or is this the only one for you?'

'Yes, I must think about it. Of course, as you say, there's no certainty about it, but at least it's a plan and a reasonable one and it would give me a chance, hope. . . .'

'That's right. Think about it and let me know.'

A thought crossed Bonniot's mind. 'By the way, what about the food I wouldn't eat?'

'What about it?'

'How would I dispose of it?'

De Forge considered Bonniot from a great height over his heavy nose, a slight smile on his lips, a malicious light in his eyes, and said serenely, 'Nothing could be simpler: you will give it to me and I will eat it. I will need the strength for my own escape.'

SIX

Bonniot pondered the matter and told de Forge the next day that he had decided to go along with the idea. But to Bonniot's surprise, de Forge would have no part of it.

'You can't really have thought it out,' de Forge told him. 'This isn't a decision anyone can take lightly.'

'I thought about it half the night.'

'Did you think of the consequences, of how agonizing it will be?'

'I want to get out; I'll do it. There's no other way.'

'You've never been hungry, really hungry. You must imagine what that means, to suffer hunger every day, day after day, and by an act of will. There's nothing else you can think of. It eats at you; it twists, consumes and changes you; you become different. And you suffer. . . . I had a taste of it, oh, only a small taste, but it was enough – in my campaigns in the Sahara. You must think of it very hard. There's time, plenty of time. You must visualize the torment and then tell yourself truthfully whether you'll be able to go through with it for weeks and months. It's only after you've thought of it that way that you can make a real decision.'

Two days later Bonniot came back with the same decision. 'I'll do it,' he said firmly. 'I'll do it.'

De Forge bowed in his way before a serious decision. 'I hope you survive,' he said.

'I hope I get out,' Bonniot replied.

From that day a change came over Bonniot. For the first time since his captivity had begun he had hope, and the old Bonniot seemed to be reborn. His eyes brightened; he walked more erectly and with a firmer step; his face no longer fell apart in repose but instead was suffused with a dreamy look; he began to laugh again. Life was no longer meaningless.

De Forge took charge of Bonniot's starvation campaign. 'I will be responsible,' he told Bonniot. 'You won't die; I'll make sure of that. What we have to ensure is a maximum chance of success. It would be too stupid for you to go through all this and then not get out.'

De Forge began by fattening Bonniot up. It was the happiest part of the operation. The orderlies would come with their platters and the two generals would eat together. In that period de Forge gave Bonniot a good part of his own ration; and he added to that many of the delicacies he received in packages or bought with scrip at the canteen. Bonniot prospered. At the same time de Forge guided him in a psychological assault on the German staff. He suddenly became the totally adjusted prisoner, placid, contented, uncomplaining, the man who had accepted his fate and given up fighting or propitiating the unkind gods. Bonniot's colleagues as well as the Germans were surprised by his transformation.

'He's a new man,' Palisse remarked to de Forge. 'Absolutely amazing. And it happened overnight. My hat's off to him. In fact, I'm taking his change as an example for myself.'

'He's really gotten a grip on himself,' Reboux remarked. 'And him of all people, separated from his bride of a night.'

Von Bardsdorf himself, who was aware of everything at the fortress, remarked the change in Bonniot. One day when he met de Forge near the canteen he said, 'I see that some of you are happier than others and that some of you have even taken to this place as if it were a vacation spot.'

'I can't imagine anyone who would go that far.'

'And your good Bonniot! Just look at him. He's getting fatter from day to day. Just look at him. A couple of months ago he was dour, bitter, and miserable. Look at him now. Baden-Baden couldn't have suited him better.'

'Nobody is complaining about how you run this place,' de Forge said soberly. 'We all agree that you're absolutely fair and even generous. Bonniot has simply adjusted to imprisonment. It's the better part of wisdom. After all, what else is there to do?'

These words from the man Hitler had said was worth forty divisions made von Bardsdorf glow. There was, moreover, no reason to doubt de Forge's sincerity. Von Bardsdorf had done everything in his power to make the lives of these French generals as pleasant and painless as possible. Indeed, life at the fortress was less like prison than an enforced stay at a seedy club. The generals had their three meals a day, meals that were sufficient if not gastronomic; they had their canteen to supplement the meals and supply all sorts of necessities; and they had their club room, where many of them spent the better part of the day and evening playing bridge. The only sensible policy a rational man could adopt was to make the best of such conditions. Von Bardsdorf was delighted to hear de Forge express the view he had expended every effort to impose on his prisoners.

De Forge immediately told Bonniot about his encounter.

Pacing his room, de Forge rubbed his hands together. 'It couldn't be better,' he said. 'The stage is now beautifully set, much more beautifully than I could have imagined.'

'We ought to be able to start on my diet now,' Bonniot said. 'The sooner we start the faster it will be over.'

But de Forge was more cautious. 'We mustn't be over-confident. Let the impression sink in. Let it be so strong they can't erase it. We must go on like this for at least another month.'

And so they did. During this period the weather changed. Summer ended and soon the fine days were but a memory. The snap of autumn with its hint of winter came into the air. In the morning a heavy fog covered the valley below the fortress, and when it lifted towards noon the leaves on the trees were gold and scarlet and were falling. It rained.

The generals huddled against the damp and the cold and, miserably, faced the prospect of their first winter of captivity. Those who thought England would collapse, and even hoped for it and a quick end to the war and with it their freedom, were changing their perspective. At first in their national pride and chauvinism, they had assumed that if the French army had collapsed so quickly, the British could not stand for long. De Forge had never held that view. He had argued with a number of the others, always insisting on the fortitude of the British with their backs to the wall and upon his conviction that the Germans could not cross the Channel against the British fleet and the RAF. 'The Boches are now dominant,' he would say. 'But time is on our side. If the British hold out, and they must, the Germans cannot win. Sooner or later they will have both the Russians and the Americans on their necks.'

So the weeks passed. The generals were bored, restive and

unhappy. Their existence was meaningless; it consisted in an interminable wait for an issue over which they had no control and about which they could do nothing. They passed their time in listless discussion between rubbers of bridge. The more energetic ones, and they were not many, tried to use the time to study. They read the German newspapers and ordered and read whatever books in German they were interested in; they could order no others. Reboux and Palisse were among those who put their time to use. But it was a struggle; however much they tried, their lives were empty. Often they had days of such despair that it took all their will plus the sense of so many others suffering the same absurd condition not to let go and fall to pieces.

De Forge and Bonniot alone lived with hope and in a framework of meaningfulness. They knew, or thought they knew, what they were about. At least they had the sense that they were acting and were not merely passive subjects of the will of others and of circumstances nobody could control or predict. De Forge continued to fashion his cable, but as it progressed he worried that it would not be strong enough to hold his weight. He had obtained a hammer and screwdriver, had loosened a plank in the floor of his room, and there he hid the growing length of rope.

At the same time he tried to work out a concrete plan for his escape. He knew that he must go over the wall during the day; but difficult as that would be, it was only then that his real problems would begin. How would he negotiate eight hundred kilometres of hostile territory to reach and cross the French or Swiss border? He could not walk that distance; it was out of the question. De Forge wrestled with this problem and at last found a bold and brilliant answer. He was naturally secretive but finally decided that Bonniot had to know.

'There will be messages I'll want you to take with you when you get out,' de Forge said to Bonniot one day.

'*If* and when I get out.'

'Impatience won't get you out any faster,' de Forge said mildly. Bonniot had been complaining about the delay in starting the diet part of the operation. 'We can begin just as soon as you have your next medical checkup and they weigh you.'

'That should be next week. I guess I can wait that long.'

'Just get the messages to my wife in Lyons. I think the best thing would be to sew them into the collar of your jacket.'

'No problem.'

'I've worked out a simple code so that I'll be able to communicate at least in a primitive way.' He paused. 'I've also worked out a plan of escape – a real plan.'

'I hope it's easier than the one you worked out for me.'

'More dangerous but less painful. For one thing I have to get over that wall.'

'How you're going to do that really baffles me.'

'I'm working on a cable.'

'A cable? With what?'

'Pieces of string.' To Bonniot's stare of disbelief, de Forge added, 'From the packages we receive.'

'It won't be strong enough. It can't be strong enough. You'll need a cable one hundred and fifty feet long with a tension resistance factor of two hundred pounds. You won't get it with pieces of string. If you go over with that kind of a cable, it will be suicide. Don't do it.'

'It's all I've got. What else can I do?'

Bonniot thought for a while. 'With that kind of cable,' he said, 'all you need is reinforcement. If you could get that length of wire, say of telephone wire, you would be in good shape and there'd be nothing to worry about.'

'But how?'

'From the outside, of course. That's something I could look into.' Bonniot rubbed his cheek reflectively. 'If I got out,' he said as an afterthought. 'Yes, it would take three or four long lengths of wire in different packages.'

'But they look into all the packages. It would never get by them.'

'It's a technical problem. Each length of wire wouldn't take up that much space. Perhaps it could be hidden, camouflaged in food somehow. I don't know, but it doesn't seem impossible to me.'

'You're right of course,' de Forge said reluctantly. 'It won't do to rush matters any more for me than for you. And if everything were prepared and laid on and the rope broke when I was ten feet from the ground and all I could do was lie there with a broken leg until they came to scoop me up . . .'

'Or if it broke sooner and you came down with a broken neck. . . . You'll need the wire reinforcement – that's a certainty.'

De Forge looked unhappy, 'No doubt. It hadn't entered into my equation.'

'And what about the plan? What happens when you touch ground outside?'

'That's the extraordinary part. Obviously I can't walk the distance; and even if I could, how far would I get? I don't even have the clothes, let alone the money, the accent, the food or sympathizers along the road.'

'So?'

'So the mountain will have to come to Mohammed.'

Bonniot regarded de Forge, not quite certain he understood. 'How so?'

'Since it's impossible for me to get out of this country on my own, someone will have to come in and get me out.'

Bonniot gave the idea some time to sink in. 'And then,' he said, reserving comment, 'what then, if someone did come for you, knowing that if he's caught, he'll get twelve bullets in his body for his trouble?'

'He would come in a car with neutral plates, Swiss plates. As you know, there are only two checks of our presence every day, at nine in the morning and at nine at night. I would get over the wall and out within half an hour of the morning check. We would arrange a rendezvous within an hour's walk of the fortress. The car would pick me up and we would speed to the frontier. When we got near it we would abandon the car and walk through with prearranged guides. I figure it would take, conservatively, twelve or thirteen hours to get to the border with a fast car. With any kind of luck the Germans won't know I'm gone until nine at night. They won't have the time to give the alert before I'm out of the country.'

'But there are bound to be police checks along the road. You'll be stopped. Automatically.'

'We'll have papers. That's for the people back home to organize. I'll have a passport, everything in order, a Swiss passport. I'll be a businessman from Geneva, whatever they can make me that makes sense and won't arouse suspicions.'

'It's simple, all right,' Bonniot said after a moment's consideration. 'But there are a lot of places where it could go wrong.'

'That's the nature of the beast – especially this one.'

The following week Bonniot had a medical checkup.

'Did they weigh you?' de Forge asked when Bonniot returned.

'Did they weigh me though?' Bonniot was jubilant. ' "Our resort agrees with you," the doctor said with that particular quality of light German humour. "You have gained three kilos since the last time." Oh, we joked and had a fine time. And they pronounced me in perfect shape.'

'Good. Then we're ready to begin.'

De Forge oversaw Bonniot's diet. Over Bonniot's objections – he naïvely wanted to starve fast and get the ordeal over with – de Forge cut his food ration gradually.

'It must be progressive,' de Forge insisted. 'The doctors must have a history with a clear chart – evidence, in short, something solid on which they can base their ignorance. We have to give them time to be puzzled, then confused. And finally time to draw conclusions, to decide that they don't have the remotest idea what's wrong with you and that the faster you leave the safer they'll be against a corpse they are unable to explain.'

Bonniot went along with de Forge's reasoning. And as Bonniot ate less and de Forge more, Bonniot lost weight and de Forge put some on. Bonniot quickly went down to his original weight and then went down below that. He was hungry but steadfast. De Forge made a point of not being seen with him too often. Von Bardsdorf appeared to know so much about the imprisoned generals that de Forge took the precaution of not being conspicuously linked with Bonniot. That could do neither of them any good.

When Bonniot came back from his next medical checkup he was elated.

'You should have seen his face when he weighed me,' Bonniot told de Forge. 'He looked at me in his white coat and he said, "Herr General, you have lost a lot of weight." Then he looked at the scale again. He asked me how I felt, if my appetite was good, things like that. I told him my appetite was fine and I felt all right except that from time to time I had attacks of nausea. He noted everything down and asked me to come back and see him next week.'

De Forge was elated too. 'Next week, eh? They've bitten. This means a weekly checkup at the very least as long as you keep losing weight.'

Bonniot laughed. 'That's what makes me feel so good. They're now paying attention.'

'No suspicions?'

'None apparent. And of course I played it bland just as we agreed. Not the hint of a suggestion that I was anything but an innocent victim. Only when he was through with the examination I asked him, looking just a little worried, if there was anything wrong with me. He shook his head and told me not to worry, that they would keep an eye on me.'

The hopes of both men were high and, in both optimism and caution, de Forge began to prepare the messages for Bonniot to take out with him. De Forge baptized his escape operation 'Cristine.' It was the name of his youngest daughter. He worked out a series of code phrases and a simple code in which messages would consist of the first letters after each break in script. Such a code was aimed at communicating short messages through censorship. He suggested that longer messages be written out and sent to him camouflaged in food.

One afternoon in late autumn, the messages completed, de Forge left his jacket in Bonniot's room and took Bonniot's jacket to his own room. There he quickly slit the seam of the lapel of Bonniot's jacket and carefully folded the messages inside. Then, his heart pounding, he hastily began to sew the lapel together. He felt exposed, was awkward with the needle and thread, and tried to race against his premonition that one of the German officers would walk in while he was sewing. Lieutenant Hetzel fulfilled de Forge's premonition: he walked in as de Forge was putting the finishing touches to his work. But even as the door opened de Forge's anguish dropped away.

'I didn't realize you sewed, *Herr General*.'

'As you see, I do.'

'It is not a general's work; that is for one of your enlisted men to do for you.'

57

De Forge looked straight up at Hetzel, his needle poised, and said coldly, 'Some generals sew better than some enlisted men, *Herr Leutnant.*'

Then de Forge went calmly back to his sewing. The lieutenant stood indecisively at the doorway, finally bowed formally and left. De Forge congratulated himself on the precaution of having left his jacket with Bonniot.

The winter cold came early that year. At the beginning of November a flurry of snow fell on the fortress. Prisoners and guards huddled in greatcoats against the icy wind that swept the fortress plateau. The trees were soon bare. The sky was low and sullen. The elderly generals felt more isolated than ever from the world. One heavy snowfall covered everything in white. It was like a white hush on the universe. Often it seemed that not a sound could be heard except the deep sound of silence.

More and more the generals remained indoors, but de Forge, Reboux and Palisse continued their daily walks, their boots crunching in the snow. They had less and less to talk about, and Reboux and Palisse became increasingly glum. De Forge, as always, maintained a certain distance, outwardly serene. He said nothing of his plans either for himself or for Bonniot; but both, he felt, were progressing favourably.

At this time the Bonniot operation went into a new phase. De Forge cut Bonniot's food allowance sharply, putting him on little more than liquids, the most nourishing of which were the soups. Bonniot weakened quickly, but took his punishment astonishingly well. Each day, he told himself, he was one day closer to his goal, the image of his bride fortifying his spirit. He became used to his starvation diet as to a natural condition and was even, in a way, exalted by it; hunger was the cardinal virtue that would shower him with munificent rewards. He cheated, the fantasy of repatriation constantly in mind, eating even less than de Forge prescribed to hasten his debilitation and speed his release.

Soon the fortress doctor asked Bonniot to see him daily. It gave the weakened little general increased courage. He had faded and shrunk, and his clothes hung absurdly on his diminished figure; his legs were so shaky that he no longer left his room except to see the doctor.

As de Forge had foreseen, the doctor had been puzzled at first and now was frankly confused. He put Bonniot through all the tests he could elaborate, but no hypothesis produced a disease to explain the symptoms. Bonniot had developed the nausea symptom with such skill that he could retch at will. He also admitted now to loss of appetite. That hardly surprised the doctor. He was baffled. Finally, he brought in two specialists. The specialists listened to the fortress doctor, examined Bonniot, shook their heads, consulted, and left without being able to illuminate the mystery.

Through it all Bonniot appeared alternately listless and worried. 'What's the matter with me, *Herr Doktor*?' he asked. 'I feel weak all the time. I can hardly move. Is it serious?'

The word *serious* had a special meaning on Bonniot's lips. He never pronounced any other word, but the doctor understood the word he meant and kept assuring him that the tests showed no sign of any serious ailment or indeed of any ailment at all.

Bonniot played it low key. 'Then why have I lost so much weight? Why am I so weak? Why do I have these bouts of nausea? Why am I losing my appetite? There must be a reason and it can't be good.'

As the doctor mumbled unpersuasive generalities, Bonniot turned away as if he knew he was being deceived and reverted to listlessness.

It was the scenario de Forge had imagined for him. Never did Bonniot affirm that he was sick. Never did he plead or even hint that he should be sent home for medical reasons. Never was he unpleasant or critical of the doctor. He was a model patient. But he asked good questions – unanswerable questions for those who did not have the key.

Towards the end of November, however, they had a scare and thought their elaborate deception would fail. Bonniot was suddenly shipped out to a hospital for observation and more complete tests. De Forge spent a bad week, but at the end of it Bonniot was back looking even worse than when he had left.

'Well,' de Forge asked, 'did they find you out?'

Bonniot grinned weakly. 'They examined me right-side up and upside down,' he said, 'inside out and outside in, every test in the book. I passed them all.'

'What did they conclude?'

Bonniot shrugged. 'They were mystified. How could they treat me when they couldn't find anything to treat? So they sent me back.'

'But how about the food? You had to eat it, didn't you?'

Bonniot smiled feebly. 'Oh, I had to eat the first two meals with the damned nurses around me, but I threw both of them up halfway through. Made myself. After that nobody was likely to question my nausea and loss of appetite, and I ate as little, even less, than here.' He looked up at de Forge with burning eyes out of a gaunt face. 'I've gotten into this so deep,' he said, 'sometimes I wonder if I really am sick.'

Everybody thought he was, and although the extensive hospital examination disclosed no known disease, none of the doctors, in the face of the recent medical history and the current symptoms and state of the patient, suspected fraud.

A few days after he returned from the hopsital Bonniot took to bed and stayed there. He was very weak. De Forge felt that bedridden, he would seem weaker still and more pathetic. The moment had come for his big scene. It was not much, but de Forge assured him that it was psychologically important.

'Maybe they're working on your release already,' de Forge said. 'Maybe they just need this little push.'

The doctor now came to see Bonniot, who lay in a bed of quiet but insistent despair.

'Well, how are you?'

'The same.'

The examination proceeded. Heart. Pulse. Throat. Eyes. The doctor simply shook his head. He had never had a case like this and knew no colleague who had.

'Well, *Herr Doktor*, how am I?'

'The same.'

Bonniot turned his face to the wall. '*Herr Doktor*, if it's serious, you must tell me.'

'Really, it's a mystery. None of us has found anything.'

'But there must be something.'

'Yes, of course, but it is not what you might think it is.'

'But whatever it is, if you can't find it, you can't cure it.'

Bonniot might have been talking to himself. 'I think,' he murmured, 'that I am going to die.'

'Well, you know, *Herr General* – '

'I have thought about it and I have watched myself. I can see it happening slowly, slowly. But it is plain. I am a lucid man, *Herr Doktor*. I know that I am going. I will not deny that I have had a bad time. The prospect of death alone, in captivity, when one has loved ones outside, a wife waiting, after only days together . . .'

The doctor's head was bowed. 'I know how hard it is, but there's no reason for despair.'

'What reason is there for hope?' With this question Bonniot turned and faced the doctor, looking him hard in the eye.

The doctor's eyes fell. 'Well, we can follow the symptoms and – '

'*Herr Doktor*, you are speaking to a general. I have followed the course of the disease with you for two months. It is clear even if we do not have a name for it. Must I be in my coffin before we look at matters plainly? I'm now so weak I can barely get out of bed. There is just one thing I regret. . . .'

'Yes?'

'Nothing. In any case it is beyond reach.'

'If there is anything I can do . . .' He was human and perhaps had a sense of guilt that he was unable to fathom what was wrong with Bonniot and could not treat him.

'No. Impossible. But if I can't see her, I will write – and it can be sent afterwards. I haven't mentioned this in my letters. It would just make her worry when there's nothing she could do about it.'

The doctor rose. 'I will see what can be done,' he said as he left.

Two days later de Forge met von Bardsdorf near the canteen.

'I hear General Bonniot is in bad shape,' von Bardsdorf said.

'He's probably dying,' de Forge said flatly.

'What makes you say that?'

'All you have to do is look at him. He looks like death warmed over. And he looks worse all the time.'

'Yes, yes, *Herr General*, something will have to be done about it.'

De Forge reported this exchange to Bonniot.

'But suppose they send me back to one of their hospitals for observation?'

'No, they won't do that. Once is enough. If they knew what was the matter with you and you were curable, they would. But they don't know and you're obviously sinking fast. The doctors must have recommended you be shipped home before you become an embarrassing corpse. They don't want you around dead.'

'Where do you suppose the papers are now?'

De Forge shrugged. He did not want to raise Bonniot's hopes too high or his own, for that matter; but he expressed his conviction. 'They could be sending them to Berlin for a decision; maybe they've already sent them. You know how it works: if the doctors recommend it and there's no overriding reason to reject the recommendation, they'll approve it.'

Like the German doctors and everyone else who had any contact with Bonniot, Reboux and Palisse were convinced he was dying. Reboux was sure he had cancer. 'Just look at him, he said. 'He's wasting away. He has the look on his face.'

He wanted to talk to von Bardsdorf.

De Forge dissuaded him. 'They'll see it themselves. Perhaps they already have. Any pressure, any talk that our doctors might cure him where theirs don't even know what's the matter with him, might just stiffen their backs. Let it ride. They're not stupid. They must have drawn their own conclusions by now just as we have drawn ours.'

The break came just before Christmas. One morning von Bardsdorf himself, accompanied by the doctor, came to see Bonniot. The presence of the fortress commander made it evident that this visit was something special. Bonniot's stomach fell away and he could not control his trembling. Both von Bardsdorf and the doctor looked at Bonniot gravely but with slight encouraging smiles.

'I have a Christmas present for you, *Herr General*,' von Bardsdorf said bluffly. 'You're going home. The orders just came in.'

Bonniot looked searchingly from one to the other, his heart

thumping, as a silence settled around the room over the echo of von Bardsdorf's booming voice. 'Then you think I'm going to die,' he whispered.

Protests and reassurances volleyed at him. He listened with wordless resignation, fearful deep down that even now they might be testing him and could reverse the verdict. He was pleasantly surprised at being able to look at himself from the outside with calm lucidity and his instinct of preserving the German decision. For six interminable months he had dreamed, hoped, despaired and finally starved for this moment, and now that it was upon him he allowed himself no emotion. Instead, he remained cautiously sunk in listlessness.

'When will I be going?' he asked lethargically, almost without interest.

'As soon as you are ready,' von Bardsdorf replied. 'You will be driven to Wiesbaden and turned over to your people on the Armistice Commission.'

'Thank you, *Herr Oberst,* thank you very much.'

Von Bardsdorf left disappointed. He had expected an outpouring of joy and thanks. Nothing would have pleased him more. Outside the building he paused for a word with the doctor.

'How many weeks do you give him?' he asked.

'At this rate, not many, *Herr Oberst.*'

Bonniot was more profuse with his thanks when he saw de Forge a few minutes later. He was now coming out of his self-imposed emotional numbness but controlled his feelings; he could hardly voice what he felt to those who had to stay on. De Forge congratulated him.

'You played it superbly,' he said.

'I will get everything to your wife immediately. You can be certain of that. And I will do anything else that's possible.'

The word of Bonniot's release spread quickly.

'We all envy you,' Reboux told Bonniot. 'Get well quickly.'

Palisse shook Bonniot's hand warmly. 'Have a wonderful honeymoon,' he said.

They laughed. It did not take much time for Bonniot to be ready. An hour after he learned of his good fortune a Wehrmacht staff car was in front of the building. A group of generals waved him off. He was wearing the jacket that

63

contained de Forge's messages.

Christmas passed; January came and went. De Forge received one letter from his wife, but it had been sent before Bonniot could possibly have seen her. This was the most difficult time for de Forge. The days dragged. Not even fashioning the slowly developing cable gave him the same satisfaction as in the past. He was focused on one thing only. Would he at last establish contact with the outside? He thought about it as he went to bed at night and even before waking it was in his mind again. He was jittery, absorbed. In repose his face was no longer a mask: his concern was written on it. Reboux coolly noted the change and wondered if the mighty de Forge could be cracking. The lofty serenity was certainly gone. Something had plainly happened. There was a crack in what had seemed to be a monolithic façade. 'The man's human,' Reboux said to himself. 'Just like the rest of us.'

The letter came one leaden day in early February. De Forge opened it when he was alone in his room. He read it quickly, savagely, his eyes racing through the pages of script. In the middle he came upon this sentence: 'Cristine is now here, and I hope to have news of her for you soon.' It was the prearranged message he was looking for. Liaison with a base in France was established.

De Forge was exultant. Clutching the letter in his hand, he told himself that now it would be possible to do the impossible.

PART TWO

The Escape

SEVEN

'It's impossible,' Rivet said.

'Suicidal,' Galland echoed.

'And for both of them,' Rivet added.

'Especially the guide,' Galland said.

Bonniot looked depressed and Madame de Forge acutely unhappy. She was still a handsome woman with a small delicate nose, a creamy complexion and the soft expression of someone constantly ready to be helpful. The three men, all in civilian clothes, were meeting with Madame de Forge in her apartment in Lyons. Glasses had been filled and emptied; cigarette smoke hung in the air over the Louis XV furniture. It was a month after Bonniot's release; he was still pale and gaunt.

'One way or another,' Madame de Forge said softly, 'he's going to do it. I know him; we all know him. He's incapable of just staying there and waiting for whatever is going to happen. You know yourself he's going to do it.'

Rivet returned her look of inquiry with a gesture of agreement. He was a prematurely silver-haired general who had been de Forge's chief of staff during the Battle of France and took a bitter pride that their army was the only one, until the flanking armies gave way, that had driven the Wehrmacht back in a sweeping attack. Madame de Forge had called upon him as soon as she learned her husband's intention to escape. In addition to the close ties between the two men, she knew that Rivet was in a good position to be effective. The Vichy Ministry of Defence had appointed him to run the Social Centre of Information in Lyons, ostensibly an office to give technical aid to army personnel but in fact a cover for what amounted to a staff school for carefully selected officers in view of an eventual reorganization of the French army. Rivet thus had many contacts and possibilities for action. What Madame de Forge did not know, and he did not tell her, was that he had organized a network to help French prisoners of war escape. But nobody in France had ever considered engineering an escape from the fortress where the generals were held.

'But it won't work,' Rivet said to Madame de Forge. 'Not with the plan he's sent us. There are too many places where it can go wrong.'

'That's what I told him right off,' Bonniot said. 'His answer was what you would expect: the risks are built in; they must be taken.'

'Too many in this case,' Rivet said. 'A plan has to have a certain probability of success to justify the risks. A car with Swiss plates crossing all of Germany first in one direction, then in the other. Police and army on the road to check just this kind of thing. In addition, there are already petrol restrictions, and by the time we would get around to the operation there would be even more severe restrictions if petrol could be got at all. No, it's just impossible.'

They were all silent for a while.

'The plan as it stands is unworkable, I agree,' said Galland. He was a handsome and dashing major who was chief of intelligence of the Military Area of Lyons, and he worked closely with Rivet. 'But I like the idea, the basic idea. It's fascinating, really seductive. Just think: the idea of sending someone in to get him out!'

Rivet frowned. 'Sending someone in doubles the risk. Two can be lost instead of one.'

'But the one we're interested in can't get out without the other,' Bonniot said.

'It's the transport part of the plan that won't work,' Galland said. 'Getting in and out by car is out of the question. But I like the idea of going in to get him out.'

'Then perhaps another way can be found,' Madame de Forge said.

'There's only one other way,' Rivet said. 'To go by train,

and that could be as bad and maybe worse than going by car.'

'Maybe not,' Galland objected. 'So many people travel by train; they could be lost in the crowd. Of course we would have to face train checks, but with the right papers and clothes they should have a good chance of getting by.'

'It's possible,' Rivet agreed. 'We'll have to study it more closely.'

'There's time,' Bonniot said. 'It will take him several months more to finish his cable. And he's going to need wire to reinforce it, as I've been telling you.'

'We'll have to work on that too,' Rivet said.

'There's a communications problem as well,' Galland said. 'We'll never be able to get back and forth on all the problems with his code. We're going to have to find another way to get longer messages to him.'

'I'm afraid you won't see him again that quickly,' Rivet said to Madame de Forge.

'I know it won't be tomorrow,' she said, 'but it will be sooner than the Germans imagine.'

She looked less unhappy than she had earlier. Whatever the problems, they were plainly going to work on them.

Rivet and Galland rose to leave. 'We'll be in touch,' Rivet said.

On the way down the stairs Galland said, 'What I wonder is who will be mad enough to go in to get him out.'

That winter and spring Madame de Forge wrote encouraging letters to her husband. In each of them there was a coded sentence or two to the effect that Cristine was progressing. But in fact progress, if any, was extremely slow. The problem was difficult to come to grips with. It had to begin with a revision of de Forge's plan, which Rivet and Galland decided was unworkable; but to revise the plan they needed information which they did not possess.

Galland took charge of the operation and Cristine was re-baptized Marianne. Only two elements of Cristine survived: first, that de Forge would get out of the fortress by his own means; and second, that a guide would be sent in to lead him safely out of Germany. But who the guide was to be and how it was to be done Galland did not know. What intrigued Galland was the challenge. He was in his middle thirties, single and exploding with energy. Routine bored him. He was constantly on the lookout for problems against which he could test his ingenuity. In Marianne he had found it. He was bewitched by the boldness of de Forge's conception. To send someone right into the lions' den to pluck their Daniel out was a spectacular way to thumb a French nose at the Third Reich. Such an escape by a man of de Forge's stature would be splashed in headlines around the world. Quite apart from the essential point of liberating de Forge so that a general of his unique quality would be available to lead French troops at a subsequent opportunity, the escape would dent German prestige, demonstrating that the seemingly all-powerful German police state was not powerful enough to prevent an ageing general from making it look foolish.

Galland discussed the problem exhaustively with Rivet. Though the sober, silver-thatched general kept stabbing holes into his proposals, Galland's enthusiasm never wavered.

'The instant they learn that de Forge has fled the fortress,' Rivet repeatedly told Galland, 'the entire country will be alerted. It will go right to the General Staff, straight to Hitler himself. He will surely fly into a rage, and the police and army apparatus will be unleashed to get de Forge back, dead or alive. From this, a principle follows, which must be the basis of your plan: at all costs the Germans must lose every trace of de Forge from the very foot of the fortress and have no idea what direction he has taken or at what point he hopes to get out of Germany.'

It was easier to define the principle than to elaborate the elements that would put it into effect; but Galland finally put together a plan and committed it to paper. The plan projecting de Forge's escape covered three typewritten pages. It bore no resemblance to more conventional escapes by younger men with the hunted riding the rails and hiding in freight cars. De Forge's escape was conceived as an escape de luxe; it followed Rivet's principle to put the Germans off his track by its very conception.

It began with the familiar premise that de Forge would get

out of the fortress on his own, although Galland noted that he would somehow have to supply a metal cable to reinforce the cable de Forge was fashioning. The plan then specified that a guide who spoke fluent German would go by train from unoccupied France through the occupied zone and all of Germany to the area of the fortress. The guide would travel with a double set of forged official papers. He would go through occupied France as a wine dealer, but once he crossed into Germany he would become a free worker for the Third Reich, an electrical specialist working for the Archimedes Gesellschaft in Breslau, where he would be returning after a holiday in France. He would carry with him a valise containing de Forge's own clothes as well as fabricated papers for de Forge enabling him to travel through Germany as the representative of a firm in Lyons manufacturing artificial silk. The guide would also have negotiable German money.

The guide and de Forge would meet near the fortress, but not too near, at a place, day and hour to be specified by the organizers in France; if for any reason de Forge was unable to make it, the guide would return the following day to the same place at the same hour.

Should the second rendezvous be missed, the guide would return to France and the operation would be cancelled.

Once the two men were together they would take the first train for Berlin. Galland reasoned that that was the last place the Germans would suspect de Forge was fleeing, right into the mouth of the lion. In Berlin de Forge and the guide would take the night express to Strasbourg, reserving compartments in the wagon-lit. Once again Galland reasoned that it would never occur to the Germans that a man in flight would travel in that style.

In Strasbourg the guide would put de Forge in contact with a special network that would lead him across the border of Alsace-Lorraine, which had in effect been annexed by Germany. If anything went wrong in Strasbourg, de Forge and the guide would proceed to Mulhouse, the town closest to the French and Swiss frontier, and another part of the network would get de Forge across to safety.

The final part of the plan provided that de Forge would hide somewhere in France, living with his family under a false identity, in an isolated house that could be defended against attack at least long enough for de Forge to get away in the event that the Nazis, enraged by his escape, should attempt to kidnap or kill him. Here de Forge could work in secret and make the necessary contacts against the day that France would once again take up arms in a war that was by no means yet ended.

'Not bad,' Rivet pronounced after he read the plan. From Rivet that was high praise. 'How do you propose to proceed?'

'Well, the first thing is to get de Forge to approve it.'

'What else can he do?'

Galland grinned. 'I know,' he said. 'But obviously –'

'Yes, yes. He has to know and he has to say yes before we can go ahead. Have you worked out a way to communicate with him?'

'In the clear and in a cake,' Galland said. 'There's some risk to be sure, but the probabilities are on our side.'

Galland copied the plan in a small clear hand on narrow bands of extremely thin onion-skin paper which he pasted end to end and rolled into a small tube of pencil lead. Then he paid Madame de Forge a visit.

'I want you to bake me a cake,' he said with a smile, holding up the tube of pencil lead. He explained what he had done without telling Madame de Forge what the plan was. 'The fewer people who know the better, and it's especially important that you do not know. But we think it's a good plan and we're hopeful it will work.' He paused. 'There's just one thing I'm not sure of. We want you to send this little tube to your husband lovingly baked in a cake. But the thing that's troubling me is whether the ink will withstand the baking.'

Madame de Forge busied herself in the kitchen. Galland directed her to place the tube in the dough at the outer edge of the cake, pointing towards the centre so that a probing German knife striking from the centre would be less likely to hit the tube. When the cake was baked and had cooled down Madame de Forge cut it in slices. Her knife never touched the tube. Finally they had to search for it. The baking had not affected the ink. Galland rolled the long band of onion-skin paper back into the tube and handed it to Madame de Forge.

70

'It's yours,' he said. 'Treat it with reverence.'

'I shall,' she said. Then she asked with a smile, 'Won't you have a piece of cake?'

In the next letter Madame de Forge sent her husband she wrote: 'I'm sending you a cake for your birthday. I hope it arrives on the right day. I'm sure you'll enjoy it. While you're eating it please remember that the entire family took part in preparing it. Cristine was especially helpful. Eat it all religiously while thinking of us.'

The letter also contained in code this phrase: tube in cake.

Madame de Forge was a very cautious woman. She wanted to be doubly sure that de Forge would not offer the right slice of cake to the wrong person.

Two months later she was reassured. The day de Forge's answer arrived was doubly memorable. It came on a day that gave Frenchmen a new perspective in their hope for Hitler's defeat: on that morning Germany attacked the Soviet Union. De Forge's letter was full of sunshine and sparkle. It was the happiest letter Madame de Forge had received from him since his imprisonment. Within the letter the coded message read: agreed send long very long cable.

One of Galland's schoolfriends, Pierre Bertal, had become the owner of a canning factory at St-Etienne, about thirty-five miles southeast of Lyons. Pierre Bertal had developed a paunch and begun to lose his hair at an early age. He was a solid family man who had an adoring wife and six children. Every Sunday morning, rain or shine, he went to mass. Pierre Bertal described himself as a patriot.

Galland's path and his had not crossed for many years. In early July, Galland thought of Pierre Bertal. When he called, Bertal was away on a business trip. Later he was off on vacation with his family. It was not until the end of August that Galland succeeded in reaching him. They saw each other over a gay and copious family lunch at Bertal's home. Bertal was well organized. The canning factory was working at full capacity, in large part for the Germans. But, as Bertal explained, there was nothing he could do about that since the Germans had come to him and there was no way he could refuse their orders. Rich farms were spread around the area, and for the Bertals there was no lack of food. The lunch recalled peacetime; it was as if there were no war and no occupation. After lunch when he was alone with Bertal in the study over snifters of *vieux marc* Galland came to the point of his visit.

'I need your help on a problem,' Galland said. 'I want to ship some wire to someone, and I want to be sure he gets it and that nobody knows he's getting it. It's extremely delicate. You follow me?'

'Perfectly,' Bertal said. The smile was now gone from his prosperous face.

'May I continue?'

Bertal hesitated just an instant, then nodded.

'The only way I can figure this wire will get to its destination is in a can.'

'That's easy enough.'

'But it mustn't be detected.'

'Somebody else might open the can?'

'Exactly.'

The two men considered each other across their snifters of *marc*.

'It's not much of a trick to make a can with a double bottom,' Bertal said.

'That's the trouble. It's too well known. They would be looking for it.'

After a moment's thought Bertal asked, 'How much wire do you want to send?'

'Quite a lot. About one hundred and fifty feet.'

'You'll never get that much in a can under the conditions you're aiming for.'

'Of course. But there's no reason not to put the wire in more than one can, say three or four. The question is can it be done – how shall I say – discreetly?'

'That depends on the purpose of the wire, on how thick it has to be.'

'Do you really want to know the purpose?'

'No.'

'Your knowing wouldn't help in any case.'

'How about the thickness?'

'I was thinking in terms of telephone wire,' Galland said. 'Something strong enough to hold a weight of two hundred and fifty, three hundred pounds.'

'And I suppose you want to send it in food cans.'

'Yes, sardines, tuna fish, something of that sort.'

'The way to do it is to roll the top edge of the can and solder the wire inside it,' Bertal said. 'But the wire must be very thin or the rolled edge will be too bulky and obvious.'

'Will you do it?'

'I'll be happy to.'

'But nobody must know about it.'

'Nobody will. I'll do the soldering myself; and I'll do it when nobody is around.'

'No marks on the cans?'

Bertal smiled. 'Once they leave the factory nobody will ever be able to trace them back. My security, and yours, will be fully protected.'

'Good,' said Galland as he rose to go. 'I'll get the wire to you in a day or two.'

'And I'll get it back to you in the cans just as quickly.'

'In as few cans as possible.'

'I think four will do the trick.'

The following day Galland sent Bertal a package containing one hundred and fifty feet of telephone wire stripped of its insulating jacket. At the end of the week Bertal phoned him.

'Impossible,' Bertal said.

'Why?'

'Much too thick. It should take about half the space.'

'I'll work on it and come back to you.'

Galland consulted with Rivet, who had a good idea.

'If anybody knows about these things,' Rivet said, 'it's the engineers. I'm having lunch with General Toulon next week. I'll raise the question with him.'

General Toulon, who commanded the engineers, knew of just the thing Rivet was looking for. It was an extremely thin strand of copper wire with a tension resistance of about four hundred pounds, much more than enough to carry de Forge's weight. A week later the wire was delivered to Rivet. In turn it went to Galland, who sent it to Bertal. This time there was no problem about the thickness of the wire. Bertal soldered it into the rolled top edges of four cans and sent the cans to Galland. Galland brought them to Madame de Forge.

'Here they are at last,' Galland told her. 'He'll be happier with what's rolled around the edge of the can than with what's inside it.'

'But what if the Germans find it?'

'They're not likely to. Just look at them. Would you suspect anything was inside?'

They were fairly large cans that were sturdily made but though the roll at the top edge might have been fractionally bigger than normal, they looked like any other cans even to an attentive eye.

Madame de Forge sighed. 'I'll put them into his Christmas package,' she said. 'It's the next one he's permitted to receive.'

'It's the best one he'll get – his ticket to freedom.'

What neither Galland nor Madame de Forge knew was that a new rule had gone into effect at the fortress: prisoners were not permitted to receive cans; they were blocked at the fortress post office.

EIGHT

A year had passed since the prisoners were herded together, and General (formerly Colonel) von Bardsdorf was very pleased with the way things were going at the fortress. The generals were behaving in exemplary fashion. As von Bardsdorf had anticipated, none of the generals had tried to escape, nor was there any indication that any of them even had the idea in mind. Von Bardsdorf was as confident as ever that it was beyond their powers and that they knew it. After all, they were not fools. They could see as plainly as anyone else that the fortress was escape-proof. But beyond that, the generals were perfectly docile. Not even de Forge, the most redoubtable of them, had caused any trouble. There had been no complaints about the routine or their treatment; there had been no opposition. In short, the generals were behaving like officers and gentlemen. This was not surprising, von Bardsdorf thought. For if their behaviour was exemplary, so was their treatment; the effect had the quality of the cause. Nobody could deny, and the generals least of all, that von Bardsdorf followed a liberal policy. He did as much as he could for his prisoners, saw to it that they had sufficient and decently prepared food, and the maximum of freedom and comfort within the limits of their confinement. If there were no complaints, von Bardsdorf told himself, it was because there was nothing to complain about; if there was no opposition, it was because there was nothing a reasonable man could be opposed to.

When the fine days of spring came von Bardsdorf decided to reward the generals for their docility and co-operativeness. His idea was to allow the generals, on their word of honour as French officers not to use the occasion to run away, to leave the fortress for part of the day and go for walks in the surrounding countryside. Von Bardsdorf had more than one reason for the gesture. For one thing, he wanted to demonstrate beyond any possibility of contradiction a German's liberality and humanitarianism. For another, he was certain he was running no risk, that none of the generals would break his word of honour as a French officer and try to escape. It was made plain that if any of them did make such an attempt, the others would pay for it. In any event, von Bardsdorf was confident that if the attempt was made, the escapee could never cross Germany without being caught. Moreover, in such a case the propaganda value would be worth the bother: it would show a French general taking dishonourable advantage of German generosity. Finally, the walks would serve to swing some of the generals to a more sympathetic attitude towards the Third Reich. Von Bardsdorf presented his idea to the appropriate officers of the General Staff and won their approval. Then he announced the proposal to the generals. They were surprised and delighted. Only de Forge was reticent.

'Well,' von Bardsdorf said to him after the announcement, 'are you pleased to be able to get out of our little hotel from time to time and have a good walk in the country?'

'I doubt that I'll be taking advantage of the opportunity', de Forge said dryly.

'And why not?'

'A matter of principle.'

'Principle, principle!' von Bardsdorf sputtered. 'What principle?'

'The principle,' de Forge replied, 'that one doesn't – at least I won't – sign my name to any agreement not to escape, whatever the restrictions or the length of time – even ten minutes.'

'But you don't expect me to let any of you out without your agreeing not to use the opportunity to escape.'

'Of course not.'

'And so long as you stay locked up in here you have no possibility of escape.'

'The fact that a person may not be able to escape doesn't mean he should agree not to do so. And to agree not to escape even for a limited time in return for a favour is a form of complicity.'

Von Bardsdorf did not try to hide his irritation. 'The purpose of my offer,' he said, 'is not to endulge in any complicity with my prisoners but –'

'It may not be the purpose. I grant you that. But it would be the result.'

'It's aimed quite simply at making the conditions of your life here more tolerable, and therefore your principle makes no sense.'

'But my dear general,' de Forge said with a wan smile, 'principles aren't intended for our comfort but to guide our actions – especially when we're tempted to do something that will increase our well-being.'

Von Bardsdorf left de Forge, muttering angrily.

The other generals disagreed with de Forge, who did not press his point. His attitude was that each man would have to make his own decision. As for himself, his decision was taken and he would stick to it. The only one he talked to about it at any length was Reboux, towards whom he had drawn somewhat closer with the passing of time. Reboux also dreamed of escape but he had no plan.

'Why not take the walks?' he said. 'Von Bardsdorf is getting over-confident. I don't see why I shouldn't take advantage of that.'

'You can't use the walks to escape in any case,' de Forge

replied. 'Every time you leave the fortress you'll have to sign out.'

'But I'll be able to learn what the entire countryside is like. It could help. It would certainly facilitate the break if I could ever get out of here.'

'They would use it against you afterwards. They would say they let you out and you ran away.'

'Who gives a damn! As long as I get away.'

'I can't do it that way,' de Forge said. 'It's got to be clean and straight, otherwise they'll crucify me when I escape.'

'*If* you escape. And they'll crucify you anyway.'

'Yes, but I'll know and they'll know that I did it by the rules and whatever they say will be a pack of lies.'

All that spring and summer, while de Forge remained in the fortress, Reboux and the others took advantage of von Bardsdorf's offer. Reboux systematically combed the area. He came to know the roads and towns in a radius of ten to fifteen miles around the fortress. Von Bardsdorf even authorized him to have a map of the region so that he could find his way and see the more interesting sights. Reboux also obtained a railway timetable, and when de Forge found out about it he persuaded Reboux to get one for him too.

The timetable was de Forge's joy. He studied it by the hour, committing much of it to memory, as if the place names and the figures beside them contained the secret wisdom of the ages. How those names thrilled him! Especially those in Alsace-Lorraine – Strasbourg, Colmar, Mulhouse . . . These were places he had been to and knew. And now, locked up in the fortress, he dreamed of them. He could visualize the stations, smell the station smells and dream of arriving there – stepping off a train, striding out of the station and into the town, a free man going where he chose.

He received the plan for Marianne in late May and immediately accepted it, putting all his confidence in the organizers of his escape. How could he do anything different? The trick was the timing of the train for Berlin. He would get out of the fortress in the morning, would walk to a nearby town, take a train there for Berlin somewhere around noon or shortly thereafter, arrive in Berlin in the early evening, then take the overnight express for Strasbourg. The timetable told de Forge that it could be done. The town of Bad Danschau was less than ten miles from the fortress. There was a train for Berlin every day except Sunday at one-fifteen. He would have no problem getting there on foot well before the train left. It arrived in Berlin at eight forty-five. The night express to Strasbourg left at ten twenty-five. His travel service seemed to be functioning efficiently.

But by the middle of the summer, about six weeks after Hitler attacked the Soviet Union, de Forge became nervous. He was suddenly unsure of the entire enterprise. What if he succeeded in getting out of the fortress but was unable to find his way to the point of rendezvous? What if he got there and the guide who was to lead him across Germany failed to show up? He would have to improvise. It was the most dangerous form of escape and the one least likely to succeed. But he knew he had to prepare for that possibility. There was little enough he could do. He needed money, clothes, identity papers. The German guards were fond of chocolate, and de Forge had been selling his own ration for some time now for negotiable German money. But there was little he could do about clothes and nothing he could do about the indispensable papers he would be asked to produce every time he had the bad luck to run into a police authority. De Forge told himself the guide had to be there and so did he at the appointed hour. These were imperatives. He could only do whatever was in his power to fulfil them and trust that on their side the organizers of his escape would fulfil them too. Finally, he decided to enlist Reboux's help. As a result he confided in him.

Reboux was surprised and impressed by the elaborateness and progress of de Forge's plan. He confirmed the judiciousness of de Forge's choice of Bad Danschau as the place to meet and take the train. Unlike the town closest to the fortress, Bad Danschau was a tourist attraction. Reboux had walked there a number of times and had observed that there was considerable activity in the town and at the station. At the fortress town de Forge would be seen and remembered since it was so desolate, but he would be lost at Bad Danschau among the many travellers who passed through the town. Reboux brought out his map and showed de Forge how to get there from the fortress along a small country road running through a forest. It was a road where few people passed and where he would be unlikely to be seen. Just before the town the road curved and descended in a slight decline at the end of which was a narrow wooden bridge running over a stream. It would be an ideal place for the rendezvous.

'But first you've got to get out,' Reboux said. 'Where are you with the cable?'

'It could be ready by Christmas, certainly by February or March.'

'Have you chosen the spot for the drop?'

'Of course,' de Forge replied. 'Months ago when I first began to weave the bits of string.'

De Forge led Reboux there. At that point the parapet rose about four feet to an opening in the wall about five feet wide curving gracefully upward and arching to a close six feet above. Across the opening and embedded in the stone was an iron bar. De Forge grasped it, and his arm shook back and forth as he tested the solidity of the bar.

'You see,' de Forge said. 'It doesn't budge. The cable goes over the bar, then I go over the bar and after that I'm in the hands of the gods.'

'But how will you get down?' Reboux asked. 'You won't be able to do it hand over hand. It's far beyond your strength.

De Forge smiled. 'Those who help me will need the strength, he said. 'I shall be seated. You see, I have a little stick, a sort of wooden bar, that I've hidden away with the cable. I shall tie that to the end of the cable, climb over the wall and sit on the wooden bar. Then the generals who will be good enough to help me – two of them will be enough for that part of the job – will pay out the cable with me at the end of it until I touch the ground.'

Reboux nodded; he was looking out into the scrub and wooded area below. 'It sounds reasonable,' he said. 'The planning is good. Now what you need is a little luck.'

'And lots of patience,' de Forge added. 'That's the hardest.' He pointed to a clump of trees. 'If I survive the descent, I'll slip into that thicket and transform myself as well as I can. Then off I go to whatever God has in store for me.'

The summer and autumn passed with surprising speed for de Forge. He kept busy. De Forge had learned that there was no death like that of an unoccupied existence; the purposeless passage of time crumpled and crushed the soul, leaving a man diminished. De Forge filled his time. Early on he had suggested to the more collaborationist of the generals that they request a series of courses in German. They had adopted his proposal with enthusiasm. The idea had delighted von Bardsdorf, and one of the staff reserve officers, a teacher by profession, took on the assignment. With several other generals, de Forge attended the courses regularly. He also studied the language and spoke it at every opportunity with the German officers and guards. He was much more fluent than he had been, although he still spoke with a marked accent.

The German attack on Russia also made a huge difference in de Forge's daily occupations. It was one of the major events he had anticipated, and he followed it as closely as he could in the German newspapers made available to the generals at the fortress. Shortly after the attack began, as the Germans drove the Russians back, Palisse made a proposal to de Forge.

'Everybody is talking about the Russian campaign and nobody knows what's going on there,' he said. 'Most of the generals can't read German and only know what they can get, if anything, from the headlines. The rest, with one or two exceptions, read it primitively and inaccurately while moving their lips. They know just enough to get everything wrong. What we ought to have is a daily discussion of the war, but somebody would have to lead the discussion. Will you do it?'

De Forge accepted. It turned out to be a daily orientation lecture that varied in length with the news, after which there was a general discussion. De Forge took the assignment seriously and spent three or four hours a day preparing it. It filled the empty time admirably. The exercise kept him intellectually alert, reading between the lines of army communiqués and field reports, sorting out the propaganda from fact, and in the end making his own daily synthesis in an effort to create a true picture out of a jumble of half-truths, shrewd omissions and blatant lies. The discussions were lively as the generals analysed the tactics and the strategy of the opposing armies. Many thought that Hitler would take Moscow and Leningrad and impose a German peace on the Russians. From the beginning de Forge stood with the small group who maintained that space was Russia's great ally, that space would give her the time she needed to hold and eventually turn back the Germans. It was the difference, de Forge insisted, between the Russian and the French campaigns.

So the summer and autumn passed and winter came. Then, late one Sunday night just before lights-out, a rumour swept the fortress that the Japanese had attacked the United States at Pearl Harbour, destroying the American fleet. A few days later the generals at the fortress learned that Germany had declared war against the United States. The daily orientation discussions took a new turn. The question that absorbed the generals now was how soon and in what manner the weight of American power would be felt in Europe. The strategic perspective was transformed. The generals agreed that there were two possibilities: either England would be used as a base for a direct invasion of Europe through France or the Allies would go for North Africa with the threat of then smashing into Europe from the south.

The second possibility electrified de Forge's imagination. For him it meant that France would be in the war again with an army in the field. It was the army he wanted to lead. Despite his imprisonment, de Forge's hopes soared. He envisioned all sorts of possibilities, both strategic and political, and all of them led to one point: a France risen again to full glory.

Shortly afterwards, in the middle of December, de Forge received the letter from his wife advising him in code that the wire for his cable would be arriving hidden in the top edge of four cans included in his Christmas package. De Forge immediately sought out Corporal Picoche. The little Parisian was willing but pessimistic.

'You know the rules, *mon général*,' he said. 'They don't let any cans go through. They stop all of them.'

'It's a Christmas package,' de Forge said. 'Maybe they'll make an exception.'

'You know how they are, *mon général*. A rule is a rule. They aren't French.'

De Forge looked depressed.

'I'll do what I can,' Picoche said. 'Those German guards will do almost anything for cigarettes and chocolate.'

The package arrived at the fortress the day before Christmas. All the packages for the prisoners were directed to a large room called the *Paketstelle*, which was located in one of the outer buildings that served as the fortress post office. The procedure called for Picoche and another French corporal to assist the German soldiers who were in charge. The Frenchmen opened the packages on a long broad table in the middle of the room. The German soldiers checked the contents of the packages to see that all was in order. They then handed them all back to the French corporals, who at that point were authorized to deliver the packages to the generals to whom they were addressed. Everything always went smoothly; the atmosphere was friendly and cheerful; everything was always delivered to its intended destination – except for canned food.

Early on, a few months after the packages began to arrive, von Bardsdorf had become suspicious of the large number of cans included in the packages for the prisoners. They might contain anything in addition to food. As a result, each can was separated from the rest of the contents of the packages, noted in a ledger, and put aside in a special slot under the name of the general to whom it was destined. When the general wanted what was in the can he went to the *Paketstelle*, the German soldier in charge opened it before him, emptied the contents into a dish and handed it over. The can was thrown out with the rest of the garbage.

When Picoche undid the package that had come for de Forge the two German overseers were, as usual, on one side of the broad table and Picoche and the other French corporal were on the other side. One of the Germans was a slim blond youth wearing steel-rimmed spectacles; the other was older, a heavy-set, swarthy man with bushy eyebrows. Picoche unloaded the contents of the package on the table. It fell in a heap, then spread helter-skelter towards either side. Most of it was food – cake, paté, nuts, dates, figs, chocolate; there were also many packs of cigarettes, Gauloises Bleues, and a grey knitted woollen sweater; the four cans had fallen on the table too. Picoche's eyes lingered on the cans. They were big ones. The steel-rimmed German casually eyed the cans. Two of them had fallen close to Picoche's hand, but it was already impossible for him to pick them up and put them back into the carton. Picoche's heart sank. He smiled across the table at Steel Rims, who was now watching him.

Then Picoche noted that Steel Rims' eyes shifted from him to the table. But his eyes did not go to the cans; they went to some bars of chocolate. Picoche turned to the older German with the bushy brows. He was observing the packs of cigarettes with a kind of lust. 'So that's how it is,' Picoche said to himself.

The Germans began shoving items across the table towards Picoche and the other French corporal, items they approved and that Picoche was to put back into the carton for de Forge. But there was a peculiar reluctance to their gestures and that look of unmistakable craving in their eyes. Steel Rims finally sent a bar of chocolate sliding across the table and at the end of the same gesture drew aside a can that was in his reach. The instant the chocolate touched Picoche's hand he sent it swiftly sliding back across the table straight into Steel Rims' hands. Then Picoche lifted the can closest to him and dropped it into the carton.

'It's Christmas,' he said with a laugh. 'Presents for everyone.'

Steel Rims looked startled, then echoed Picoche's laugh.

'Presents for everyone,' he cried. 'It's Christmas.'

He pocketed the chocolate and slid the can under his hand across the table at Picoche. Picoche slid a bar of chocolate across the table towards Steel Rims with his right hand and another bar of chocolate across to him with his left hand, crying, 'Presents for everyone. It's Christmas.' The German with the bushy brows and the other French corporal watched the scene with smiles on their faces. Picoche was in very good form. He nudged his comrade. 'Don't you understand?' he said. 'It's Christmas. Presents for everyone. Send him some cigarettes, registered letter express. He's a smoker.'

The French corporal laughed. He sent three packs of cigarettes whirling across the table. Bushy Brows scooped them up. One second they were in his hands; the next they were in his pockets, gone.

'How about a present for us?' Picoche teased. 'A little something to eat.'

Steel Rims motioned to the can near Bushy Brows. The man laughed. He spun it across the table, and with either hand Picoche sent another bar of chocolate and another pack of cigarettes towards the Germans. All the cans were in the carton. The table was cleared. The carton was set aside. The next carton was on the table. The four men laughed. It had been a gay, profitable incident for all of them and now they could forget it. Steel Rims and Bushy Brows were smiling. Ah, those Frenchmen, they were thinking. They were also thinking of the chocolate and the cigarettes. Later they would divide the loot. It was the most appreciated present either of them would get this Christmas.

Picoche tried to keep a straight face when he handed the Christmas package to de Forge. The general, standing stiffly in his room, could not bring himself to ask the question on his lips.

'You will find some things missing, *mon général*,' Picoche told him. 'It's my fault.' Picoche slyly watched de Forge's face darken. 'But after all, *mon général*, it *is* Christmas and even the Boches are our brothers in this season of love for all men. So I gave them your chocolates and cigarettes. A lot of it anyway.' Picoche paused as de Forge regarded him uncomprehendingly. Then, relishing the moment, Picoche pixielike delivered his punch line. 'In return,' he said, 'they were good enough to let you have the four cans.'

All things considered, it was a fine Christmas for de Forge. His mood was festive. The cans were emptied and consumed as he shared his riches and celebrated Christmas with Reboux and Palisse. With some trouble he twisted the top edges of the cans open and, his eyes momentarily closed at first and praying, found the copper wire soldered within. A wave of triumph rippled over him. The wire was ever so thin, but the four lengths together were long, long, and plainly the strand of copper both strengthening and supported by the cable of twine would be more than enough to hold his weight. Grasping the wire in his hand, de Forge felt a surge of power. Freedom was now in his hands. He had outsmarted von Bardsdorf and the whole damned German military establishment. He would get out of their rock-bound, sky-high, escape-proof stone fortress, and nothing in the world, not Hitler, nor his army, nor his police, nor any force on earth would stop him.

NINE

In the first months of the following year, 1942, Operation Marianne took on another dimension. It had begun as a private affair, merely as an idea in the mind of a singularly wilful man determined to escape and convinced that he was destined to play the pre-eminent rôle of the saviour of his country. Then Operation Marianne had swiftly grown into a broadly French national affair: it was organized by a number of key military figures connected with the Vichy regime who aimed eventually at using de Forge, once free, to head French forces in the field against Germany. Now Operation Marianne took on international ramifications. Suddenly it reached out across the sea to Washington, to the White House.

The Americans and the British were in the planning stage of operations for the conquest of Europe. At the time, President Roosevelt and his advisers were hesitating between two strategic conceptions. On the one hand, they were tempted by the prospect of a swift, bold invasion of the European mainland. But on the other hand, caution tempered audacity as they considered a landing in North Africa prior to opening a continental second front. Both conceptions involved allied operations on French territory. In either case French support with the co-operation of a prestigious French leader for political as well as military reasons was indispensable. It was considered particularly important in the event of a landing in North Africa to produce an eminent French military figure around whom would immediately and loyally rally the French divisions defending the North African coast, cities and military installations; in which case the landing could be made with a minimum cost in lives, a maximum guarantee of success, and without the painful prospect of battling against French troops.

It was not the opinion of the State Department or of President Roosevelt that their man was General de Gaulle. Relations with the leader of the Free French in London, whom the Americans regarded as outrageously difficult and not necessarily the incarnation of France, were frankly bad. The Americans hoped to find a man who was less prickly and more conciliatory. Above all, they wanted a military man of high rank and outstanding prestige who had the size and experience to take command of the French army and who would be accepted by the army – that is, the officer caste – as their leader. Did such a man exist? Was he the kind of man who would fight with the Allies against Germany?

Alerted to the problem, the American embassy in Vichy made discreet inquiries. Invariably the man indicated was de Forge. The Americans were told that in 1940 de Forge had first led one army, and though circumstances were such that he could not emerge a victor, it was the only army that had advanced, however briefly, against the German machine; then de Forge had been suddenly transferred to retrieve a desperate situation at the head of another army in full retreat, but before he could act he had been overwhelmed and captured. There was little doubt, however, that in different circumstances he had the ability to reverse the roles and avenge himself on the enemy who had defeated him. All judgments concurred: de Forge was a great soldier; he was respected; he would be followed. Unfortunately, he was in German hands, a prisoner, out of circulation.

One day in March, quite by chance, General Bonniot, resplendent in his uniform and almost back to his normal weight, attended a diplomatic reception in Vichy where he met a bright and enterprising young counsellor of the American embassy named James McKesney. As they chatted over a glass of champagne, de Forge's name came up. McKesney said he had heard a great deal about the man, that de Forge fascinated him. Bonniot replied that he knew de Forge well, that they had been prisoners together. The conversation proceeded cautiously on both sides, but enough was said for each to infer that the other had more to add. McKesney was particularly intrigued by one exchange.

'What a shame,' he remarked at one point, 'that a man like

that is a prisoner of war and therefore nonexistent for the duration.'

'De Forge may not be quite that nonexistent – at least not for the duration.'

'But he can play no role.'

'That's true as long as he's a prisoner,' Bonniot said in an even, neutral voice.

McKesney looked puzzled.

'After all,' Bonniot added, 'I was a prisoner too but the Germans were kind enough to release me.'

'And do you expect them to be kind enough to release de Forge as well?' McKesney asked in the same ironic tone.

Bonniot shrugged. 'Who can predict in these times what the shape of the future will be?'

McKesney asked to see him again. Bonniot made the appointment in an obscure little outlying café where there was small chance that he would be recognized; he wore civilian clothes. This time, having the approval of his superiors at the embassy to probe more deeply, McKesney lost little time in coming to the point. The military attaché had been consulted and had assured McKesney that General Bonniot was 'safe.'

'We're interested in de Forge,' McKesney said, 'very interested. You suggested when we spoke last that he might get out of the fortress as you did.'

'Not as I did,' Bonniot said with a smile. 'But I did suggest he might get out.'

McKesney wanted to know more, but Bonniot refused to go into any of the details.

'It's enough for you to know,' he declared, 'that de Forge is not necessarily out of the way, as you put it, for the duration. For the rest, if you're really interested, I'll put you in contact with other people who are more directly involved.'

So it happened that the American embassy was put in contact with Rivet and Galland.

The Americans were told that the organization of de Forge's escape was in an advanced stage, that while the outcome of such an enterprise could not of course be forecast, everything possible was being done to assure its success and the result would probably be known some time in the spring – that is, within the next few months. The Americans wanted to know if de Forge was disposed to work with them. The best way to find out, they were told, was to ask him. But were communications secure? Until now, the Americans were told with explanations, they had been. The French officers were finally asked to put the following question to de Forge: would he agree to work with President Roosevelt for the liberation of France and under what conditions?

Rising tall as trees, both Rivet and Galland felt as if they had picked the sweepstakes winner. The question told them everything they could possibly have hoped for. It was no secret, of course, that the Americans were planning operations that would ultimately result in the liberation of France. But Rivet and Galland now felt they had a direct confirmation. Beyond that, it was plain to them that the Americans had picked their man as the Allies' principal French military comrade-in-arms. That was the least that the question could mean. For the Americans could not have in mind anything but the top job in applying this way to a man of de Forge's stature; and they must know that de Forge was not the man to demand or accept anything less. Thus, like a flash of lightning that suddenly illuminates the darkness and holds everything sharply clear in its flare, the question revealed for its organizers the full significance of Operation Marianne: it would release the man who would lead French troops in battle beside their allies for the liberation of France.

At the fortress de Forge was having a hard time. Ever since America had become a belligerent he had felt that great events were being prepared that directly involved France, and this sense of history passing him by when he was meant to be fashioning it drove him into a state of impotent despair. Each passive day was a torment, his inner turmoil boiling up and his mask of serenity began to crack. He developed a tic blinking nervously; at times he was unable to hold his temper in check. On two occasions he savagely ripped into collaborationist generals, who tried to reduce European policy to a choice between Nazis and Communists, humiliating them before witnesses and needlessly inviting their hatred and enmity

Instead of becoming more relaxed as the preparations for his escape progressed, de Forge became jumpier. Trying to calm himself with work, he plunged into his study of German, pored over the German press, devoted himself to preparing his orientation lectures, exercised daily to be in good physical shape for whatever ordeal might be ahead of him. Alone at night in the dark silence of the sleeping fortress, he toiled long hours over his cable, splicing the copper wire into the twine, meticulously linking and twisting them together with puffed, burning hands and sore muscles. But he had no inner peace. The sense of time crawling in the fortress and of history in full flight outside was too strong.

But if time crawled for an impatient de Forge, it also advanced. One lonely March night, a year and a half after beginning it, de Forge twisted the last strands of his reinforced cable and with a triumphant sigh told himself that his cable to freedom was completed. The next morning, aware that he was casting himself blindly into the dark, he conveyed the news by code to his wife: *ribbon ready awaiting order proceed rendezvous*. In the same message he reminded her that the picture on his false identity card should be without moustache and with spectacles. Then, wound up tighter than ever, he waited for an answer.

A week later a letter arrived from his wife. He knew it was too soon to be the answer to his message, but could not imagine that it would turn what until now might have been fantasy into reality. As he deciphered the code in the letter, the question the Americans put to him exploded in his mind like a thousand Roman candles, splendidly confirming his greatest expectations. For how many deadly hours in the impotence of captivity had he dreamed of such a proposal! But never in his wildest reverie had he imagined that they could come to him while he was imprisoned behind thick stone fortress walls in the far reaches of Germany. Then they must know of his plan to escape! And they must expect him to make it!

Excitedly, he sat down at his table. He knew exactly what his conditions would be; he had thought about them often enough. The isolation of captivity screened him from the reality of France's defeat and the German occupation, and he lived romantically in an intellectual world of his own illusions. France, momentarily prostrate, was still a first-class power, her former grandeur within reach if it could be grasped, her military leadership still to be asserted. He quickly scribbled his answer to the American question:

'General de Forge accepts President Roosevelt's proposal of co-operation under the following conditions:

'1 – The territorial integrity of France, both inside and outside metropolitan France, as of September 1, 1939, will be re-established.

'2 – French sovereignty will be complete on French territory wherever French troops fight beside American troops.

'3 – General de Forge will be commander in chief of Allied forces in the theatre of operations where French troops fight.

'4 – The rate of the franc in relation to the dollar will be the equivalent of the rate of the franc in relation to the pound granted by England to General de Gaulle.'

Condition three conformed with French rank in both world wars.

Having committed his answer to paper, de Forge slipped it into the pages of his big French-German dictionary. It was too long to send by the simple code established with his wife and although he had no idea how he would send it, that did not trouble him; he was sure in his present mood that he would find a way. He left the building, driven out by his excitement, unable to remain alone. He had to share his mood with someone and looked for Reboux, but he could not find him. On his way back to his room he ran into Palisse.

'Something's up,' Palisse said. 'Have you seen Reboux?'

'I've been looking for him for half an hour.'

'Von Bardsdorf called him in. He must still be with him.'

'Do you know what it's about?'

'No,' said Palisse, 'but I can imagine.'

Reboux was the only general apart from de Forge who was making a serious effort to escape.

'Do you think one of our people could have denounced him?' Palisse asked.

'We'll have to wait until he gets back and then try to piece it all together.'

They walked back to their building. De Forge worried. It was not only Reboux; it was himself. The factor that immeasurably increased his chances of escaping was von Bardsdorf's certainty that no prisoner could even attempt it. If von Bardsdorf knew that Reboux had plotted a way of getting out, his suspicions would be aroused about other prisoners. The result could be a disaster. Security would be tightened, freedom of movement restricted; perhaps worst of all, they would fine-comb the place with search parties. De Forge's heart dropped as he imagined such a party discovering his cable. He put the image out of mind. It was sheer morbidity, he told himself. There was not one chance in a million that they would find it so long as it remained hidden under the planks in his room. With Palisse, de Forge waited an eternal half-hour in Reboux's room before Reboux turned up.

'It's incredible,' Reboux announced calmly in response to the inquiring looks of his two friends. 'I've been sprung.'

'They're letting you go?' Palisse said unbelievingly.

'That's what von Bardsdorf said. It appears that the Japanese are not happy with our military attaché in Tokyo, and of course I got on quite well with them during the years I had the job. They remembered me and suggested that relations would be considerably improved if I were to return. The whole thing has been negotiated and settled, so off I go back to the world.'

Reboux spoke coolly, betraying none of the emotion he felt. To show his joy would have been too cruel to those remaining. Reboux soberly accepted their congratulations. 'If you have any messages, written or verbal,' he said, 'I'll be glad to deliver them.'

'Come into my room when you have a moment,' de Forge said. 'I'll have something for you.'

Later de Forge gave Reboux two messages to deliver to his wife. One was the answer to the Americans; the other said that he was ready to go, urged that the date be quickly set and that it be a Friday since weekend leaves for the guards were in effect at the fortress and security slackened from Friday night to Monday morning; de Forge added that the rendezvous be made outside the town of Bad Danschau, specifying the little wooden bridge crossing the stream west of the village, and concluded that Reboux would convey to them certain details and confirm that he, de Forge, had complete confidence in their arrangements and committed himself blindly to their plans. Reboux put the messages inside the lining of his kepi.

'Tell them I'm ready and depending on them,' de Forge said for the third time.

And for the third time Reboux assured de Forge that that would be the first thing he would do when he got to France.

'And now,' Reboux said, 'I have a few things you may find useful.'

He handed de Forge two hundred negotiable marks, a German railway timetable, a map of the area surrounding the fortress, a map of the German-Swiss border, a compass, a soft Tyrolean hat complete with a feather, a raincoat without stars of insignia and a small stock of food.

'As you can see,' Reboux said with a smile, 'my plan for escape had made some modest progress.'

Soberly de Forge tried on the Tyrolean hat.

The effect was comic. Reboux laughed. 'It's perfect,' he said. 'Nobody could possibly recognize you.'

'It's something I can use,' de Forge said, flushing and quickly taking it off. 'How did you get it?'

'My wife sent it to me wrapped in a package of grease.'

De Forge studied Reboux for a moment. 'Your good fortune is mine,' he said. 'So obviously I'm doubly pleased.' He paused and his smile brightened. 'I'm also pleased for you,' he added, 'because your plan was no plan at all and couldn't have worked. Believe me, the surest way of getting out of here and back home, free, safe and in one piece, is to have the Germans as your accomplices.'

Everything was ready. De Forge had tested every inch of his cable and had made all his other preparations for the escape. He had paid a very high price in reichsmarks to one of the fortress gardeners for a pair of grey pants that had not only long since seen their best days but were on the verge of seeing their last. The gardener had been unable to resist taking so much money for a pair of pants that not even he could wear much longer. De Forge did not mind. The pants would complete his outfit until he met his guide and could get into his own civilian clothes that the guide would bring with him. Meanwhile, in addition to the pants, de Forge would wear a sweater, the Tyrolean hat and Reboux's brown gaberdine raincoat, which, unmarked by any military insignia, had the look of a civilian costume and would allow him to pass for a tourist. The only item that clashed was de Forge's boots. But that would have to do for the walk to the rendezvous. With luck, he would meet nobody; his luck would have to be extraordinarily bad if the one or two people who might cross his path on that country walk happened to notice his boots.

De Forge also bought a switchblade knife from the gardener. The towering, dignified general handled the knife and admired it, and the gardener offered it, once again at an exaggeratedly high price, at the same time that he sold the grey pants.

'It's a very good knife,' the old and stooped little gardener told de Forge, showing him its qualities. 'You see, I've kept it sharp and pointed. A knife always comes in handy, and someday when you need it you'll be sorry if you don't have it.'

The gardener's last simple statement decided de Forge. To be caught with a knife meant that he would be accused of being armed, but the knife could prevent him from being caught. The decision was a test. He told himself he would rather die than be brought back in humiliation to spend the rest of the war a prisoner while the fate of France was being decided without him. If he was laying down his life to get away, anyone who stood in his way would be taking the same risk. The knife gave him an odd consolation.

For some weeks after Reboux left, de Forge lived in a state of suspension. There was nothing more for him to do but wait, and patience was the least of his virtues. Every night he went to sleep with the same thought as the one he woke up with, and between waking and sleeping the thought never left him. When, when, oh God, would word of the rendezvous come? He was like two men in one. Inwardly, he was coiled upon his obsession as tightly as a high-tension spring; outwardly, he plodded through the daily fortress routine wearing an air of placidity. But he ruffled easily, and the other generals left him alone. Many, as always, felt resentment because of his haughtiness. But now they misread him. What put a distance between him and the rest of the world at this point was the agony of waiting. Nothing happened; he had never lived so intensely. But he communicated none of this, not even to Palisse, the only person he frequented; and this self-imposed silence served to intensify his anguish.

He had more to be anguished about than he suspected as a new danger to his enterprise developed from an unexpected quarter. It came from Paris, where no less a personage than Otto Abetz, Hitler's ambassador to France, was tipped off that de Forge planned to break out of the fortress. Abetz immediately sent a telegram to Consul General Krug von Nidda, the liaison officer between the Ministry of Foreign Affairs in Berlin and the German High Command, telling him a member of the French government had advised him that, according to a person close to de Forge's circle, the general intended to escape. Abetz added that the French government insisted on issuing the warning since it realized that an escape by a man of de Forge's eminence would obviously be bad for Franco-German relations.

The warning sped through channels to an incredulous and indignant von Bardsdorf, who suppressed his anger but not his disbelief as he listened to that outrageous suggestion from the outside with its dubious implications about the quality of *his* fortress as a prison, not to mention the efficiency with which it was run, and its irrational presumption that any man in his right mind, including a de Forge, could question the 'inescapability' of his situation. Having controlled his emotion on the telephone, von Bardsdorf leaped to his feet when he replaced the instrument in its cradle and paced his office, allowing his rage to explode.

'Escape, escape!' he cried. 'How can he hope to escape?' And von Bardsdorf raised his arms in helpless exasperation at the folly of his superiors and let them fall, slapping resoundingly against his thighs.

For a satisfying quarter of an hour von Bardsdorf indulged his petulance, storming and flirting with the idea of doing nothing about the warning from the High Command. But even as he spluttered about Abetz's ignorance and Berlin's stupidity to the corpulent colonel who was his second in command, von Bardsdorf knew that something would have to be done. Finally, having vented his bile, von Bardsdorf gave the order to search de Forge's room.

'See what you can find,' he sarcastically told the colonel. 'Maybe there's a homemade helicopter in his closet he intends to fly off in.'

At five o'clock that afternoon the door of de Forge's room swung open without warning. De Forge dropped the German newspaper he was reading and looked up, startled. From the doorway a German noncom barked out that the room would be searched. De Forge rose with a sinking heart as the colonel marched into the room followed by Lieutenant Hetzel, the noncom and a private.

'Make yourself at home, gentlemen,' de Forge said with massive irony. 'I beg you to look at anything and everything. There isn't much and it won't take you long.'

But as he played the unconcerned host, he worried that they would find all the things he had gathered for his escape and wondered bitterly which of the collaborationist generals could have swung them on his track.

The search began with the closet, and the colonel himself looked into it, handling some of de Forge's clothes with a casual, gloved hand. As he groped among de Forge's things, the colonel smiled over von Bardsdorf's image of a helicopter in the closet; he would report that none was there, anticipating his chief's amusement. De Forge's face twitched when the colonel's spotless glove brushed the more pedestrian grey pants and gaberdine raincoat, civilian clothes that were *streng verboten*. But, his expression again severe, the colonel turned back to the room without mentioning these items.

He noticed some kitchen utensils on a shelf above de Forge's washbasin and ordered a pot to be taken down and examined. The private reached up for it, placed it on the basin and lifted the cover. Again de Forge's face twitched. Five pairs of eyes saw that the pot contained potatoes and raw carrots. They could not see the German railroad timetable hidden under the carrots.

'I don't believe it's forbidden to have vegetables, *Herr Oberst*?' De Forge's comment was so gentle it was less a statement than a question.

The colonel bowed from the waist in agreement.

The private put the pot back on the shelf, but before de Forge could relax the colonel pointed to another pot he wanted to look into. Reboux's Tyrolean hat was hidden in the bottom of it. This time the five pairs of eyes observed nothing more than a large amount of white beans. Nobody ordered the private to shake the pot or dip his hand into it.

'As you can see,' de Forge remarked, 'I'm richly equipped.'

The search, as von Bardsdorf had led the colonel to expect, uncovered nothing out of order. The search party was therefore ready to leave, having faithfully executed its duty, when Lieutenant Hetzel noticed the big Sachs-Villatti dictionary on de Forge's table and picked it up. De Forge's heart sank. Between the thin pages of the thick volume he kept the reichsmarks he had accumulated for his escape by selling his chocolate, through the discreet Picoche, to guards with a sweet tooth. The money was all there in ten- and twenty-mark notes. The marks Reboux had given him were there too.

'We all know, *monsieur le général,* that you translate entire articles from our press,' Hetzel said. He hefted the volume and added, 'You have chosen the best dictionary that exists.'

'Watch out, *monsieur le lieutenant,*' de Forge said. 'You're playing with my safe.'

The one thing de Forge feared was that Hetzel would drop the dictionary and that the reichsmarks would scatter before their eyes.

'Your safe?' Hetzel said. 'Aha, very interesting.'

He let the dictionary fall open in his hands. As de Forge was certain it would, the thick book fell open towards the centre where de Forge had purposely placed his French money – two bills, one of a thousand francs, the other of five hundred francs.

'Well, well, it *is* your safe,' said Hetzel. 'But how do you happen to have this money?'

'I had it when I arrived. The Geneva Convention gives me the right to hold on to the pocket money I need, and as an army general, I was authorized by the fortress officials to keep these fifteen hundred francs.'

'True enough,' the colonel said.

'Thank you, *Herr Oberst.*'

'None the less, *monsieur le général,*' the colonel added, 'you can't do anything with this money here; you can't spend it since it isn't negotiable in the fortress, so in your own interest you ought to deposit it at the Kommandatur instead of leaving it, as you say, in your safe.'

'That is my affair, *Herr Oberst.* In any case, *monsieur le lieutenant* can now see that I spoke the truth when I baptized this excellent Sachs-Villatti dictionary my safe.'

And fearful that Hetzel, who had been distracted by the exchange, might begin thumbing through the dictionary, de Forge snapped it from his hands, shutting it noisily at the same time. He put the dictionary on the table and, laughing, sat on it, his feet swinging clear.

'I told you, *monsieur le lieutenant,* that you mustn't touch my safe. Now I am obliged to protect it.'

'Don't be upset, *monsieur le général,*' Hetzel said with mock contriteness. 'I had no intention of robbing you – and certainly not before witnesses.'

'No doubt, *monsieur le lieutenant,*' de Forge said, leaning at the edge of the table on the heels of his palms and bowing his head slightly with ironic condescension.

But then his expression changed abruptly as if an official mask had been set over his face and his voice became steel as he turned towards the colonel. 'I must admit, *Herr Oberst,*' he said, 'that I am extremely offended by this manifestation of suspicion and mistrust which has plainly motivated your distasteful search of my quarters. You have of course found nothing since there was nothing for you to find. I beg you to convey my displeasure to the general in command of the fortress.'

De Forge rose as he spoke. When he finished he was at the door, which he opened to let his visitors know that the comedy had lasted long enough. They made their exit in the same order as they had made their entrance.

The next day at the same hour General von Bardsdorf appeared in full dress; he wore all his decorations across his chest, a sabre at his side and spotless white gloves. This time de Forge's door was not flung unexpectedly open; the commander of the fortress knocked softly for admittance. De

Forge received him very coldly.

'I have come, *monsieur le général*,' von Bardsdorf said with admirable dignity, 'to offer my apologies for the ineptitude some of my subordinates have displayed.'

De Forge icily accepted his jailer's apology.

Then, with considerable hemming and hawing, von Bardsdorf philosophized at some length about how important it is not to put any faith in baseless rumours. De Forge solemnly agreed. But none of his probes elicited any indication of what the source of those rumours might be. The conversation slipped into less sensitive subjects and von Bardsdorf finally left, his sabre clattering against his leg, assured that he had appeased his star boarder and salvaged the honour of the Wehrmacht.

Three days later in a letter from his wife de Forge received the message he had been waiting for. It came in a formula he had agreed upon with Reboux about de Forge's oldest daughter, Adele. De Forge's wife wrote, 'Adele will be leaving on a trip on the last Friday in May and will meet her uncle that day at one p.m. at the railway station in Marseilles.' The translation of the sentence was that de Forge was to get out of the fortress on the last Friday in May in time to meet his guide at 1 p.m. on the same day at the bridge near the Bad Danschau railway station.

As soon as he had read the key sentence de Forge looked at his calendar. The last Friday of the month was ten days away. In his exultation, de Forge failed to return to his wife's letter for some time. He was on his feet and about the room, unable to be still. Inwardly he kept repeating, 'Ten days, only ten days.' He had been a prisoner just a few weeks short of two years, and now at last he would be able to cast off the paralysis that had bound him and become a man again. 'Ten days, only ten days.' He was less flesh than spirit, unaware of his members, of what bound him to earth and this fortress. Suddenly he felt, now that freedom and action were within reach if he would but stretch for them, that he was alive again. The fortress was no longer his universe; vast horizons opened up to him and though everything on them was vague and nothing could be defined, de Forge felt he had the size, growing every second, to deal with any obstacle, threat or challenge that appeared. 'Ten days, only ten days.'

When his euphoria subsided de Forge returned to his wife's letter. He quickly saw that it contained a coded message and hastily decoded it. Once again his spirit bounded and soared. De Forge had before him the terse reply to his message to the Americans. It read: *conditions accepted.* The signature told him the level on which he was dealing: FDR.

The next ten days flew past; de Forge floated weightlessly towards the last Friday of the month.

Fortunately de Forge had no inkling of the problem that now beset the organizers of Operation Marianne. Had he been in contact with Major René Galland, who was operationally responsible for Marianne he would not have felt euphoric at all.

Galland was an energetic man with enormous verve, but on the day de Forge received the message about the escape rendezvous Galland was not his normal self. At about the same time that de Forge learned about the rendezvous Galland arrived at the office of General Rivet, his chief, in an unusual and pitiable state. The peppery and dashing officer felt as deflated as a toy balloon whose air has escaped. For just as everything was organized and in place, simply waiting for Galland to push the button for the machinery to turn, everything fell apart.

Galland had spent himself on Marianne. He had involved thirty-four persons in the operation to organize the escape of one man, and they were geographically spread from Vichy to Strasbourg. He had arranged successive places to cross the artificial frontiers that existed as a result of the German occupation of France: there was the border between Alsace, in effect absorbed into the Reich administratively, and Occupied France proper; then there was the line between Occupied France and Unoccupied France. In addition, a small contingent had been assigned to find a house where de Forge, once safely in Unoccupied France, could not only live with his family and work in security but also be protected to the extent possible, should the fury of Hitler be so excessive that the Nazis would attempt to kidnap or kill him. Most critical of all, Galland had found a guide with the indispensable qualifications who was willing to risk his life by going into Germany to get de Forge out. But on this morning, only ten days before the rendezvous at Bad Danschau, the guide had disappeared.

'Are you sure?' Rivet asked.

'Certain. I checked all possibilities. He's vanished.'

Rivet gnawed at his lip. Galland looked away. It was a bad sign; Rivet felt backed into a corner too. 'There's no backup?'

It was as much a statement of fact as a question. Galland shook his head unhappily. Rivet knew there was no backup. They had been through all that. This was a military operation without an army. The whole affair, everybody involved including themselves, was on a voluntary basis. Call it resistance if you're on the left; call it patriotism if you're on the right; or mix it all up in a salad *à la française*. Whatever you called it, it was a hell of a way for a professional to fight a war. Of course they had found someone to agree to go in for de Forge. There was always somebody to take on the wildest assignments; and he had been so sure of his man and so reluctant, with Rivet's reserved approval, to put another man on standby in view of the job and the problem of finding anyone, that now he was caught short and the entire operation was compromised. Galland understood the man who had run out, understood him profoundly – and hated him anyway. The man had had the time to think things out; he had found his senses and lost his head. It all turned on the guide; without one they had nothing.

'And we were so lucky,' Galland said morosely, 'to have Reboux turn up and give us just the detailed information we needed.'

'It was going too smothly. It couldn't last.'

'But this! If I could get my hands on the bastard, I'd throttle him.'

'Can we call it off? Postpone it?'

Rivet knew that was impossible. He was whistling in the dark. There was no way they could get to de Forge in time.

'We must do something,' Rivet said against Galland's silence. 'You remember what Reboux said: "Give him the order. De Forge told me just before I left – they were his last words to me – that once he gets the order, no matter what the problems might be, he would execute it." '

'I remember,' Galland said miserably. 'I worked like a madman after those meetings with Reboux.'

'De Forge will be a pigeon if someone isn't there to meet him with clothes and papers to take him back to France through the network.'

'Of course. We can't leave him high and dry.'

'We've got to find another guide.'

'It's late,' Galland said. 'It's – '

'So much the better. He won't have time for second thoughts.'

'If he's the type who's going to have second thoughts – '

'I know,' Rivet said angrily. 'But we've got to produce a guide.'

'All right,' Galland said, 'we'll produce one.'

'Do you know who?'

'No, but I know someone who does.'

The two men regarded each other in silence. Neither was pleased with himself or the other. It was the eleventh hour and they were improvising; they were improvising an operation both knew was critical for the future of their country. They were juggling with the freedom, and perhaps the life, of no ordinary man, but with that of General de Forge, whom President Roosevelt had personally accorded the prime French military role in Allied operations to liberate France. Neither Rivet nor Galland mentioned the American commitment, but both were thinking of it. That made their bumbling even less forgivable. They were professionals; they felt they had acted like amateurs. Galland had to control himself not to be physically sick.

'Whoever he is you'll have to get him fast,' Rivet said at last.

'I have a meeting about it an hour from now.' Galland hesitated. 'With Sister Elisabeth,' he added. 'If she can't produce someone fast, nobody can.'

Sister Elisabeth was a patriotic Alsatian nun who had helped dozens of prisoners of war escape, had been caught by the Gestapo and imprisoned, escaped herself, and gone right back to work for an escape network, simply changing her headquarters from a convent in Strasbourg to one in Lyons.

'Didn't she supply the last one?'

'He was my contribution,' Galland said sourly.

Galland wanted to end the painful meeting and, rising brusquely, he went to the door. His hand was on the knob when he turned and saw another expression in Rivet's eyes; the ice had thawed.

'You don't seem very enthusiastic,' Rivet said.

'How could I be?'

'Well,' Rivet said, 'this is a funny business. . . .' And as he paused, groping for words, Galland was touched to see that he was embarrassed to raise a matter of sentiment about their work, which they had always accomplished as a job to be done, like breathing, without grand words or the need to verbalize any justification. 'You see –'

'I know,' Galland said gruffly. 'It'll come back. It's just that I feel so awful about this mess I've got us into. You expect the impossible of people, and when they fail you you can't forgive them.'

'You'll find someone else because you have to.'

'Yes, I'll find someone else,' Galland echoed without conviction.

Rivet's clear blue eyes were worried. 'Still,' he said, 'I don't like it.'

'Neither do I.'

TEN

Without underestimating the danger, Galland told Sister Elisabeth no more than he had to about Operation Marianne, but Sister Elisabeth told Galland even less. All she would say was that she would find the man for the job. Galland insisted.

'Is it that important?' she asked. 'Really that important?'

'It couldn't be more important.'

It was the way Galland said it that impressed Sister Elisabeth; as a result the words were burned into her brain. Still she refused to take him into her confidence.

'Trust me,' she said. 'I'll have him here for you in twenty-four hours.'

'But it's urgent,' Galland insisted, trying to find out more. 'It's very, very urgent.'

Even as he urged her to tell him more, Galland saw in her closed, if placid, expression that she had made up her mind not to give him the reassurance he so badly needed. That simply made him try harder. At this stage he could not face twenty-four hours of total ignorance about the man on whom his entire operation depended. Besides, depending on what she said, he might put those twenty-four hours to use. There was so little time.

While he spoke, he tried to stare Sister Elisabeth into submission, matching the intensity of his regard with that of his words. He thought she was impressed, but she remained unmoved. Sister Elisabeth was a heavy woman and, in her cowl and habit, of indeterminate age; at first sight her well-washed face with its irregular, unfeminine features seemed, if one was charitable, at best plain, but when she spoke the naïve goodness that shone from her pale blue eyes made her appear almost attractive.

'I can't tell you any more now,' she repeated, but with less conviction than before. 'It's only overnight. You'll have to trust me.'

'All right, *ma soeur*,' Galland said, seemingly resigned but playing his best card. 'But this isn't a matter of trust.' Then mildly but in the form of an irrevocable sentence, 'You're being unprofessional.'

Sister Elisabeth wavered: with considerable justification, she prided herself on her professionalism in the escape business. 'I can't tell you who he is before he commits himself. That would be immoral.'

'Just tell me *about* him.'

She accepted this compromise between professionalism and morality and said he was an unemployed and, in these times, unemployable journalist.

'He's not well known, I hope.'

'Not embarrassingly.'

'How old is he?'

'Thirty-one.'

'Education?'

'Ecole Normale Supérieure. Top of his class.' She said it with a certain pride.

'Then why isn't he a professor or a diplomat or in government or even in industry?'

Sister Elisabeth sighed. 'People say he has a flaw that neutralizes his gifts: lack of ambition.'

'But . . .?'

'But, well, of course he isn't ambitious, that's true. Not in the ordinary sense. Not for a conventional career. He has a quirk. He's an oppositionist. Always has been. Intellectually, he's against all the standard thinking, all the orthodoxies – right, left and centre – religious, social and political. He thought it was important, wanted to do something about it. So he refused the normal opportunities. He wrote, started a small weekly with some friends. But of course that ended with the war.'

'Then he's political.'

'Very.'

'Where does he fit?'

Sister Elisabeth shrugged. 'Nowhere really. Maybe independent left. But very independent. He had reformist ideas, rather utopian. But the Communists didn't like him any more than the Fascists. That must be why he isn't in jail today. The Communists dismissed him as an ineffectual nihilist. The Fascists attacked him as an irresponsible anarchist.' She smiled. 'And needless to say,' she added, 'he's an ardent antimilitarist.'

Galland made a face. 'He sounds like exactly the man we don't want.'

'On the contrary, he's just the man you want. He can do the job.'

'Does he speak German?'

'Perfectly.' She hesitated. 'His mother was German.'

Galland looked pained. 'That too. It's too much.'

'But he's as French as – as I am.'

Galland shook his head. 'I don't like it,' he said.

'Do you have anyone else?'

They regarded each other for a few moments without a word.

'But is he loyal?' Galland asked. 'If he took it on, would he follow through?'

'If I didn't think so, would I suggest him?'

'Have you known him long?'

'All my life,' Sister Elisabeth replied.

Galland mulled it over while Sister Elisabeth waited patiently. 'If it weren't you –' Galland left the sentence hanging in air. 'Why do you insist on him?' he asked.

Sister Elisabeth thought for a moment. 'For two reasons,' she said, 'apart from the fact that I don't know anyone else for the job. First, he can do it – if he agrees to go. Second –' She paused. 'Second, because he should do it, he needs to do it and it will make a better man of him. You see, he's lost now, he's having a bad time, but he's really a most remarkable human being.'

'I appreciate your candour, *ma soeur*,' Galland said, and added with a touch of irony, 'We're not practising therapists, you know. But the first reason is enough.'

'I thought it would be, in the absence of any other candidates.'

They smiled. They understood each other.

'You seem to feel very strongly about this fellow,' Galland remarked.

'Of course,' Sister Elisabeth replied. 'I love him.'

There would be time enough to say he was her brother once he had committed himself, as she hoped he would, at least to meeting Galland.

Sister Elisabeth's *pneumatique* had not told Maudet a thing except that she had to see him and it had to be immediately. If someone had suggested that his sister might offer him a rendezvous with destiny, he would have replied with an indulgent smile of scepticism at such a grand and hence misleading phrase. Maudet was too weighted down with his own problems to give much thought to those that might be raised by his sister.

He walked through the noon-hour throng towards his furnished one-room flat as if he were blind, his clear blue eyes turned inward under an unshorn mop of wavy blond hair. It was a fine spring day, but to judge by the way he was hunched over his thoughts it might have been December instead of May. Nothing was working out; nothing could work out. This morning had been another example of it on top of so many other examples. The editor had listened to him blandly, with an appearance of sympathy, but in the end he shook his head and turned down all three ideas. Not that Maudet was surprised. How could he infuse an editor with enthusiasm when he had none himself? He was not meant for free-lancing. Especially when he felt the atmosphere around him to be hostile. Of the three men in the editorial offices who had known him in earlier days, two had ignored him and the third had barely acknowledged him with an embarrassed smile before turning quickly away. His pre-war Paris reputation had followed him; he was poison. Maudet felt no bitterness. He understood that nobody was in a hurry to expose himself to what might be sudden professional extinction. One or two editors, more courageous than the rest, gave him occasional assignments and published his nonpolitical pieces under a phony by-line. It was enough for him to exist, but it was hardly a life. Maudet knew that he could expect no more until the war ended. What discouraged him was that he saw no end to the war. It would drag on and on and on.

Towering over everyone else, he moved automatically through the crowd, unaware of the scurry of people, all his attention concentrated within him. He did not become aware of the outside world again until a quarter of an hour later when he came to the building where he lived and saw Sister Elisabeth waiting for him. Maudet bent down and kissed both her cheeks. The stiff cowl brushed his face; there was the familiar clean smell of soap.

'You were dreaming again,' she said.

'I can't hide anything from you.'

They looked into each other's eyes, smiling. Their meetings often began that way. That searching look, to seize their moods, was like a caress. Each was opposed to the path the other had taken – Maudet was an atheist – but they were wedded by a commitment beyond family, perhaps beyond life. Of late Maudet had even begun to think that, whatever the metaphysical and institutional facts, his sister was meant to be a nun – to do what would most inspire goodness and charity to flower.

'Actually,' he said as he led her into the building and up the stairs, 'I was thinking about a most depressing subject: myself.'

'So was I.'

'Poor thing. Worrying about her little brother again.'

Maudet was six years younger than his sister, and it was true that she worried about him; he often teased her about it.

They climbed up and around, up and around. Maudet's flat was rather bare with nothing on the walls, which had not been painted for years, and the furniture was very worn; but the room was spacious and airy. Nothing in it belonged to him except for a scattering of books he had salvaged when he moved from Paris.

Sister Elisabeth sat in the one comfortable chair catching her breath from the climb. Maudet sat on the edge of the divan, which he turned down and slept on at night; he leaned gracefully towards his sister, his arms on his knees, his hands clasped. He did everything with grace, even the simplest gestures. Without effort or affection, he also had size and the authority that flowers from it. He was a man who occupied the space he filled: you knew he was there. Maudet's head, topped by the unruly shock of blond hair, was in proportion to his large body and had an animal impressiveness; a crooked nose emphasized his rugged good looks, which women found especially appealing because of an almost saintly expression of candour when his face was in repose.

Sister Elisabeth came to the point quickly. She told her brother what Galland had told her: that they were organizing the escape of a very important person from a German prison, that they needed a man who was absolutely dependable, speaking fluent German, to go into Germany, and lead their man back to Unoccupied France, that obviously it was dangerous. Above all, Sister Elisabeth stressed the importance of the operation.

'So,' she concluded, 'I thought of you. It seems made for you. But I didn't tell them I had you in mind.' She paused, plainly unsure of his reaction, and anxious not to push him since she knew that pressure should work in reverse. 'Well,' she added, 'if you don't like it, I can always try to find someone else. But still I think it's for you.'

He thought about it for a while, taking his time. 'Who could it be?' he wondered aloud. 'Its importance is obviously a function of who it is. They didn't say, of course.'

She shook her head. 'They wouldn't tell anyone who didn't have to know.'

'But suppose it turns out to be someone – awful.'

She knew he would think of the political angle. She never did. 'It won't be,' she said. 'And anyway they'll have to tell you and you can always say no.'

'I'm tempted,' he said. 'For the first time I'm tempted.'

'I thought you would be.' As she spoke, Maudet rose and paced. 'I thought you would be because it's important and – and special.'

'That's only part of it,' he said. 'Of course it's an important part of it but still, between us, there's something else. . . . I haven't told you what a dead end I've reached.'

'Why do you think I thought of you for this operation?'

'You suggested one or two others.'

'They weren't like this one.'

He considered her. 'You saw this thing in me coming on all along.'

She shrugged. 'It's been coming on for a long time. I didn't need any special powers of observation.'

He sat down again on the edge of the divan, leaning towards her. 'Sometimes it seems to me that it's been coming on forever. Ever since I was a child. But I didn't know it. I always took myself for granted, a fact of nature, like a tree or a flower. I suppose I never *truly* thought about myself until things started to go wrong, and then not really until a few months ago.'

'It was bound to happen,' Elisabeth said gently. 'You were so happy and wrapped up in what you were doing that you had no reason to search inside yourself. It took me a while to understand that, and that's when I stopped beating at you.'

They had a shared memory of their early discussions and battles: the older sister, overweight and plain, who was struggling for some kind of spiritual salvation, trying vainly to lead the younger brother, gifted and good-looking, in her wake. Maudet had shied away from the start. Without articulating it, he had attributed Elisabeth's spiritual needs to her physical handicaps. He needed no more than he had: the gift of the joy of living. But now that life had soured and the gift had been removed, Maudet was discovering that his former self was insufficient for the problems he faced. Sister Elisabeth had long felt he couldn't do anything unless he did something; meditating, agonizing over himself might enlighten but would hardly deliver him from his devils. Only action could do that. But he was a loner and the right action had not been easy to find.

'Somewhere along the road,' he said, 'I lost control. I suddenly realized one day that I no longer dominated my situation but was its victim. The things I was doing weren't the things I wanted to do but had to do; they were forced on me by all the things I had done before and could no longer retract. The past, my personal past, weighed on me like a mountain, pinned me down.'

'That happens when you take a wrong turn.'

'But how awful when you see quite suddenly that you're closed in by a set of conditions that are imposed on you and all you can do is react to them. Sometimes I've felt as if I were no more than an amoeba, a bit of protoplasm, that budges in one way or another as it's prodded. And for how long did it go on without my even being conscious of it!'

'But now you have a way out,' Sister Elisabeth said, 'a good way out, and a completely new direction to take.'

Suddenly Maudet's expression changed and Sister Elisabeth was warmed by his luminous smile. 'You're a fine sister,' he jested, 'to be sending me on a mission like this.'

She returned his smile. She saw that he would at least take the first step and see Galland, and the first step would lead on to the others. Neither of them could imagine where each small successive step could lead to, to what risks or fatalities. They did not know enough about the mission to measure the danger if, indeed, it was measurable, if the unforeseeable could be foreseen; but since the mission was fabulously attractive in itself and was a noble exploit for her and a spectacular coup for him, they subtracted the negative factor. There would be time to put that back into the equation, Maudet thought, if it proved necessary before a final commitment was made.

'These are very professional people,' Sister Elisabeth said. 'I have faith in them – and in you too. Besides, I'll pray for you.'

'That's practically a guarantee that I'll come back.'

'Of course you'll come back.' She was as serious as he was light.

'Luckily,' he teased, 'we can depend on the professionals if God doesn't hear your prayers.'

'He will.'

'And if He ignores them because He doesn't approve of this sinner who has strayed from the path of righteousness?'

'Don't tease,' she pleaded. 'It's too serious.'

She would not utter the word, but in her mind was the thought that death is far from our worst fate. She had already said it many times in discussions with her brother. She felt that the important thing was how one lived, not when one died, that the way one died could consecrate the life snuffed out. As passionately patriotic as she was passionately religious, she was totally dedicated to laying low the Nazis, the very image of evil, and could imagine no death more noble than one suffered for that holy cause. But in any case, she did not look upon death as a tragedy. She contemplated it with serenity and the unshakable conviction of her faith. Death, too, was a deliverance.

'Do you suppose,' Maudet was wondering aloud, 'that it's possible to escape the person you are, simply to run away from him, and to find at journey's end that you're someone else, someone you'd much rather be?'

'It happens all the time,' Sister Elisabeth said with assurance.

Sister Elisabeth led Maudet directly to Galland. It was not far and they walked. On the way she asked her brother whether he had heard from Monique. He shook his head. Maudet had lived with Monique Noirault for two years in a hectic relationship that had been broken by the war. Despite an overwhelming physical attraction, the liaison had probably been doomed by violent personal differences, but the forced wartime separation had been premature and poignant, especially for him.

'Not a word,' Maudet said.

'Is it still important?'

'I hope not.'

But peeking up beyond her cowl, Sister Elisabeth saw the expression on her brother's face and knew it was.

'You still think of her,' she said sadly.

'I can't just erase it.'

'After all this time?'

'After all this time.'

It had been a defeat, he thought. You don't forget a defeat that quickly.

'She's still in Mulhouse?'

'So far as I know.'

Before Maudet's reticence Sister Elisabeth dropped the subject. She had never liked Monique and had always thought she was wrong for her brother. That was evident to everyone but him. Maudet knew how she felt; he did not like to discuss Monique with anyone – the subject was too painful – and least of all with his sister. They walked the rest of the way in silence.

Galland was waiting for them. Sister Elisabeth was hardly surprised at *his* surprise when she introduced Maudet as her brother. Galland made no effort to hide his pleasure; all of his teeth showed in his grin.

'I hadn't imagined there was another like her in the family,' he remarked.

Maudet smiled thinly. 'There isn't,' he said.

Sister Elisabeth left and the two men proceeded to Rivet's office.

'He's her brother,' Galland said as he introduced Maudet to Rivet.

'Whose brother?'

'Sister Elisabeth's.'

'Ah, good, good . . . Why, that's splendid.'

'I've always congratulated myself, too, on being my sister's brother.'

They laughed.

'You understand,' Galland said, 'that it's a great comfort for us that you're her brother – and a very high recommendation too.'

So the meeting got under way on a good note. They asked

Maudet about himself, already knowing the answers. It was mainly for the form but also to get the feel of the man. On the previous day, after speaking to Sister Elisabeth, Galland had had a long and exhaustive talk with Rivet about their prospective candidate. On the basis of Sister Elisabeth's information, they had sadly and reluctantly agreed on two propositions: 1) that he was the wrong man for the mission; 2) that they would give it to him. The non sequitur was inescapable: since he was the only candidate, they had no choice. Still, it was not an easy decision and both felt a little guilty about it. They were therefore doubly delighted to discover that Maudet in no way conformed to the pessimistic inferences they had drawn from Sister Elisabeth's description of him. Assuming the worst for their purposes, they had anticipated that Maudet would be a weak and irresolute intellectual. Instead, he impressed both Rivet and Galland as a man of substance and decision.

Finally Rivet began to describe Operation Marianne and the role the guide would play in it.

Maudet stopped him. 'If I may say so, you're going at this the wrong way around. You think I may be hesitant about the danger of the mission, so you want to describe it to me first. Then, if I back away from it, you won't have to reveal the identity of your man. In fact, it's the man's identity that's important to me, not the danger. If he's a certain kind of politician, I wouldn't take any risk at all for him. Tell me who he is. It might save the trouble of describing what has to be done.'

Rivet and Galland glanced at each other, then turned back to Maudet with new respect.

'He's not a politician,' Rivet said. 'He's military, a general. I would say, and I'm not the only one, that he is France's best soldier. I'm talking about General de Forge.'

'Ah, yes, of course,' Maudet said, acknowledging the familiar name.

'Whatever his personal political opinions may be, he has kept them private,' Galland said. 'This much we know: he has never accepted the defeat and is dedicated to continuing the fight against Hitler. That's why he wants to escape.'

'What's more,' Rivet said wryly, 'you must not imagine that

112

de Forge is just another general. He is the man who will be the commander in chief of French troops when they take the field again against the Germans. That is, if we can free him.'

'And that isn't simply our own point of view,' Galland added. 'The Americans support that position too.'

'So you see why we attach so much importance to our little operation,' Rivet said.

For a while none of them said anything more. But what had been said seemed somehow to remain in the air, to fill the room.

'In short,' Rivet said, 'de Forge is our man. We think he is unique and irreplaceable, that no other Frenchman can do what he can do or make the contribution he can make in fighting the Germans. If we can manage to free him, the feat will not only be spectacular, it will be historic. That's why we've gone to such trouble to organize his escape.' Rivet paused. 'Would you be willing to go into Germany to lead him out?'

Maudet did not hesitate. 'For such a man, of course.'

'You are aware of the risks,' Galland quickly cautioned.

Almost at the same time Rivet said, 'If you're caught, they'll stand you against a wall and put twelve bullets in your body.'

Their eyes plunged into Maudet's, whose answering stare was a firm, limpid blue. 'It's worth the risk,' he said. 'I agree on the principle. But now you must tell me exactly what I am to do and then I'll be able to say whether I'll take on the mission itself.'

Rivet and Galland spent an hour describing the operation in detail and answering Maudet's questions. When Maudet grasped the plan and the role he would play in it he felt a certain relief. For a moment he had feared that he might have gone too far to retreat gracefully from a plan whose risks would prove overwhelming and whose chances of success would be minimal; but now he was reassured. There were no battlements to scale, no prisons to storm, no cloak-and-dagger manoeuvres to execute. It all seemed quite straightforward. He would go in by rail with 'absolutely authentic false papers' showing that he was an electrical technician employed as a volunteer worker at the Archimedes Gesellschaft in Breslau, and the justification for his trip would be that he was returning from a vacation in France. He would meet de Forge and deliver the things the general needed to travel through Germany – his civilian clothes, German money, and 'absolutely authentic false papers' showing he was an industrialist in artificial silk from Ste.-Marie-aux-Mines. Then, with other false papers permitting him to return to France because of ill health, he would deliver de Forge to the people in Alsace who would get him across the border, and tranquilly return to Lyons by rail. Two trips. In and out. And no violence. That was important: Maudet hated violence. It all seemed simple enough, almost childishly simple. Of course he would do it. Moreover, he was to be coddled and protected wherever possible like a movie star whose dangerous scenes are done by a double.

'You're not expendable,' Galland said. 'You're too precious for us to take any unnecessary risks with you. So we've decided not to use you to take de Forge's clothes and papers across any frontiers. Someone else will do that. We don't want to take the chance of having you picked up before you even get to de Forge. You will go to Mulhouse with complete security; after that there are no frontiers. When you get off the train at Mulhouse you will be met and taken to a safe place to spend the night. There you will be given the valise with de Forge's things in it. You will take the train the next morning to Strasbourg, where you will meet the man who will be there to get de Forge away on your way out; he will also give you reichsmarks, ration tickets, et cetera – what you will need in Germany. After that you will take the train again via Frankfurt, Leipzig and Dresden to meet de Forge at the bridge outside Bad Danschau.'

Maudet's heart leaped when he heard that he would be going to Mulhouse and spending the night there, so close to Monique, but he quickly realized that he would not be able to see her.

'You'll recognize de Forge,' Galland said. 'He will be looking for you at the bridge, but of course he won't know you. You'll say the password to him: "*Morgen*, Fritz." His answer will just be "*Morgen*." There you'll be, the both of you,'

Galland said, suddenly smiling to lighten the tone, 'two French-men deep in the heart of Germany most improperly intro-duced.' Maudet smiled too at the strangeness of the scene. 'With luck the Germans still won't know what happened to them. You'll take it from there – the train to Berlin, the sleeper to Strasbourg, you hand de Forge over to our people there and they will whisk him to safety right back here and put you on the train home as well.'

'It sounds easy enough,' Maudet said.

'The scenario, if it's a good one, is always easy. Acting it out is harder. It's reality, what you can't foresee, that spoils the best scenarios. That's what you have to watch out for. When it hits, and it will, you'll have to improvise. Just keep one thing in mind: your mission is to bring him through. What-ever happens, I mean whatever happens, that is what you are to do – get him through. That doesn't mean you should be with him. On the contrary. Keep him in sight, keep him tied to you as if you were attached by an umbilical cord, but keep apart – as if you happened to be in the same place but had nothing to do with each other. It will cut the risk in half. If he's caught, you'll be able to get away and vice versa. They mustn't know there are two of you. Remember they'll be looking only for him.'

'I'll remember.'

'Then you're still with us; you'll do it.'

'Of course. It's a brilliant plan – simple, sensible, misleading to the Germans, and not least of all it's safe.'

'I hope so,' Galland said.

After Maudet left to get identity pictures for his false papers, Galland asked Rivet what he thought of Maudet.

'Better than I expected, less good than I might have hoped,' Rivet replied. 'It won't make any difference if the operation goes smoothly. But if it doesn't, there could be problems. He's a personality with a mind full of ideas. There could be a clash with de Forge.'

'De Forge will handle him,' Galland said confidently.

'He's strong,' Rivet said. 'I like that. Too gentle, but big and strong, which could help in a pinch. And I don't think he's the kind who would crack under pressure. Not with de Forge there to buck him up.'

'He's all right,' Galland said. 'I found him impressive on all counts.' Galland was vastly relieved. 'It will work. It's got to work.'

ELEVEN

While Major Galland under the authority of General Rivet was the organizer of Operation Marianne, the man on whom de Forge's flight from Germany hinged was a lieutenant of the reserves, Lucien Blanchard. Blanchard was responsible for getting de Forge's civilian clothes and papers to his guide in Mulhouse and for getting de Forge back across the border to safety in France. It was he who would establish contact with Maudet when the mission began; it was with him that Maudet would establish contact when it ended.

Blanchard was a man who lived dangerously. He was a much decorated officer who had fought courageously in 1940 and now ran a remarkably well-organized network that passed escaped prisoners of war into the free zone. He frequently crossed the demarcation line between the occupied and unoccupied zones and often went as well into the annexed region of Alsace. In view of these activities and the consequent need for anonymity, he had a singular disadvantage. During the battle of France two years before, he had been shot in the face and the bullet wound had left a long scar on his right jaw. It made him easy to identify. But when urged to undergo surgery to remove the scar he steadfastly refused. 'Never,' he cried. 'It's my most beautiful decoration.'

Everything about Blanchard was small except his heart. He was very short and thin with tiny feet and dainty hands and a lean face that sparkled with well-being. His hair was thin and sandy, his eyes blue and his smile sunny. He was also enormously energetic.

The day after Maudet accepted his mission Blanchard went to Lyons to meet him and to pick up de Forge's things. Madame de Forge had prepared her husband's clothes – a dark

116

blue topcoat, an oxford grey suit, a pair of black shoes, three shirts, six pairs of socks, four sets of shorts and undershirts and four ties as well as a packet of handkerchiefs and a pair of gloves. Galland examined each item to check that none bore de Forge's monogram, then took them all out of the handsome bag stamped with de Forge's initials and put them into a nondescript dark brown valise he had brought for the purpose.

'More than enough for a short trip,' Galland said. 'You should be seeing him soon.'

'Whatever happens, you'll let me know.'

'As soon as we have word.'

'I'll be waiting. . . . It's my role.'

Galland handed over the valise to Blanchard in Maudet's presence. Galland also gave him de Forge's false papers, which were made out in the name of Albert Forveille, manufacturer of artificial silk at Ste.-Marie-aux-Mines. Blanchard had been told that his new 'client' was very important, but he had not been told who he was. Blanchard asked no questions; it was one of his many virtues. But Galland emphasized and re-emphasized the extreme importance attached to the success of the operation.

'We'll do our best,' Blanchard said. 'Everyone has been alerted; everything has been laid on. I will personally get the valise and the papers across the demarcation line and the border. I will leave it in a safe place and pick it up next Tuesday when I meet our friend here at the railway station in Mulhouse. He will have it all the following day when he takes the train for Strasbourg.'

'It's the way out I'm concerned about when they return,' Galland said.

Blanchard went over the plan again. 'We'll meet them right at the station in Strasbourg,' he said, 'the minute they get off the platform. We've borrowed a small truck for transportation. The itinerary to the border has been checked and should be absolutely secure. We'll cross the frontier at Chavannes-sur-l'Etang. The German Customs man there is in our pocket; we've bought him. After Belfort it's hard to tell; we could run into something we don't expect. But by then we'll be followed by a carful of well-armed friends with at least one and probably two small machine-guns in case of need. We hope there won't be any need because that would be messy and we like a clean operation. As I told you, this is the first time we've made arrangements of this sort. We don't particularly like it because if there's violence, it could blow up our network. But if our client is as important as you say, it's a case of noblesse oblige.'

'And what if they don't get to Strasbourg, at least when you expect them?'

Blanchard shrugged. 'We'll keep meeting trains from the east for a couple of days afterwards just in case. There's a contact point in Mulhouse too if they turn up there instead of Strasbourg. Mulhouse makes more sense anyway: it's practically on the border.'

Blanchard was pleased that Galland had nothing further to ask and no suggestions to make. They had been over the same ground many times in the past few weeks, but this part of the operation was Blanchard's and, having created it, he had the pride of a thing well done which could not be improved by anyone else. He knew from experience that the success of these operations depended on foresight, planning, organization. He also knew that there was a point beyond which one could no longer plan. There would be contingencies no one could foresee. Flexibility and luck would then be the decisive factors. Above all, once you had meticulously done everything you rationally could do, you had to be lucky. He would rather work with someone who was lucky than smart.

He found himself saying it to Maudet. 'Galland is a head-quarters man,' he said. 'He thinks he's God and all the events out in the world we inhabit must conform to his will. But we know better. The unexpected will happen; you can be sure of it. My advice to you is to be lucky. Of course it doesn't hurt to be smart; that can always help. But if an operation of this sort is to succeed, believe me, you've got to be lucky.'

Maudet smiled. 'I'll try,' he said.

'Then relax. That's the best way to be lucky. Be relaxed. I look them right in the eye and I'm saying to myself all the time, "I'm innocent. I have nothing to be afraid of." It relaxes me. That's why I've been lucky.'

The next day Blanchard took the train to Mulhouse carrying

the nondescript brown valise that contained de Forge's clothes. The general's false papers and a small packet of reichsmarks were hidden between the cardboard lining and the outer covering of the suitcase. At the border a German Customs official examined the bag, poking about suspiciously among the shirts and underclothes. He unfolded the suit to see if anything was hidden in the pockets. Very relaxed, Blanchard looked at him, wide-eyed and innocent. The Customs official looked from little Blanchard to the big suit and back again.

'That's not your suit,' he said accusingly.

'It's my son's,' Blanchard replied easily.

'He's a lot bigger than you.'

'So is his mother.'

The Customs official didn't even smile, but he handed back the suit and chalked the bag.

Blanchard deposited the bag at the station in Mulhouse, where it would be safe until he picked it up the following Tuesday. Then he took the next train back home and spent the better part of two days fulfilling another assignment Galland had given him. He scribbled and typed out a fictitious correspondence to conform with de Forge's assumed profession of a manufacturer of artificial silk. When he was finished he was satisfied that, short of verification of names, companies and addresses, the correspondence had a convincing air of authenticity.

On Tuesday, the correspondence in a briefcase under his arm, Blanchard set out again for Mulhouse. But this time he was unlucky. The train was stopped at the border for five hours. Everybody had to pass through the German police strainer. Fortunately, Blanchard had nothing compromising on him; the correspondence was innocent enough and nobody questioned it. But when the train was allowed to move it was far too late for the rendezvous with Maudet.

Blanchard hoped Maudet was resourceful; he would damned well have to be if he was going to survive. He would have to find a safe place to spend the night, and he would know that the hotels, constantly checked by the police, were dangerous. Blanchard worried. He hoped Maudet wouldn't panic. The important thing was that Maudet have the bag with the clothes, papers and money when he took the train for Strasbourg the next morning. They would meet at the station then as if they had never missed their rendezvous and everything would fall into place. Blanchard sighed. It was a hell of a way for the operation to begin.

Maudet was inexperienced, and none of Galland's or Blanchard's warnings about accidents, the unexpected, the need to improvise really got to him. He never imagined that the mission would not go according to plan; the plan made sense, and he naïvely expected reality to conform to logic. Galland saw Maudet daily and came to understand him.

'He's absolutely fearless,' Galland explained to Rivet. 'No nightmares of arrest, torture, firing squads. Not an ounce of morbidity, unlike our last candidate. He's really remarkable. But' – Galland paused a beat for effect – 'it's not because of courage. He's simply opaque to danger. What's out there isn't real; only the plan is. He's in love with it. He thinks it's all going to work just as I planned it.'

'Don't you?' Rivet asked.

'I'm betting on it too, of course, or I wouldn't have planned it this way. But I know the odds.'

'And he's betting a little more.'

'But he's not even worried. I'm worried – aren't you?'

'I'll feel a lot better when it's over.'

'Did you ever know an operation like this one to work exactly as planned?'

The two officers considered each other silently.

'I guess we're lucky to have him after all,' Rivet finally said. 'That kind of ignorance, or optimism, or whatever you want to call it, is positive.'

'It's men like him,' Galland said, 'who have the makings of heroes.' There was no trace of cynicism in his voice.

That Tuesday morning Galland accompanied Maudet to the station. They shook hands on the platform and Maudet, carrying a small bag with a few changes of linen, swung up on the train.

'We're counting on you to bring him back,' Galland said.

Maudet smiled confidently. 'See you in a week,' he said.

The train was packed when it left Lyons. From his second-class compartment Maudet watched the fat green countryside of Bresse roll past, *Le Progrès de Lyon* unopened on his lap. He was on his way and on his own and he had never felt so good to be in his own skin. Ten days ago he had been at the bottom, an unemployed free-lance going nowhere; now he was launched on an enterprise of historical dimensions and the world stretched before him full of rosy promise and star-studded dreams. Maudet lost himself for a long moment in the spell of those dreams before returning to reality and opening his newspaper. Everything was right, he felt, down to the train smell and placid May landscape floating by.

People got on and off the train at each station, but as it approached the demarcation line, the train gradually emptied until only a handful of passengers remained. It was the first test. Maudet felt a pinch at his heart when he handed over his papers to cross into the Occupied Zone. The official examined his papers closely but scarcely looked at him. In a few moments he handed the papers back and passed on. Richard Maudet, become Roland Morand, was verified, stamped and authenticated for travel and could continue on his way at his own risk and peril.

The train filled up again. Some German soldiers got on, and Maudet knew he was in the Occupied Zone. With a mixture of shame and guilt, he turned away and looked out the window. An image flashed into his mind that had not come to him for a long time. Shortly after the occupation began he had gone to Royan on the western coast of France. One sunny summer morning he had passed in front of the local brothel with its charming sign, AU CLAIR DE LA LUNE. On the edge of the road about two hundred German soldiers were lined up in perfect order in rows of three, waiting their turn in complete silence. Maudet had been told that rain or shine, day or night, there was always the same long line of German soldiers in front of the brothel with its drill-field order and impressive silence. It was a sight that caused the French no little amusement and made them feel less defeated. The image improved Maudet's mood. It made him feel that the enemy he would face was less inhuman and more vulnerable.

The train emptied again as it came to the border, but this time it was a German official who checked Maudet's papers. As the man examined the *Ausweis,* Maudet again felt a squeeze at his heart and a small ball of fear in the pit of his stomach. The man took his time, studied the papers, glanced at Maudet, examined the papers. Maudet sank into a numb calm. Something was wrong. His heart fluttered; he girded himself. The man passed the papers back to him and saluted. Tucking the documents in his pocket, Maudet knew that to the last stamp he had 'absolutely authentic false papers.'

At Mulhouse, Maudet strode down the platform to the exit, his small bag feeling light in his hand. He looked for Blanchard among the few people at the gate waiting for arrivals and was surprised not to find him. Maudet waited a few minutes, then made a turn of the station. No Blanchard. The ball of fear was back in his belly. Bigger this time. What if he had been arrested? Maudet had a sensation of hanging alone in emptiness, naked and vulnerable as an infant.

He made another quick turn of the station, then another more slowly. Then he sat on a bench in the waiting room facing the entrance, prepared to wait. But he noticed a portly man observing him and unhesitatingly rose, picking up his small suitcase, and left the station. Still looking about for Blanchard, he crossed the street and went into a café. He was about to order a glass of beer when he remembered that the currency was reichsmarks and that he had none. He swore to himself and left the café.

Walking back and forth opposite the station, he kept an eye on the entrance for Blanchard. He gave Blanchard half an hour. When the time passed he gave him another half-hour. Maudet crossed the street twice and looked for Blanchard in the station. The portly man was gone. The last fifteen minutes Maudet spent waiting on a bench next to the Buffet de la Gare.

When he gave up he was worried but hopeful. Blanchard knew his schedule; if he had not been arrested, he would deliver the bag with de Forge's clothes and false papers in the morning when Maudet left for Strasbourg to meet the local contact, Max Reiber, before going on; and go on he would, with or without the bag, though he could not imagine how de Forge would get across Germany without documents. Whatever Galland and Blanchard had said about improvising, the idea of subtracting the plan from the mission was like a knife stab in the gut. Without the plan the mission made no sense. It was suicide.

Maudet had heard and remembered an address in Mulhouse that Blanchard had mentioned to Galland: 9 rue Vauban. He might find Blanchard there or at least a bed for the night. He asked a passerby directions and began walking. It was quite far. The name of the street had been changed, Germanizing it, but a young boy pointed it out to Maudet. At number 9, the door was opened by a young man with brilliant black eyes; he did not hide his suspicion and hostility.

Maudet talked fast. 'I'm a friend of Monsieur Blanchard. He was supposed to meet me at the –'

'Monsieur who?'

'Blanchard, Monsieur Blanchard.'

'Don't know any Blanchard.'

'But –'

The door slammed. Maudet rang the bell again – hard. The door opened only wide enough for Maudet to see one of those hard black eyes.

'I told you I don't know any Blanchard; it won't do you any good to insist.'

And Maudet was again staring at the blank closed door. He turned away, muttering aloud, 'The bastard,' but as he walked off he thought wryly, No wonder nobody in Blanchard's damned network ever gets caught.

He posted himself far enough from the house not to be seen from it but close enough to see anyone go in. Nobody did. He finally concluded that Blanchard would not appear. It was early evening. Reluctantly, he turned back towards the station and the prospect of a hotel for the night. There would be a police check, but he felt reasonably safe. His papers were in order and he had nothing incriminating on him. Suddenly he stopped in his tracks. Monique! Incredibly, he had been so preoccupied since arriving in Mulhouse that he had not thought of her.

His heart lifted. He began to walk quickly. He stopped at the first café. Impossible to phone. He hadn't a pfennig. Couldn't change money there. He would surprise her. Rue de l'Espérance. A perfect name for the occasion. At the café the woman behind the cashbox gave him directions. The name of that street was changed too, Germanized like all the others, but it was a long street and he couldn't miss it. It wasn't far away, closer to the station than the rue Vauban.

Maudet hurried. If only she was at home. She had to be home. But what if she had a lover? And what if he was there? It was two years since he had seen her, and she hadn't written in months. For all he knew she was married – or engaged. He would face that when it came. They had told him to improvise; he was improvising.

Maudet slipped past the concierge's loge unseen. Quickly and silently he climbed the stairs. On the third floor he found her name on a door. He took a deep breath and rang the bell. Nothing. His heart dropped. Then a sound far off, coming closer to the door. The glorious sound of a woman's clicking heels. It had to be her.

'Who's there?'

'A friend.'

The door swung open. She stood there a long moment, petite, trim, a crown of black hair heightening the stark white face with the finely chiselled nose and the huge dark eyes, staring up at him in disbelief, immobile, petrified; then his name was on her startled lips and they were in each other's arms.

In the living room they talked as if they were satisfying a deep hunger, devouring every morsel as they caught up with each other and all the things they had in common, their eyes saying what did not come to their lips; but when she asked what brought him to Mulhouse he put her off, saying, 'Later, later.'

The physical thing was still there; that was evident instantly. The contact was powerful, but at first they were almost shy about it, talking around and through what both felt and neither would mention. They were both very animated, yet for two people who had lived together, rather formal. However, there was nothing shy or formal in their eyes. They sat at opposite ends of the divan, out of reach but as close as if they were clinging to each other. Then they were. It needed no more than for him to lean forward, putting out

124

his hand to touch her, and she came to him. She came to him because it was impossible for her not to. It was as sudden and violent as straw bursting into flame. He loved her body; it opened to him and closed to hold him, tight and possessive. He let himself be held and caressed, and, moved by her caress, he teased and vexed her lovingly and as she rose to it and rose again and higher still, he roiled her brutally, hearing her cries against his own.

It ended too quickly; it almost always did when things were less than perfect. He had blindly wanted it to go on and on, knowing at his nerve endings, as he knew now in his again functioning mind, that this was the best they had and that the rest could not work. So he came out of it badly, conscious, alert, his mind active. Drugged, replete, snuggled against him, she did not sense it.

Later she was mock repentant. 'I didn't even offer you anything to drink,' she said, 'or ask you if you were hungry. You have to watch out when you visit bachelor girls. They attack.'

'Why don't you ask me if I'm hungry?'

'Are you hungry?'

'Famished.'

She said she didn't have a thing to eat in the house. That's what everybody said in those wartime days. Too often it was literally true, but Monique had reserves. She brought out the remains of a tasty rabbit pâté, broke open a can of sardines, mixed a salad of tomatoes and tuna fish, whipped up a light runny omelet flavoured with bits of onion and set out a platter of cheese and a bottle of red wine. It was a feast. They ate in the kitchen wearing robes, intimate as in the old days, and plunged into the food ravenously. For a while they were gay, but then she asked him again why he was in Mulhouse and he could no longer evade the question.

'Do I have to tell you?'

'Of course.'

'You won't like it.'

She stopped eating and gazed at him with a look of foreboding. 'It's not politics,' she said with a kind of despair.

'In a way.'

She put down her fork with an air of resignation, of false patience, and waited for the worst. He knew that expression

125

from a thousand quarrels, all of them, it seemed to him, about the same subject: why he was eternally involved in projects unfavourable to him instead of in those that might spring him out of his poverty. It was the rock on which their liaison had broken. Monique was practical, unpolitical; she automatically absorbed the conventional dogmas in the air around her and had a fierce hostility to the others as representing a personal threat. Maudet knew she wouldn't like it but told her at last why he was in Mulhouse, leaving out names and details but confiding the general lines of his mission.

'You're mad,' she said. 'I always thought so.'

She sounded so genuinely convinced that he smiled.

The smile infuriated her; she felt he was being mockingly superior.

'You haven't lived with them,' she said intensely. 'You don't know how they are. It's your *life*.'

'You mustn't get so upset. Of course it's a risk, but it's important. There are some things you can't refuse to do.'

She made a gesture of impatience. 'You're risking your life for this man. Why should you? One life is worth another. It's the only one you have, and you treat it as if it wasn't worth any more than an old pair of socks.'

'You don't understand. This is something I want to do and I have to do. It's not easy to explain, but I *have* to do it.'

'And if they catch you?'

'I don't expect them to.'

'But if they do?'

She had a way of saying the wrong thing. Maudet smiled. 'They can't – it's not part of the plan.'

She wasn't amused. 'Spare me your wit,' she said. 'If your precious plan doesn't work, you'll need it.'

He watched her as she cleaned up. He loved to look at her. He loved the curve of her breast and of her hips, her high bottom and the whiteness and softness of her skin. He loved her face and all its expressions, in joy, in tenderness, in anger too. Despite their quarrels, he loved to be with her; he always felt good when she was there, at peace, in harmony with himself. He did not know why, but he knew it was so. They were hopelessly different, and he knew that made her unhappy and that they could never work out their problems.

126

But he knew that with his mind. By some other means that he could not describe he knew he needed her and that when she was by him everything was right. He watched her move efficiently and sulkily back and forth. He loved her face when she sulked. But now he reproached himself that he had upset her.

'Don't be angry,' he pleaded.

A tenderness in his voice softened her expression. 'You haven't changed a bit,' she said. 'It's for you, not for me that I'm worried. It's your life, not mine.'

It hurt him to hear her separate them that way even though it was a fact that they were not together and for so long had not been a couple; but he hated to hear her define their relationship, or lack of one, because that seemed to kill something or make it less likely to come to life again.

'I had to get away from Lyons. I simply had to leave that place.'

'For Germany?'

'Well, I had to go there too as it turned out. But first I had to get away from where I was. It was no life; it was non-living, a kind of purposeless existence, like an animal or an insect. I had to break out of it or it would have broken me. It *was* breaking me, little by little, a bit every day. After a week I was smaller, after a month smaller still. I felt I was disappearing, that soon I wouldn't even exist. Nothing can be worse than that.'

'And how do you think I feel? Do you think it's any better here? At least you were in the free zone. You had the Marshal; I have the Fuehrer.'

He granted her the difference but not in a way to satisfy her; he was sardonic. From the very beginning, by instinct, principle and reason, he had abhorred and opposed Marshal Pétain and everything he represented. But like the great mass of Frenchmen at the time, Monique fervently supported the Marshal and approved his policy of collaboration. It was not that she, or they, liked the Germans, let alone their Nazi leaders, or wanted to collaborate with them; but they wanted all the unpleasantness to go away and they thought that this was the quick and easy way for things to come back to normal.

It put Monique's back up when Maudet told her that it

127

couldn't work out that way, that she was suffering from an illusion. That was not what she wanted to hear; she couldn't bear hearing it. The war wearied and bored her and made her utterly miserable and she desperately wanted it to go away. That was why she couldn't bear to hear the word 'resistance' or the name of de Gaulle. That only brought the war closer and made it last longer. She had had enough.

Maudet tried to change the subject. It always made him unhappy to discuss politics with Monique. There was never any true discussion since they had no common ground, and in any case he had nothing to learn from her apart from her rationalized prejudices and she wouldn't listen to him, finding it all too abstract and theoretical. But she would not be stopped. What she had to say lay heavy on her heart, and now it all poured out. It had nothing and yet everything to do with politics. For it had to do with her and her situation, her miseries and yearning, and like everyone else living under Nazi domination in the midst of a war, she could not separate her own condition from the general political situation and the way it would develop. Her lament and hope were simple and indeed commonplace, but they were no less deeply felt for that. It came down to this: what the war had taken away peace would give back. But she was impatient; there was so little time and it passed so quickly. She was young but that wouldn't last forever. What the war had taken away was life, the possibility of living, the joy of living, movement, travel, all sense of ease and expansiveness. Meanwhile, her best years were passing in a kind of nothingness, closed up in this hole, in Mulhouse, which it was impossible to get out of, and where she had to scrounge for every little thing, an egg, a can of sardines, as her life eroded.

There was much more of this, and as he listened Maudet felt both compassion and a deep personal hurt, the one because she was so genuinely unhappy, the other because nothing she so passionately desired included him. He could sleep with her but he had lost her; he was outside her dreams.

Quite apart from how he felt, Maudet was saying to himself, 'She wants to escape too. Everybody wants to escape. Mulhouse is a prison; all of France is a prison; the times are high walls and nobody can leap over them.' He felt very special, very lucky. He had escaped.

But as he listened, Maudet was also thinking that the defeat, the occupation, even the annexation had touched her only superficially, that what she suffered from were the privations and the quality of life that were their consequences. He thought that by temperament she was first of all a woman, then a bourgeoise, and only after that French, and was astonished, in view of the cynical between-the-wars climate about nationalism and *patrie* in which he had grown up, at how French he felt. He reflected sadly that though she protested that she was as French as the next one, she could accept the defeat but found it intolerable not to be able to wear silk stockings or drink a cup of real coffee. But he confided none of these reflections or emotions to her, simply showing his sympathy for her problems by a certain tenderness.

They went to bed in a sober mood, their quarrel, at least on the surface, patched up. It was only then that he told her he had to leave the next morning. He was pleased to see her disappointment.

'Can't you stay longer?'

'If only I could.'

'For me?'

He loved her to cajole him, but he preferred it when he could be cajoled.

'Impossible, darling. If I'm not on that train tomorrow morning, the whole operation is shot.'

She sulked, and then he was cajoling her. She came around and they made love again, but it was different this time. Before it had been sudden and explosive, complete, a thing in itself, a thing apart. Now it was tormented. He could feel her turmoil and sense her struggle in the midst of her pleasure, and somewhere behind his consciousness he knew he must still be important to her; but at the end, engulfed by him and beyond her conscious self, she cried out obscenities, grasping at his body as if she wanted at once to possess and destroy him.

Maudet fell into a deep sleep, unsure whether they had made love or hate.

He woke up suddenly, instantly wide awake, his heart pounding, with a feeling of terror. Monique was not beside him; he heard her in the next room.

'What time is it?'

But before she could answer he saw the clock beside the bed and leaped out, virtually jumping into his clothes. He was furious.

'Why didn't you wake me?'

She came into the bedroom and watched him dress. 'Aren't you going to take a bath?'

'You know I don't have the time.'

'You don't have the time to make the train either.'

Still dressing and as much in a rage against himself as against her, he said, 'So that's it. What happened to the alarm?'

She did not have to tell him; he saw in her provocative, almost triumphant expression that she had turned the alarm off before it rang. The bitch, he thought; but at the same time his sense of guilt, her air of complicity, his lingering desire for her as he hastened to leave, her brazen attempt to hold him back, the sheer crudity of it all with Monique standing loosely there in that whore's posture, naked under her thin blue robe, flaunting her body, and that half-smile on her lips – all of it combined suddenly and electrically to shoot a powerful sexual charge through him. He stopped an instant, almost dressed, surprised and irritated at his automatic physical reaction. He was torn between hitting and hugging her. Each impulse cancelled the other; he glared and turned away, twisting his tie into a quick knot.

'There's coffee all ready,' she said.

'No time.'

He swung into his jacket. No time even to shave. He snapped the suitcase shut, straightened up and stood there irresolutely a second. No time, no time.

'I have no money,' he said. He tried not to show his embarrassment – or his haste; he wanted to scold her, punish her like a wilful child who had just knowingly done something wicked, and here he was forced to ask for her help.

'There's some in my purse on the dresser.'

Maudet took what he thought would be enough for a one-way ticket to Strasbourg and then a bit more to be on the

130

safe side; the entire amount was not very much. She watched him from the door. To her, he was like a child too, an irresponsible child who did not know what he was doing but was too big now to be spanked and put on the right path. She let him do what he had to do; she knew she could not stop him.

He turned back to her with the same inextricable mixture of emotions and need to rush. They looked at each other across the room and he saw that her smile was decomposing and tears brimmed her eyes. He crossed the room and embraced her. She clung to him.

'I love you,' he said, his voice husky. 'I love you.'

She held on to him tightly, so tightly. All the while he was thinking, No time, no time. He pressed her very closely, then broke away and without turning back, his throat choked, was out of the apartment, racing down the stairs and into the cool, placid May-morning street.

He ran; holding his suitcase stiffly, he ran until he was out of breath, then he trotted and when he recovered his breath he ran again. He dashed into the station three minutes before the train was to leave.

Blanchard was there. He had been nervously waiting, pacing and constantly looking at the station clock.

'What happened?'

The same words tumbled out of both their mouths at the same time. They laughed, each relieved to see the other. There was no time for talk. Maudet bought his ticket and hurried to the train with Blanchard at his heels. Blanchard handed him the de Forge valise and something light wrapped in paper.

'What's this?'

'His hat. I bought it yesterday. It should fit him; it's his size.'

Maudet's hands were full. He strode briskly forward, reaching the gate to the platform.

'Reiber is expecting you,' Blanchard said as they were parting. 'Don't miss him.'

'Don't worry; he has money for me.'

'There's plenty in the valise too. . . . By the way, that was you, wasn't it, who came to the rue Vauban yesterday? I was sure of it from the description. You scared hell out of them. When I got there they were ready to take off.'

'I waited for you but obviously not long enough. That boy of yours with the hard eyes should use a little imagination.'

'You can't use what you haven't got. But you'll be known the next time – if there is one. Just remember to go there if Mulhouse is where you wind up.'

Maudet nodded. He was moving again. 'See you soon,' he called over his shoulder.

'We'll be waiting for you.'

Maudet took off his jacket and sank into his seat; he was drenched and quivering. He had not had the time to worry about what had gone wrong and might become worse. It was just as well. He was back on the track now and his sense of guilt about having overslept had evaporated. He had seen Blanchard; he would see Reiber; he had the valise with de Forge's things. In short, the plan was functioning again. That was the essential thing. He gradually unwound and regained his composure. But it took him a long time to put Monique out of mind. Preoccupied as he was, Maudet lost all sense of time and was surprised when the train chugged into the station at Strasbourg.

Loaded down with his two suitcases and the package containing de Forge's hat, Maudet left the station looking very much the innocuous traveller. He was aware of the effect and delighted with it. With a smile, he wondered whether the most accomplished actor could make himself look suspect even to the most alert policeman if he were carrying two suitcases and a package without a handle.

Reiber was waiting for him, as arranged, on the terrace of a café across from the station. They recognized each other immediately from descriptions of what they looked like and would wear. Reiber was a chunky man, about fifty years old, and wore a black Hitler moustache.

'They were right,' Reiber said as Maudet, huge and blond, settled into a wicker chair. 'There aren't two like you.'

Maudet smiled. 'They were right,' he echoed. 'There are two of you, and the other is in Berlin.'

Reiber laughed. 'I had this moustache before I ever heard of that son of a bitch, and I won't shave it off until the day he dies – may it be soon.'

They did not have much time before Maudet's train left for Frankfurt. Maudet ordered a .pâté sandwich and a glass of beer; it was the first thing he had had to eat that day. Reiber handed him some German money, enough to live on modestly for about ten days; if the plan worked on schedule, it would give Maudet plenty of margin for everything, including travel. Reiber also gave him ration tickets for food, and some samples of artificial silk and illustrated catalogues to lend some authenticity to de Forge's cover as an artificial silk merchant. It was quickly done, quickly explained. Reiber crossed the street with Maudet, helping him with his suitcases.

'We'll be expecting you,' he said. 'And don't worry; if you don't get here the day we expect you, we'll still be meeting trains for another couple of days.'

In the train Maudet settled down with a feeling of well-being. Reiber was solid, Blanchard sure – both capable men you could count on; if there was danger, they would block it out, bodily, like protective walls. And they cared. Maudet felt he could depend on them as he once felt he could depend on his father, completely and in any circumstance. Although in fact he was supported only by a puny handful of men, he felt that he had behind him and around him, blocking the Germans and protecting him from them, a solid organization with unseen but impressive ramifications. What touched and won him to this illusion was that those in support whom he had met were men committed to an enterprise for which they could lose their lives but gain no more than the satisfaction of succeeding. Why did they do it? From what inner source did their action spring? They never talked about it; they only talked about *what* they were doing and *how* to do it. Maudet was proud to feel a kinship with them, something more than comradeship, something more like a kind of love, a feeling that they had all joined to bet their lives for the same unexplained reasons on the same turn of fate.

The train rolled up the Rhine valley to Frankfurt, where, after a wait of several hours, Maudet changed trains to go directly east across the breadth of Germany. It was a long, slow trip, repeatedly broken by unexplained delays, that lasted all night and brought him through Erfurt and Leipzig to Dresden in midmorning. The train was packed; all the

133

trains were packed, it seemed, and many men in uniform were on all of them. Maudet saw some damage in the Frankfurt rail yard which he assumed had been caused by bombs from RAF night raids, but the massive systematic raids had not yet begun and the damage Maudet saw impressed him as being a mere pin prick beside the vast claims Allied propaganda was already making about the crushing effectiveness of the bombing. Nor did he see any evidence to support analyses he had heard on the BBC and the Voice of America to the effect that Germany's economy was in imminent danger of falling apart. Despite the expectable restrictions of a wartime economy, everything had looked close to peacetime normal to Maudet in the little window-shopping tour he had taken in Frankfurt while waiting to change trains. The people in the streets, the station and the train appeared to be subdued, but they also impressed Maudet as being passive and disciplined. It depressed him. They're like sheep, he thought. They don't even cross the street when the light is against them, not even if there's no traffic and not a cop in sight.

He decided to stop in Dresden and spend the day and night there rather than go straight on to Bad Danschau, which was only thirty miles away. In a small town he would be conspicuous whereas in a city like Dresden he could pass unnoticed. He deposited de Forge's valise and hat at the station, and, carrying only his own suitcase, he emerged into the street.

It was a fine, sunny spring day, and Maudet had nothing to do but kill time. He walked. He enjoyed the walk, enjoyed the texture and lift of the old buildings, stained and yet fresh from the centuries, enjoyed gazing into shop windows and observing the midday throng of people hastening about their various errands, enjoyed breathing in the feel of a city he was seeing for the first time and probably would never see again; enjoyed, above all, a sense of leisure, of temporary irresponsibility before plunging into the heart of the mission that had brought him here. So he wandered aimlessly, feeling relaxed and strong, and that the job he had to do was an important part of a much bigger thing, something so big and important that eventually it would bring down everything around him, this city, this country, its army and government. He felt he was part of the movement of history.

These high-flown reflections so entranced Maudet that it was almost one o'clock before he suddenly realized how hungry he was. He stopped in front of the first restaurant he found and studied the menu pasted on its window. Soup, spinach, marmalade and, for those with ration tickets, meat. Maudet decided not to shop around for anything better and went in.

He came upon a bare antiseptic room that practically guaranteed a tasteless, mediocre meal at best. All the tables along the walls were occupied and Maudet was obliged to sit at one in the middle of the room. From the stir he created as he went to the table and sat down Maudet felt as if he had just walked on stage and was on display front and centre with all spots burning on him. It was unnerving. But the waitress who took his order, a pretty but rather faded blonde, flirted with him. Daring finally to look around, Maudet saw that there were about twenty-five or thirty customers in the restaurant, all of them elderly. Why did they stare at him? Was it because he was young and not in uniform? Something in his clothes? In his manner? Or was his sense of guilt so strong that he was imagining an interest in him that did not in fact exist? Maudet would never know. Nothing about the food surprised him: the soup was watery and without taste; the meat was tough and stringy. Maudet bolted the meal and left, many pairs of eyes following him out the door.

After lunch Maudet walked until he was tired; it was less enjoyable in the afternoon than it had been in the morning. Because for once he had nothing better to do he went into a barbershop for a haircut.

'Not too short.'

After a pause, the barber's gambit: 'Nice day.'

Maudet refused the gambit with a grunt and pretended an inextricable interest in the newspaper he held in front of him.

Towards evening he found a small third-rate hotel not far from the station and asked for a room.

'They're all occupied,' the hotelkeeper, a sour-faced man of about sixty, said. 'But if you don't mind being in a room with somebody else, I have one bed free. A sailor on leave already has the other bed.'

Maudet hesitated.

'Don't take it if you're fussy,' the hotelkeeper said, 'but you'll have a hard time finding a room in Dresden tonight.'

Maudet felt weary, incapable of trudging from hotel to hotel. He filled out the registry card and went to the room. The sailor was not there. Maudet hid his identity papers and money under the mattress and to avoid having to talk to the sailor went to bed early. Later he heard the man stumble in, plainly drunk, but pretended he was asleep. In the morning, once again to avoid his German roommate, Maudet was up early. The man was sprawled in his bed snoring quietly. At seven o'clock, his suitcase in his hand, Maudet tiptoed out of the room.

It was two hours before the train for Bad Danschau was scheduled to leave. Maudet passed most of the time strolling along the banks of the Elbe. Once again it was a superb day, the sky a cloudless blue, the air balmy. It would make things easier for de Forge, Maudet thought, and said to himself, 'Hitler weather – anti-Hitler weather.'

The train swung down the Elbe valley into the glory of the May morning. It chugged along in the direction of Prague, winding through the spring-green countryside, and crawled lazily from town to town, all of them sprawled contentedly on a carpet of rich brown earth and grassy meadows and glittering in the sun. The train stopped at most of the towns as if it found each one irresistible, remained there a while embraced in its arms, then reluctantly slipped away to nestle long and happily in the breast of the next one. The ride, with its local commuters getting on and off and its city trippers on an outing in the country, seemed to Maudet interminable; but he felt a rising excitement as the train progressed with agonizingly deliberate slowness towards his destination.

After a long stop at Pirna, where Maudet could see the smoke stacks of the town's synthetic petrol factory, the train rolled towards Bad Danschau. Then suddenly, his heart leaping out of him, Maudet saw far off in the distance the fortress looming high over the valley. Even so far away the towering mass of rock topping the mountain was impressive. It seemed to dominate the universe, fearsomely solitary, like the abode of an ogre in a tale of horror. From the slow-rolling train Maudet saw the fortress rising dark and foreboding directly out of the

136

mountain of rock towards the sun, and with a little shiver he noted the long sheer drop along the flat rock side of the mountain straight down into the woods at its foot. From where he was he could not see how anyone could get down that unbroken mountain wall; it did not seem possible. Seeing the reality de Forge had to face, Maudet wondered seriously for the first time whether the general would be able to fulfil his part of the bargain. By this time, if de Forge had gone into action on schedule, he was either outside and on his way to the rendezvous or lying broken at the foot of the pile of rock.

When the train pulled into Bad Danschau, Maudet was wondering what had happened. Was de Forge at this moment walking through the woods to meet him? Did the Germans already know? Were they combing the area, alerting the countryside, stopping and questioning all strangers?

There was no sign of anything out of the normal as Maudet stepped off the train with his suitcases and package. The station dominated the Elbe from one side of the river, and the small town spread out in the valley on the other side. Maudet checked the trains, then deposited his suitcases and package and stepped outside.

The sun was higher and hotter now. In front of Maudet was a narrow country road; to the left it ran along the rail line, rose in a slight incline, curved to the right and some distance farther on disappeared into a high-treed forest. It was out of that forest that de Forge should soon appear. If he did not, Maudet would have to return for him the next day, Saturday. If de Forge again failed to come out of the forest, Maudet would make his way back to France without him, his mission aborted.

Maudet strolled leisurely along the road, turned the curve and came to a worn wooden bridge that ran over a stream, a tiny tributary of the Elbe. It was the rendezvous point. He looked at his watch. Not much longer to wait. He looked around. This spot, which until now he had known only as an inked cross on a map, was not as he had imagined. It was pastoral. Trees in full leaf lined the stream and one side of the road. To the right a grassy field dipped into a line of the poplars outlined against the milky blue sky. To the left an endless stretch of farmland with its quilted pattern of ploughed earth and meadowland. Ahead of him the narrow tarred road with dusty dirt edges and shallow ditches. At first Maudet's city ears heard only a depthless silence, but then the murmur of the stream came up to him and with it the cries of birds and the whisper of the trees when a breeze brushed their leaves. The breeze also brought him the sweet smell of May. Maudet sighed. It was so peaceful, so distant from the clash of armies, from plotting men.

Maudet looked at his watch again, then fixed his eyes on the road. It curved to the left ahead of him and about two hundred yards beyond was swallowed in the shadows of the forest. A figure emerged from the shadows. Maudet's heart beat faster. The figure approached him, closer and closer. No, much too short. Another figure appeared and approached. Still another disappointment. Each time Maudet busied himself to appear to be a tourist enjoying the scenery, his back turned so that he would not have to greet or be seen by the passerby.

He was now looking at his watch almost constantly, engulfed by anxiety. It was only minutes before one o'clock, the rendezvous time. Galland had told him time and again that de Forge prided himself on his punctuality. 'He is never late.' The words, tone and accent were still in Maudet's ears. This time he will be, Maudet said to himself. He kept wondering, demanding, 'Where is he? What's happened to him?' and imagining the worst possibilities. He also realized darkly, with harsh self-criticism, that he did not want to return to Dresden and come back here again the next day.

As Maudet brooded, the whine of a siren from a nearby factory filled the air. A moment afterwards the chimes of a town clock rang out. Maudet looked at his watch once again. One o'clock. He had a premonition that something had gone wrong, that de Forge would not appear that day, and began puzzling over whether it would really be too imprudent to spend the night in the village as a tourist to avoid the trip to Dresden and back.

TWELVE

Unlike Maudet, de Forge took nothing for granted. Nobody had to tell him that even the most meticulously prepared plans can go wrong. During his long career he had presided over too many that had aborted for the most unpredictable reasons. He would not, therefore, bet all his marbles on one plan without being ready to abandon it for any mediocre improvisation that might have the superior virtue of working. Such elementary but far-reaching wisdom had first been impressed upon a youthful de Forge when a long-nurtured battlefield plan demanded that he lead his company to the right and he had quickly discovered in the face of heavy fire that the plan could only succeed if he led his men to the left. This seminal experience, combined with not a few others like it, brought him to what he lightly called in his younger days de Forge's first principle: if the facts don't fit your plan, make your plan fit the facts.

De Forge also knew that the best improvisations are those that are the most rehearsed. So he did everything he could to rehearse whatever he might have to do if the plan failed. He expected to be met by a guide who would provide him with false papers, clothes and money; but if the guide missed the rendezvous, a possibility which de Forge did not exclude, he believed he could still get to the border with the clothes he had acquired and the money he had accumulated, though the lack of false papers and help at the border would admittedly set the odds strongly against him. De Forge also foresaw the possibility that the Berlin night express exit to Strasbourg might not work and studied alternative routes on his German railroad timetables so assiduously that he knew virtually by heart the train schedules of Saxony, Bavaria and Wurttemberg. Fleeing by that route, he figured that in three days at the most he ought to be across the border. To be on the safe side he laid down a provision of black bread, Gruyère cheese, sugar and schnapps. It would make him independent of the German economy and its food-ration tickets. In addition, de Forge had his armoury; it was not much of an armoury, but it was the best he could manage. He had the switchblade knife he had bought from the gardener, and he also had one last strong length of cord that had not gone into his cable; it could serve, in case of need, as a garrotte.

By the Thursday before the last Friday in May all de Forge's preparations were completed. On that day, at the same time that Maudet was killing time walking the streets of Dresden, de Forge made the rounds of the fortress seeking out individually eight of the French generals whom he had long since carefully chosen. Knowing them as one knows men one has lived with in captivity for two years, de Forge trusted each one of them completely. They were the *durs* – the tough ones. Each rejected the defeat, abjured collaboration with the enemy, embraced acts and symbols of resistance, repudiated compromise, steadfastly believed or said he believed that France would triumph. In short, they were the resolute, unredeemable bitter-enders.

Quickly, succinctly, de Forge told each of them he planned to escape. They were stupefied. Except for Palisse, none of them had had the remotest suspicion. Faithful Palisse was surprised too, but more than that he was disappointed and hurt that de Forge had not confided in him earlier. Whatever his feelings, however, Palisse recognized that in matters of this sort it was always wisest to say nothing to anyone unless and until that person could do something about it.

De Forge told each of the generals that he needed his help. He told them about the cable and said that he would make his break the next morning, jumping the wall between nine-thirty and ten o'clock, timing it to avoid the round of guards that circled the battlement every fifteen minutes. He needed two men to pay out the cable and others to stand guard.

All the generals, once they had recovered from their astonishment, instantly approved what de Forge was doing, and although they were all aware of the reprisals that they together with the rest of the prisoners would suffer, none of them mentioned it. Some of the generals, however, pointed out to de Forge the risks he was running. They did not think he could make it. 'Better to be a live prisoner than a dead fugitive,' one of them advised him. Another said, 'What good is anyone dead?' De Forge quietly answered their objections, and when they saw he was determined to go ahead they did not try to dissuade him.

Later de Forge led them on a casual stroll to the point in the battlement where he planned to make his drop to the outside. He positioned each general so that, using whatever pretext came to mind, they could block anyone from the area during the critical few minutes of the drop. De Forge told them he did not think there would be any problem unless they were very unlucky; he had been observing the area and nobody ever came by at that hour of the morning. Finally, just before they broke up, he told them that the operation would begin when he signalled them by taking out his handkerchief and wiping his forehead with it.

In the early evening, when the German staff was eating, de Forge took the cable out of the hiding place under the planks in his room. It was neatly rolled into a large loop and was very heavy. Palisse was with him to help carry it. De Forge patted the cable fondly.

'I never desired an object so passionately in my entire life,' he said. 'And I'll never leave one behind me with more joy.'

Some of the other generals ran interference for them as they carried the cable and a small wooden bar to the place in the parapet where de Forge was to make his drop. They masked the cable as well as they could between them and under their open coats, crossing the width of the fortress plateau and sidling along the battlement behind the building where the orderlies lived; but de Forge had picked his moment well and nobody crossed their path or saw them. The escape embrasure was at the edge of the wooded area at the far end of the fortress plateau, and they deposited the cable for the night in some bushes only a few feet from the spot where de Forge would jump the wall.

After the evening meal de Forge gave the generals assembled in the common room his daily orientation lecture as usual, analysing the German press on its reports and commentaries about the course of the war. Nobody could have suspected from de Forge's even, professorial tone and majestic calm that beneath fluttered a heart that like a bird about to be freed could scarcely wait to take wing.

In his room afterwards de Forge quickly destroyed his remaining papers, then, very agitated, paced a while to quiet his nerves. Committed beyond recall, he cut the wish from the thought and, with a lucidity he had suppressed until then, considered the many places where the plan could misfire. It was a long way from the iron bar embedded in the embrasure to Unoccupied France. And to begin with, there was the drop over the wall. It terrified him. He felt himself floating weightless in the chasm and his stomach flipped as, dry-mouthed, the vertigo hit him. I'm mad, he thought, to hurl myself at the impossible. He did not think he would survive the drop, but nothing could stop him from making it.

Brooding, de Forge sat at his small table to write two letters. The first, brief and formal, was to the doyen of French generals at the fortress who, because of his rank, length of service and age, officially represented the imprisoned Frenchmen in their dealings with the fortress administration. De Forge begged the general to excuse him for the trouble he was about to cause him, adding that he was sure the general would understand de Forge's motives and take them into account.

The second letter was to von Bardsdorf, announcing and explaining his decision. He told the fortress commander that he could not endure imprisonment and that it was his duty to escape. He readily admitted that what he was doing no doubt amounted to a stroke of madness and would probably cost him his life. He asked that when his body was found, instead of the customary official notification, his wife be informed with delicacy. De Forge closed the letter by thanking von Bardsdorf for the correctness of his behaviour and assured him that he appreciated and would not forget the special consideration he had shown towards him.

He considered writing a third letter, to his wife, but quickly decided not to. A letter of farewell would put a curse on the operation and struck him at this stage as melodramatic. Besides, having put into words to von Bardsdorf the worst of his fears and having prudently asked that the blow be softened for his wife, he felt he had done all that was required.

He felt much better when he rose from the table. He was

142

ready to go. It had taken him two years, but now, at last, he was ready to go. He undressed and slipped into his prison cot – for the last time, he thought. It took him a long time to unwind, lying there wide-eyed, taut, and when at last he fell asleep he remained on the edge of wakefulness, impatient all night to be up for the newest, freshest day of his life – for all he knew his last one.

The new day began like all the others. De Forge's orderly, Gabory, woke him at seven o'clock. Ersatz coffee and black bread. Above the fortress hung a limpid, milk-blue early morning sky. Not a cloud. It was the first day of creation. De Forge took a deep breath. He was strung tight. He turned to the devoted Gabory, affecting a studied casualness.

'This time,' he said, 'I have news for you.'

The chunky Norman orderly stood there like a rock as de Forge told him that within three hours he would jump the wall; only Gabory's eyes showed his surprise. De Forge told him that he would be closely questioned and advised him what to say and what not to say.

'Stick to the truth wherever you can,' de Forge told him, 'and embroider as little as possible. The important thing to keep in mind is that you must not do anything that would lead them to suspect I've gone before they find out for themselves at the evening roll call. For the rest, you saw nothing, heard nothing and you weren't the general's confidant.'

'It's true.'

De Forge smiled. Gabory was a good man, a very good man, and de Forge looked at him fondly. 'I'll miss you, Gabory,' he said.

'I'll miss you, *mon général*.' His eyes glinted. 'But not as much as von Bardsdorf.'

Following his normal routine, de Forge put on his uniform – khaki trousers, dress jacket, field cap. He carefully prepared his little bundle, neatly packing the food, secondhand civilian clothes, two pairs of socks and underpants, toothbrush, razor and a tiny mirror. It was held together with a string he would put around his neck so that the bundle would dangle in front of him; a military cape that would hide the bundle was also ready to be thrown around him.

143

At nine-fifteen Lieutenant Hetzel arrived for the morning roll call. De Forge received him as he did every morning with old-world courtesy. As he did every morning, the general chatted in German with the lieutenant. They might have been old friends across two generations, or professor and student. Unhurriedly, casually, as if this day were like any other day, de Forge exchanged ideas with the lieutenant. This time they happened to light on child education and de Forge critically analysed the balancing roles of father and mother. Lieutenant Hetzel nodded sagely; he had come to take an immense pleasure in these morning chats. After ten minutes de Forge glanced at his watch and gave the lieutenant to understand that he could leave.

De Forge waited until he was certain that Lieutenant Hetzel had left the building. Then he picked up the bundle and suspended it from his neck, took the cape and threw it around his shoulders, carefully buttoned the cape and stepped outside. Although de Forge's heart was pounding, he was icy calm.

Without undue haste, he started towards the parapet. He glanced once again at his watch just as he turned the corner of his building, noted it was precisely nine-thirty, and ran head-on into General von Bardsdorf. Both men were forced to stop short. De Forge felt the blood run out of him. He swore to himself as he bowed his head slightly and greeted his captor.

'Up and about early,' von Bardsdorf said.

'Like you, *Herr General*.'

'Fine day.'

'Superb.'

'You're a cautious man, *Herr General*, to be buttoned up like that on such a day.'

'You can never tell what you'll run into.'

Von Bardsdorf laughed. 'You should let yourself go. There's nothing to fear today.'

'I hope you're right, *Herr General*.'

Von Bardsdorf swept by. De Forge relaxed and went on. None of the generals were about at that hour except for those de Forge had alerted the previous day. As he strode across the deserted open area de Forge met the middle-aged reserve lieutenant who had just completed the nine-thirty turn of the guard. They saluted each other and passed on.

Palisse joined de Forge and they walked together to the escape embrasure. A younger general, named Frainet, who was almost as big as de Forge and powerfully built, was already there; he and Palisse would pay out the cable while the others stood guard. Nobody said anything. De Forge checked and saw that the cable and wooden bar that would serve as his seat were still where they had been placed for the night. The cable stuck out a bit into the path circling the battlement. He pushed it with his foot but could not shove it completely into the bushes.

'No point in being seen with me this morning,' he said. 'It can only cause problems for you later. Come back as soon as the guard passes.'

Palisse and Frainet moved off.

At nine forty-five the sergeant doing the next turn of the guard appeared and came up to de Forge. He was a man of about fifty-five, a photographer in civilian life, who often complained to de Forge about how his shop in Leipzig was running down in his absence and about the war which would never end and allow him to return to his wife and five children and the portrait work he did so well.

De Forge greeted him gaily. 'Where's your camera, Herbert?'

'No cameras on guard duty. Why do you ask, *Herr General*?'

'What a shame. I would have been happy to have had my picture taken on a day like this against the magnificent background. For my memory book. To recall these happy days at the fortress.'

'You're pulling my leg as usual, *Herr General*. And that picture I took of you when you arrived here came out so badly. I'm still upset about it, and you always find an excuse not to let me take another one.'

'Don't be upset, Herbert. Bad subject, bad picture.'

'You're out of focus, unrecognizable. Well, one day we'll do it over properly, but now I must make the round.'

But instead of directly circling the battlement, the elderly sergeant stopped a few yards from de Forge just where the cable jutted out into the path from the bushes; his right foot missed it by only an inch or two. De Forge closed his eyes; an enormous weakness overcame him. It was finished; Herbert, good, fine, sentimental Herbert, would bend down and pull out the cable and de Forge would be back where he had been two years ago when he first arrived at the fortress. He opened his eyes. Herbert's back was turned to the cable. He was simply standing there admiring the splendid panorama as the sun evaporated the mist in the valley below. In a moment the sergeant turned away and proceeded on his round.

It was all clear now; they had fifteen minutes before the next guard would appear. Palisse and Frainet returned to de Forge. The other generals hovered casually in the background in sight of de Forge close to the positions they were to take. De Forge looked around him once, then again. Everything seemed normal; nobody who should not be there was in view. He was suddenly aware that he was breathing heavily, noisily. For a moment he held his breath to regain control, to calm down. This was the moment; not an instant's further delay. De Forge reached into his pocket and drew out his handkerchief. He looked around still again, then very deliberately brushed the handkerchief across his forehead twice, three times.

The generals went to their positions. At the same time Palisse and Frainet grabbed the cable. They attached one end to the iron bar embedded in the embrasure and tied the other end firmly to the centre of the round stick of wood, which resembled a shortened broom handle. Then they placed the stick on the far side of the iron bar with the cable resting on top of the bar and turned to de Forge.

'Ready. Let's go.'

Without a word, his face set, long moustache aquiver, de Forge threw off his cape, leaving it beside the parapet, and with the bundle now visible, swinging from his neck, jumped up on to the stone ledge of the embrasure. There he hesitated a beat, grasping the iron bar with both hands; he made the mistake at that instant of looking out at the vast chasm that opened up below him. All that immense empty space for a body to fall through and smash on the ungiving rocks below! 'Oh God,' he said to himself, and quickly shut his eyes. For another beat he was paralysed; the vertigo had hit him and, as tightly as he held on to the iron bar, he felt himself swaying. His fear of heights clamped him to the iron bar and the ledge. 'I mustn't look,' he kept repeating to himself. 'I must keep my eyes shut.' To Palisse and Frainet, who could feel the Germans crawling up their backs, de Forge's momentary, terrified hesitation, which they could not understand, seemed endless.

'Let's go, let's go,' Frainet whispered urgently, keeping his voice low as if they might be heard.

Awkwardly, his eyes tightly shut, de Forge carefully lifted one foot, then the other, and put them on the far side of the iron bar, grasping it all the while with both hands, with the knowledge that he was holding on to his very life. Only when he was fully turned around facing the fortress did he open his eyes. At his back he felt the broad, deep, unending emptiness, the vast space to fall through; he felt it at his anus, in his bowels.

'The stick,' Palisse whispered; he did not want to be overheard either. 'Get on the stick.'

'Lower it a little,' de Forge said hoarsely.

Palisse saw the whiteness of de Forge's knuckles around the iron bar and understood. He lowered the cable slightly.

'There you are,' he said softly. 'Easy does it.'

It helped. De Forge held solidly on to the iron bar with his right hand and, steadying the stick with his left hand, managed to get his legs around it and into a sitting position on the wooden bar. His shins were now crushed against the outer edge of the embrasure, his bottom out into the void. He tightened his buttocks. He felt defenceless against the empty space. He was mad, mad, out of his mind. He would never survive the drop. He felt the dip, felt the void hit him again in his anus and his bowels. He now grasped the cable with his left hand and the iron bar with his right hand; he hated to release his right hand.

'Are you holding it?'

'We're holding it.'

Palisse and Frainet were braced to hold de Forge's weight, their hands firmly gripping the cable.

'Then let's go.'

He forced his right hand to drop from the iron bar and

147

grab the cable, his armpits soaked. Then, clutching the cable with both hands for his life, feeling the bump on his behind as his weight hit it, his knees and his toes scraping the wall of rock, feeling the void below in his entrails, feeling the end had come, de Forge looked up and found himself gazing directly into Palisse's eyes. One thought was suddenly in his mind, one phrase on his lips: *'Vive la France!'* but from that instant everything happened too fast, and the words were blocked in his throat.

Seeing de Forge's right hand sweep from the iron bar to the cable and feeling the weight of the man hit his hands, Palisse held tight a moment, his eyes flashing. This was it. *'Merde!'* he said and, in unison with Frainet, dropped the cable an arm's length.

De Forge froze, mistaking the cry of good luck for a curse because the cable had slipped. But he only sank just below the edge of the embrasure and came to a stop with a bump, dangling there and feeling the great emptiness beneath him at the tip of his spine, waiting helplessly, muscles taut, breath held, for the plunge through space to the rocks below. To his surprise the cable held. He swung out from the wall, then back towards it, hanging above the chasm, and out of the corner of his eye saw the void around him, feeling it all the while between his squeezed buttocks. Then he shut his eyes tight again, straining to control his blind fear of heights, he who had never flinched under fire, and exerted all his will as if tugging fiercely at a rope of steel to bind body and mind so that his terror would not burst out of him.

Seated with the flat of his thighs over the wooden bar, de Forge held on to the cable with both hands as he swung out and around, out and around, hanging and turning in space, dangling from the thin strand of rope that twisted as it slowly lengthened, turning him with it as he swayed towards and away from the wall, feeling his body become heavier and freer in its movements as the cable became longer. Once he opened his eyes and saw the earth and sky and wall of rock twirling around him and he shut his eyes tight again. The two generals above paid out the cable slowly, very slowly, almost tenderly, an arm's length at a time, feeling the weight at the end of the cable swing and sway more and more as they let it out but could not control it. Twisting and swaying, his eyes shut, de Forge floated slowly down. Then suddenly he was rolling over on the ground; he had been lowered so gently that he had slid to the earth without a jar.

De Forge yanked the cable once very hard and let go of it. He watched it rapidly jerk upward but did not wait until it had disappeared. Quickly he scrambled to his feet and rushed, stumbling, down the open scrubby incline where he had landed into a clump of trees. He threw himself on to the ground, hidden at last, feeling safe and protected, and caught his breath. He was certain he had not been seen. Automatically he looked at his watch. Nine fifty-four. How could so much happen in so little time? But he knew that Palisse and the others would easily dispose of the cable before the next guard came around.

Having rested a moment, de Forge sat up and proceeded to transform himself. He undid his bundle, spread its contents around him and, holding his tiny mirror in his left hand, he shaved off his long thick moustache. He got to his feet, removed his field cap, took off his dress jacket and khaki trousers and threw them under a bush. Then he put on the pair of old trousers he had bought from the gardener and a grey turtleneck sport shirt his wife had sent him. On top of that he drew on the raincoat Reboux had given him; it was small for him but it would do. Finally, he put on the Alpine hat with the feather and a pair of heavy tortoise-shell glasses. He had a feeling of acute pleasure that he was so totally changed as to be unrecognizable. Who would see in him anything but a fatuous tourist? At the same time he experienced a surprisingly sharp pang of vanity: he was not a man to stoop to disguise – it offended his dignity.

He redid the small bundle, which now contained only his provisions and few personal effects, put it under his arm and started walking. He walked through a grove of tall pines that descended to the foot of the hills out of which the fortress rose. At the edge of the wood he crossed a small bridge over a tributary of the Elbe and then turned left to take the road towards Bad Danschau.

It was only a little after ten o'clock. De Forge walked along without hurrying. He had plenty of time. There were few

people on the road or in the fields. Along the entire way he met
no more than half a dozen women and children. Each time he
returned their friendly greeting – *'Morgen.' 'Morgen.'* – and
passed on. Nobody took undue notice of him; he plainly had
no interest for them.

At twelve-thirty he came to a wooded height from which
he could see Bad Danschau in the valley below astride the
Elbe. De Forge sat down at the foot of a pine tree and
contemplated the scene before him. His rendezvous was at one
o'clock, and he did not want to arrive ahead of time. The
train for Berlin was scheduled to leave Bad Danschau at one-
fifteen. He would go into the station and directly out on the
train with no waiting around and a minimum chance of being
observed.

At twelve forty-five he rose and strolled slowly, casually,
along the road to Bad Danschau. Coming out of the shadow
of a thick wood into the May sunlight, he heard the sudden
whine of a siren from the town and moments later, mingled
with it, the chimes of a clock. He did not have to look at
his watch to know that it was one o'clock. A couple of hundred yards ahead he saw a small wooden bridge, and on the
bridge he saw the tall figure of a bareheaded, blond young
man. The young man was looking in his direction, and he
guessed even at that distance that the young man was waiting
for him, that this was his guide. His heart rose in a burst of
elation, his main concern during the long morning walk erased,
but he did not quicken his step; without haste, slowly, steadily,
he approached the bridge and the young man. De Forge's
elation was not unalloyed. He did not like to be seen in his
get-up by anyone who knew him. It was bad enough that
without the generous flowing moustache he had worn since
he was a young man he felt naked; much worse was the
feeling that in the old trousers, the short raincoat and above
all the Tyrolean hat he looked ridiculous. So de Forge unhurriedly advanced with a small cloud cutting across his sunny
mood. The young man's eyes never left him. When de Forge
got to him at the wooden bridge the young man spoke.

'*Morgen*, Fritz.'

'*Morgen*.'

They shook hands. At the same time de Forge's small,

bright brown eyes took in Maudet with a clinical intensity that froze and shrivelled the younger man. It was a hard, cold all-business regard searching for what the surface hid that made Maudet feel he had encountered a man from another planet and been found wanting. His smile died and he dropped his eyes, vaguely annoyed and disappointed. This wasn't how he had imagined their meeting. They started walking towards the station. With no effusions or small talk, de Forge went straight to the point.

'At what time is the train for Berlin?'

'At six o'clock.'

'How about the one-fifteen?'

'Cancelled.'

The joy ebbed out of de Forge; only the irritation remained.

'What time is the next train out?'

'In twenty minutes.'

'We'll take it.'

'But it's going east – to Prague.'

'Unimportant. We'll change later and swing around.'

'We can't do that.'

'Why not?'

Maudet drew a deep breath. 'There are people waiting for us in Strasbourg to take us across the border.' He did not succeed in keeping his growing annoyance out of his voice. 'If we take the first train in the wrong direction, we'll miss them.'

'And if we stick around here for five hours only ten kilometres from the fortress, the Germans *won't* miss us. They may already know I'm gone.'

'It's a chance worth taking. They won't necessarily come by here. We can stay out in the woods until just before the Berlin train leaves, then – '

'Nothing doing.' De Forge was a rock. 'The important thing is to put as much distance as possible between me and the fortress in any direction – especially to the east, where they'll never look for me.'

'The important thing is to get to our friends as fast as possible so they can get you over the border before the Germans clamp it shut.'

Riding over Maudet impatiently, de Forge snapped, 'Whatever we may think about the Germans and their damned government, they run their trains on time. With their help we'll get to our friends before it's too late.'

Frustration choked Maudet. He had an impulse to throttle the man walking beside him for whose life and freedom he was risking his own. To wait was of course a risk, but to be stampeded east seemed to Maudet pure folly. Once they climbed on that first train all the arrangements he depended upon, all his security, the means and solidity of the mission evaporated. Maudet felt like a one-legged man whose crutch was being snatched from him and smashed. He stopped abruptly. De Forge stopped too. They faced each other.

'But if we don't go to Berlin,' Maudet argued, indignation high in his voice, 'if we don't go to Berlin, we'll be lost. What about all the arrangements? What about the plan?'

De Forge exploded. 'Fuck the plan! We'll make another plan as we go along. Ten other plans!' He glared at Maudet. Maudet glared back. 'Understand one thing,' de Forge said. 'In an operation like this someone has to take command.'

'Of course, *mon général*,' Maudet said sarcastically. 'But with an army of one man you'd do better to consult than to hand down orders.'

'What do you do in civilian life?'

'I'm a journalist.'

De Forge snorted. 'I might have known!'

'I'm not exactly enchanted with generals either.'

'Well, you're stuck with this one.'

Maudet decided to start all over again, persuasively. 'Look, General,' he said, his effort at patience too obvious, 'once we get on that train to Prague –'

De Forge cut him short. 'Don't you know when a decision is taken and a subject is closed, young man?'

Maudet flushed, but before he could say anything de Forge had turned and begun walking again. Soon Maudet caught up. They walked a way in a leaden silence. De Forge's head was thrust forward. Maudet's jaw was clamped.

'Where are my clothes and papers?' de Forge asked after a while.

Maudet hesitated, then shrugged, defeated. 'The valise is

deposited at the station.'

'If you'll get it, I'll go into the woods here and change.'

'I don't think you will; I won't let you – you'd be seen.' The last sentence was a concession. Maudet's voice was hoarse. He did not look at de Forge; he could not look at him. He looked straight ahead. A few moments later he added, 'Much better to change in the toilet on the train and go to another compartment afterward.'

They stopped in front of the station. A lot more people were there now than earlier.

De Forge looked Maudet directly in the eye and spoke in a level, neutral voice. 'You don't have to come any farther if you don't want to. With the clothes and papers you've brought me –'

'No, you'll need me. I came here to guide you out and that's what I'll do. Only –'

'Good. Then let's try to make it work.'

'That's what I was coming around to. It'll work better if you remember that I'm not in your army and I'm not under your orders.'

'I'll try to remember that,' de Forge said ironically.

The train whistle howled close by and they heard the train chug towards the station.

Maudet kept up his attack. 'This decision of yours is a disaster. It throws everything off. We're reduced to improvisation. I'm going along under protest. Because I have no choice.'

'It's coming in. Hurry!'

'I'm afraid we won't miss it.'

'How about the tickets?'

'You get one to Prague; I'll get one to Munich. Then if they do come around here looking for you, they won't be able to add one and one and discover it makes two.'

'But if I –'

'They won't recognize you,' Maudet said. 'I wouldn't have known you except that I was expecting you and they told me you'd be wearing that hat.'

Each bought his ticket to a different place. They had to hurry, but, running along the platform, they boarded the train heading east. Galland's simple, brilliant plan was shot. De

Forge did not seem to mind; Maudet sat rocking with the train, sunk in misery. It was not only that they were speeding away from France instead of towards Berlin and the wagon-lit of the night express to Strasbourg. Maudet was also aware that he had never before met a man to whom he had had such an instant reaction; what disturbed him was that it so closely resembled hate at first sight.

PART THREE

The Chase

THIRTEEN

The train was not at all what Maudet or de Forge had imagined. It was an old wooden model, and the toilet was not at the end of the car but in the middle. All around were German officers. It was impossible for de Forge to go into the toilet, change his clothes and come out without being noticed. Both men, sitting apart but in view of each other, understood that immediately. They could do nothing but ride it out and hope de Forge would not be challenged. From under his Tyrolean hat de Forge shot accusing looks at Maudet before subsiding into the rhythm of the train. Maudet ignored the looks, pretending a serenity he did not feel. It had been his decision and he sweated over it; he swung between a cringing fear that police would come through checking identity papers and a fruitless yearning that they had waited and taken the train to Berlin. Suddenly he froze: a drunken lieutenant in a group of noisy officers had noticed de Forge and was making him his butt.

'Quite a hat, old man. Who are you going to tickle with that feather? Ah, if I had a feather like that, I'd tell you what I'd do with it.'

His companions roared. De Forge stared ahead, unamused.

'Come on, old boy, loosen up. If I were a tourist like you and had that feather and the time to put it to use, I'd look happier than that. Come on, yodel us a tune, something to go with the hat. Here, have a drink, it'll set you off on the right note.'

The lieutenant's friends grinned and added their own pleas,

sensing easy amusement and a good laugh. De Forge stood up, his bleak dignity blunting their taunts. The laughter died.

'Excuse me, gentlemen.'

De Forge bowed his head towards them, turned his back and walked to the other end of the car. They looked uncomfortably at each other and two or three of them shrugged, but after that they were more subdued.

There was no police check before Bodenbach, fifty kilometres down the line. Feeling lucky, de Forge and Maudet got off to change trains and direction. They would switch west through the Sudetenland towards the rail junction of Eger. There they planned to change trains again going south to Munich, then transfer once more to shoot straight across to Strasbourg. De Forge was pleased with the new itinerary; he felt that his prolonged study of German railway timetables was paying off.

'So far, so good,' Maudet said. Some deep recess of his mind had succumbed to the myth of the total efficiency of the police state and he was still amazed that on a fifty-kilometre run there had been no check of identity papers.

'No thanks to you.'

Maudet flared back. 'On the Berlin train you'd have been able to change.'

'If we had got on the Berlin train.'

The train they boarded at Bodenbach was an express with normal main-line metallic cars that had toilets at either end. The train was packed; all the compartments were filled and the overflow of passengers, a noisy, bustling mixture of soldiers, officers and civilians, jammed the passageway. It was what de Forge and Maudet, climbing into the only second-class car, had hoped for since their best chance of going unnoticed was in this hubbub and confusion. They jostled their way next to the toilet at one end of the car and as soon as the train had left the station Maudet went into the toilet with the valise containing de Forge's effects and the package with his hat. De Forge sank out of sight on a seat that folded out from the wall next to the toilet.

In the toilet Maudet opened the valise, dug into it, lifted the bottom flap and took out the papers and money hidden there. He put half the reichsmarks into a pocket of his trousers,

156

carefully placed the rest of the money and de Forge's false papers on his clothes in the valise, and put his own new false papers authorizing him to return to France as an invalided worker into the inside breast pocket of his cheap brown tweed jacket. Maudet then took out his other false papers, the ones authorizing him to come into Germany, tore them into little bits, threw the bits into the toilet and flushed them out of sight. He tore the wrapping off de Forge's brand-new black fedora and put it on top of the money and false papers.

De Forge was at the toilet door the instant Maudet opened it. As de Forge went into the toilet, Maudet glanced nervously around; nobody seemed to have noticed them or to be paying attention. The train rocked and roared westward. Maudet elbowed through the crowd of passengers to be able to observe at a short distance whether anyone would notice de Forge when he came out.

Five minutes later the toilet door opened and de Forge emerged, a different man, the oddly garbed traveller transformed into an elegant gentleman from the black fedora, old-fashioned starched collar, fitted dark-blue topcoat, and smart pearl-grey gloves to the shiny black shoes. No moustache; heavy tortoise-shell glasses. He carried the valise. Maudet released his breath and relaxed. Nobody gave any sign of being aware of his existence. Beyond that Maudet felt a surge of confidence in the disguise: there was no resemblance between this conventional though aristocratic-looking figure and the famous mustachioed general. Except for his height.

De Forge raised an inquiring eye towards Maudet, who replied with a cold nod of reassurance. Then they ignored each other, sinking into the rhythm of the speeding train and a relaxed sense of well-being. They had the papers to prove they were legitimate travellers and they were headed in the right direction. It was quite an improvement. They would arrive in Eger at midnight and take the train for Munich at three in the morning, then on to Strasbourg. Instead of arriving on Saturday morning with the overnight express from Berlin, they would arrive on Saturday night or at worst on Sunday morning. Maudet was sure that Reiber with his Hitler moustache would be there to meet them and take them in hand; Reiber had said he would keep on meeting trains for a couple of days. Luckily they weren't all as starry-eyed as the naïve guide of the operation, anticipating a letter-perfect exercise.

Maudet glanced at de Forge, who was leaning against a window, his eyes closed. Like Maudet, he towered over the rest of the crowd. It was too bad there was so much of him to see – and hear. Maudet squirmed as he recalled their meeting. That icy, X-ray eye. The warmth of a cobra. But he was his cobra and he would have to learn to live with him. So this was the man they were so anxious to rescue, the man he was risking his life for. Maudet was obliged to admit his quality, but that didn't lessen his hostility. He resented being pushed around like an inanimate object by a man who issued peremptory orders, expecting them to be automatically obeyed. He would help de Forge; that's what he was there for. But he had no intention of jerking to attention like a puppet every time de Forge pulled a string.

De Forge was dozing on his feet. He had a sixteen-cylinder constitution, but he also had the enviable ability to turn his machinery on or off at will. With the pressure at least provisionally relaxed after an almost sleepless night, the drop over the wall and the long walk to the rendezvous, de Forge had turned himself off. Energy not in use should be conserved, he told himself, and he drowsed standing.

He had sized up Maudet in that first piercing instant and suspected that he did not fit the measure of his operational slide rule. Maudet's looks, intelligence, charm, culture, sensitivity and the rest were beside the point; the right qualities for the wrong job. He needed a machine, not a driver; someone who would submit to direction and could be used to get him off and away. For de Forge men fell into one of two categories, the leaders or managers who conceived and guided enterprises, great or small; and their instruments, those who executed the orders and did what had to be done to bring an enterprise to fruition. Maudet was an instrument. But he did not see himself as one. He was a refractory instrument and, therefore, a dangerous one that would frustrate or at least impede the operation instead of helping it along to its goal. The man had no sense of hierarchy or discipline – a journalist, an intellectual. He plainly didn't know the meaning of the word *sacrifice*. De Forge wondered if he would have time to educate him.

The train proved to be a false express. It stopped often, lurched into motion, inched ahead, finally hurtled forward, then stopped again. It stopped more often between stations than at them, but at last, towards ten o'clock that Friday night, it stopped and did not start again. They were at the town of Falkenau, fifty kilometres east of Eger. The conductor came through and announced that the train would go no farther that night, that it would leave for Eger at five o'clock the next morning.

De Forge and Maudet trooped out of the train and into the waiting room with the few remaining passengers, who were grumbling and complaining. They had put only two hundred kilometres between themselves and the fortress, and now that they were stranded until dawn they felt a lot less good than they had on the moving train.

Maudet was furious with disappointment. He plunged the knife in. 'So the Nazis run their trains on time.'

De Forge chose to ignore the remark, looking through and beyond Maudet as if he did not exist. But they both suffered the same bitter dejection as they walked into the dismal waiting room. The myth of Nazi efficiency was dying hard for them. Only now, stuck for the balance of the night in this chill and miserable room, did the obvious hit them: the overburdened German wartime railway system was a mess; they had been counting on timetables that were at best a hope, at worst a fiction.

About ten passengers, including two Wehrmacht noncoms, were in the third-class section of the waiting room. De Forge and Maudet joined them and lay down on wooden benches opposite each other. To avoid conversation with any of the people around him de Forge pretended to be asleep. He did not realize how tired he was, how much the day had taken out of him; he had hardly closed his eyes when he was fast asleep.

A bustle and the sound of boots awoke him. It was two in the morning. Through half-closed eyes he saw a patrol of *Schupos* around Maudet. He heard their gruff questions and

Maudet's submissive answers. Quickly satisfied, the *Schupos* turned towards de Forge. He shut his eyes and lay there, still as a slaughtered stag, feeling helpless. Through his closed eyes, through his pores and nerve endings he felt the presence of the patrol around him; he was chilled by the smell of leather boots a few inches from his nose. Then came the harsh voice.

'What are you doing here? Where are you going?'

De Forge lay still as still, his breathing heavy and regular, though he knew now the patrol would not pass him by. The *Schupo* shook his arm, repeating his question.

De Forge started, looked up at the man and yawned in his face. 'What's going on? What do you want?'

'What the hell's the matter, do you have shit in your ears? Are you a Czech, a Pole, a Chinaman? Don't you understand German, you ass hole? *Papiere, schnell!*'

De Forge sat up and glared at the man. 'I'm Alsatian,' he snapped. 'As good a German as you and better. For one thing, I'm polite, and you'd do well to be polite too.'

De Forge fished deliberately into his pocket for his wallet, extracted his 'absolutely authentic false papers' and handed them to the angry *Schupo* with total assurance. 'There. Have a look.'

The *Schupo* studied the documents for an interminable moment, stretching de Forge's nerves tight. Beyond the *Schupo* poring over the papers he caught Maudet's anguished eyes and turned away, irritated. De Forge yawned again, forcing it, his belly churning. The *Schupo* looked up at de Forge from the papers. 'Here it comes,' de Forge said to himself, tightening inside even harder. But then, like a surprise gift he did not deserve, the papers were thrust into his hand. He accepted the prize as if it were his due, a malicious smile on his lips.

'Well, where are you going and what are you doing here?' The voice was still gruff, but the bite and suspicion were out of it.

'I'm going to Munich. Here's my ticket. And as you can see, I'm waiting just like everybody else because our train broke down, which is hardly unusual, and we can't get out of here until the next one leaves for Eger at five o'clock.'

Put down, the aggressive *Schupo* looked sheepish. De Forge

had everybody in the third-class section as an audience for his performance and they were openly smiling at the way he had turned the tables making the *Schupo* look ridiculous by boldly stating the obvious. The *Schupo* groped to salvage his dignity.

'Next time answer right away and I won't have to raise my voice.' There was more apology than accusation in the statement.

'When I'm asleep and can't hear anything?'

The *Schupo* saluted without a word and the patrol left.

Maudet was impressed but hardly enchanted by de Forge's virtuosity. Later, as they were sitting together, he spoke up. 'You seem to be taking a lot of unnecessary risks.'

'None that have got me caught.'

'I was scared stiff when you made believe you were asleep and he shouted at you.'

'That's touching.'

'Nothing personal, but I thought he had you.'

'And he would have if he had seen your expression as I did. You should learn to hide your emotions.'

'And you should learn not to expose yourself. You didn't have to stand on your hind legs and bark at him. You're a fugitive for Chrissake; can't you forget your stars and medals?'

De Forge said very precisely, 'I stood up to the *Schupo*, but I didn't stand up.' He smiled. 'Sure, there's a limit to the risks you take. The man may remember me, but he'll never remember me tall.'

'He wasn't looking for you. That was clear.'

'They probably didn't find out I was gone until the night checkup. It'll be trickier today and worse tomorrow.'

'Which means you'll have to resist the temptation to impose yourself on every police official who looks at you cross-eyed and raises his voice.' When de Forge did not reply, Maudet added, 'We'll also have to travel a lot faster if we're going to be out by tomorrow. It's not as if we had taken the train to Berlin.'

De Forge's answer was a look that made Maudet regret having let his last remark slip out. It was below the belt. He was angry at himself. Pressures were building up – weariness, irritation at the delays, de Forge's personality – pressures that squeezed him into unfamiliar reactions. He vowed that he would keep a firmer grip on himself, but was still angry because instead of going to Berlin they were stuck here.

De Forge placidly admitted to himself without remorse that they probably would have been much farther on had they travelled via Berlin. But a lifetime of making decisions had taught him that they could only be made in terms of what you knew while you were making them and that regrets in view of what you learned later were futile. He did not think it worthwhile to point out to Maudet that everybody had 20-20 hindsight.

After a few minutes he raised a question he had been thinking about for quite a while. 'Are you armed?'

'Nobody thought it necessary in view of the plan.'

De Forge did not seem to be surprised. 'I have a knife and a garrotte,' he said casually. 'Just a bit of string but in strong hands quite enough. You can have either one.'

'What for?'

De Forge gazed over his large nose at Maudet's spontaneous revulsion as from a great height. 'You never can tell,' he said. 'The perspective of the original plan is no longer valid. It's time to have another look.'

Maudet felt in de Forge's tone and expression the condescension of the military mind; it made him aggressive. 'I wouldn't be able to use either of them anyway,' he said.

'If you had to, you'd be able to.'

'In a railway station against a patrol before ten witnesses including a couple of soldiers?'

'The next time it may be different.'

'No, thanks.'

'Just trying to be helpful. A fugitive armed is a fugitive with a better chance of making it.'

'I'm not the fugitive,' Maudet said curtly.

De Forge started to answer in the same tone, then stopped. 'Very well,' he said, tacking with a show of good humour, 'you'll be unarmed and I'll be double-armed.'

Day was breaking when the train crept out of the station, picked up speed and rolled towards Eger. They sat together for the short ride in the early morning, reasonably sure there would be no problems, and in answer to de Forge's questions Maudet described the mood in France, the mystique of the old Marshal, the vast sea of lassitude and the tiny islands of resistance.

'Resistance is beginning to spread in different forms,' Maudet said. 'There are women who go about in mourning, for example, even though everybody knows that nobody close to them has died.'

'Why? Who are they mourning?'

'France.'

De Forge was indignant. 'What sentimental nonsense! Sob-sister stuff for the misguided. As if France were dead! France will never die. The only thing wrong with France is Frenchmen. Instead of wearing black ribbons – what a uniform – they should take up arms.'

'In these times? How?'

'They have to be shown. That's why I have to get back. I will show them.'

It's his business, Maudet thought, and found himself torn between his antipathy to the general's arrogance and a reluctant admiration for his assurance, for the quality of strength unmixed with any doubt that emanated from him. Maudet suddenly realized that something was rubbing off on him; he was gathering strength from de Forge.

They chugged into Eger on time. It was six-thirty and a train for Munich was scheduled at seven. In the station they headed straight for the big information board and quickly ran through the list of departures. The seven o'clock train to Munich had been cancelled. The next one for Munich was not scheduled to leave until seven at night. De Forge swore. They looked at each other helplessly.

'You're right,' de Forge said grimly. 'None of their god-damn trains are running on time.'

'Half of their trains aren't running at all. Maybe,' Maudet added, 'that Berlin express never showed up either.'

They both smiled weakly; the situation was so bad they almost savoured it.

'I thought they were going to help us get away,' de Forge said. 'Do you suppose they're doing this deliberately to block us?'

They laughed over the feeble humour; it cleared the air somewhat.

A train from Prague was due to come through at four-fifteen going to Nuremberg and Stuttgart. It was a more northerly and direct way of going to Strasbourg and therefore more dangerous; the Germans would be more likely to be looking for de Forge on that line than along the southerly route. But they had already lost too much time and agreed that they could not afford to lose any more, particularly since they could not foretell what further delays there might be. Thus far their record was lamentable: twenty-four hours after de Forge's escape they were only 250 kilometres from the fortress. De Forge decided they should take the Nuremberg-Stuttgart train and Maudet raised no objection. Anything, anywhere, so long as they moved.

They had a wait ahead of them of almost ten hours. Luckily, even at the early hour they had arrived a horde of travellers crowded the station and they were lost among them. But time dragged and tried their nerves. They ate in the station and drank a couple of beers. Separately, they went to the washroom and shaved. While de Forge was shaving, Maudet overheard two men discussing his escape; they had heard the news on the radio. When de Forge returned from the washroom Maudet told him what he had heard. De Forge shrugged, but the worry was in his eyes. After that the empty minutes crawled more slowly than ever. The wait seemed endless; it was torment to sit still.

The news was on the front page of the afternoon papers. All of them carried the same fuzzy picture of de Forge, the one taken when he entered the fortress.

'Terrible picture,' Maudet said. 'Out of focus.'

'My contribution. You'd have to know me to recognize me.'

All the newspapers played the story big and in exactly the same way; it obviously came from the Propaganda Ministry with specific orders. Over the picture was the identifying headline: THE FLEEING FRENCH GENERAL DE FORGE. Beneath the picture was the caption: 'The French General de Forge, who was a German prisoner of war, has escaped from his fortress prison in Saxony. Anyone who helps the fleeing general in his flight will be punished with death. There will be a reward of 200,000 reichsmarks for the capture of the general. General de Forge is six feet three inches tall, slender, has grey hair and a large grey moustache and speaks German with a French accent. Information about him should be communicated to any army or police unit.'

'Two hundred thousand marks! They think a lot of you.'

'Not of you,' de Forge growled. 'Now you know what they'll do with you if they catch us.'

'I knew before. If I didn't, I've been told often enough.'

'Well, now it's official.' Through his sardonic smile de Forge looked perversely pleased.

Standing in the station just like anybody else in the middle of all the other people, Maudet could not imagine that he could be arrested and, bound and blindfolded, stood in front of a firing squad to have the life shot out of him. But he did not like to be reminded of the possibility. 'Why do you insist on it so?' He failed to keep an edge of sharpness from his voice.

'Does the prospect trouble you?'

'I don't anticipate it, so it doesn't trouble me.'

'You should anticipate it. After all,' de Forge rumbled, 'death is our destiny.'

'It's something that at my age I'm patient about.'

But de Forge would not be put off with a quip. 'It's a present reality for both of us apart from age. You should be aware of it. I'm aware of it every minute.'

'It's not easy for me to imagine.' Maudet hesitated. 'Somehow it seems unreal, something like a movie I'm watching but am not a part of.'

It was what de Forge had sensed. He felt that Maudet was like an unblooded infantryman – at the first shot, the first crisis, he would panic. De Forge wanted to make him aware of what he had to do, mould him to his mission.

'Look at it this way,' de Forge said. 'I didn't think yesterday morning I'd be alive today. I never thought I'd survive the wall; it scared the hell out of me. You see, I can't take heights. But that gives you equipment – expecting to go, then sticking around. It gives you an advantage. It's like having a second life after you've kissed the first one good-bye. Something's released; it's as if your chemistry had been shaken up and

165

rearranged. You're lighter somehow, carrying less baggage. And you're able to go freely, without reservations, for all or nothing.' De Forge paused. 'That,' he said slowly and soberly, 'is what this game you've got yourself into is about – all or nothing. Without fear; without pity; without remorse. With one purpose: to win even if you die for it.'

'I'm here. I'm doing all I can.' Maudet's voice was tight. 'I'm as exposed as you – more than you. If we're caught, you go back to prison; I get executed.'

'But if I escaped, it wasn't to be dragged back to captivity. Anything rather than that. It's what I'm getting at. I'm ready to die, but not to go back to that fortress.' De Forge's small brown eyes glittered fiercely, fixing Maudet. 'I'll do anything, anything, to get to France and do what I was intended to do. I've got to get there. It's not me; it's the nation through me. Yes, you're doing everything you can do, but so far it's been easy. The crunch is ahead. Or at least we've got to expect it. What then? If you know you can die, you'll be able to kill. But you don't really know the one and you're not ready to do the other.'

'If I had to –'

'If you had to! That's a hell of a way to go into battle.'

'It's not exactly the same thing.'

'You don't even want to be armed.'

'To knife a man, to choke him to death with a rope!'

'Forget about the damned morality that's been stuffed down all our throats. This isn't peace; it's war. These aren't Frenchmen; they're Germans.'

'But look at them,' Maudet said from his bowels. 'They're men.'

'They'll kill you if you don't kill them. And in cold blood if they take you – legally, according to all the forms.'

'But still a man's got to be able to do it. Jam a piece of steel into a man's belly – it takes doing.'

'They'd do it to you.'

'That doesn't make it any easier doing it to them.'

'You'll have to learn,' de Forge said dryly, 'like everyone else. They should have taught you before you came; it's part of the job.' He considered Maudet's hurt and angry face and told himself that the only way to make him rise to his size and

166

get anything out of him was to belittle and shame him. 'Either a man can do a job he commits himself to or he can't,' de Forge went on cruelly. 'But once he's committed he can't go half-way and stop, striking a pose and proclaiming that his sensibilities are offended; he's committed to everything that follows, to all the consequences. What he thinks he can't do or wouldn't have done under other circumstances he has to do. Because the meaning of right and wrong has changed for him – if he has the eyes to see it. Right is the mission accomplished; wrong is the mission failed. The rest is literature, which is to say, shit.'

'I know that!' Maudet exploded. He said it so loud that a few people turned and looked at them, and Maudet lowered his voice, repeating, 'I know that. I'll do what I have to do, whatever I have to do. You don't have to give me any of your goddamn sermons.'

De Forge considered him from a great height. Let him stew in the bile I've stirred up, he thought; it will prepare him for realities he's still too raw to face. 'Just remember one thing,' de Forge said. 'We may not be able to stand each other, but we can't stand without each other.'

They did not speak for a long time after that. They bought a great many illustrated magazines and newspapers, sat apart and went through them. Maudet sulked, pretending to read and hating de Forge for the condescending way he had delivered his little lesson. But the point had been jabbed painfully under his skin and could not be ignored. He quailed before the prospect of killing a man. On the other hand, the prospect of being killed held no terrors for him; he was opaque to it. That was unreal, beyond his decision or control, not easy to imagine. But he could easily imagine the physical act of putting an end to a man's life with his hand lunging at the end of a shaft of steel or his muscles wrenching at the ends of a strip of rope. Each time he visualized himself committing the violence he jerked away from it as if the violence were being committed on him. So during the long wait he turned in anguished circles that de Forge had drawn for him.

They finally climbed into the train, de Forge in second class, Maudet in third. After the bone-stiffening hours on a wooden bench in the station at Eger, de Forge observed the plush seats in the second-class compartments with a tender eye. But he knew that a vast dragnet was now being thrown around the country to catch him and thought it was probable that a search squad would at some point be dredging the train in the hope of landing him. With an instinctive sense that his pursuers might be fishing around him at any moment, he looked about carefully for a protective position. He found it in a free window corner of a compartment opposite a Panzer lieutenant, wearing the brassard of the Afrika Korps and an Iron Cross with oak leaves. At a glance, de Forge judged the man with his coarse, mottled face and dull eyes to be a former Reichswehr noncom who had gone up from the ranks and who, if need be, could serve him as an excellent cover.

At the door of the compartment de Forge brought his right arm up smartly in the Hitler salute.

'Heil Hitler,' he said, and added in his most courteous old-world manner, 'Would the *Herr Leutnant* permit me to sit opposite him?'

The lieutenant nodded coldly. As de Forge put his fedora and suitcase on the rack and took his seat, he smiled inwardly at how correct the icy reserve of the desert hero was towards the commonplace civilian. None the less, noting that the lieutenant had nothing to read, de Forge offered him a handsome publication he had bought on the fjords of Norway. Unthawing, the lieutenant accepted the courtesy.

While the train rolled towards Nuremberg, the lieutenant browsed through the pictorial beauties of Norway and de Forge read the *Frankfurter Zeitung*. About every half-hour Maudet sauntered into de Forge's car and down the corridor to glance into his compartment and make sure that all was well. He did not know what he could do if all were not well, but he had a compulsion to check at regular intervals.

During the stop at Nuremberg, Maudet stood in the corridor of his car, leaning on the open window and watching passengers get on and off. Just before the train started towards Stuttgart he saw what he had feared. At the far end of the train an officer of the S.S. Police, followed by a man in civilian clothes and a man in uniform, climbed aboard. Maudet had no doubt about whom they were looking for; by this time they were certain to be checking every west-bound train.

When Maudet got to de Forge's compartment he saw that it had filled up. On de Forge's side were a young girl and a civilian of about de Forge's age; beside the Panzer lieutenant were an elderly woman and a young Luftwaffe officer. Maudet caught de Forge's eye, and presently de Forge rose and went into the corridor. They stood casually beside each other, looking out of the window as if they were strangers.

'An S.S. search party is on board.'

'Where?'

'Way up front.'

Nobody noticed the quick, surreptitious exchange, and as the train plunged into the night, the two men returned to their places.

Like the other trains they had taken, this one was erratic, hurtling along for a while, then stopping inexplicably for long periods or merely creeping forward. The train was far behind schedule. Now and then, de Forge, at the end of his patience, left the compartment, presumably to stretch his legs, but in fact to look around and see what was going on. Only a couple of hours before the train was to arrive in Stuttgart, de Forge was standing in the corridor smoking a cigarette when he saw the search party come into the car.

He returned unhurriedly to his seat and scrunched himself down to appear as small as possible. Presently he engaged the Panzer lieutenant in conversation. His gambit was the fjords of Norway.

'Did the *Herr Leutnant* enjoy the magazine I lent him?'

'Very much, thank you.'

'No doubt that's because the *Herr Leutnant* knows the landscape of Norway much less well than a flatter, warmer landscape.'

'What makes you say that?'

'Why, your brassard. I fought in the last war, in the trenches, the mud. But to have fought with our heroic army of Africa, in the desert, under such a leader as Rommel! To have swept around the English flanks and crushed them!'

The lieutenant basked in the warmth of de Forge's admiration.

'I followed your campaigns closely,' de Forge said. 'I have a special interest in the region. You see, my business has taken

169

me to Egypt on occasion and so I am not entirely ignorant of what the area is like.'

'Then you have been in the desert.'

'Of course.'

'And you have felt the sun beat down on you.'

'Like a sledgehammer.'

'Like a sledgehammer. The sweat pouring down your face.'

'And the people, the Arabs in their flowing robes – '

'Yes, yes. Semites but not Jews. Yes, I remember one day, it was on the eve of an attack – '

The fuse was lit. The Afrika Korps lieutenant shot aloft. The conversation soared. Sketches of desert scenes followed hard on battle anecdotes, all of them fuelled by de Forge's exclamations of wonder and delight. They cruised over parched desert tracks, paused briefly with sun-darkened Bedouins in palm-shaded oases, then suddenly swerved back to Rommel and present realities.

'The secret,' de Forge said, 'is his use of tanks.'

'Like mobile battering rams. We smash through and the infantry follows up. But if you'll excuse me, it's no secret. Everybody knows what he does; the British know too, but they can't do a thing about it. It's talent. Genius. That's what it is. And behind the tanks we know that fewer of us will die.'

'Iron cavalry.'

'That's it – iron cavalry. Shooting fire and steel. Artillery on the move. And nobody knows how to use it like our Rommel.'

'What Hannibal once did with elephants – '

'Ach,' the lieutenant interrupted, 'where is the comparison between a herd of elephants and a corps of tanks? Our Rommel has been doing something that is superior even to what Hannibal did. And when history is written, you will see – '

The door of the compartment opened noisily as the Afrika Korps veteran was demonstrating the superiority of the Desert Fox over the wily Carthaginian. The S.S. police lieutenant stepped into the compartment; his two subordinates blocked the door.

The Panzer lieutenant barely glanced at the S.S. man. Aroused to a rare pitch of intellectual excitement, he pursued his demonstration, bearing Rommel in full flight towards Valhalla as de Forge interjected a word here and there,

170

gunning him to still dizzier heights. Iron-faced, the S.S. officer went about his business. He checked the papers of the young girl sitting on de Forge's side of the compartment; then he took a much longer time carefully going through the documents of the man sitting next to de Forge who was about his age.

The Panzer lieutenant's ardour never cooled; he zoomed into the outer stratosphere. 'Rommel is unstoppable. He will liquidate the British in Egypt. It's merely a question of time, but it's a certainty. Cairo will be ours, the Nile. Those we don't take will be forced to flee, like at Dunkirk. We will hold the Suez Canal, control the waterways.'

'And east of Suez,' de Forge suggested encouragingly.

'The Middle East. Of course. Logically and strategically that comes next. An entire world. Palestine, Persia. And beyond that India. The horizons of conquest are limitless.' He rubbed his hands together and laughed. 'When you circle the world you come back to Berlin. Consider this. . . .'

The S.S. man hovered tentatively over de Forge, it was his turn to be checked. But de Forge seemed unaware of him. The Panzer lieutenant arched the power of the Third Reich over the globe, and de Forge (how could he do otherwise?), de Forge concentrated all his attention on each glowing word. Indeed, everyone in the compartment, with more or less discretion, was eavesdropping. It was what they all wanted to hear and it was delivered with such passion. The S.S. man hesitated. No, it was impossible to interrupt such a conversation at such a moment; he would come back to the distinguished-looking gentleman after the others in the compartment had been checked.

The S.S. man took little time to go through the documents of the elderly woman and the young Luftwaffe officer but more than he required. He, too, was now listening. It fascinated him.

'. . . gold under the sand,' de Forge prodded.

'The material meaning of the Middle East for us. Oil. What a difference it will make for each individual German when we get that oil, and we'll get it in spite of the damned British. Oil to run our machines and factories. Oil rich. There's an ocean of oil under those sands, an ocean! Enough to drown the whole damned British army, and with what's left to run Germany for a century.'

'And the raw materials of Africa.'

'Colonies. We'll be back there. We'll show the lazy niggers how to work. With our organization we'll show them how to produce.'

'Better than the ridiculous French.'

'Or the damned British. We'll show them. What this will mean for Germany in a few years . . .'

The S.S. officer had turned once again towards de Forge and the Panzer lieutenant. Once again he hesitated. He was supposed to check the documents of everyone on the train without exception, and he was plainly a thorough man. But even the strictest rule has a cut-off point. The Afrika Korps veteran and his elegant companion were clearly the best of the nation. Ah, if all the others displayed the same sentiments, had the same vision! No, it would be excessive and ill-mannered to break in on them. The S.S. man bent forward slightly from the waist towards de Forge, raising his right hand in a salute.

'Heil Hitler, *gnädiger Herr*!'

'Heil Hitler, *Herr Oberleutnant*.'

De Forge flashed his eyes, impatient, distracted, towards the S.S. man for a fraction of a second and, plainly too preoccupied for police formalities, was instantly back to the glories that awaited the Third Reich. As the search party left, the Afrika Korps hero had completed the colonization of Africa and was descending upon India. He was surprised at how suddenly his travelling companion's eyes glazed into disinterest. With his audience slipping away, he stumbled into silence. For the rest of the trip de Forge buried his large nose in the fjords of Norway.

The train arrived in Stuttgart, the last stop, far behind schedule and all the passengers poured out. It was after midnight. In the crowded station de Forge mixed with a group of men of about his height, looked around and had the impression that the place was crawling with S.S. men, many more, it seemed to him, than could be normal. Maudet had the same impression.

'They're covering the station like a carpet,' de Forge said. 'We've got to get out of here fast.'

They looked at the big board announcing the day's departures. An express to Strasbourg was listed, but it would not leave until five o'clock; there was also a train for Metz that left at one-fifteen. The Metz train was for Wehrmacht personnel on leave.

De Forge looked around the station again and came to a quick decision. 'The Metz train.'

'Dangerous. With all those soldiers.'

'But look at all the S.S. I don't like the smell of the place.'

'We can't go all the way to Metz. It would take us forever to come back down to Strasbourg.'

'We'll get off at Landau, then straight south for Strasbourg. It'll take us just as long, probably longer, as with the direct train in the morning, but at least we'll be out of here, we'll be moving. And once we're past the Rhine we'll be in friendly country. We can –'

It was the look in de Forge's eyes as he stopped in mid-sentence. Maudet glanced over his shoulder. Thirty yards away a swarthy man was staring at them. He had the build of a wrestler, wore a tightly belted beige trench coat and a soft hat pulled over his eyes. He smelled of the Gestapo clear across the station. Maudet turned quickly back to de Forge. It's his height, he thought, his damned height.

'Is he still looking at you?'

'Let's go.'

They moved away from the main entrance of the station towards a double line of columns that would allow some manoeuvring. The trench coat was following them. They led the man up the hall of columns, then turned around one out of sight and doubled back. Trench coat was only momentarily confused. It was enough, at least for the moment. De Forge and Maudet strode rapidly out of the main entrance; but looking over their shoulders, they saw the burly man in the slouch hat hurrying after them.

They emerged from the light of the station into a street under total blackout. For a moment they saw nothing – a womblike darkness; they might have been blind. But they had to move. They stumbled ahead, groped along a building wall, then turned sharply to the right. They could now dimly make out forms and see each other's white faces in the darkling

173

light of the moon. Holding their breath, still as the shadows about them, they hid in the corner of a shop entrance. The street was deserted. In the silence they heard the click of a man's leather heels approaching them. Trench coat brushed by inches from them, his steps receded, suddenly stopped. De Forge moved away quickly, silently. Maudet hesitated. When he stepped out of the doorway a firm hand grasped his left arm. He tugged against it. Too late. Thick fingers gripped his arm like an iron clamp and pulled him around. He looked into the dark, tough face of the powerful man who had been following them.

'What are you doing here? Where's your friend?'

'Where I'd be if you hadn't stopped me. Let go. Are you crazy?'

Maudet tried to wrench free, but the man locked Maudet's arm expertly in both of his, clamping him painfully still.

'Trying to get away, eh?'

'Of course I'm trying to get away. Who are you? What do you want?'

'Don't try that on me. You know damned well who I am. And if you don't, you'll know soon enough. You don't play around with the Gestapo.'

The man pushed Maudet slightly ahead of him by his twisted left arm, marching him off. Maudet was in agony. He wanted to swing around on the man but couldn't. He felt that the slightest effort against the force being exerted on him would break his arm. I've had it, he thought. Like a rabbit being taken in by its ears. He knew that they would hold him and check his story, and find out that there was no truth in it. It flashed through his mind that de Forge had got away, but that gave him no comfort. He felt dead inside. His only feeling was the strain on his arm propelling him towards Gestapo headquarters. He wondered what he would say when they began torturing him.

FOURTEEN

The pain in Maudet's arm was too much. He started walking faster to get away from it, to play with the little distance he could put between himself and the Gestapo agent. 'Not so fast, you tricky bastard. If you knew what was waiting for you, you wouldn't be in such a hurry.'

The man jerked at his arm, yanking him closer. Maudet groaned, slowed down, pacing his steps gingerly to those of the Gestapo agent.

'That's better. That's a good boy. You just do what Poppa wants and you'll still have your arm when we get to headquarters.'

But as soon as Maudet slowed down the Gestapo agent pressured his arm to force him to go faster, and when he started to go faster the man squeezed his arm to bring him back to his side like a dog on leash. He kept it up, constantly breaking Maudet's pace, building up the pressure on his arm. Through the cat-and-mouse game the man jabbed a relentless patter into Maudet's ear.

'Faster. Not too fast, you stupid bastard. Slow down. Come on, move along. Stop dragging your ass. Speed it up. Whoa. You don't want to run. What's the matter with you? Don't you know how to walk? Get going, you dim-witted ass hole. Come back. Not so fast.'

All along the man kept roughing up Maudet, jabbing an elbow in his back just under the rib cage, throwing him off balance with his knees, and twisting and pressuring the arm he had painfully clamped, causing Maudet to stumble forward rather than walk with him.

They had not gone very far when Maudet, his face twisted with pain, complained, 'You're breaking my arm. You don't have to twist that hard. I'm not trying to get away. I have no reason to.'

'Close it,' the man growled, and gave Maudet's arm an added twist that made him hop forward. 'Come back here, you son of a bitch. In a little while you'll be glad if all you get is a lousy little broken arm.'

Maudet came back on his pinned arm and, looking sideways over his left shoulder, saw his tormentor's hard, impassive face plainly in the moonlight. He was about to speak to him again when suddenly and at the same instant the grip on his arm was released and the man's head jerked back, his face hideously distorted. The mouth opened in an awesomely deep sucking gasp that strangled in a small, croaking noise; his hands were clawing at his neck, at the thing choking him, his tongue swelling out of his open mouth, his eyes bulging wildly. For a moment Maudet was paralysed. He wanted to run, to escape. In the moonlight the Gestapo man's face was turning purple. His head was jerked back, the soft hat smashed over his forehead; his body was projected awkwardly forward and out of balance, his tongue sticking out grotesquely, his hands clutching weakly now at his throat and the dry, agonizing croaks that came from it.

'Hit him! Hit him!' De Forge's voice was an urgent breathless whisper.

Maudet swung his right fist into the man's belly. His left arm was numb. He hit the man again with his right, a wild swinging roundhouse, lower this time.

'Your knee! Kick him!'

Maudet brought up his knee sharply just once. It was partly blocked by the man's trench coat but that did not matter. The fight was out of him. De Forge felt his breath, his life, go through his hands from the rope throttling the man as his body fell back, sagging against him. De Forge supported the man's weight partly with his body, partly with hands twisted vicelike on the garrotte around the man's neck. The man's head had now fallen forward and his face was invisible under the soft hat still crushed down on his head. Standing back a bit, Maudet made out de Forge's incongruous fedora, squarely set on his head, and his elbows thrust out, stretched against the rope. In the moonlight on the silent and deserted blacked-out street the two figures remained as motionless as a monument, the Gestapo man's heavy body slumped against de Forge, following the lines of his bulky, coated form as if the two figures had been cut from the same

176

block of stone. De Forge held him like that for what seemed to Maudet many long minutes. They didn't say a word. Finally de Forge let the inert body slip away from him. It sank to the sidewalk, the hat rubbing against de Forge and falling away. The bare skull hit the asphalt. Maudet winced when he heard the sharp hollow sound.

'Is he dead?'

'He'll never be deader.'

'Let's get away from here.'

'No hurry. The sooner we get back to the station the longer we'll have to wait. And there are plenty more like this one there – only alive.'

De Forge set a deliberate pace; Maudet limped. As he walked, he massaged his left arm.

'That swine roughed you up.'

'He was a swine, all right.'

'You should have moved faster.'

Maudet said nothing. He wanted to thank de Forge but couldn't. De Forge rubbed on him like sandpaper on stone. It was his calm superiority, his perkiness; Maudet was shaky, trembling.

'What's the matter with your foot?'

'I turned my ankle when I kneed him.'

'You took your time.'

Again Maudet made no response. Finally he managed to say, 'I would have been cooked without you.'

'It would have been because of me that you would have been cooked. Nevertheless,' de Forge added, 'you're supposed to rescue me; I'm not supposed to rescue you.'

'Thanks anyway,' Maudet said dryly.

With mock ingenuousness: 'Maybe you'll be able to do as much for me.'

At the station entrance Maudet stopped de Forge. 'I've been thinking,' he said. 'If you're still willing to let me have it, I'll take the knife.'

'Good.' De Forge handed over the knife. 'Now we're both stronger.'

They did not hesitate when they got into the station. De Forge went directly to the only ticket window open and asked for a second-class ticket to Metz.

'You'll have a long wait,' the pretty ticket seller said. 'There's no train for Metz until two o'clock tomorrow afternoon.'

'But there's one in a little while – at one-fifteen.'

'That's a special train for soldiers on leave. There's an extra charge of fifty per cent for your ticket and no assurance that you'll have a seat.'

De Forge was hardly to be dissuaded; he paid the extra charge and went off with the ticket. A few minutes later Maudet bought a third-class ticket. On the way to the train they bought some newspapers. The story they were interested in was still on the front page. They read it on the platform.

The same picture of de Forge was still prominently displayed. The reward of 200,000 reichsmarks for his capture was headlined over the picture and the caption once again warned of the death penalty for anyone who helped him. The accompanying story disclosed that Hitler himself, plainly furious, had taken a number of decisions as a result of de Forge's escape. The commander of the fortress, General von Bardsdorf, had been dismissed. All other military fortress personnel, officers as well as enlisted men, had been transferred to the Russian front. All repatriations of French prisoners of war for whatever reason had been cancelled.

The story propounded the argument that the cancellation of thousands of compassionate repatriations, and all the suffering that would result for French soldiers and officers and their families, was the direct responsibility of General de Forge. It said that the cancellation order would be rescinded immediately if de Forge gave himself up and returned to captivity. More a police and propaganda tract than a news story, it concluded that if the fleeing French general had a spark of humanity in him or the slightest feeling for his own soldiers and countrymen, he would turn himself in.

'Blackmail,' de Forge sneered, but even on his sturdy shoulders it was a weight to bear.

The repercussions of the escape, especially the pitiless decision on repatriations, raising questions of state between Berlin and Vichy, were the measure of how seriously the German authorities regarded it. De Forge had been certain that their reaction against the prisoners at the fortress would be brutal, and no doubt it had been, though the story did not mention the penalties imposed on them; but he had not imagined the savage backlash on the fortress personnel or the sweeping inhumane measure affecting so many thousands of French prisoners of war.

What the generals imprisoned at the fortress might be suffering under the new commander and their new guards was suggested by a side story that went with the main one and that hit de Forge much harder. It said that the rope used in de Forge's escape had been found near the room of his friend and accomplice, General Palisse, that an S.S. unit had immediately been assigned by the personal order of the Fuehrer to transfer Palisse to a punishment prison, that on the way Palisse had attempted to escape and that he had been shot and killed in the attempt.

'The bastards. They took him out and murdered him.'

'Was he really your accomplice?'

'A pretext. It's half spite and revenge, half to discourage anyone else from doing what I did. That's Hitler. The mind of a barbarian. He runs a country the way you run a zoo – as if it were peopled with animals. He's a beast and in the end he'll die like a beast.'

De Forge raged, helpless to bring back a friend from the death he had led him to. Maudet had just seen him strangle a man but found him no less redoubtable now, his voice low and fierce in the shadows of the platform.

'Remember,' he muttered at last to Maudet, the violence still in his eyes, 'nothing is so cheap as human life, nothing so important as principle. Either we win or they win. When they stand in your way, get rid of them. If they present their throats, cut them. You'll have plenty of time for fine-spun morality when there's nothing to do but talk about it.'

The train, when it rolled into the station, was not a very long one – three second-class cars and five third-class cars. Only one passenger, a lieutenant, got off from the second-class section. De Forge hurriedly climbed on to get the free place. He found it in a compartment next to a captain. Giving the Hitler salute, he asked if the seat was vacant. The captain, more asleep than awake, said it was. De Forge sank into it and closed his eyes, shutting off any possibility of conversation by appearing to go to sleep. But though he was exhausted and depressed, he was wide awake. He opened his eyes. The other passengers in the compartment dozed; they were all in uniform, leaving de Forge conspicuously the only civilian in the group.

In a short while the noncom on duty came through and noticed the new passenger. He considered de Forge a moment, then startled the general by the way he addressed him.

'Does the *Herr Offizier* need anything?'

'Thanks, nothing now.'

De Forge took in the pleasant, rosy-cheeked young man and his eager blue eyes, impressed with his flair in discerning that he was an officer.

'Perhaps later then, *Herr Offizier*?'

'When I get off at Metz I'll ask you to carry my bag.'

'I'll be there, sir.'

And I won't, de Forge said to himself as the noncom left. De Forge and Maudet had agreed that they would get off at Landau, where they would take a train south into Alsace and on to Strasbourg.

Maudet was in the car behind de Forge's. He dozed fitfully in his uncomfortable third-class compartment. Shaking on the wooden bench with the movement of the train, he vaguely sensed the impact that the past two days and de Forge's personality had had on him. A change was taking shape in him. While he was determined to resist de Forge and his views, he was no longer sure of what only forty-eight hours earlier had been certainties, not merely ways of thought but ways of being. But he was too tired to try to sort out these changes and define them.

The train rumbled westward in the black night under a sudden torrential downpour. At about three-thirty, restless and unable to relax, de Forge left his compartment and started towards the toilet at the end of the car. To his surprise, the rosy-cheeked young noncom was hovering in the corridor. It struck de Forge as odd at that hour of the morning. The boy – he could not have been more than nineteen or twenty – had no apparent duties to perform and should have been resting in the part of the train set aside for him. They nodded as de Forge squeezed past, and it seemed to de Forge that the noncom looked at him strangely, not at all as he had earlier in a quite neutral way; this time the look was searching and there was an air of guilt about the boy's eyes, as if he were being observed doing something he wanted to hide.

When de Forge came out of the toilet the noncom was gone. De Forge went on into the next car to look for Maudet and met him on his way to see if everything was normal. Nobody was in the corridor and they spoke hastily, furtively, looking out the rain-splattered window in the dimmed corridor light.

'I may be in trouble,' de Forge said. 'The noncom on duty in my car seems to have an idea of who I might be.'

'How so?'

'We exchanged a few words. It may be my accent. He's obviously quick and smart. He sensed that I was an army officer. Then he must have thought about the accent and he waited around to see how tall I was.'

'Are you sure?'

De Forge shrugged. 'It's a question of smell. But I have a feeling that he must be trying to figure out this very minute how to confirm that I'm in fact that fleeing French general and above all how to manage the arrest so that he gets the reward.'

'We'll get off at the next stop.'

'The next stop is Landau – maybe he'll wait until Metz. That's where he thinks I'm getting off. It would make sense. There would be S.S. at the station; all he would have to do is point his finger at me and they would do the rest. If I were innocent, he could say he was sorry and wash his hands of it.'

'Our absolutely authentic false papers are fine until they start asking questions.'

'Well,' de Forge said, 'if he nails me on the train, you're in the clear.'

'Maybe we ought to jump.'

'At this speed? In this weather?'

'We'll see.' Maudet kept his eyes on the raindrops trembling on the window, away from de Forge. 'Maybe you're imagining all this.'

'I wouldn't bet on it.'

'We'll see,' Maudet repeated. 'I'll meet you in a while between our cars.'

They returned to their compartments to collect their things. All the passengers in de Forge's compartment were asleep or dozing. The captain opened an indifferent eye as de Forge slipped into the passageway. Carrying his bag, de Forge moved along the corridor and out on to the platform between the cars. He stood there solidly, his fedora sedately on his head, the blue coat buttoned, the valise set aside in a corner. He waited.

The train rattled along through the storm-swept night. Every time it slowed down de Forge's heart rose, but then the train would gather speed again. Landau can't be far off now, de Forge thought, and he began to feel that perhaps he had been too apprehensive. But how could he know? All the immense propaganda facilities of a totalitarian state had been saturated with the news of his escape and appeals to be on the lookout for him and have him arrested. Nobody in Germany who read a newspaper or listened to the radio could be unaware of his flight. And while there was little resemblance between his current face and the picture they had so widely published, his accent, age and height could not be concealed from anyone who came across him and happened to make the connection.

I have to be lucky, de Forge thought. At that instant the door of his car smashed open and the young noncom burst on to the platform. He stopped short, startled. De Forge cursed his luck. The husky, rosy-cheeked boy was a bad actor; he didn't know how to cover up that he had found what he was looking for.

'I thought you'd be in your compartment.'

'As you see . . .'

'You're not getting off?'

'Indeed I am.'

'But it's not Metz.'

A condescending smile. 'I'm aware of that, young man.'

'But you said you were getting off at Metz. You said you wanted me to carry your bag.'

'Quite so. But since then I've changed my mind.' De Forge bestowed a benign smile upon the agitated young man. 'Friends,' he said with a sigh. 'Metz will have to wait until tomorrow while I see my friends at Landau today.'

The noncom stood awkwardly before de Forge, speechless and baffled.

'However, if you're really so anxious to carry my bag, I won't disappoint you,' de Forge said kindly. 'You may help me with it when I get off.'

'That's not what I was anxious about.'

De Forge affected a puzzled expression. The boy looked at him irresolutely. Just then the door of the third-class car opened and their eyes shot away from each other, distracted. Maudet came on to the platform. He glanced at them indifferently, then put his valise down at his feet and leaned against the wall of the car facing them to wait for the train to stop. The noncom and de Forge turned back to each other.

The boy hesitated, gathering himself. He plunged. '*Mein Herr,* you must not get off at Landau.'

De Forge's heart sagged. He raised a questioning eyebrow. 'And why not?'

'You're French,' the noncom burst out. 'It's clear from your accent. I know – '

'Alsatian. And German.'

' – who you are. It's as plain as the nose on your face and your height.' He pushed himself, sure and excited, now that he had said it. 'You must come with me. I can't let you off. You must come with me.'

He stepped forward in the rocking train and took hold of de Forge's arm.

De Forge shook him off. 'Are you out of your mind? I'm an artificial-silk merchant. All anyone has to do is look at me and my papers to know. If you don't – '

'We'll see about that with the police, but you've got to come with me.'

He moved in again, putting his hand on de Forge's arm. Again de Forge shook him off. Maudet was observing the scene as the train rocked and rattled through the blackness and the downpour. He could not hear what they were saying above the noise of the train but he could imagine. He saw that now they had gone beyond words. Just as he pushed himself away from the wall of the car to move towards them the noncom turned to him for help. De Forge was backed off in a corner of the platform.

'What's going on here? What's the matter?' Maudet asked, approaching them.

'He wants to get off at Landau.'

Shrugging, smiling, 'So do I.'

'But he wants to escape.'

'Who is he?'

'That French general. General de Forge. Help me.'

The young noncom had kept his eyes on de Forge. Maudet was at his side. The noncom took a step forward. In the dim light de Forge saw Maudet's right hand come out of his pocket. At the end of it was a steel blade.

Maudet called to the noncom. 'Just a minute,' he said. 'There's something . . .'

The boy turned. De Forge saw the flash of the steel blade. A swinging right on an upward arc to the belly. The blade disappeared in the dark cloth of the noncom's shirt. He made a whooping sound, the breath knocked out of him, then, deep and urgent, sucked in a noisy lungful of air through his open mouth. The train rattled along. The noncom looked at Maudet with dull, uncomprehending eyes. Like a sheep, Maudet thought.

'But –' the noncom started to say.

'I'm sorry,' Maudet said very loudly over the noise of the train.

At the same time he pulled back his right hand and punched the boy again in the belly with the steel blade.

'Excuse me,' he said, so low this time that de Forge, a few steps away, could not hear him.

No sound came from the boy. He buckled and slipped to the floor of the platform between de Forge and Maudet.

Maudet leaned down and wiped the blade in two swipes on the noncom's trousers. 'I didn't want to do it,' Maudet said. He straightened up. 'I had to do it. It wasn't possible not to do it.'

De Forge turned the boy's head around and examined his face. 'Dead,' he said. 'Hurry before someone comes.'

He yanked the outer door half open, and a draught of pungent rain-soaked wind swept the stale train air clean. As he turned towards the body, a puddle of rain formed in the corner behind him. Maudet took the feet and helped him drag the body to the open door. They were awkward over the heavy deadweight but pulled and pushed it into the rain puddle at the edge of the half-open door. Maudet stepped back, puffing with exhaustion. De Forge gave the body a final shove at the shoulder, and as the upper part of the body tipped clear he swung the lower part out of the door. It tumbled away head-first. The noise of the train rocking along covered all other sounds, but Maudet felt in his belly the sound of the boy's body as it flew out of the door, hitting the side of the car and tumbling and bouncing away on the gravel roadbed. De Forge slammed the door shut.

Maudet leaned weak and trembling against the wall of the car, his eyes closed. He was drenched with sweat. The blood had ebbed from his face; in the dim light it looked green; it was wet with rain. 'He was only a kid,' he muttered.

'It was his fault. He got in the way.'

'Yes, he got in the way,' Maudet said wearily. He opened his eyes and looked nakedly into de Forge's.

'You did what you had to do,' de Forge said. 'You did it well.'

'Then why do I feel – unclean? Why don't I feel good? Proud? As if I'd just done something noble?'

'You'll get over it. . . . He got in the way. That's how it happens. You had to get rid of him.'

Maudet looked down and saw a small puddle of blood at his feet. De Forge followed his eyes. Maudet stepped carefully around the blood and returned to his side of the platform. De Forge swept his shoe through the blood, mixing it with the dirt on the floor. He ground his heel in it until the blood was an indistiguishable stain among others. Nobody would be able to tell that a man had just died there.

Maudet turned aside, eyes gazing unseeing out of the rain-dripping window. He clenched and unclenched his right fist in his coat pocket. The hand encumbered him; he would have washed it had he been able to and wished he could separate himself from it or at least forget it existed. It was murder really. The boy never knew what hit him. What appalled Maudet was that it had been so easy. A punch in the belly and the life was out of him. Gone. He felt his fist hit the boy again, the blade cutting into the flesh as if nothing were there. Maudet felt sick and gagged. What was life if it was so fragile against death, which was forever? Maudet remembered the boy's clear blue eyes and rosy cheeks, his pink and white complexion like a girl's, then only a moment later the body's deadweight. Out and away like a rotten log. With a tremor of terror Maudet felt his own frail mortality.

The train plunged forward into the black belly of the night and Maudet felt that he was being swallowed up; he felt the future plunging swiftly and irresistibly upon him, felt that it would freeze him in the unwanted, inescapable present before slipping away indifferently to become the past when nothing, neither wisdom nor hindsight nor the gods themselves, could change anything. No way to stop it. What happens will happen. He felt helpless, prone before lurking disasters that would pounce and strike. Doubt and foreboding gnawed at him. For the first time since the mission began he wondered if they would make it.

FIFTEEN

Maudet and De Forge were facing each other at diagonally opposite corners of the platform connecting their cars when the crash came. The train shuddered to a sudden stop with an ear-splitting clank of smashing metal and shattering glass. Maudet was propelled forward, slapped hard against the wall of de Forge's car and slipped to the metal flooring. The terrifying crash of metal and glass died; for an instant the silence was filled with the steady beat of heavy rain on the roof of the car, then came shouts and hoarse calls out of the black, storm-filled night.

'Are you all right?' de Forge asked, bending over Maudet.
'I think so. What happened?'
'Don't know.'
De Forge helped Maudet to his feet. Maudet sagged against him, then straightened up.
'What is it?'
'The same damned ankle I turned.'
'It's not broken?'
'Oh no. I can stand on it.'

'Can you walk?'

Maudet took a few tentative steps. His limp was more pronounced.

'I can manage.'

The train was awake and alive. Men moving and talking loudly, windows slamming open, glass breaking, shouts, guttural cries. The doors to both cars smashed open at the same time. Soldiers and officers trooped out, opened the side doors and peered forward. The rain poured on to the platform, drenching those at the door. Everyone spoke at once.

'It was an air raid, a bomb.'

'Ah, the damned British.'

'No, no. It was sabotage, a mine.'

'Maybe it was terrorists.'

'Who?'

'The French. This isn't so far from the old border.'

'Ridiculous. Probably just an accident. Maybe a collision or a loose rail and the engine jumped the track. Something like that.'

'What can you see up ahead? What is it?'

'Can't see a thing. Look for yourself. Let me out of the rain.'

They were all too preoccupied with the crash to pay any heed to de Forge or Maudet, but both of them felt conspicuous in their civilian clothes surrounded by so many men in uniform. The stir of men in movement continued about them amid the wildest rumours of what had happened and the number of men killed and mutilated up front. A soldier sent out by an officer finally stepped into the downpour, went forward and returned five minutes later, his uniform soaked, face shining wet, with the news that the engine was lying on its side and the first two cars behind it were partly crushed together and off the track.

'It's a mess,' he said. 'I think the engine-driver was killed. Some of the men in the first car were hurt, but they're getting through to help them from the other cars.'

One or two others braved the storm to see for themselves. But soon the rest of the men returned to their places, leaving de Forge and Maudet alone again. The rain beat on the roof of the cars like a battery of drums.

'We can't stay here,' Maudet said.

'I can't go back to the compartment either,' de Forge replied. 'They're wide awake now and we'll be here for hours, probably the whole day. Did you see how they looked at me? There wasn't another civilian.'

'But we can't go out in this rain.'

'Why not? If we have to. Landau can't be very far. This track is blocked. We'll gain time by walking there. In any case, it's out of the question for me to stay on the train. Someone is bound to recognize me. . . . But how about your foot? Can you make it?'

Maudet was sure he could. They waited a while, alone, hoping the rain would stop, fearful that someone would pass through and question them. Presently the drumbeat of rain let up a bit and they grasped their valises, stepped out into the night and began walking along a gravel path beside the track towards the front of the train. In a moment they cut across a field to a narrow but paved road and sloshed ahead along it. They could make out the train dimly in the darkness, the engine and first cars twisted on their sides beside the track like an immense felled malevolent beast.

By the time they reached the road they were muddied to their knees and soaked through. Maudet limped badly and slowed them down. They were hunched against the unrelenting downpour, plodding doggedly through the blackness with only the dim wet shine of asphalt to guide them. De Forge tried grimly through the beat of the rain to set a fast pace, but Maudet kept falling behind. He limped increasingly, his ankle tormenting him. De Forge sloshed ahead, then as they lost contact in the dark, was forced to slow down until Maudet, hobbling painfully and splashing through puddles on the road, was once again at his elbow. By now they were as sensitive to each other and their fugitive moods as if they were an old married couple, and soon, without having exchanged a word, they were both at the ragged edge of their nerves.

'Can't you go faster?' de Forge asked impatiently. 'We'll never get there.'

'I'm doing as well as I can,' Maudet gasped.

The rain slackened somewhat though it continued to fall

188

steadily; but the wind rose and whipped sheets of rain into their faces. Maudet began to sneeze and sniffle. They had no idea where they were, hoping at each step that they would arrive at the outskirts of Landau, where they could get a train coming down from the north. As Maudet weakened, snuffling and limping along almost at a crawl, de Forge became stronger and increasingly impatient. At each step he made his ill temper felt, muttering, grimacing, gesturing. Finally Maudet stopped in the middle of the road. They had been walking almost an hour. It was close to five o'clock in the morning. The eastern horizon was emerging a dirty grey. Above and behind them the sky was still black and hostile. The rain fell. De Forge had gone on. He returned towards Maudet, stood at a distance from him. They both held their valises. They considered each other coldly through the rain. There was a long silence.

'Well?'

'I can't any more,' Maudet said.

'What are you going to do – wait here in the rain until a choir of angels flies down and carries you to the station?'

'I tell you I can't. It's too much.'

'What do you mean you can't?' De Forge was indignant. 'You've got to.'

'I can't keep up that pace with my leg. Don't you have eyes? Can't you see? Don't you understand?' Maudet's voice rose in the dark. 'Tagging along at your heels! I'm not a dog. Or an ox.'

De Forge regarded him for a moment in silence. 'Intellectuals,' he sneered. 'No staying power. No guts.'

'There are limits, God damn it, and I've gone beyond them,' Maudet said. 'I'm going to sit down over there and rest.' He indicated with a nod a low stone wall just visible along the side of the road. 'I'll set my own pace from now on.'

'You fool, if you sit down now, you'll never get up. Your foot will stiffen and you won't be able to move.' De Forge's nose seemed to lengthen with the intensity of his contempt. 'You don't think I've been pushing and pulling and beating you along because it gives me pleasure, do you? I'm not a sadist. You're a child: you don't know what's good for you. Even now, standing there, your foot is stiffening. You've got to keep on moving or you're finished.'

'Go to hell with your phony concern for me!' Maudet cried. 'I'll show you who's a child. You want to set the pace? Set it! Go ahead, go! I've been holding you up. All right, you'll get there faster on your own. You don't need me. Here, take back your knife. You may need it. I'm used up, ready for the ash heap. All right. Just take what you need and go fuck yourself.'

He held out the knife. De Forge looked at him steadily from a hostile distance. Finally de Forge drew a deep breath.

'Keep the knife,' he said.

He turned and strode away.

Maudet watched de Forge's strong, broad back quickly disappear in the gloom. 'Good luck!' he shouted after the figure he no longer could see. 'Good luck! You'll need it.' Then he added aloud to himself, 'The son of a bitch! The goddamn insufferable, egomaniacal son of a bitch!'

Maudet stood there a moment longer, tears in his eyes, then limped over to the low stone wall and sat down. The rain had turned into a fine cold drizzle. He hunched into his trench coat, hands in his pockets, sat dripping and sniffling, cold and wet, and rested. His ankle throbbed, his nose was stuffed, his head ached, his body slumped over with lassitude. Despite everything, despite his pain and fatigue and discomfort and the bitterness in his heart, it was good at least to be sitting, not to be moving, to be at rest.

A quarter of an hour passed. During that time Maudet did not budge. Nor did he think. He was overwhelmed with rage and weariness. Every part of his body ached. He wanted to do no more than remain where he was. He shivered, sneezed, took out a handkerchief and blew his nose. He told himself that he could not remain there forever. But he could not gather the strength to get up and move. 'I must, I must,' he said aloud. He was alone and felt his loneliness with an aching poignancy. What was he doing there? Alone and nowhere? His heart sagged with a sense of opportunity missed, of failure. He hated de Forge, bitterly, fiercely. 'The son of a bitch,' he repeated aloud. 'The supercilious, hateful son of a bitch.'

The edge of grey sky on the horizon crept into the black, smudging it and casting a dirty light below. The rain continued to fall, heavier now. His shoulders hunched, his hands in his pockets, his head down, Maudet gathered himself despondently to rise. He sneezed, shook his head, heard a noise, saw a pair of muddy black shoes at his feet, looked up. De Forge towered above him, tall, solid, close. His face was impassive but his eyes were no longer hard. Maudet blinked, swallowed, looked away. His heart soared, his throat choked.

'*Allons*,' de Forge said gently. 'Let's go.'

He bent down and helped Maudet rise. Maudet picked up his valise in his right hand; de Forge held his valise in his left hand. He put his other arm around Maudet to support him. Slowly, painfully, his foot as stiff as de Forge had said it would be, Maudet began again where he had left off, limping along the rain-swept, deserted road. But this time de Forge's arm was around him.

A chill dawn wind rose from the west driving sheets of rain before it, and the wind-driven rain cut into their faces. They put their heads down and plodded ahead at the same limping pace. It was hard, slow, tedious going. Maudet leaned heavily on de Forge, using him as a crutch. Both men were soon exhausted. They kept sloshing forward, making very slow progress, still not knowing where they were. The sky hung low above them, half of it now a heavy sombre grey, the rest still black. The light was a dark dirty grey and the entire world was wet. The rain lashed at them. The wind ripped at the dripping trees, and its whoosh through the leaves sounded against the rush of water racing in the ditch beside the road. Maudet, soaked through, limped along holding on to de Forge, his eyes closed with pain and fatigue, indifferent to puddles and the driving, slanted rain which had become a part of his existence like the air he breathed.

They came to a rise at the peak of a curve in the narrow road and to their dismay saw spread below them the panorama of a huge valley, a dark wet green expanse stretching to the gloomy horizon: Landau, if it existed, was nowhere in sight. They started down the hill. A short distance below, a cart drawn by a fat farm horse emerged from a rutted dirt road. It turned in a downhill direction and stopped. When de Forge and Maudet came level with it they saw on the raised wooden driver's bench holding the reins a bulky figure in a shiny yellow rubber raincoat under a broad-brimmed yellow rubber hat. They started to pass, but the figure called out to them. To their surprise, it was a woman's voice.

'Climb on,' she cried. 'It's better than walking.'

De Forge helped Maudet get into the back of the cart and then followed him. They sat gingerly up forward near the woman on the outer edges of the cart. It bounced down the hill into the valley, the iron-shod wheels making a racket on the bumpy asphalt.

'Where are you going?' the woman asked over her shoulder.

'Landau,' Maudet replied. 'Is it far?'

'Fifteen kilometres,' she said. 'Too far to walk, especially – ' She hesitated, not knowing whether Maudet's limp was a permanent affliction it would be indelicate to refer to, and then turned and looked at him curiously. She had a pleasant, open face with a suntanned complexion and pale blue eyes.

Maudet explained the train accident and their haste to get to Landau to see friends who were expecting them. 'We thought it was just a short distance away.'

'You've gone off at an angle.'

'Is there a bus that can get us there?'

'Not from here. Not at this hour.' She looked back at them curiously, kindly once again. 'You've been out in this storm half the night? Yes, of course, you both look it. You're soaked through.' The rain still fell and Maudet had hardly stopped sniffling, sneezing and blowing his nose. 'The best thing you can do is find some shelter, get dried out and have some rest. My farm is close by. If you wish, you can come with me. Later I'll show you where you can get transportation to Landau.'

Maudet looked at de Forge, who nodded, and Maudet accepted the invitation.

They were chilled to the bone when the cart stopped in front of the farmhouse. The woman led them into the kitchen. It was cosy and spotless. A low fire was burning in a big, old-fashioned stove, and the woman stirred it to life, poured on some coals from a pail and put a big kettle on. Then she turned and considered her guests. De Forge had removed his hat, which he held in his hand. Maudet's nose was red and he was so chilled he trembled. Rain water dripped from their clothes, forming puddles at their feet.

She smiled warmly and shook her head. 'You men,' she said. 'You're all the same. Like children. Come, you'd better take your things off. You'll catch your death of cold. Do you have dressing gowns? Here, I have rooms for you where you can change. I'll draw a bath for you. That's what you need. A hot tub.'

She led them upstairs into tidy little bedrooms, talking all the while.

'Come along,' she said. 'Just follow me. We'll have to hurry now; I have chores to do. But I can see that you're both fine gentlemen and I can leave the house to you. I'm all alone now; my men are gone. Off to the war like all the others. This way, please. There. Change in here and hand all your clothes out to me. They're soaked. I'll dry them over the fire. I'll draw the tub and you can take turns one after the other. You'll find the bathroom here. The door is open. That's it. Hand me your clothes. I'll be out when you come down but I'll be back soon enough, as soon as the chores are done. You'll find coffee, it'll be good and hot, and bread and butter and jam and cheese. Just help yourselves.'

Maudet thanked her effusively through the door.

'Don't thank me,' she said. 'It's a pleasure to have men in the house again. I just hope someone is doing the same for my men right now. I'll be back. Make yourselves at home. Just open the beds when you've eaten and get a few winks of sleep.'

One after the other de Forge and Maudet soaked the chill out of their bones in tubs of hot water. Then, barefoot and wearing robes, they went down to the kitchen, where their clothes were being steamed dry over the stove. The woman was not there. But she had left a pot of coffee on the stove. It was ersatz but hot. On the kitchen table she had left a big loaf of crisp homemade rye bread, a huge chunk of sweet country butter, a jar of her personal brand of strawberry preserves and a light cream cheese so fresh it could only have been whipped up on the spot. They sat down before these unexpected delights and feasted. As their bellies filled, their spirits lifted.

'We must have hidden virtues,' de Forge said, sitting back and sighing as he finished. 'God is watching over us.'

They felt replete but very tired and sleepy. It was eight

o'clock. The rain fell in an unrelenting drizzle from a low gloomy morning sky. They thought of the beds upstairs with their fresh white sheets. How long had it been since they had slept in a bed? De Forge yawned; watching him, Maudet yawned too. They rose together.

'She'll surely wake us when it's time to go,' Maudet said.

'In any case I'll be up in an hour or two,' de Forge replied as they trooped up the stairs to their bedrooms.

But they did not realize how exhausted they were.

It was late in the afternoon when de Forge woke up. He jumped into his dressing gown and crossed the hall into Maudet's room. Maudet was snoring away. De Forge called to him, then shook him awake. He came out of his deep sleep slowly and badly, grumpy and sullen.

'It's late,' de Forge said angrily. 'That damned woman didn't wake us. Go down and get our clothes. We've got to get out of here and on our way. The less she sees and hears of me the better, otherwise I'd be down there myself. Come on, wake up. It's late, I tell you.'

De Forge hovered over Maudet, nervous and agitated, as Maudet, still sodden with sleep, got up. De Forge watched Maudet climb automatically into his robe and limp towards the stairs. 'How is your foot?' he asked.

'Better,' Maudet mumbled. 'But my cold is a lot worse.'

The woman was in the kitchen over an ironing board, pressing Maudet's trousers. Maudet noticed in a corner his shoes and de Forge's, side by side, polished to a high shine. The kitchen was warm and cosy. It smelled good. The window was open to the afternoon breeze and the warmth of the setting sun. The rain had stopped; the sky was blue. Despite his stuffed nose Maudet could sense the smell and feel of spring. He wondered if any of the things he had been through the previous day had really happened. The white curtain bellied in on the breeze, and he saw in quick flashes the contorted face of the Gestapo man as he strangled on de Forge's garrotte, the puzzled look on the boy's face as he punched the steel blade into his belly, the rain pouring upon him in the darkness as he sat in misery by the side of the road. None of it seemed real so soon afterward in this homely kitchen with the handsome blonde woman energetically applying the iron to his trousers. She looked up as he came in, a smile on her lips, then went back to her ironing.

'You look better now,' she said. 'Rested. But that's a bad cold you have.'

'You've been very kind,' Maudet said. 'But we must go now. We've imposed on you too much as it is, and we're very late. We thought you would wake us and we overslept.'

'Wake you!' She laughed. 'I tiptoed upstairs when I came back and you were both sleeping like a regiment. I didn't have the heart to wake you.'

'Well,' he said, 'we do have to go. It's wonderful of you to take such good care of us, to press our clothes and to receive us so generously. I won't forget it. Neither will my friend.'

'But you can't go now,' she said serenely, not looking up and continuing to press the trousers with considerable energy. 'Not unless you want to walk.' She stopped and looked at Maudet with her clear, untroubled blue eyes, very light and blue against her bronzed face. 'There are only two buses to Landau, and the afternoon bus has already gone.' She laughed at the disappointment he did not try to mask. 'What difference does it make if you get there a day earlier or a day later? You'll stay here a bit longer and fill my solitude. You'll be my prisoner. The both of you.' She laughed again. 'My prisoners of war.'

Maudet's lips parted in a pallid smile. 'I guess we are — until tomorrow. There isn't very much we can do about it.'

'You can enjoy it. It isn't such a bad prison.'

'Nor such a brutal guard.'

She laughed with pleasure. 'That's better. Now you're getting into the spirit of your sentence.'

They chatted for a moment. Maudet begged her to excuse him for his boorishness; he had been thinking only of getting to his destination but he was really delighted to be her guest. She chided him but confessed that she was even more delighted to have them in the house; the house seemed empty with her alone in it and there were so few distractions; it was an agreeable change. While they talked she finished her ironing and handed him his clothes and de Forge's. He saw that the shirts, underclothes and socks had been washed, dried and pressed.

'It's too much,' he protested. 'How could you do it all so quickly?'

She glowed. 'It's a professional secret.'

Maudet made his way back up the stairs burdened with clothes.

De Forge was waiting for him impatiently. 'What took you so long?' he wanted to know, taking his things.

Maudet explained that they would have to stay overnight. He was surprised at how calmly, apart from a fleeting look of exasperation, de Forge took the news.

'I was afraid of that,' de Forge said. 'Very well, we're blocked. But I can't spend an entire evening with that woman. We can't assume that by the end of it she wouldn't know who I am or at least have good reason to suspect it. I'll stay right here in my room. You must tell her that I'm not feeling well — a splitting migraine — that I'm obliged to stay in bed and try to sleep it off.'

Maudet dressed and joined the woman in the kitchen. But she would not have him there. She was preparing dinner, when her domain was sacred. Maudet was taken aback. He liked her because she was so warm and feminine, and he could not remember when he had encountered anyone with her un-affected simplicity and open-hearted generosity. A bit mother, a bit wife, she treated him in heavy-handed and intimate fashion, as if he were already a member of her family, and banished him to the tidy, unlived-in living room.

'Out, out!' she cried the moment he appeared. And as he backed away, startled, she pursued him to the door, a rolling pin in her floury hands, shooing him off with gestures and laughing blue eyes. 'You can't stay here now. It's all top secret. Go away! Into the living room with you. I'll call you when it's ready.'

'Can't I set the table?'

'You can't do anything. I do the serving in this house. All you can do is wait outside until I call you.'

He turned about the living room, bored and impatient to be with her again. She communicated an ease of spirit, and he felt at home with her. After a while he left the house and strolled around it in the soft May evening. He found a wooden bench under an elm in a flower-rimmed garden and sat there watching the sun, big and red, sink gracefully behind a hill far off to the west. The crickets all around him were noisy. He felt at peace.

Presently the woman came out looking for him. He sat quietly admiring her as she approached, unaware that he was there. She wore a simple light blue cotton dress that was snug at the waist, emphasizing the curve of her hips, and she walked with a free, girlish stride swinging her bare plump arms. A pink light from the flaming western sky bathed her face and full figure. Her silver-blonde hair worn loosely up in a bun caught glints of the dying rose-coloured light. When she came upon him looking up at her from the bench she was startled and stopped suddenly with a surprised little gasp.

'How naughty of you,' she said, pretending to scold him. 'You've been hiding here all along. . . . Dinner's ready. Where's your friend?'

She was disappointed to hear that he would not be dining with them. 'What a shame,' she said. 'It's a special occasion and three would have made it more festive.'

'What's the occasion?'

She would not say. 'Later,' she insisted. 'There's a time for everything. I'll let you know soon enough.'

They started back towards the house.

'Your friend is very quiet,' she said. 'I don't think I've heard him utter a single word.'

'It's because he hasn't been feeling well.'

'What does he do?'

'What do you think he does?'

She shrugged. 'He looks so distinguished, so important. I feel rather small beside him.' She pondered. 'If I had to guess,' she ventured, 'I'd say he was a diplomat or maybe a surgeon, but a great specialist. Or perhaps even a general. Except that he can't be a general.'

'Why not?'

'You don't find generals wandering around in civilian clothes completely lost in the middle of the night while a war is going on. That wouldn't make sense.'

Maudet laughed. 'No sense at all,' he agreed.

She smiled indulgently. 'Well, what does he do?'

'He's a silk merchant.'

'Oh,' she said. 'I was way off. He looks more impressive than that. But being a silk merchant isn't bad either, is it? Not if he's good at it, and I'm sure he must be. And you?' she added, looking at him rather shyly.

'Me?'

They went into the house at that moment, and Maudet followed her into the kitchen. Contact was momentarily broken, and when Maudet entered the kitchen he exclaimed at how lovely it was. The woman had set the table with a sparkling white tablecloth and in the centre of the table had put an elaborate silver candelabrum. Colourful sprays of gay spring flowers she had picked from the garden were spotted around the room. It was simple and charming.

Although it was not yet dark when they sat down, she lit the candles. The soft light flattered her strong tanned features, the wide mouth, firm chin, aquiline nose, all framed by the silken crown of her light blonde hair. It was a Roman face, womanly but imperial.

'It's an heirloom,' she said, sitting back from the candelabrum. 'I bring it out for special occasions. Do you like it?'

He admired the intricate silver swirls and baroque elegance of the glittering antique. She looked as shyly pleased as a little girl being admired. As he uncorked a chilled bottle of Rhine wine, she brought the soup steaming to the table. It was a perfectly simple and simply perfect potato and leek soup. Maudet filled his plate full a second time from the tureen on the table between them. She did not have to urge him on. The light aromatic wine lifted their spirits and they chatted gaily about food and wine, about delicious dishes they had eaten and unforgettable bottles they had drunk.

'I hope you like it,' she said as she served the *coq au vin blanc*. 'It's made with the same wine we're drinking. It's a speciality of the house.'

'Served,' he announced, 'only on special occasions.'

She laughed. 'That's true, but you mustn't mock me.'

He tasted the tender flesh of the bird stewed in the wine and cream sauce and pronounced it succulent.

'Can you taste it through your cold?' she asked.

'My head has cleared with the wine and hot soup,' he said.

198

'The texture is perfect. Worthy of a French *cordon bleu.*'

'It's a French recipe.'

He hesitated, then looking at her through the glow of the candlelight, said, 'I'm half French, you know.'

'No, I didn't know. How would I?'

'My father was French, my mother German. Alsace.'

'Now that you say so, it doesn't surprise me.'

'Why?'

'Little things. . . . That's what makes you different,' she added. 'I like it.' She paused. 'I like the French,' she said. 'I always did. They have something special. But I think every people must have something special. Even the Russians, even the Jews.' She looked automatically over her shoulder as she said it. 'We had some Jews in the town here. They were good people. But they're gone now, God knows where. My family came from the east. We were brought up to see the good in people. But that isn't the way most of us here see it now. Everything has changed. It's not the way it used to be when I was a child and growing up.'

'It will change again when the war is over.'

'Whenever that will be. We've had so many victories. One after the other. Victories for the nation. You know I've thought about this a great deal. The nation and the people who make it up are two different things. The people buy the nation's victories and pay for its defeats. And the price is always too high. Even if you survive the war, you never survive it whole. There are the days and the nights, and the months and the years you lose that are gone forever, that you can never recapture.' She spoke softly, sadly, with the quiet assurance of having paid dearly for her knowledge. 'What then if the nation wins?' she went on. 'What's it all for? We'll all be six feet under soon enough anyway. And now with what's going on in the east with the Russians, who knows when it will end?'

'Or how,' Maudet said. 'The German nation may be different from the German people, as you say, and of course it is, but it will make a big difference to the German people if the Reich wins or loses the war. Generally speaking, a people pays more for a nation's defeat than it costs them for a nation's victory. Indeed, there could be a very high return for you,

199

whatever the cost, if Germany wins.'

'I never wanted more than I had,' she replied simply. 'It was enough. I never wanted to go around like a highwayman on a horse striking my neighbours and taking what was theirs for myself. And now I just want to go back to where I was. We had a good life. A good life until they took my men away. First my husband all the way back in the beginning. It's just a year since I've seen him, since he's been back on leave. And now my twin boys are gone. Only a few months ago. Eighteen years old. Boys. Children. But they dressed them up in uniforms and taught them to shoot a gun. That isn't why I put them into the world.'

She stopped abruptly. Her eyes glistened. She brought the wine-glass to her lips and drained it. Maudet poured for both of them from a second bottle.

'This will not do,' she said, managing a smile. 'I'm incomplete without them. It's very hard and I must not think about it, not tonight. We must talk about other things.' She rose, raising her arms in an eternally graceful feminine gesture and patting her hair in place with large strong hands. 'I have a surprise for you,' she said, leaving the table.

She went to a cupboard and returned bearing a small cake covered with chocolate cream. In the middle of the cake was a single candle. Solemnly she placed the cake on the table and lit the candle.

'What's this?' Maudet asked. 'Why, it's sumptuous.' She was still standing, smiling luminously, her deep-set eyes glittering in the candlelight. Maudet smiled up at her. 'The special occasion,' he said.

'I can't hide anything from you,' she said mockingly. Then she cleared her throat and announced portentously, 'It's my birthday.'

Maudet rose, congratulating her. He moved around the table and embraced her on both cheeks, wishing her a happy birthday. Then he insisted that she blow out the candle and make her wish. She did. Maudet poured more wine and drank to her while she cut the cake. He protested as she served him copiously a second time that he was eating too much cake, but in the same breath declared it irresistible.

They finished the dinner in a festive mood and rose from the table tipsy.

Both thought of de Forge at the same moment.

'He's probably asleep,' Maudet said.

'I'll prepare a platter for him anyway,' she insisted.

'Of course. I'm sure he'll be happy to be awakened for it.'

Maudet carried the platter up to de Forge while the woman cleared the table and tidied up in the kitchen. As Maudet had expected, de Forge was wide awake, waiting for him and hungry.

'You'll like it,' Maudet said, setting down the platter.

'How is it going down there?'

'Nothing to fear. She has no idea who you are.'

'Nobody else around?'

'Nobody. There's no danger at all. She's really quite simple and charming. It's her birthday. We've been celebrating and you've got the last of the birthday cake.'

De Forge was already attacking the soup with appetite. 'We leave early in the morning, right?'

'Yes.'

'And she'll wake us?'

'That's right.'

De Forge was talking between gulps of soup, but now he looked up at Maudet with a quizzical smile. 'Don't let me keep you,' he said. 'The operation is on the tracks, which is the important thing, and I'm sure the birthday celebration isn't finished yet.'

Maudet was not as sure as de Forge, but when he returned to the kitchen the woman had switched on the radio and the strains of a Strauss waltz filled the room.

'He's awake?'

'Devouring his dinner.'

'Perhaps he will want to come down and join us.'

'Oh no. He wants to get back to bed.'

Maudet had told her earlier that his limp was caused by a turned ankle, and she had prepared a basin of hot water and herbs for him to bathe his foot in. He protested a bit and she pressed him gently but firmly.

'Come now,' she said. 'Off with your shoe and sock. It will

soothe your ankle, and tomorrow when you leave it will be new again.'

He did as she demanded, and as he sat there with his foot in the basin she brought out a bottle of schnapps.

'That will soothe your ankle,' she said, 'and this will soothe your soul. It will kill the bugs.' She laughed. 'We're attacking your troubles from both ends – head and foot.'

She fussed over him, jesting but tender. She seemed to need someone to fuss over and mocked him and herself as she did so, but was happy caring for someone who needed her attention. He basked in her solicitude; it was sweet to be tended with such womanly warmth, to have his needs anticipated before he was even aware of them, in short, to be pampered. They spent a cosy evening, slipping into a warm hazy glow over their schnapps to saccharine melodies from the softly enveloping sound of the radio.

Later, when the news came on, they listened to it, the spell of their intimacy suddenly broken as they were invaded by the outside world. Bombings, dog fights, battles on the Russian front, preparations for invasion from the west, Fortress Europa. It all seemed very far away and to have nothing to do with them. But the voice went on, evoking the violence around their little circle of peace in the softly lighted kitchen isolated in the perfumed countryside under the stars. A French general named de Forge was in flight and it was the duty of every German citizen. . . . Dead or alive. 200,000 reichsmarks. Six feet three inches, grey hair, moustache, et cetera. Three killed when a train crowded with troops jumped the track near Landau. No accident. A mine. Terrorists. Vigilance against the enemies of the Reich. The caramel-sweet voice finally stopped. Music.

Maudet watched the woman as the news of de Forge was broadcast. Her face was impassive until she noticed him staring at her and then she smiled, her eyes blue and filmy. It was plain that she had not made the connection.

When the newscast ended she spoke to him teasingly of the way he had turned up. 'If you hadn't been on the train,' she said, 'I'd think you were the terrorist.'

'Oh?'

'Well, what were you doing fleeing in the middle of the

night from the scene of the crime?'

'Fleeing from the scene of the crime, of course.'

She giggled. 'It's all very suspicious, isn't it?' She was quite tipsy and slurred her words somewhat. It amused her not to be able to speak crisply, and she played with it rather like a child. 'Yes, I must say it's very suspicious.'

'Very,' Maudet agreed, smiling with her.

'I could be shot for what I'm doing,' she said, lifting the snifter of schnapps to her lips. She sipped, put it down, took aim with an imaginary rifle, and said, 'Ping!'

'You're quite right,' Maudet agreed.

'Harbouring a terrorist. Two terrorists. I don't know which is more dangerous – the silent one or the one who keeps secrets.'

'Secrets?'

'You *could* be a terrorist for all I know. You could be anything. We've talked and talked, and you haven't told me a thing about yourself.'

'It would be too terrifying,' he said compassionately.

'I don't know who you are, what you do or why you're here.' She hiccuped.

'Because I'm a prisoner,' he said. 'Remember?'

She laughed. 'Yes,' she said, her cheeks flushed and her eyes bright. 'I do remember. You're my prisoner. You're here to keep me company on my birthday.'

From the radio a couple crooned a sentimental tune in close harmony with strings and saxophones behind them oozing a syrupy accompaniment. The spell of intimacy in the kitchen was woven again as if the newscast had never broken it.

'You never asked me which birthday.'

'Is it important?'

'That's the French part of you,' she said with a smile. 'You know it's important. Thirty-nine.' She sighed. 'If times were normal and my man and boys were here, perhaps it wouldn't be important. It never was before. The seasons passed. I asked no questions. I was complete. But a woman alone is incomplete.'

She paused over the statement as if staggered by an illumination and seemed to be examining it, or herself, from all sides.

In the absence of talk the banal music from the radio was intrusive, jarring. Maudet glanced at his watch. She saw it.

'You're sleepy.'

'A little,' he understated.

What intrigued and troubled her bored him; it was a familiar story.

'Then a last small sip for me, please, while I prepare my own special hot little cold killer that you'll drink in bed when you're under the covers.'

He poured some more schnapps for her and with a quick gesture, head thrown back, emptied his own glass in one large gulp. There was more in the glass than he had thought. He felt warm and good; his head was light, his body weightless.

'I never used to think,' the woman was saying, back to her former theme, to her gnawing concern, the emptiness, the depths of nothingness of the life she led alone. 'Now,' she said, 'I think all the time. I ask myself questions, so many questions. But I have no answers. Why are we here? What's it all about? Why should life be like – like nothing? Empty. Like a wonderful-looking dish without salt? So promising and such a tasteless disappointment? You're an educated man. Why?'

'I don't know.'

'Somebody must know.'

'Nobody knows,' he said flatly.

'The professors, the priests.'

'They least of all. Doctrinaires. They have *their* answers, not yours or mine.'

His head was whirling. The room spun around him. He kept seeing two of her, sometimes more, the images fanning out, then blurring together like an agitated accordion.

'The libraries, the books,' she was saying. 'The answers must be in all those books I never had the time to read. The answers must be waiting there for anyone to see. But which books? What authors?'

'They'll tell you how far away the moon, the sun and the stars are and how to measure the distance,' Maudet said, slurring his words drunkenly. 'They're very strong on that. Or how to boil an egg or grow a rose. But if you hurt inside with the pain of your mortality and want to know why life has turned flat, stale and insipid, all the authors in all the libraries of the world will turn their backs on you. There are no answers to the ultimate questions. They'll tell you to decorate your house or cultivate your garden; the *Weltschmerz* will pass.'

'Then what's the good of it?' she asked. 'What good is it if in the end we die and they can't tell us why we lived, or only half lived, and what it's all about?'

'The good of it, the good of it!' he muttered, struggling to his feet. 'I'll tell you the good of it.' He fell back into his chair. 'It's so that the road to the grave may be paved with good sensations. That's the good of it.' He swayed aloft again, very unsteady, the room turning, and leaned with his knuckles on the table for support. 'The idea is,' he said, 'that if we *have* to pass through this vale of tears without understanding where we came from, why we got here or where we're going, if anywhere; if we are unable to satisfy our aspirations to godhood, to knowing, as you say, what it's all about, but are condemned to sink helplessly and forever into our ignorance of mere humans incapable of grasping our condition or so horrified by its cruel meaninglessness that we refuse to comprehend it –' He paused in midflight, looked at her oddly as if clutching for words beyond his reach, then his grave face, his eyes, lit up in a smile. '– at least,' he continued, 'at the very least we can satisfy the beast in us, our animal urge and instinct, that profound need and imperative' – his face was now fully illuminated – 'which is,' he concluded triumphantly, 'to be scratched when we itch.'

His luminous smile erupted in laughter and he fell back again into his chair. With an effort he choked back his mirth. 'That,' he pronounced with a flourish, 'is the tickle theory of man's mission on earth.' And he let out a bellow of laughter.

She considered him soberly, shaking in his seat with laughter, his eyes glistening with tears, and shook her head. 'You don't know what you're talking about,' she said. 'You're drunk.' Watching him gradually recover from his fit of laughter, she smiled wanly and added, 'I think I'm a little drunk too. Come, you must go up. I'll help you.'

He insisted that he could do whatever had to be done by himself and stood up at his place swaying and smiling a brittle, pasted-on smile. He lifted an index finger high and said, 'Lots of people believe in my tickle theory, more people than you imagine. Raw materialism, that's what it is. What most people live by. Why, the entire elaborate structure of society has been erected to that end.' The laughter bubbled briefly in his throat again and softly died. Grinning wildly, he announced, 'All the citizens of all the countries of the world demand their share as an inalienable right.' He stumbled over the words. 'You can't blame them. Who doesn't enjoy a good tickle? Who doesn't want to be scratched when they itch? Don't you ever believe those puritanical old hypocrites who deny it. And when the noble statesmen feel the time is ripe to grab a greater share of the tickle-factor, they go to war to redistribute the available but always limited means of scratch to satisfy the national itch.'

He roared again with contented laughter, bent down and picked up the shoe he had removed to bathe his foot, and straightened up unsteadily as she watched him indulgently. Weaving but not staggering, a touch too stiff in his effort to walk straight, he limped out of the kitchen holding one shoe, wearing the other, and talking all the while.

'Itch, scratch and tickle. That's what it's all about. That's what they're all after. That's what it all comes down to. Itch, scratch and tickle. They can call it what they want, dress it up with fancy names and make it look like what it isn't, but in the end it's nothing but that underneath all the sauce they cover it up with.' His laughter trailed behind him down the stairs.

Maudet undressed slowly, his movements poorly co-ordinated, and had just fallen heavily into bed and pulled the covers to his chin when the woman came into his room with the hot toddy. He was not so drunk that he failed to notice she was no longer wearing her blue dress but a light pink cotton robe. She looked at him curiously, intently, to decipher, he thought, whether he was still in the same ebullient mood as a few minutes earlier. Her eyes were very blue and very bright.

He grinned at her. 'Happy birthday,' he said.

She smiled, then tried to look severe. 'You must drink it all,' she said, handing him the steaming glass.

Holding the hot glass close to the rim between his thumb

206

and index finger, he took a tentative sip and grimaced. 'It tastes like arsenic,' he said.

'How would you know? You never tasted arsenic.'

'Oh, yes, I did,' he said. 'I used to be the chief arsenic taster at the local arsenic works. That's how I got this way.'

She laughed with him, sitting on the edge of the bed, watching him drink.

He continued to make a face as he sipped the brew. 'Actually,' he said, 'it's rather a good arsenic. A bit pretentious, of course, but in a friendly way.'

'Never mind your jokes,' she said, smiling. 'Just drink it.'

'It's going to my head.'

'That's where it's supposed to go.'

'You're sure it won't kill the patient with the bugs?' he asked, still sipping.

'You're taking too long,' she said impatiently. 'Drink it faster while it's hot.'

Obediently, he gulped the hot liquid, took another swallow, a bigger one, still another. When he had drained the glass he handed it to her.

'That's a good boy,' she said, looking at him with a bright, fixed, blue-eyed smile.

He saw her sitting close to him through an alcoholic mist, filmy, blurred, her eyes glittering and liquid. Waves of heat ran over him; his face was flushed; sweat beaded his forehead.

'I'm hot,' he said. He puffed his breath out of his open mouth making a whispering sound. 'Pure alcohol,' he said. 'Did you see it?'

She laughed. 'It's working,' she said. 'That's good.'

'It's working, all right.' He smiled a stiff, crooked smile out of a face that had lost all feeling, and he thought he saw the same smile on her blurred face a couple of feet away. 'I'm not drunk,' he said. 'I'm *very* drunk – pickled.'

'That makes two of us.'

Maudet's hand fell on her thigh. Through the thin material he could feel the warmth and firmness of her flesh. He squeezed gently. She did not push his hand away; she seemed to ignore it. But to his disappointment she rose, leaving his hand on the bed-cover, abandoned.

She put the glass she had been holding on the night table

and went to the door.

Frustrated but befuddled, Maudet wished he had the means to hold her back. 'Aren't you even going to say good night?' he asked.

She turned at the door and stared at him across the room with that same bright, fixed, blue-eyed smile.

'I'm going to turn out the light,' she announced.

He was so befuddled with drink that he did not realize what she meant. But as she reached for the switch, her robe slipped away. Then instantly, on the image of her naked body flashing into sight, the room went dark. The blood throbbed in his ears and he did not hear her cross the room. But in a moment he felt the covers on the other side of the bed being pulled back. Then she was upon him, her body warm and fragrant, her mouth moist and clinging. He soon understood what she meant when she said that she was incomplete without a man.

The morning bus for Landau passed through the village near the farm at about seven o'clock, and by six-thirty they had eaten a hasty breakfast and climbed into the horsedrawn cart, de Forge high up on the bench beside the woman, Maudet in the back. In her farm clothes the woman lost her singularity and once again took on a nondescript look; like the horse, she seemed to belong to the cart, the farm, the earth. Maudet had to find her eyes, her bright, light blue eyes, to connect this stranger with the warm-bellied woman in whose arms he had passed the night. He wondered if she had been avoiding him since they had awakened or if it was simply morning-after shyness. She had busied herself with chores while de Forge and he ate breakfast; then, in the flurry of getting on the road, there had been no time to say the slightest word. But her eyes avoided his and she seemed preoccupied.

De Forge and Maudet felt conspicuous in the cart and indeed, dressed as they were in city clothes, they looked totally out of place. It was therefore just as well that they left so early, that so few people were about and that the ride to the village was so brief. They attracted some curious stares as the cart clattered along in the light haze of the May morning, but nothing more.

When they arrived in the village they had little time, for

the bus came along minutes afterward. De Forge shook the woman's hand as soon as he climbed down to the road, and said good-bye very formally, thanking her for her hospitality. She turned to Maudet and led him a few steps aside.

'What is it?' he asked. 'You look troubled.'

'It will pass.' She smiled wanly. 'No hangover?'

'No hangover.'

'And the cold?'

'Your cure worked. You should give me the recipe.'

'I think it was a double cure,' she said.

They both laughed.

'My foot is much better too,' he said. 'I hardly limp at all. I don't know how to thank you for everything.'

'You mustn't,' she said. 'You were dragooned. I'll make a confession to you because I'll never see you again: from the beginning I knew how it would end.' She flushed. 'I never thought I could speak like this, so openly, to a man. Anyway, I'll never forget my thirty-ninth birthday. You were wonderful to me – and for me.'

'I'll never forget it either,' he said.

Out of the corner of her eyes she saw the bus approach. 'One other thing,' she said quickly. 'I know. That's what's been troubling me.'

'You know? What?'

'Who you are.'

Maudet felt the blood drain out of his face.

'It came to me this morning when I left you, suddenly,' she said. 'Suddenly everything was clear: why you were out in that terrible storm; why you were in such a hurry – not to get to Landau, but back to France; why you never said anything about what you do or even told me your name or asked for mine, knowing that if you did, I'd ask for yours. All that.'

'Listen –' he began, grasping her arm.

She drew away. 'You should never have done it,' she interrupted. 'Blow up a train. Kill innocent people, people you don't even know, women perhaps, children. It's murder. Senseless.'

A smile of nervous relief started to form on his lips, in his eyes. But then he was stuck. He was aware that behind him the bus had stopped, and he did not know how to convince her quickly that she was wrong without telling her the truth he was so relieved she did not know.

'It could have been anyone,' she said. 'It could have been me.'

He grasped her arms in both hands and said with all the conviction he could put into his voice, 'We couldn't blow up that train; we were on it.'

'If you had been on it, you would never have got off in that storm in the middle of the night.'

He could find no ready answer. Despite her distortion of the facts, he felt, as he hesitated awkwardly, that she was looking at him bare. He hastened to fill the leaden silence.

'As I told you –'

'I know,' she said wearily, and raised her eyes over his shoulder towards the bus. 'You had better hurry if you want to get safely back to France. It's leaving.'

He glanced back at the bus, then at her. Her expression was closed and pained. He picked up his valise. 'Your suspicions –'

'Yes, yes,' she cut in sceptically.

He bent and kissed her on both cheeks. Rocklike, she did not respond. He turned unhappily, hurried to the bus and got on. As it started moving, he looked out the window from his seat in the back beside de Forge. Standing stolidly in the road in her nondescript farm clothes, she watched the bus and Maudet in it move away, out of her life. She did not wave. Neither did he.

'Well,' de Forge said dryly, observing Maudet's gloomy expression, 'that was a touching farewell.'

'Not what you imagine. She thinks we blew up that train.'

De Forge's irony evaporated. 'Will she denounce us?'

Maudet shook his head. 'I don't think so. But it took the bloom off a red, red rose.'

De Forge was uneasy when they arrived in Landau, but no squads of S.S. were waiting to greet them when they got off the bus. At the station Maudet played the advance scout and only after he had checked that the enemy was not in sight did de Forge join him. There was a train for Strasbourg at eight o'clock, in another ten minutes.

'Our luck is changing,' de Forge said. 'For once we don't have to wait.'

Few passengers were on the train when they got on, but at Wissembourg, the border town between Germany and Alsace, it filled up. A fat Alsatian woman took the seat beside de Forge, and her husband sat opposite her. De Forge read the *Voelkischer Beobachter*, pretending to be so engrossed in it that he was aware of nothing else. The woman glanced at de Forge, then leaned far over towards her husband to caution him.

In a loud whisper and in heavily accented French she said, 'Hey, the type beside me, the one with the thick glasses, watch out for him, don't say a word. He's got the mug of a Boche, a real Prussian.'

De Forge quickly put up his newspaper to hide his smile. Later, when he lowered the newspaper, he saw the woman eye him distastefully and her husband look at him with suspicion. He stared back at them icily, meanly, partly out of some pixie quality that rarely came to the surface, partly to keep them on what he regarded as the good path of their prejudice. He was secretly amused when they turned away uncomfortably and angrily under his glare.

There was no police check on the train and, apart from the scornful parting look the Alsatian couple threw at de Forge, nobody took any note of him. The train rolled into Strasbourg at ten forty-five. But Reiber with his Hitler moustache was not there to meet them. It was too much to expect him to be at the station for every train from Germany, including one coming in from the north. None the less, Maudet was disappointed and felt lost.

'We can't wait around for him to show up,' de Forge said. 'The one place they're sure to watch is a railway station, and especially this one.'

'We have the address I told you about in Mulhouse,' Maudet said. 'That's where Reiber would probably have taken us anyway. We can do it on our own.'

Their luck held out in Strasbourg: a train for Mulhouse was leaving in only another half-hour. Maudet waited for the train in the station, reading the newspapers. The story about de Forge's escape was still on the front page. The German authorities were keeping it alive, picture and all. There was a great deal of repetition from the previous stories, but it

211

described with painstaking detail a variety of false leads across a large part of Germany, implying with dabs of evidence tied together with hopeful logic that the fleeing French general was running into a dead end. At the same time it appealed to all good citizens to be on the lookout for the fugitive and to alert the police about any individual who might prove to be the man in flight. It cited as well half a dozen arrests in various German towns, but unfortunately none of the men denounced had turned out to be de Forge.

De Forge went for a brief stroll outside the station. The sun had burned off the morning haze and the sky was a translucent blue. De Forge felt wonderful: he was back home. The Germans occupied this city, but the French inhabited it. Walking with the Monday morning crowd in the streets of the capital of Alsace and breathing the clean, washed air of May, de Forge enjoyed a springtime lilt and the lift of finding himself in friendly territory. He had crossed all of Germany, and the only barrier that now stood between him and his goal was the border. He began to think ahead – to the American proposal, the agreement he had concluded with President Roosevelt, the Herculean job of organizing, equipping and leading an army. The prospect galvanized him. He felt that this was what he had been born and brought along to this point in time to do.

De Forge returned to the station in a reflective mood. He bought a first-class ticket, Maudet a second-class ticket. The train for Mulhouse, coming from Berlin, rolled into the station on time. Maudet went ahead and climbed aboard. But just as de Forge was about to go down the steps from the station to the train platform he saw a squad of S.S. police making a spot check of the train. De Forge was standing opposite one of the first-class cars. He waited there until he saw the head of the squad come out of the far end of the car, then quickly crossed the platform, his spine tingling, climbed up the steps at the other end of the car, and sat down in the very first compartment. As he sat down his heart was pumping as if he had been racing and his breath came in gasps; he had no way to disguise his height and he was afraid that one of the S.S. men might have spotted him.

But nobody came to arrest him, and a few moments later

the train jerked to a start and began slowly rolling out of the station. Looking out the window, de Forge observed the sturdy, uniformed S.S. men on the platform below. Some of them looked back at him, their faces blank, as they would look at any unknown object. From the moving train, it gave de Forge a peculiar sense of security.

That did not last long. As the train rolled into Sélastat, de Forge saw another group of S.S. police waiting on the platform. Instinctively, he reached for his valise. He had no doubt that they were looking for him and was convinced, simply on the face of things, that they were now saturating the railway lines with search parties to flush him out. He saw the S.S. men board the train at the far end of his car, where the others had got off earlier in Strasbourg, and like a tracked animal sensing he was being brought to bay, de Forge took to heel, climbing down at his end of the car. Then, walking casually down the line, he saw the S.S. men start checking the identity papers of the passengers. The train began to move. In the next car Maudet was at the window of his compartment. His eyes widened in surprise as he saw de Forge on the platform. De Forge made a sign with his head towards the other end of the train, a sign indicating some danger there.

'The next train,' he called out.

Maudet read his lips and nodded that he understood. He swept by and the train quickly disappeared, leaving de Forge alone on the platform. He was not sorry; he had the feeling that neither his identity papers nor anything else could get him by a search party that was alert.

He checked on the next train to Mulhouse and was told that the one scheduled to leave at two o'clock had been cancelled; the only other one that day did not leave until eight-fifty and would bring him to Mulhouse at 11 P.M. His luck had turned again: there was no alternative to spending the day in Sélastat.

De Forge deposited his bag at the station and strode away as if he knew where he was going, groping all the while for a way to be inconspicuous in a small provincial town where he well knew that nothing was more conspicuous than a strange face. Not far from the station a poster on a kiosk solved his problem. It was a local holiday, and the event of the day was a soccer game. De Forge found his way to the sports field. By the time he arrived a large crowd was gathered and de Forge quickly got lost in it.

He enjoyed the spectacle. The two amateur teams were evenly matched, and what they lacked in skill they made up in youthful energy; the fans were just as entertaining, jumping up and down on the sidelines and urging their teams on with shouts, cheers and wisecracks. But at the end of the game sport bowed to propaganda before a captive audience. The sports leader gathered both teams around him for a political pep talk, haranguing them on all that the youth of Alsace owed to the glorious Fuehrer, while his girl friend, short and heavy, wearing two bejewelled shiny red hearts pierced by silver arrows on her ample breasts, gazed at him with adoring eyes.

During the speech, only minutes before the crowd would break up, de Forge had the uncomfortable feeling of someone staring at him. He looked around and saw to the left a short distance away across a solid bank of faces a large, fat man regarding him intently. De Forge quickly looked away. A few moments later he glanced over again. He was not mistaken: all the other faces were directed with more or less interest in the direction of the sports leader; the fat man was looking across them at him. He caught de Forge's eye just as de Forge turned away and seemed to be giving some sort of sign of recognition. De Forge did not turn back again to find out. As the sports leader finished speaking and the crowd rose to its feet with rather tepid applause, de Forge was already pushing his way to the right through the mass of people to get away. He looked over his shoulder once, over the heads of the crowd, and saw the fat man struggling to penetrate the packed mass of fans, straining to reach him. De Forge elbowed his way to the edge of the crowd and with the feeling that his massive pursuer was at his heels, quickly left the stadium and strode rapidly, half running, towards the centre of the town without a backward glance.

When de Forge slowed down to catch his breath and looked around, the fat man was nowhere in sight. It had been a bad scare. De Forge wanted to disappear until his train left. He passed a movie house, retraced his steps, bought a ticket and went in.

214

The screen was alive with screaming dive bombers, bursting shells, grimy Russian villains and fearless, blond German heroes. De Forge sank into the dark anonymity of the holiday audience. During the newsreel his picture suddenly filled the screen as the announcer's voice intoned a brief version of the caption material de Forge had read in the German papers under the same picture. He sat stoically through the entire show and left with a large group of others when the lights came up for the interval.

Outside the theatre de Forge turned to the left and ran straight into the arms of the massive fat man. De Forge was too startled to move; in any case, it was impossible to break and run. He was caught.

The fat man grasped de Forge's arms with his huge hands and said, 'You were too fast for me back there at the soccer game, but I have you now. I never saw anyone in such a hurry.'

De Forge looked into the fat man's eyes. They twinkled.

'I don't understand,' de Forge said.

'Don't you recognize me? Toto. Three years ago. Cannes. In August.'

'I wasn't there then,' de Forge said. 'I'm afraid – '

The fat man's smile faded. 'I could have sworn it was you. Excuse me.'

De Forge found a park and sat on a bench in the peace of evening to kill the last hour or so. He was hungry. His small stock of food was gone and he had not eaten since breakfast, but he would not risk going to a restaurant where the owner and other diners could study him for an hour. A couple of pieces of sugar remained and some schnapps. He dipped the sugar in the schnapps and sucked it. It gave him the feeling that he was less hungry.

The hour came at last to go to the station. This time no S.S. police were there. He found when he sat down and the train set off that he was exhausted; the strain on his nerves was telling.

At eleven o'clock the train arrived at Mulhouse. The station was practically empty. So far as de Forge could see, there was no Gestapo or S.S. on the lookout. But Maudet was not there either. De Forge did not wait for him. The only familiar face he saw in the station was his own – on a poster. It was the same picture as the one in the newspapers and in the newsreel, and it bore the same price – 200,000 reichsmarks – for delivery of the subject.

Although Maudet had given him Blanchard's Mulhouse address, de Forge decided not to go there until morning. He preferred the risk of a hotel to that of encountering a police patrol while wandering through deserted streets in search of the address so late at night. As a young officer, de Forge had once stayed at the Hotel de l'Europe, which was not far from the station. He walked to it, following a Wehrmacht major. The name of the hotel had been changed to the Europaeischer Hof. The major took a room that cost six marks. After a brief discussion with the night clerk, de Forge settled for a room that cost four marks.

Handing de Forge a registration blank, the clerk apologized. 'It's the regulations,' he said. 'These days we're obliged to follow them.'

The severest judge could not take exception to the substance of what he said, but the tone was one of complicity from one Frenchman who recognizes another.

De Forge filled out the blank under his false identity. The Gestapo would be reading it the next day, but de Forge knew it could not lead them very far.

'The police check the blanks around six in the morning,' the clerk said casually. 'If you wish, I can wake you a bit earlier.'

'As a matter of fact,' de Forge replied blandly, 'I have to catch an early train for Strasbourg. Please don't fail to wake me at five.'

De Forge tumbled into bed and slept deeply until he was awakened at five. He dressed hurriedly and, without bothering about breakfast, paid his bill and went out into the cool, early morning light. He walked towards the station. Mulhouse was still asleep, but he came across a young girl on her way to work and she directed him to the street he was searching for. It was on the other side of the station. De Forge now walked quickly, anxious to get there.

Shortly after six he stood before the house. He walked up the front steps and was about to ring the bell when the door opened and a short, stout, elderly woman came out holding a little prayer book in her hand and plainly on her way to early mass. She was startled to come upon a man on her doorstep. De Forge was immediately sure of her.

'Excuse me, madame,' he said, 'but I believe you were expecting someone here yesterday?'

'Why, I don't know,' she said doubtfully. 'I don't know anything about it.' She looked up at de Forge, considered him for a moment with her mild brown eyes, then suddenly made up her mind. 'Yes, I do,' she said. 'Come right in, quickly, quickly.'

When de Forge was in the hallway and the door was safely closed, she said, 'It's you, General. Oh, I'm so pleased. Come in. Sit down. Your friend is here. We were so worried about you. My son will be so relieved. I'll call them.'

De Forge felt light and joyful. 'But madame,' he said with a smile, 'you're going to miss mass.'

'It doesn't matter, General. God won't hold it against me.'

The woman bustled off to find Maudet and the others. De Forge settled back and sighed. He had a feeling of luxuriant homeyness in that simple, middle-class house. He felt he was no longer out in the cold, no longer alone. He had at last made physical contact with his base.

The worst is behind me, de Forge was saying to himself when Maudet and Blanchard rushed into the room smiling and calling out greetings. There's only the border to cross.

SIXTEEN

'A case of *force majeure*,' Blanchard said as he rubbed the long scar on his lean jaw. He was explaining why he had not met de Forge at the station. 'One of their damned patrols stopped me. If you had waited three minutes, I would have seen you; but it's just as well. Very dangerous to be out at night. I wouldn't let Maudet here go to look for you. My own papers, of course, are legitimate.'

They sat around the dining-room table drinking steaming

hot chocolate with huge slabs of thickly buttered country bread. De Forge was ravenous and ate with immense appetite as he listened to Blanchard, small and energetic, describe the situation, occasionally running a dainty hand through his thin, sandy hair. De Forge was impressed with the scope of the network's intelligence service. Blanchard's group had friends in the local administration who fed them information.

'They've used every conceivable means to broadcast word of your escape to pull you back again,' Blanchard said. 'The Fuehrer's personal order. He seems to have gone into a tantrum. All the police organizations, all the frontier stations, all the border guards and Customs officials are watching for you; and innumerable respectable gentlemen answering to your general description have been stopped, arrested, questioned and inconvenienced in various parts of Germany and Alsace, all to no avail.'

Blanchard's blue eyes twinkled and de Forge and Maudet smiled; but quickly coming to the point, Blanchard shifted to a more sober tone.

'As you know,' he said, 'we expected you three days ago, on Saturday morning. It's now Tuesday. We kept the line of escape through Chavannes into Occupied France organized and on the alert through the weekend. But now we've dismantled it, called everyone off. It's too late to get you through that way. The Gestapo and the Deuxième Bureau anticipated that your line of escape would be through Occupied France. The patrols are lined up along the border there like a guard of honour. Solid. It would be suicide to try it.'

'What do you propose?' de Forge asked.

Blanchard spread his hands in a gesture of impotence. 'What is there to propose? The best thing is to sit tight until things cool off.'

De Forge would not hear of it. 'They'll maintain the emergency situation at the border for weeks, for as long as they know I'm still on this side. That's what I'd do.'

'Isn't it better to remain safely hidden for a couple of weeks?' Maudet put in. 'By that time they'll be getting careless; it will be easier.'

De Forge pounced on him. 'It's better yet to find a way to get across now.' He turned to Blanchard. 'How about the

218

Swiss border?' he asked.

'They've increased patrols and vigilance on the Swiss side too,' Blanchard said. 'But it's not as bad there. If you're going to get through now, it would have to be through Switzerland.'

'I'm ready,' de Forge said.

Blanchard hesitated. 'You realize,' he said, 'that at this point we're improvising. It would have to be done with a different network through a different line of escape. No connection any more with our base in Lyons and Vichy. I don't know if they would approve, and it's their operation.'

'Do you care?'

'Not really.'

'I didn't think so. Bureaucracy, the chain of command – that's the last thing we have to worry about,' the general said. 'The point is to get through, and as fast as possible. Let's improvise.' But then de Forge had a second thought that checked his enthusiasm. 'How about security?' he asked.

'They're not my men,' Blanchard replied. 'But I wouldn't put you in their hands if I thought there was a security risk. It's a private network – a restaurateur, a priest, some local farmers and young men from the villages near the Swiss border. They have no connections with anyone. It's pure benevolence towards anyone who has to get away from the Boches. You see the type: the Boches kicked us in the ass – shit for the Boches.'

'Frenchmen,' de Forge intoned, 'one hundred per cent. . . . Let's go then for the Swiss border.'

Blanchard disappeared for several hours. Shortly before noon he bounced back into the house, his tiny figure brimming with energy.

'It's all set,' he said. 'They think they can get you across in a day or two. You'll hide at the priest's house until they organize it. Then they'll move you to a farm that's even closer to the border, right on it, in fact. Then over you go. It shouldn't be more than forty-eight hours from now.'

'Where's the priest's house?' de Forge asked.

'In a village not far from the border, about twenty kilometres from here.'

'When do we go?'

'I'm to deliver the package at two o'clock.'

'The package,' de Forge said, 'will be ready.'

The delivery point was not far away, in front of a factory in the rue du Port along a canal. Maudet had accomplished his mission, having delivered de Forge to Blanchard, who had the responsibility of getting him across the border; as relieved to have the hot general off his hands as he was pleased to have delivered him safely, Maudet was prepared to return to Lyons on the three o'clock train, the necessary documents in his pocket.

'Come along with us,' Blanchard suggested. 'As soon as we drop the general, we'll drive you to the station.'

They set out in an ancient Peugeot sedan. Blanchard sat in front beside the driver, his nineteen-year-old nephew, a sturdy, bright-eyed boy who owned the car and was proud and excited to take part in this enterprise of men. De Forge and Maudet sat in the back. They were concentrating on the problem of putting de Forge across the border, and none of them anticipated any trouble before getting him to it, certainly not in the short ride through Mulhouse at two o'clock in the afternoon. The day was fine and sunny, and the streets, with many people still at lunch, were uncrowded. The black Peugeot sedan moved smoothly through the centre of Mulhouse and headed towards the outer part of town in the direction of the canal alongside the rue du Port. De Forge looked about with great interest, but nobody in the street paid any attention to the old Peugeot. It was a routine ride, just as Blanchard had expected. Then the Peugeot turned into the street leading to the rue du Port and, too late to be able to turn back, Blanchard and his nephew at the wheel saw a police barrier blocking their way about fifty yards ahead.

A big Wehrmacht truck was parked sideways across half the street. Four or five uniformed S.S. men armed with rifles stood there stopping traffic, and three men in civilian clothes were checking the documents of everyone who was stopped. As the Peugeot with the four men in it approached the barrier, one of the S.S. men signalled it to stop. Blanchard's nephew, his face white, glanced to the right at his uncle, not knowing what to do, automatically slowing down. Blanchard stared ahead, his small figure crouched and tense. He had no time to think, only a second or two to make up his mind as the car rolled towards the roadblock.

'Go through them,' Blanchard whispered hoarsely to his nephew. 'Go through them. If they stop us, we're cooked.'

The Peugeot approached the group of uniformed men, heading straight towards the one flagging them down. It slowed as it approached, the men in uniform, with their rifles, looking more imposing as the car drew nearer. And yet the S.S. men were relaxed. They were on a routine detail; nothing ever happened. Then it did.

'Step on it!' Blanchard hissed in the car. An instant afterward, his voice hoarse and louder, he repeated, 'Step on it.'

The car, in low gear, was only a few feet from the S.S. men. Suddenly, with a whine of the motor, it accelerated. The car swerved away from the truck blocking the street. At the same time the S.S. men, startled and swearing, leaped out of the way. The right wheels of the car, one after the other, bounced up on the kerb. One of the men in civilian clothes, unable to step aside fast enough, grabbed on to the mudguard of the accelerating car. The Peugeot quickly gathered speed, its motor screaming. It slanted to the left, half in the gutter, half on the pavement, shooting forward, the man still clinging to the mudguard. Then, as the car turned left back into the street and the right wheels came down with two bumps, one after the other, the man fell off.

The Peugeot screamed forward, the noise from its motor piercing the air, shrieking, as the car strained for more power, forward faster and faster, screeching fearsomely, inconceivably persisting in its ever rising scream beyond physical resistance as if it would burst, with Blanchard now shouting at his nephew, 'Go! Go! Faster! Faster!' Then he turned back, shouting fiercely at de Forge and Maudet. 'Down! Down!' They ducked. Rifle shots cracked out behind them and the terrifying whistling whine of bullets whipped past them, cutting through the relentless scream of the motor. Bullets thumped into the body of the car. Only seconds passed, but each second seemed to hang motionless, unending, through the high metallic screech of the motor, the crack of rifles, the whistle of bullets, the movement of the car lumberingly slow though accelerating, agonizingly stationary in its accelerating speed, with every man in it trying to scrunch himself into the tiniest untouchable particle against the terrifying noise and the deadly projectiles whistling around him. Suddenly, as their bodies told them they would never survive that hail of fire, the car turned hard to the left on squealing rubber and skidded around a corner.

People scattered, frightened and furious, turning and cursing as the Peugeot sped away. It turned right at the next corner, then left. De Forge and Maudet were holding on to the backs of the front seats. The car swerved wildly, passing cyclists and cars, barely missing others that crossed in front of it, motorists and cyclists shouting and shaking their fists. Nobody in the car spoke. Blanchard's nephew was hunched over the wheel, speeding into the centre of the town. Maudet's face was drained; de Forge was grim.

'Where are you going?' de Forge asked.

No answer. The boy did not seem to hear. De Forge had the impression that he was driving automatically, not knowing where he was going, too shaken to have his wits about him. It was Blanchard's job to get them out of this mess. Suddenly de Forge was aware that lively little Blanchard had not said a word since they had cut out of range of the S.S. rifle fire.

'My uncle,' the boy said at that moment. 'He's been hit.'

Blanchard was sitting back in his seat, leaning against the door. De Forge bent forward in the speeding car and gently took Blanchard's shoulder in his hand. There was no response. He bent farther forward and looked into Blanchard's open, empty blue eyes, then glanced down and saw the blood, profuse, richly red in the sun, alive, drenching Blanchard's lap.

'He's dead,' de Forge said flatly. Almost in the same breath he said, 'We've got to abandon the car,' adding silently, *and the body.* 'You've got to think of where we can go.'

It was not very far. They were at full throttle in the rue de Strasbourg, a broad street running towards the downtown area. A woman crossing the street froze when she saw the Peugeot racing down upon her. The boy turned the wheel sharply to avoid her, stepping on the brake at the same time. The car skidded, tyres squealing against asphalt. A small truck darted out of a side street from the left and the boy swung the Peugeot back to the right. He lost control. The car swung completely around, skidding, slowing, turning on itself but remaining upright. It crashed to a stop against a metal pole with a sickening smash of metal, the radiator crushed into the motor. The motor died. Blanchard was slightly turned to the left, seeming to observe his nephew, who was frantically trying to bring the motor back to life. De Forge and Maudet bounced out of the car from each of the back doors. Out of nowhere a crowd began to gather.

'Come on, let's go!' de Forge cried.

'My uncle,' the boy moaned, still working frantically at the ignition.

'Leave it, come along!' Maudet hurled at him.

The boy looked up at them, his face a torment. Blanchard looked on with his vacant, staring blue eyes, strangely silent.

'Come on,' de Forge commanded. 'He's dead. You can't help him any more. Hurry or we'll get it too.'

The boy swung out of the car. A crowd had already gathered around it, everybody chattering; but nobody had yet noticed that the figure in the front seat was a corpse. De Forge and Maudet were already moving away; the boy followed them. People in the crowd stared at them asking what had happened.

'We're going to find a cop,' de Forge muttered.

Turning the first corner, hurrying away, they ran head-on into one. The cop, who had heard the commotion, looked at them suspiciously without recognizing de Forge.

'What's going on?' he asked in German.

'An accident,' de Forge said. 'You ought to get there quickly. A man's been hurt – badly.'

'He's just back there,' Maudet added. 'Looks urgent.'

The cop thanked them and ran towards the Peugeot. De Forge and Maudet exchanged a look of relief, and with Blanchard's nephew behind them began running too – in the opposite direction. As he fled, Maudet kept seeing Blanchard inert and blank-eyed in the front seat of the Peugeot and imagining himself as the corpse; he felt both guilt and elation to be alive. Blanchard's nephew was in shock; he followed the others like an automaton. The older men would have liked to be gentle with him, but they simply hurried him along as he dragged behind; they had to hurry, had to think of survival; there was no time for compassion.

'We have to get off the street,' de Forge said, still striding briskly away from the accident though they were now reasonably sure they weren't being followed. He turned to the boy. 'Can you take us somewhere safe? Anywhere.'

The boy shook his head.

'Don't you know any of your uncle's friends?'

'My uncle lives on the other side, in the free zone. He just visits.'

'Don't you know any of the people he sees here?'

The boy shook his head again, looking at de Forge with dead eyes. 'Today was the beginning for me. He said it would be a baptism without fire or water.'

De Forge and Maudet exchanged a worried glance. It was worse than they had thought. All the while they strode quickly away from the accident. The street they turned into looked familiar to Maudet. Then he remembered.

'I can get us off the street,' he said. 'I know someone who lives near here.'

De Forge's eyes lighted up. 'Good,' he said. 'We'll go there.' Then he added, 'We ought to split up. They're looking for three of us by now.' He turned to the boy. 'There's no point in our staying together and every reason to separate,' he said as gently as he could. 'Do you have a place to go?'

'Home,' the boy said in a dead voice.

'Any place but there,' de Forge said sharply. 'They'll be looking for you there. Through your car, the licence plate. They could be there already.'

The boy seemed absorbed with something else. He did not react, did not seem to hear de Forge.

'Do you understand?'

'Yes, I understand.'

'You have a friend, don't you? . . . Good. Go to him and then get out of Mulhouse as fast as you can. Go to the free zone. Don't write to your parents; get word to them about yourself through friends.'

De Forge would have liked to say more, to guide the boy, coach him. But there was no time. They had to break off. 'Courage,' de Forge said, patting the boy on the shoulder.

'Just get away and keep your wits about you.'

The boy had tears in his eyes.

'Courage,' Maudet said, shaking his hand. 'It couldn't be helped; it might have been you or me.'

Maudet wanted to tell him not to feel guilty, that the risks had been equal but that his uncle had been the unlucky one. But Maudet, usually so articulate, could find no words, not then, not quickly, not in the face of the boy's emotion. He had a sour feeling of dissatisfaction as the boy left them and he and de Forge turned towards Monique's apartment.

'Where are we going?' de Forge asked.

Maudet told him. De Forge said nothing but did not seem happy about it. Maudet didn't blame him; he didn't feel very happy about it either. There was nothing to say; they had no choice. Maudet had no idea how Monique would receive them – or whether she would receive them at all. He felt it best to warn de Forge and told him.

'When there's only one thing to do,' de Forge growled, 'no matter how bad it is, the thing to do is to do it.'

Maudet thought he heard the voice of an old battlefield commander who more than once had been forced to do what he could not avoid, knowing the cost would be prohibitive. He suddenly had a surge of deep and futile regret for Blanchard, overwhelmed by human frailty and the finality of death. It was so stupid, so absurd. A bit of flying lead and Blanchard was erased. Like a rabbit or a bird under a hunter's gun – or an insect under heel. And in one way or another it would happen to them all. He felt vulnerable, alone; nobody could do anything for him.

They walked the rest of the way in silence. When they got to the building they went in quickly, stepping around two bicycles in the hallway. As they passed the concierge's loge, the concierge glanced up from her dishes but did not challenge them. Maudet looked at his watch. It was two twenty-five. Only half an hour had passed since they had burst through the German roadblock. Life, Maudet thought, was not duration but intensity. But one of them was dead – forever.

They climbed the stairs. Maudet knocked. The same sound as before: a woman's heels clicking towards the door. It opened. The expression of surprise again on Monique's handsome face. It was like a film Maudet was seeing for the second time. Nothing surprised him. He pushed past her, knowing that this time she would not welcome or want him. De Forge followed. She knew instantly who he was. The door had hardly closed when she was demanding that they leave.

SEVENTEEN

'Get out, get out!' Monique cried, following them helplessly into the living room, furious that she had not seen de Forge before they barged in, and slammed the door in their faces. 'You can't stay here.'

'We can't leave,' Maudet said firmly. 'We have nowhere else to go.'

The colour rose in Monique's pale cheeks; she was trembling, undone. 'You don't expect to stay here, the two of you, do you?' Disbelief, incredulity was in her voice, and an undercurrent of panic.

Maudet shrugged. 'For the moment we're groping,' he said candidly. 'It's not that we want to stay; we have no alternative.'

Her fury burst over her fear. 'I knew it was you, I knew it,' she cried. 'The minute I heard it on the radio, the minute I read about it in the papers. But I never thought you'd bring him here. How could you do it?'

'We had no choice,' Maudet said calmly.

'Throwing your own life away is your affair, but how could you bring me into it?'

Her voice was shrill, almost out of control, and Maudet did not know how to quiet her except by setting an example of placidity. But it wasn't working: Monique kept turning nervously about the room on the razor edge of hysteria. De Forge went off to one side away from them. He stood near the window, apart from the scene, listening to what they said, but it was as if he were absent. The problem was Maudet's; it was up to him to solve it, if he could. And if he couldn't? Well, there would be time to see what they

226

could do then.

'You must go somewhere else, you must,' Monique was saying. 'I have errands to do. There will be people here this evening. You must go now, immediately.'

'You can call them off,' Maudet said.

'I won't call them off,' she snapped. Suddenly, instead of anger, her eyes were flashing tears. 'Why do you do this to me? I have nothing to do with politics. I don't want to be involved. You know what they'll do to me if they find out that you were here with him, and I'll have you to thank.'

She was trembling again, shaking with fear and frustration.

'You've got to understand,' Maudet said, 'that we don't want to stay here either, but we can't just walk the streets. They'd pick us up.'

'That has nothing to do with me,' she screamed, tipping over the edge of hysteria. 'You've got to get out now. NOW! NOW! NOW!'

Maudet and de Forge glanced at each other wordlessly. She glared at them, her eyes darting from one to the other, quivering, beyond reason, searching in desperation, like a trapped beast, for a way out.

'All right,' she said, her voice lower but harsh and unnatural, 'if you're going to stay, I'll leave.' She started for the door.

Maudet blocked her way. She tried to push past him. He thrust her back. 'Don't be a damned fool,' he said.

She stood in front of Maudet, trembling, clenching and unclenching her little fists, her eyes wide and staring and brilliant, her breath coming in short gasps. It was like watching a live bomb gathering energy to explode.

'I'll scream,' she said finally, menacingly. 'I'll scream.'

'Don't be a damned fool,' Maudet repeated, but this time in a cajoling tone.

She opened her mouth and closed her eyes and let out a piercing scream. Maudet pounced on her, clapping his hand over her mouth and muffling the ear-splitting scream. She bit his hand hard and he jumped back, swearing in pain. Panting and screaming, Monique ran towards the window. But this time de Forge blocked the way. She raised her fists and hammered them on his chest, sobbing and shouting, 'Let me past, let me past.' As he reached down to pin her hand, she

slipped by him and in one step was at the window. De Forge
grabbed her arm and jerked her back, swinging her around
with a sweep of his left hand. She was still turning, coming
towards him, with her mouth open in another animal scream
when he slapped her just once, very hard, with his right
hand, so hard that she staggered back to the left towards the
window. Her voice was cut dead in midscream; she made a
whispering, sobbing sound as she sucked in her breath with a
gasp, raising her hand at the same time to her cheek. The
white skin was already inflamed with striped marks from the
impact of de Forge's thick fingers. She turned away, whimper-
ing, and put her hands to her head. With her back to them,
she crouched in her misery and her sobs became louder,
painful to hear.

Maudet was furious – not least with de Forge for pre-
empting his function. Ignoring de Forge, he led Monique to the
divan and sat her down, saying, 'Are you going to be sensible now?'

She shook her head, sobbing. 'I want you to go, I want you
to go.' She could not stop repeating it. 'I want you to go.
I want you to go.'

De Forge was at the window looking out, worried. 'Do you
suppose anyone heard her scream?' he asked.

'We'll know soon enough,' Maudet said in a tight, angry
voice.

De Forge loomed over Monique. 'If anyone comes to the
door,' he growled, 'you're to say it was nothing, just a silly
scare. It will keep you out of trouble as well as us.'

She looked at him defiantly through her tears, but at the
same time she cringed. She was afraid of him, like a little
girl under the authority of a severe father. It made Maudet
angrier.

'I'll say what I please,' she sniffled.

'He'll just go back to prison,' Maudet said, 'but you'll
hang like me – and I'll give them the evidence to hang you
with.'

She thought as much of Gestapo justice as he did, and her
eyes filled with tears of terror and self-pity. They expected a
knock on the door, expected a horde of neighbours to come
pounding on it, calling out for an explanation of those terrible

screams, ready to break down the door to lend aid and succour against the horror that had caused them. But nobody came. Still they waited, hovering over Monique, not knowing what she would do, fearing the worst. Then, suddenly overwhelmed by what was happening to her, Monique broke. She began thrashing about against Maudet, who was beside her on the divan, and burst into a fit of uncontrollably hysterical weeping. Maudet tried to take her in his arms to comfort her; she would not have it. He shook her; she sobbed and wept even harder. He slapped her; instead of quieting her, it brought on a paroxysm. She heaved about, out of her senses, with such strength that Maudet had trouble holding her down. He was afraid that she would collapse in convulsions.

De Forge observed them with a sombre eye and the dark realization that he had been led into a dead end. Worse, he faced a vicious dilemma: he could not stay, but he had nowhere to go. And the longer they stalled, the more likely they were to be victims of events they could not foresee. First, the girl, that little bundle of concentrated disaster, had to be got out of the way. De Forge slipped into the bedroom, rummaged in a bureau drawer, and came back to the living room with several pairs of stocking in his hands. Monique was still struggling sporadically and moaning but had visibly weakened, the peak of her fit past.

'Hold her hands together behind her,' de Forge commanded. 'This will quiet her down.'

Monique made one last effort, wriggling and trying to bite Maudet; then, as suddenly as the fit had come on, the fight went out of her. De Forge quickly and expertly tied her up with the stockings, knees together, ankles to hands behind her back. She lay helpless on the divan, trussed like a fowl for roasting.

'If you keep on making those noises,' de Forge said, shaking a stocking in her face, 'I'm going to gag you. You won't like it.'

She shut up, looking at him with fear and hatred, then turned away from his hard stare.

De Forge led Maudet to the far end of the room. 'We're up a blind alley,' de Forge said so softly that Monique could not hear him. 'We've got to get out of here.'

'But where? How?' Maudet whispered.

'I don't know, but we've got to move. Coming here has been a terrible mistake. We would have done better to have started walking out into the open country towards the border.'

'Without knowing where it is or how to get there?'

'We're not getting anywhere here.'

'We're not getting into the Gestapo's arms either.'

'That remains to be seen,' de Forge said, his voice still very low. 'We don't have any chance at all here.'

'It's better than throwing ourselves at them.'

'With this girl here that's just what we're doing. We're going to have to do something about her – she's in the way.'

The phrase rang in Maudet's mind like an echo; then he remembered the boy, the young German noncom in the train. 'What do you suggest we do?' he asked indignantly. 'Kill her?'

'It's an idea you ought to get used to,' de Forge said. 'We may have to.'

The discussion became heated, but their voices remained low, too low for Monique to understand though she strained to catch their words. While they were arguing she had time to think. It was an exercise she had not indulged in since they had crashed into her apartment. She came to some quick, panicky decisions.

'Untie me,' she called out. 'I hurt all over.'

They looked around at her doubtfully.

'Untie me,' she repeated. 'I'm all right now; I won't make any trouble. . . . I have an idea for you.'

Maudet went over to the divan; de Forge followed standing behind him. 'What kind of an idea?' Maudet asked.

Lying trussed up on her side, she looked up at him. 'If I give you a place to go, will you leave right away?'

'Of course,' Maudet said. 'Where?'

'Untie me.'

Maudet turned and looked at de Forge, who shrugged.

'Now behave yourself,' Maudet said, and untied her.

She rubbed her wrists, stretched her arms, massaged her ankles and took a few paces around the room to get her blood circulating again. When she sat down in a corner of the divan and faced them she was nervous and trembled as if she had caught a chill.

'All right,' de Forge said. 'What's this place of yours?'

'How long will you stay there?'

'We haven't even got there yet,' de Forge said.

'Come on, Monique,' Maudet said. 'You know we'll move on as fast as we can.'

'Only overnight,' she said. 'No more.' She was still shivering.

'All right, only overnight,' Maudet agreed.

'I didn't send you,' she said. 'You just came on the place by chance.'

'It goes without saying,' de Forge said impatiently.

'It doesn't at all go without saying,' Monique snapped.

'You can depend on us,' Maudet said placatingly. 'If you play straight, so will we. It's obvious.'

She took a deep breath. 'It's a chalet not far from the border,' she said, 'a hut, nothing much, a couple of kilometres from the frontier. Nobody's in it now. It's a lot closer to where you want to go than you are now.'

'Why didn't you tell us about it in the first place?' Maudet asked.

She looked at him with impenetrable eyes and said nothing.

'Who does it belong to?' de Forge asked.

'My friend,' Monique said, and now she looked at Maudet boldly, aggressively.

'So that's it,' Maudet said. A pang of jealousy hit him like a fist in the heart.

'What do you expect me to do,' she said defiantly, 'retire to a convent?'

De Forge cut in. 'Will your friend be going there in the next day or two?'

'Not until the weekend,' Monique said. 'We ride out on our bicycles on Friday. But remember you promised you would only stay overnight.'

'How far away is it?'

'Twenty-five kilometres. That's the problem. I don't know how you'll get there.'

'Isn't there a bus?' de Forge asked.

231

She shook her head. 'Not any more today.'

'We can get out there the way you do,' Maudet said. 'On bicycles.'

'The ones downstairs in the hall,' de Forge said.

'No, you don't,' she objected. 'They're mine and my friend's. What will I say when he comes here tonight?'

'That they've been stolen,' de Forge said.

She thought about it. 'What if they pick you up with the bikes?'

'We stole them,' Maudet said. 'It can't involve you.'

'And if they pick you up in the chalet of the owner of one of the bicycles?'

'We'll say we walked there, hitched a ride from Mulhouse. But are there so many police patrols on the road and around the chalet?'

'We've never been stopped,' Monique said. 'But neither of us is a fleeing general at the centre of the biggest manhunt this region has ever known.'

Maudet turned to de Forge. 'What do you think?'

De Forge's answer was to ask Monique how to get to the chalet. She told them where it was and gave them exact directions.

'The key to the back door is under the mat,' she said. 'I don't think anyone will stop you on the way. But if anyone does, tell them you're going to the Arnaud farm for provisions – butter, eggs, that kind of thing. The farm is beyond the chalet. Old man Arnaud may be helpful too, if you need any help. But better yet is the pharmacist in the village. He knows everybody and everything, and he hates the Germans. His name is Walmer.'

'How about your friend?' de Forge asked. 'You're not going to tell him about this, I hope.'

'Not if I can help it.'

'Can you?' Maudet asked.

'I don't know.'

'It would be a lot better if you didn't,' de Forge warned.

'I can't promise,' she said. 'It won't be easy if he begins to ask questions.'

'Is he on our side or theirs?' Maudet asked.

'He's not on their side,' she said sharply, 'but he's even less on yours.'

'A patriot,' Maudet said sarcastically. 'Long live France, but let's not do anything about it.'

De Forge rode over his words. 'Then you mustn't tell him. It will be better for all of us, especially for you.'

'I'll try,' she said. 'He can be awfully insistent, but I'll try.'

She led them to the door. 'Don't forget,' she said. 'You only stay overnight, then you leave.'

They nodded their agreement.

'You'd better go ahead of me,' she said. 'The bikes are locked together. I'll roll them out for you.'

'And the concierge?' de Forge asked.

'I'll find some story for her. That's easy. She likes me.'

The door was open when Maudet turned to Monique with resentment and regret. His face betrayed him, but the naked hurt did not move her. She regarded him coldly, ungiving. He caught himself, pride overriding weakness.

'Thanks anyway,' he said.

The *anyway* with its taste of bitterness and contempt wounded her and she struck back. 'Don't thank me,' she said. 'I'm not helping you; I'm getting rid of you.'

He started to answer hotly, but de Forge put a hand on his arm and interrupted sternly. 'We don't have time for this. We must go – right away.'

Maudet turned abruptly, and de Forge and Monique followed him down the stairs. The concierge did not seem to notice them; in any case, she said nothing, turning her back in her loge. Maudet and de Forge waited in the street. It took Monique only a moment to release the gadget locking the bikes together and roll them into the street. They took the bikes from her in one motion and mounted.

Just before pushing off de Forge turned to Monique, standing in the doorway. 'I wouldn't get cute if I were you,' he said. 'So far as the Gestapo is concerned, you *have* helped me, however "pure" your reasons may be. And if I get caught because of anything you say or do, I'll make sure that from one side or the other you'll regret it for the short time you'll have to live.'

As de Forge rode away he was grimly pleased by the look

on Monique's face. The fear he had thrust into her gave her a stake in their safety – at least for a while. 'If she prays,' de Forge said to himself, 'she'll pray for us tonight.'

Maudet pedalled in the lead with de Forge about one hundred yards behind him. With luck, they felt, they could get by. They were fairly sure the police had no description of them since they had ducked out of sight when the Peugeot broke through the roadblock, and they doubted that in the confusion when the car smashed up anyone had observed them carefully and reported their observations to the authorities. For what it was worth, Maudet took a beret out of the pocket of his trench coat and put it on. De Forge wore his fedora flat on his head. Pedalling along straight-backed in his blue coat, he had an air of incongruous dignity – old France on a bicycle. He was not unaware of the bizarre effect, nor was he wrong in thinking his just-out-of-mothballs look a perfect camouflage.

De Forge noticed one or two people smile as they saw him go by. Some police cars swept past, and he followed Maudet in a detour around a knot of people where the police apparently were making a spot check of passersby. Towards the edge of town a policeman on a corner watched him approach, and de Forge's heart dipped at the prospect of his questions; he was ready to draw out the false driver's licence Maudet had brought him as an identity paper, but when he went by the policeman merely smiled and even put his hand to his helmet, perhaps as his personal tribute to a fragrant survival of the past.

Soon afterward they hit the open road. It stretched endlessly before them, a thin strip of black macadam rising and falling, gently turning between green meadows and cultivated fields. From time to time they pedalled out of the warm May sun into the shade of trees lining the road for stretches of a few hundred yards. There was little traffic in either direction; more often than cars, other cyclists went by. Farmers worked the fields. The villages they went through seemed to be deserted. It was very peaceful.

By the halfway point Maudet had a lead of about half a mile. It was just as well; that way no one could assume they were together. They pedalled on under the huge blue sky, fat white clouds floating by under a mild spring breeze. At times, peasant women in the fields by the road straightened up, their hands on the backs of their hips, and watched them go past. In the villages children sometimes stopped their play and waved to them. It was more like an outing than flight.

They were lucky. There were no roadblocks, no police checks. Nobody challenged them. Monique's directions had been simple and precise. Following them, they arrived at the chalet in the evening before nightfall without having to ask anyone their way. They found the modest wooden construction Monique had described on a rise half a mile along a country road off the main highway and on the edge of a thickly wooded area. It was completely isolated; no other house was in sight. Maudet found the key to the back door under the mat. They trudged wearily through the kitchen and in the living room sank exhausted from the long bicycle ride into deep armchairs. For a minute or so they were quite content to rest there without saying a word.

'Are you as hungry as I am?' Maudet asked at last.

'I could eat,' de Forge said.

In the kitchen Maudet found a small stock of canned food, a package of biscuits and some bottles of wine. He opened a bottle and large cans of sardines and tuna fish and brought it all into the living room on a tray, and they ate as if no food could have been better than that simple fare. When they finished it was almost dark, but they sat in the gathering gloom, having decided, despite the isolation of the chalet and the improbability of anyone passing by, not to risk putting on a light.

They spoke quietly in the darkness, spoke of many things; de Forge did most of the talking in a long, flowing monologue, urged along occasionally by a word from Maudet. He spoke of Blanchard with a depth of feeling and an eloquence that amazed Maudet, who at the same time sensed de Forge's need to talk in this first respite they had had, safe, sheltered and for a few hours at least not on the move, an interlude in their flight.

De Forge spoke of the many other 'comrades-in-arms' who had fallen by his side, comrades he had survived a quarter of a century ago but never forgotten and never ceased to

235

mourn. He spoke of the guilt that had infected him at surviving the fallen, of the sense of triumph at emerging whole being diluted by the feeling that with each comrade he had left something of himself behind, that a part of himself had died. As de Forge spoke of his idea of France, of what he hoped to do, of Europe and of Germany within the European community, 'the beast slaughtered so that the angel could fly (after all, they produced Beethoven, Goethe and Kant),' Maudet realized that his feelings towards de Forge had changed. What they had been through together had eroded the rough, sharp edges of conflict; it was smoothed over. They, too, were comrades-in-arms. This long and, for Maudet, exquisite moment of intimacy when, for the first time since their meeting on the country road, de Forge was completely relaxed and spoke to him with simplicity and from the heart crystallized Maudet's feeling towards him. He became aware that something of de Forge had rubbed off on him, that he had absorbed some part of de Forge and that a part of de Forge was forever more a part of himself. So, in closeness and warmth and in a kind of comradeship, among the shadows of the room and then in the darkness of the enveloping night, de Forge communicated himself to Maudet, entering into him like a wave of the sea into sand.

They did not speak of practical matters, and then almost reluctantly, until they were settling down for the night, de Forge in the big double bed in the bedroom, Maudet on a cot. 'We've come far, but there's still the border,' Maudet said. 'Tomorrow's the day.'

'The last barrier, the most dangerous time.' De Forge's low-pitched voice was assured. 'It's not the way any of us foresaw it. We're out in the open. And without support. To-night we can sleep soundly, but tomorrow not even this house will be safe. By this time your friend will have spoken to her friend – or at least we have to assume she has. He can't denounce us without first coming here and discovering us or he will compromise her. Unfortunately, we have to assume the worst, that however she may feel about it, he will impose his will – and the way she spoke indicated he usually does – that he will be tempted by the reward, will find an excuse and a way of getting here tomorrow and will call the police.'

Maudet sighed unhappily. 'We have to be out of here in the morning,' he said.

'And I have to be across the frontier by tomorrow night.'

It was evident and for Maudet scary. Neither of them had to say that it would be up to Maudet to find the frontier and a way to get across; de Forge would have to disappear into the landscape, not be seen.

'I couldn't have gotten this far without you,' de Forge said. 'I'm very grateful.'

'I simply did my job.'

'You did it very well. If I get across, I'll owe it to you. I want you to know how I feel about it, how deeply I feel about it.'

For a while they were silent.

'And you?' de Forge asked later. 'There's no point to your going over with me.'

'I'll turn around and take the train like everyone else.'

'You'll know how to reach me.'

'Of course.'

'There will be much to do,' de Forge said. 'We will need you. . . . There will be much to do tomorrow too. We must sleep.' He paused. 'It won't be easy and we're going to have to be lucky. The last step, like the first, is almost always the hardest.'

De Forge fell asleep immediately, but Maudet lay awake a long time. He did not know how he was going to manage that last step, but he knew he would manage it. He had to. As he lay there with his eyes wide open in the dark, he also knew why. It was because de Forge demanded it of him, and de Forge had a texture, an imperative of being he could not deny. Yet only a few days ago – was it only a few days ago? – de Forge had repelled him. But then, only a few days ago his crutch had been the plan without which he had felt he could not move; and here he was improvising from moment to moment, from crisis to crisis as if uncertainty had always been his way of life.

He saw that their roles had been reversed, that though he had come along as de Forge's guide, de Forge had guided him all the way – guided him, blooded him, formed him. All this Maudet became aware of as he lay sleepless in the dark room.

Small wonder that his attitude towards de Forge had changed. He realized that de Forge was a man who took knowing, an uncompromising man of old-fashioned integrity whose inner complexities and animal tenderness were deeply hidden under a seemingly impenetrable ramrod exterior. Maudet would never have suspected he could feel any sympathy for such a man; but now he had lived with him and fought with him and come to know him; and before falling asleep at last, he knew that the emotion he felt for de Forge was more than affection and something approaching what people call love. It vaguely troubled him that he could not explain the depth of his feeling, yet the most obvious fact of all, as so often happens, never occurred to him: he had wedded his life to de Forge's; his reason for being had become the success of the mission.

They woke up early to a superb spring morning, the sky cloudless and vaporous blue. It was one of those mornings, the air washed clean, when the heart could burst at the joy the earth seemed to offer.

'The weather is with us,' de Forge said. 'It's a good sign.'

He would have said the same thing had it been pouring, and with better reason; fewer people would have been about to see him and visibility at the border would have been lessened. But morale was important on this day of all days, and at least it would be comfortable being out of doors.

Their muscles hurt from the long bicycle ride the previous day, but they were both so preoccupied with their thoughts that neither mentioned it. They washed quickly and ate a Spartan breakfast of dry biscuits washed down with tap water.

'I'm going to have to play it strong, take chances,' Maudet said. 'There's no choice. If I fall on the wrong type, it's curtains.'

De Forge nodded. 'You won't,' he said. 'Use your judgment. We're in Alsace, in France not in Germany. It will work. There's the pharmacist, Walmer, and the farmer, Arnaud. You'll work something out. Try to get a guide if you can, but for yourself alone, of course; just leave me out until I have to turn up.'

De Forge's calm confidence amazed Maudet, who had awakened feeling rather nervous and lost; but as de Forge had intended, his mood was contagious; courage and resolution flowed from the older to the younger man.

They locked the house and put the key back under the mat after rolling the bicycles into the kitchen. 'We'll walk,' de Forge had said. 'If that bastard shows up, let's not give him an excuse to put the police on us as bicycle thieves.' Then they walked off into the sparkling May morning. But they had not gone very far when de Forge stopped near a wooded area off the dirt road that led to the chalet.

'I'll wait for you here,' he said. 'Take your time, but don't be too long.'

He turned, walked off the road and disappeared among the trees. Nobody, Maudet thought, will find him there. Then, under the rising sun and warmth of the day, he strode towards the village. It was only a short distance away around a bend of the paved road, a longish stretch of attached stone buildings with low-slanting tile roofs and in the midst of them, around a square, some run-down shops. The pharmacy stood proudly in the middle of the square next to a grocery store. It was closed. Maudet looked at his watch. Eight-twenty. He crossed the square to a stationery store that was open and bought a newspaper, then walked through the village, which seemed deserted except for a few preschool children, and into the open country. Not far outside the village Maudet turned off the road into a field. He sat leaning against a small, shady tree that hid him more or less from passersby on the road and opened the newspaper.

The war news – German advances on the Russian front, the sinking of an Allied convoy in the Atlantic, dogfights over the Channel, a naval battle in the Pacific, the impregnability of Fortress Europa – took second place to the big local story of the day: the Peugeot sedan with its mysterious passengers that had broken through a police barrage, leaving one dead in the fusillade. The story identified Blanchard as a bandit and terrorist and described with a mixture of fact and fancy the suitcases left behind (de Forge's and Maudet's) filled with revolutionary documents and arms and the 'four' men who had abandoned the car and their dead accomplice; despite the multitude of police barriers thrown up immediately after-ward in the centre of Mulhouse, none of the fugitives had been caught, but the police were pursuing a variety of leads. The story gave no indication that the authorities had made any connection between the Peugeot incident and de Forge. Maudet's greatest relief was that Blanchard's nephew had got away.

There was a smaller story about de Forge at the bottom of the front page. It said that he was now probably in Alsace despite a variety of false reports of his presence elsewhere in Germany, and added that the frontier was now a solid wall blocking his escape; the article ended with a direct appeal to all loyal citizens to be on the lookout for de Forge and to notify the police immediately of his whereabouts. They're whistling in the dark, Maudet said to himself. But he did not like the line about the frontier being a solid wall.

He left the newspaper in the field and returned, without hurrying, to the village. It was eight forty-five. The pharmacy was open. Maudet walked in. As the door closed, the bell attached to it clanged behind him. No customers. Only the pharmacist, short and roly-poly in his not very fresh white jacket behind the counter among his bottles and the anti-septic pharmacy smell. The pharmacist looked questioningly at Maudet above his ample double chin, his moist, thick lips, bristly moustache, and ruddy cheeks, through bright, malicious eyes that seemed amplified by the thick lenses of his glasses. He looked like a man who sucked pleasure out of life the way a child sucked soda pop from a straw. Maudet knew the type at a glance, before he had said a word, and liked what he saw with the reservation that he might be too much of a talker. He decided instantly to be open. To hell with discretion. He had no margin for that.

'Monsieur Walmer,' he said expansively. 'How do you do?'

The man's eyes twinkled; not the suspicious type with a laugh in sight. 'And yourself?' he asked on an amused but more subdued note.

'You've been most highly recommended to me,' Maudet said, 'and I should like to purchase a small package of aspirin.'

Walmer smiled with Maudet. 'That must have been some recommendation to bring you all the way over here for a package of aspirin – a small one.'

He handed the aspirin to Maudet, who paid him.

'Ah, my friend,' Maudet said, 'that is the least of the reasons that brought me here. An old and charming family friend, Monique Noirault, suggested that if I had any insurmountable problems, you could help me surmount them.'

'It's quite a trick. Mademoiselle Noirault flatters me.'

'She believes in you – in the farmer, Arnaud, too. She says that both of you have the same attitude as I towards the noble and dashing Germans, uncontested rulers of Alsace – admiration, respect and loyalty.'

'If Mademoiselle Noirault says so,' Walmer said with an expressive shrug.

'The trouble is,' Maudet continued, 'that they make so many rules. They demand so much discipline.'

Walmer raised his eyes to heaven: silent, pained acquiescence.

'It soothes the soul to break a rule from time to time,' Maudet persisted as Walmer nodded his head with the understanding that forgives all trespasses. 'It lifts the heart to march out of step. It's exhilarating.'

'Ah, but don't let the sergeant see you,' the fat, little pharmacist said from the heart, and Maudet knew he had reached him.

'I must get to Belfort,' Maudet said, and quickly added on a stroke of inspiration, 'I must get there to see my girl friend.'

'Why don't you take the train from Mulhouse?'

'Without an *Ausweis*?'

'You can apply for one.'

'The Herr Direktor is not romantic enough to accept the real reason, and I don't have any other valid one. They've annexed me and occupied her. The only way to get together is to walk across the border – out of step.'

'Difficult.'

'With a guide?'

Walmer shook his head with such conviction that his double chin wobbled. 'Not now,' he said. 'Nothing will help now. Don't you know they're trying to catch that general who got away, de Forge? A regiment of guards must have gone up last night. One of the woodcutters was down and told me about it. A guard every hundred yards and plenty of patrols. They even have searchlights, big ones, they turn on after dark every time a rabbit scurries across a field. We never see cars of the Gestapo or gendarmerie around here. Yesterday they were racing through all day long. Look!'

Maudet turned quickly to glimpse two cars full of gendarmes roaring through the village and out of sight. When he turned back to Walmer, the chubby little pharmacist was again shaking his head.

'The border is crawling with them,' he said. 'You'll do better to get yourself an *Ausweis* or a new girl.'

'Do you know where the border is?' Maudet asked.

'I've lived here all my life.'

'Just tell me how to get there.'

Walmer hesitated, considering Maudet with his clever eyes behind the thick-lensed glasses. 'That's easy,' he said at last. 'All you have to do is follow the gendarmes on that road. In ten minutes you'll be there.' He paused. 'But of course that's as far as you'll get without a passport and an *Ausweis*.'

Maudet stood there perplexed as the roly-poly pharmacist slowly and casually came out from behind the counter and went to the shop window. Maudet followed him and stood at his elbow.

'On the other hand,' Walmer said, 'there's another way of getting to the border – out of step. I used to be up and down it all the time when I was a kid playing at smugglers. It was us against the border guards. Pam! Pam! We used to run across into Switzerland, just a few yards, then back again. It was easy. Then when I was older I used to go up there with girls on summer nights. That was even better. . . . Where are the summer nights of yesteryear?' he wondered aloud with a sigh.

Then, suddenly, he stopped rambling, and with many gestures of either or both hands he explained very carefully to Maudet, standing at the shop window, how to reach the path leading up the hills to the border. It started back in the direction where de Forge was waiting.

'It's a secret path in a way,' Walmer said. 'Of course we all know it, but you're not likely to run into anyone until the top. You'll see a farmhouse on the left. The border guards are always hanging around it; they always did, for a little distraction, a snooze in the hay or a bowl of milk. You go to the right along the line of woods and about three or four hundred yards along you'll see a huge fir tree smack out in the middle of a meadow. You can't miss it. That's Switzerland. There's nothing to show it, no markings, but that's it. Beyond the fir tree there's an open, uphill stretch of about a hundred and fifty, two hundred yards where you can still be seen and shot even though you're across the border. You're not safe for your true love until you cross that open stretch and reach the trees on the top of the hill.'

'How about cutoffs on the path? Can they mislead me?'

'It's straight up. A child would find the way. The cutoffs are dead ends. You can't go wrong.'

'How long should it take to get to the top?'

Walmer thought about it for a moment. 'For a husky young fellow like you,' he said, 'maybe an hour, maybe an hour and a half. It's a nice walk.'

'Thanks,' Maudet said at the door. He smiled radiantly. 'I'll remember you in my will.'

'That gives me a better chance than being remembered by you in Belfort,' the pharmacist said with a wink.

Maudet laughed as he left. The man hadn't believed his transparent story for a moment, but there were conventions one had to observe even if they were only a joke or a shallow pretence.

He had some food ration tickets in his pocket and bought some tomatoes at the grocery store that they wrapped in an old newspaper. A little farther on he bought a loaf of bread at the bakery. There he asked at what time the first bus left for Mulhouse and was told at eight in the morning from the square.

He sauntered back along the route he had taken earlier, holding the tomatoes in the newspaper wrapping in one hand and the long naked loaf of bread in the other, not hurrying, and feeling good. For the first time since he had got up to this glorious May morning he was aware of the day and of his existence in it. He had done what he had to do, had done it quickly and well, and for a while now at least, he had nothing to worry about. The border problem could wait until they got to it; the important thing was they now knew how to get there. He walked back to de Forge, happy to be alive, enjoying each step, each breath, enjoying the touch of the sun and the fragrant air. He could no longer understand what concerns could dull a man to such a day.

De Forge saw him as he approached and came out of the wooded area to meet him.

'Let's go,' Maudet said. 'I know the way. Here, you'd better take the bread. It'll make you look domesticated, on your way to a family lunch.'

'Go ahead,' de Forge said, taking the bread. 'I'll follow.'

Maudet appreciated de Forge's thoughtfulness in separating them. He walked at a good, purposeful pace. The path that Walmer had indicated was not far off, and Maudet found it easily off the departmental road to the right between a stream and a large, low-eaved stone house. They passed few people on the way, and nobody took undue note of them.

Maudet waited for de Forge a short distance into the path, and for a little while they walked side by side. At the beginning the path was fairly wide and the terrain flat, but it soon began to climb and the path narrowed between trees and underbrush so that there was barely room for them to walk abreast. Maudet told de Forge what he had learned from Walmer, and de Forge told Maudet he had seen a man he assumed to be Monique's friend arrive at the chalet in a Citroën, load the two bicycles on it and leave without putting the key under the mat.

'We've been dispossessed,' he said with a wry smile. 'You should have seen his face.'

'It's a good thing we weren't there,' Maudet said. 'We've got enough problems.'

They soon stopped on the edge of a clearing, sat down, divided the bread and the tomatoes and ate ravenously. Even without butter or salt the food was delicious. When they rose they proceeded more cautiously. Maudet took the lead and de Forge followed about forty yards behind; if they came upon anyone descending the path, de Forge would have the time to hide in the underbrush.

As they progressed, the path rose more and more steeply, twisting in zigzags among tall, full-leafed trees and thick underbrush. In places the path narrowed so that there was just room for one person to pass. They pushed aside branches of young trees blocking their way and pressed on. Higher up, the terrain became rough and rocky and rose more steeply. It was hard going and they stopped frequently to catch their breath and rest. But Walmer had been right; there was no going wrong. Towards the top the terrain flattened out, running into a grove of fir trees. The air was clean and pungent. Maudet stopped. Through the trees to the left about fifty yards away he saw the farmhouse, a sprawling group of buildings with a wire enclosure for the cows. Once again Walmer was right: a couple of border guards were there talking to a peasant woman.

Maudet waited for de Forge. Then, cautiously and stealthily, they moved to the right well behind the line of trees fronting an open meadow. They stopped after a few hundred yards when they saw out in the open, far beyond the line of trees that hid them, a tall fir tree, solitary and noble. It stood there splendidly, isolated, its branches raised as if in prayer or exaltation to the eternal blue sky. It was more than a tree; it was a beacon guiding the wayward home. Their hearts rose.

'Switzerland,' Maudet whispered.

De Forge gazed across the fat green meadow, contemplating the rising breast of land that gently swelled beyond the fir tree to a wooded ridge whose lofty trees were greenly etched against the tranquil sky. His heart swelled. It looked so peaceful, so gentle. There lay his harbour a step away. There lay the port he had steered for since his capture two years before.

They had seen no border guards apart from those in front of the farmhouse, but they sensed their presence. They crawled to the edge of the meadow. Off to the right and to the left were guards. They stood there casually, relaxed; they carried rifles.

'They must be all along the line,' de Forge whispered. 'It's worse than I thought.'

'At least they don't have machine-guns.'

'They can kill you just as dead with a rifle bullet.'

At de Forge's suggestion, Maudet went off to the right to check how far the line of guards extended; to the left they were blocked by the farmhouse.

Almost two hours passed before Maudet returned, shaking

his head. 'They're posted all the way down as far as this forest goes,' he reported. 'You're just as well off crossing here.'

'After dark,' de Forge said. 'It can't be done in daylight, but after dark my chances are a lot better than theirs. I'll crawl to the tree, then walk up the hill. It should be easy.'

It looked as if it would be easy – at least in the dark.

'They made a mistake,' de Forge said professionally. 'They have no dogs. Very unthorough for the methodical Germans. I'd never get through if they had dogs.'

Later he asked Maudet how he planned to return.

'I'll spend the night up here, a little farther in the woods,' Maudet said. 'When daylight comes I'll go back down the path to the village and take the morning bus to Mulhouse, then the train to Lyons. I should be sleeping in my bed tomorrow night. I'll let them know where you are.'

They settled down to wait for nightfall. De Forge dozed for a while as Maudet, unable to sleep in any case, kept watch. He was edgy and envied de Forge's ability to turn off his energy and store it for later use. The long wait tired Maudet. He was restless, the sap rising irresistibly in him, but was forced to remain immobile. He kept looking at his watch and at the sky. The minutes dragged; the sun hung motionless in the west. It was the slowest, laziest sun Maudet had ever seen.

From time to time two-man patrols passed. At such times Maudet tightened up and scarcely dared to breathe; de Forge, awake, rested and clear-eyed, watched them impassively. At sundown a patrol paused only a few feet from where they lay, so close that they could hear their conversation. In the midst of griping, their talk came around to de Forge.

'I hate this kind of duty,' one of them said.

'It's pointless! That's what I don't like.'

'He'll never come through here, not during the day and not at night.'

'Never.'

'Why should he go into Switzerland when he can go straight into France? It can't be any more complicated crossing that border than this one.'

'We're here for nothing if you ask me. Special duty, double duty, and all for a general nobody'll ever lay eyes on.'

'Six hours on, six hours off. I'm dead. I could really use a good night's sleep.'

They moved on.

De Forge smiled coldly. 'There's nothing a guard likes more than sleep,' he whispered.

The sun finally dipped, immense and orange, behind the horizon and the night gradually closed down over them. It was very quiet. A half-moon hung high in the sky, casting some light but hardly enough to illuminate the obscurity. De Forge waited. It was the hardest moment. Maudet, staring out into the meadow, thought he could make out the top branches of the fir tree, a darker black against the blackness of the sky.

Still de Forge waited. An hour passed. Maudet did not mind any more, not since night had fallen. He felt comfortable in the darkness, protected. It gave him confidence as de Forge, with his patience and judgment, gave him confidence. He was breathing easily now. With each minute that passed he felt better. He thought of the distance they had come, of the feat they had accomplished. It was not too bad. . . .

De Forge nudged him. 'It's time,' he said.

They shook hands. To his surprise, Maudet found he could not speak; his throat was choked. He was glad it was dark; it would have disconcerted him if de Forge had seen him.

'Thanks,' de Forge said. 'Tell them where I am and get in touch with me. There's still everything to do.'

De Forge wriggled out into the open, on to the grassy meadow, and Maudet watched him disappear.

Gradually his emotion subsided and his heart was light. It was done; they had succeeded. He lay there a while longer, relaxed now, just a bit longer to be absolutely certain that de Forge had crossed over before moving back towards the path to wait until dawn, perhaps to sleep. He thought he could sleep now. He had unwound. A luxurious feeling swept over him, the feeling of having completed a difficult assignment and of facing the delicious emptiness that follows.

He had started to rise from his prone position when he was ripped from his euphoria. On the meadow night was suddenly transformed into day. A brilliant white beam of light swept the open space and came to rest to the left of the fir tree, pointing like a diabolical finger of accusation at the figure incongruously wearing a fedora nailed in its glare.

Maudet was on his feet, moaning, 'No, no. They can't; they mustn't. He's beyond the tree. He's in Switzerland.' Through his moan he heard the hoarse, shouted, guttural commands. How had they known? He had heard nothing. Was it luck? De Forge must have just stopped crawling and risen to his feet. He was pinned in the blaze of light. Those damned commands. He was turning. He would have to come back. It was all for nothing, all thrown away.

Maudet couldn't stand it. He couldn't let it happen. In another moment it would be too late. He had to do something, had to do it now. He burst into action.

'*Nein, nein, nicht da!*' he shouted, running into the meadow. 'Not there, over here! There are five of them here! That one's a decoy!'

His voice filled the night. As he ran he kept shouting. The voice of a guard to the right picked up his cry, yelled for light in his sector. The cries were imperious, urgent. The finger of light swung off de Forge and to the right, chasing Maudet. He zigzagged away, to the left, to the right, feeling light and free, the beam of light bouncing after him. He raced across the meadow, tacking across the violently swinging flare of light, parallel to its source to keep it from catching and holding him. He ran, the finger of light finding, then losing him. They were firing now but the blood pounded in his head, his breath coming in deep gasps, and the crack of rifles sounded distant and unreal. He ran, and each time the finger of light seized him he wrenched away. But he was slowing and the farther he ran the longer the beam of light held him. The firing was heavier now, the rifle cracks covering each other, their explosions erratically filling the air, bullets whistling and howling around him. He ran, but at last the flare gripped and held him. He was well beyond the fir tree when the bullet brought him down. He plunged forward, his face in the dewy grass, heaving to draw breath into his lungs.

They held the light on him, fearful no doubt that he might rise and run again; and though he lay on Swiss soil, they came running, rifles in hand, to collect him. He heard a gruff voice ask about 'the other one,' and heard another voice say, 'Gone, but we got one of them.'

His eyes closed, and inert but conscious, Maudet smiled.

He said to himself, 'You got the wrong one. We're the ones who got you.'

When they turned him over he was dead.

From the ridge in Switzerland at the far end of the meadow de Forge saw the guards carry Maudet's body back to their side of the border, guided by the shaft of light. What he could not see, and had not seen, he was able to infer. Silently, motionlessly, he saluted Maudet, who would not take the morning bus to Mulhouse nor sleep in his bed in Lyons. A doubt assailed him. Some things are beyond reach. Was the cause already lost while they died to catch a star? He had a glimmering of the world he cherished changing beyond recapture, of a France that would never glitter with her old glory, of the millennial civilization that had cradled him being crushed between the Russian and American giants. For a long time de Forge stood immobile on the ridge looking down at the border post, hearing across the expanse of the meadow the vague and distant murmur of voices. The current of history swept multitudes, and its flow was not easily turned. He recalled everything he knew about Maudet as if he were committing it to memory. His eyes sparkled in the obscure light of the half-moon.

Presently de Forge raised his eyes higher. There would be other battles, other Maudets, and he would reach for the star, higher, ever higher, and if he stretched for it, really stretched, who knew, perhaps in the end he would catch it. He gazed towards the horizon behind which, under the black, starlit sky, the Third Reich crouched, its cities darkened, its battalions on the march, its legions ruling the continent from the steppes of Russia to the Atlantic, and his face grim, his eyes cold, he raised his fist and cried aloud, 'Now it's my turn to pursue you.' Then he turned and strode off to the formalities of freedom.

AFTERMATH

That is the story of General de Forge's escape. But the reader may be curious to know what happened afterward. Was the purpose of the escape fulfilled? Did de Forge serve France as he felt he was destined to, or was the escape, with its risks and sacrifices, in effect for nothing?

This is what did happen.

The weeks immediately after he returned to Unoccupied France were busy ones for de Forge. No one knew how he had managed to escape, but the headlines told everybody he had done so. That was enough. The exploit thrust de Forge upon the scene as the most heroic of French generals, and a wave of admiration spread around the world. Here was a man alone, and a prestigious general, who had realized every anti-Nazi's fantasy: he had challenged the seemingly invincible machine of the Nazi police state and won. But in reaction pressures correspondingly mounted for him to climb down from his pedestal and crawl back to the fortress.

The pressure came from the top. The Vichy chief of government, Premier Pierre Laval, told him his escape had poisoned Franco-German relations, which was true enough, and demanded that he give himself up. The German ambassador, Otto Abetz, raged and insisted that he surrender. A personal envoy from Hitler tried to persuade him with honeyed arguments. Even the Vichy chief of state, Marshal Pétain, put the weight of his authority in the balance and urged him to return to prison 'for the sake of France'.

In the face of this enormous pressure and a virulent press and radio campaign to discredit him, de Forge stood steadfast. He maintained contact with a handful of army followers and through them with the Americans. Despite Gestapo surveillance, word came from the Americans that their need for him was imminent. Another escape was in the offing, this time by submarine. De Forge made his preparations and quickly sent his wife and children to Switzerland, out of

250

reach of the avenging Nazi regime. He was ready. The command of armies was about to be his again, but this time he was to be the supreme commander. He would meet with General Eisenhower and it would be arranged.

The star that de Forge was reaching for, higher, ever higher, seemed now to be within his grasp – he had only to stretch just a bit more and he would seize it. But that was when Hitler lost his patience. The Gestapo report about the sudden departure of de Forge's family was a signal; something was in the air; de Forge had to be checked. Hitler made a personal and imperious demand that de Forge be handed over. Under this pressure Vichy collapsed, but wanting to maintain the illusion of French sovereignty, insisted on the legal niceties. The legal niceties meant extra-legal means. It would be done without the French government's official knowledge. The Gestapo would kidnap de Forge, transport him to Germany and deliver him to his jailers. De Forge was warned by an anonymous phone call only minutes before a dozen agents, in the dark hours of a late October morning, crashed into the house he had rented outside Aix en Provence; they found it empty, de Forge's bed still warm.

For months de Forge was on the run, moving from apartment to apartment, from town to town, his link with the Americans broken, contact lost. By the time he escaped to North Africa the following summer history had passed him by. The Americans had replaced de Forge with General Henri Giraud, a fine soldier but without political gifts or the charisma for leadership; the French had swung behind the towering figure of General de Gaulle, who was slowly breaking Giraud's hold on power. With de Gaulle running the government and Giraud the army, de Forge could play only a subordinate role with no function to his measure. 'He was born to give orders not to take them,' de Gaulle was to write of him later, but while anxious to use his talents, would give him no rope. 'If I do,' he was reported to have said, 'he might hang me with it.'

In war nothing is more dispensable than talent. As armies clashed and new leaders rose and played their parts, de Forge was held in the background, then eliminated from command and put on the shelf for the rest of the war. The worst of it was that nobody missed him. His fairy princess had other knights to protect her.

The rest of de Forge's life was spent in obscurity and he died in 1957 at the age of seventy-five. After sketching his career and recalling his celebrated escape, an editorial on the front page of *Le Monde* sent him to his grave with these words: 'As it turned out, History, the most implacable of judges, after hesitating over General de Forge's exceptional gifts, finally turned him away. No doubt he deserved better. He was a man of undeniable and immense courage; and when the times demanded defiance, when all hope seemed vain, he displayed it in the grand manner and in the best French tradition.'

No monument was erected to de Forge's memory; no boulevard, avenue, square or street bears his name.

Famous War Books in Fontana

Rommel Desmond Young *35p*
'As the life and adventures of a swashbuckler and superb leader of men, *Rommel* can hardly be too highly commended to the public.' *Evening Standard*

The First and the Last Adolf Galland *30p*
The rise and fall of the Luftwaffe—by Germany's greatest fighter pilot. 'Some of his air-battles read almost as fast as the Messerschmitts he flew, and his staff-battle accounts give the clearest picture yet of how the Germans lost their war in the air.' *Time Magazine*

Winged Dagger Roy Farran *30p*
The thrilling account of Captain Farran's amazing career in the Special Air Service during World War II. 'Strongly recommended.' *Evening Standard*

Malta Convoy
Peter Shankland and Anthony Hunter *30p*
The fantastic saga of the tanker *Ohio*. It tells of the men who sailed her and also of the ship herself, who, broken-backed and sinking, carried not only the oil, Malta's sole hope of survival, but, the fate of the war itself.

Ten Thousand Eyes Richard Collier *30p*
The incredible exploits of the French Underground. 'A magnificent story, splendidly told.' *Evening News*

Underwater Saboteur Max Manus *30p*
The thrilling story of Max Manus and his tiny band of Norwegian underground fighters in World War II, who crippled German shipping against enormous odds.

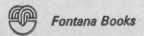 *Fontana Books*

Famous War Books in Fontana

Bridge on the River Kwai Pierre Boulle *25p*
One of the finest war novels ever written—the famous story of
three remarkable men: *Col. Nicholson*, who was prepared to
sacrifice everything—except his dignity; *Major Warden*, a
modest hero and deadly killer; and *Cdr. Shears*, a man who
escaped from hell and was ordered back.

Reach for the Sky Paul Brickhill *35p*
The unforgettable story of Douglas Bader, legless fighter
pilot of World War II. 'This is a handbook of heroism . . .
there is no medal yet for courage such as his.' *The People*.
'Moving and enthralling.' *Evening Standard*

Carve Her Name with Pride R. J. Minney *30p*
The story of Violette Szabo—wartime Secret Agent who, in
solitary confinement, suffered atrocious tortures, but never
gave away any of her secrets to the enemy. 'She was the
bravest of us all.' *Odette Churchill*

The Phantom Major Virginia Cowles *30p*
The astonishing exploits of David Stirling—commando hero
of the desert war. 'An inspiring adventure story—the S.A.S.
exploits were so fantastically daring that they can hardly fail
to make exciting reading.' *The Times*

Sinister Twilight Noel Barber *35p*
'We may never have a better book about the fall of Singapore.'
Sunday Mirror. 'An entirely fresh light on what was regarded
as a scandalous betrayal . . . so freshly and readably different.'
Evening News

The War of the Running Dogs Noel Barber *40p*
A vivid, comprehensive book about the British defeat of the
Malayan Communist guerrillas. 'Exciting and engrossing . . .
a superlative slice of lucid, living history.' *Sunday Express*

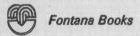 *Fontana Books*

Famous War Books in Fontana

The Tunnel   Eric Williams   *30p*
The story of the author's two dramatic escapes from prisoner-of-war camps that were unable to hold him. 'The atmosphere of prison-camp life is made more vivid than anything that one has read before. The excitement is maintained to the end.'
Glasgow Herald

The Wooden Horse   Eric Williams   *30p*
'An unusually good and gripping tale of a clever and courageous break from captivity and a nightmarish journey to freedom.' *The Observer.* 'It may be said with confidence that nothing better of its kind is likely to emerge from the Second World War . . . An amazing story.' *Glasgow Herald*

The Escapers   Eric Williams   *30p*
Breathtaking epics of escape collected by World War II's boldest escaper. 'Must surely represent the cream of escape literature. All his episodes are well chosen . . . They are long enough to be satisfying, and particularly, to give us a glimpse of the writer's character.' *The Listener*

More Escapers   Eric Williams   *30p*
'Few authors have written more vividly about wartime escapes than Eric Williams. In *More Escapers* he widens his scope to include peace-time escapologists.' *Coventry Evening Telegraph.* 'The reader is likely to find each of these escapes more enthralling than the last.' *Times Literary Supplement*

Send Down a Dove   Charles MacHardy   *35p*
'The finest submarine story to come out of either World War.' *Alistair MacLean.* A British sub in the closing years of World War II fights off mines, the Germans, and a mutiny below decks.

 Fontana Books

Fontana Books

Fontana is best known as one of the leading paperback publishers of popular fiction and non-fiction. It also includes an outstanding, and expanding section of books on history, natural history, religion and social sciences.

Most of the fiction authors need no introduction. They include Agatha Christie, Hammond Innes, Alistair MacLean, Catherine Gaskin, Victoria Holt and Lucy Walker. Desmond Bagley and Maureen Peters are among the relative newcomers.

The non-fiction list features a superb collection of animal books by such favourites as Gerald Durrell and Joy Adamson.

All Fontana books are available at your bookshop or news-agent; or can be ordered direct. Just fill in the form below and list the titles you want.

- -

FONTANA BOOKS, Cash Sales Department, P.O. Box 4, Godalming, Surrey. Please send purchase price plus 5p postage per book by cheque, postal or money order. No currency.

NAME (Block letters) _____

ADDRESS _____

_____

_____

While every effort is made to keep prices low, it is sometimes necessary to increase prices at short notice. Fontana Books reserve the right to show new retail prices on covers which may differ from those previously advertised in the text or elsewhere.